# JAMES HERBERT

# THE SECRET OF CRICKLEY HALL

PAN BOOKS

First published 2006 by Macmillan

This edition published 2007 by Pan Books
an imprint of Pan Macmillan
20 New Wharf Road, London N1 9RR
Associated companies throughout the world
www.panmacmillan.com

ISBN 978-0-330-41168-4

A CIP catalogue record for this book is available from
the British Library.

Typeset by SetSystems Ltd, Saffron Walden, Essex
Printed and bound by
CPI Group (UK) Ltd, Croydon, CR0 4YY

Visit **www.panmacmillan.com** to read more about all our books
and to buy them. You will also find features, author interviews and
news of any author events, and you can sign up for e-newsletters
so that you're always first to hear about our new releases.

*'From the darkness let the
innocent speak so that the guilty
may know their shame.'*

ANON

*'The evil that men do lives after them . . .'*

SHAKESPEARE

*'Train up a child in the way he should go:
and when he is old, he will not depart from it.'*

PROVERBS ch 22, v 6

THEN

*They scattered into a darkness scarcely tempered by oil lamps, the soft glow easily repressed by the deep shadows of the house.*

*The shrieks and cries of the fleeing children rose above the noise of the storm outside. The sound of their stockinged feet was soft on the hard stone floor of the cavernous hall.*

*Some of them took to the stairs, scurrying past the tall, almost ceiling-high window at the turn, rain beating at its glass, the fierce wind rattling the frames, lightning flickering outside and casting darker shadows across the stone floor.*

*The children found refuge wherever they could – behind furniture, beneath tables, inside cupboards, anywhere they might sink into the umbra and be hidden while they prayed they would not be found. There in their hopeless sanctuaries they held their whimpers but were unable to control the chattering of their teeth and the nervous fidget of their limbs, for they knew that eventually he would find them, that he would seek them out one by one.*

*Silent tears drenched their cheeks and glacial fingers seemed to squeeze their small hearts.*

*He would snatch them from their hideaways and punish them.* And this time, *a cruel knowing voice whispered in their minds*, this time it would be the worst punishment of all . . .

*They heard his approach even though he wore no shoes, for he* swished *something through the cold damp air, each swish ending in a sudden violent* thwack, *the beating of cane against bare flesh.* Swish, *then* thwack, *cane on flesh*, swish, *then* thwack, *two individual sounds that could be clearly heard over the raging storm outside.* Swish-thwack! *Louder*, swish-thwack! *Louder, coming closer.* Swish-thwack! *Almost becoming one sound.*

*They tried to be very, very quiet . . .*

NOW

# 1: ARRIVAL

Although the rain had ceased for the moment, single thick globules, as if too heavy to be held by the blanket cloud overhead, splattered against the windscreen like miniature water bombs, and were quickly reduced to smears by the intermittent sweep of the wipers. Eve's spirits had felt as low as the weather during the earlier part of the five-hour journey (including the break for lunch) from London, and now they dropped to an even lower level.

The big grey-stone house on the other side of the narrow rushing river looked grim, more like an ancient sanatorium or resthome for the indigent elderly than a family home.

Gabe had parked the Range Rover in a small clear area beside the lane that led a mile or so downhill to the harbour village of Hollow Bay. Despite the miserable weather, Eve had felt her heart lift a little (as much as it was capable of lifting these days) once they'd left the motorway – interstate, Gabe, her American husband, kept calling it – and reached the West Country; she had almost enjoyed travelling through sheltered lanes with close beech hedges that frequently gave way to wide sweeping moorlands of fine heather and bracken, distant woodland-clad hills their pastel backcloth, not even the dark louring skies spoiling the splendour. Rather than announce nature's retreat towards winter, the autumn colours

– the reds, greens, browns, golds and yellows – of woodlands and fauna boasted their glory as the Range Rover sped through deep valleys and crossed rough-stone bridges over tumbling streams.

Gabe had promised them healthy long walks (much to the exaggerated groans of their daughters, Loren and Cally), especially along the beautiful deep-sided and tree-lined gorge – he called it a ravine and the map called it Devil's Cleave – in which their new temporary home was situated; they would either follow the river down to the sea or climb towards its source on the high moors. It would be fun. On weekends they could explore the craggy coastline, the rugged clifftops and the small sheltered bays and sandy coves. Weather permitting, they could even take out a sailing boat and ride the waves. Or maybe do some horse riding (because his homeland was the States, Gabe had convinced their youngest daughter, Cally, that he had once been a cowboy, a fib for which he would have to answer when she discovered he'd never been on a horse in his life, Eve had thought wryly). If the weather was bad, they could just explore the countryside by car.

There'd be plenty to keep them occupied on weekends, he had assured them. And it might help the healing, he told Eve when they were alone.

Now they were here and this was her first sight of Crickley Hall, which was not quite large enough to be called a manor, but was much too big for a normal home. Gabe had visited twice before, the first time in summer when he'd scouted the locale for a property close to the job to which his engineering company had been sub-contracted, and a second time a week ago when he'd hired a van and, with Vern Brennan, a fellow-American buddy of his, had delivered most of the bulky items the family would need for their stay (the house itself was already furnished with old-fashioned stuff, according to Gabe, which was good enough to get by with).

Through the Range Rover's windscreen, Eve saw that a sturdy wooden bridge traversed the swift-moving, boulder-strewn Bay River, which Gabe had described as no more than a wide, gentle stream when he had returned from viewing the property a couple of months ago. But then, it had been late August; now the boisterous waters threatened to overspill the raised banks. The bridge itself was made of rough timber, the sides crosshatched with thin lengths of rustic logs beneath thick rails; while it appeared strong, the structure was not wide enough to accept the Range Rover – nor any other largish vehicle – hence the parking bay on this side of the river.

On the opposite bank, the house – or Hall, as it was called – occupied a level expanse of cut grass and shrubbery with the odd tree here and there (one tree near the front had a child's swing dangling from a stout branch). The far thickly foliaged side of the gorge loomed impressively steep, high over the stark building.

'It looks a bit grim,' she found herself saying, immediately regretting the criticism; Gabe had tried so hard.

Her husband looked across at her from the driver's seat, his wide tight-lipped smile concealing any disappointment.

'Guess it looked a little different in summer,' he said.

'No, the weather doesn't help.' She touched his hand on the steering wheel and made herself return the smile. His wonderfully blue eyes, darkened by the gloom of the car's interior, examined her own for reassurance.

'It's just a change, hon,' he almost apologized. 'We all need it.'

'Can we get out now, Daddy?' came Cally's impatient voice from the back seat. 'I'm tired of sitting.'

Switching off the engine and thumbing open his seatbelt, Gabe turned and gave his younger daughter a grin. 'Sure. It's been a long haul and you've been pretty good all the way.'

'Chester's bin a good boy too.' The five-year-old squirmed in her seat, searching for the seatbelt button.

The black, lean, coarse-haired dog, who slumped on the back seat between the two sisters, sparked to attention at the sound of his name. When Gabe and Eve had picked him out at the south London dogs' home six years before, they had been told that the year-old puppy was a crossbreed, something of a Patterdale in there somewhere, but Gabe reckoned the scruffy orphan was all mongrel, without an ounce of breeding in his runty little body.

Chester (Gabe had chosen the name) had grown to almost fifteen inches high: he was cow-hocked with turned-out feet, back and front, and there was too little angulation to his hind legs for dog show events; there were now grey and brown hairs among his short black fur, especially under his muzzle, chest and the untidy tufts around his neck. Seven years old, those dark-brown eyes still held their puppy appeal and, even though he was generally a happy-natured dog, his turned-down mouth gave him a perpetual cast of sadness. When they lost Cam almost a year ago, Chester had howled for three nights running as if he knew more than they did, as if he were aware their son was gone for ever.

Gabe acknowledged the now-alert dog with a slight upward tilt of his chin, the opposite to a nod. 'Yep. Chester's been pretty tight. Not even a small leak all this way.'

'Only because I told you every time he looked uncomfortable,' reminded Loren, who had that pretty but gangly appearance of many twelve-year-old girls, pre-teenage and just beginning to take a greater interest in what was worthy of 'cool', be it in music, clothes, or Mother's make-up. Sometimes she assumed a maturity that should not yet have been learned, while at other times she was still his 'princess' who loved her dolls and frequent hugs (the latter more occasional than frequent these days).

Loren had been adamant that no way was she leaving her friends and school in London to live in a place thousands of miles from anywhere, a place where she didn't know anybody, a place she'd never even heard of. It took some persuasion, plus a promise of having her very own cell phone so that she could keep in constant touch with all her girlfriends, to convince her things would be okay down in Devon. That and the quiet one-to-one chat Gabe had with her where he'd explained that the deal was to get Mummy away from their regular home and its constant reminders of Cameron for a while, just long enough maybe to allow Eve some closure to a year that had been horrendous for them all. Loren had understood immediately and had put aside her reluctance to leave – until the last few days, that is, when imminent departure had drawn out long goodbyes and floods of tears between her and her closest friends.

'Good thing you decided to come along then,' Gabe responded with only mild teasing.

'Thank you,' he added seriously, looking directly into his eldest daughter's eyes, and she knew he was thanking her for more than just watching over Chester.

'Okay, Dad.'

He realized at that moment that he missed the extra 'd' and the 'y' at the end of 'Dad' and wondered when it had started happening. Was Loren, his princess, growing up so fast that he hadn't noticed? With a jab of melancholy that perhaps only fathers of growing daughters can know (sons were way different, except to doting mothers), he swung back in his seat, glancing at Eve as he did so. There was a

11

moistness to her gaze as she studied the big house on the other side of the bridge.

'You'll like it more when the sun comes out,' he promised her softly.

'Daddy, can we get out?' came Cally's pleading voice again. Cally was seven years junior to Loren and now the same age as Cameron when he'd disappeared almost a year ago. Five. They'd lost their son when he was only five years old.

'Put your hats on first. It might pour again.' Eve was instructing them all, Gabe included. He reached into the glove compartment for his woollen beanie, pulling it down half over his ears against the chill he knew waited beyond the cosy warmth of the Range Rover. Eve checked their daughters were following suit before pulling the hood of her rainproof jacket over her own dark hair.

Beneath her untidy fringe lay deep-brown eyes that until a year ago had reflected warmth and a sly humour; but now grief had shadowed them and dulled their vibrancy so that feelings were no longer exposed, were curtained by perdurable sorrow. As the girls obeyed hat orders and reached for door latches, Chester standing on the seat and pawing at Cally's shoulder to get past her, Eve stepped out of the SUV and surveyed Crickley Hall once more.

She heard Chester's yelp and Cally's whoop as they tumbled out of the other side of the vehicle and something bit into her heart as child and pet headed straight for the wet bridge.

'Gabe,' she said apprehensively, drawing in a sharp breath.

'S'okay.' Louder, at Cally: 'Hey, rein in, Scout. Wait for us.'

Cally skidded to a halt on the wet planks of the short bridge, but Chester continued, yapping with pleasure at the sudden release, only pausing when he was halfway across

12

the lawn. The child's swing close by stirred in the slight breeze. The dog looked back over his shoulder uncertainly.

Eve eyed the rough latticework of the bridge, then the beleaguered riverbanks. They would all have to keep a watch on Cally: the diamond-shaped openings between the diagonal struts were wide enough for a child to slip through on the deck made greasy by rain and spray, and the riverbanks were not fenced, their edges unstable. Cally would have to be warned never to use the bridge or go near the water on her own. They could not lose another child. Dear God, they mustn't lose another child. Eve raised a hand to her mouth as a latent sob caught in her throat.

Gabe hunkered down in his black reefer jacket, collar turned up round his ears, which were mostly covered by the beanie, and hurried towards their youngest daughter, while Loren followed just behind. Cally waited midway across the bridge, unsure whether she'd been silly or naughty. She looked questioningly at her approaching father and smiled when she saw him grinning. He scooped her up in his arms and together, Loren pausing to wait for Eve, they left the bridge and walked towards the tall grey house.

The building was constructed of simple dull-grey granite blocks, even the quoins at each corner and the windowsills of the same drab shade. Most of the other old and largish residences they passed in the last half hour or so of their journey had been built with limestone or sandstone, even flint: none had been as plain, nor as dour, as this place. The only embellishment, such as it was, seemed to be the shallow pilasters on either side of the huge nail-studded door, these bridged by an equally plain stone lintel which offered precious little cover for any visitor waiting in the rain on the two meagre cracked steps that led up to the entrance.

There were four sizeable windows to the ground floor, with six smaller windows along the upper storey, and four more even smaller dormer windows jutting from the slope of the slate roof, the slope itself quickly squaring off to accommodate four brick chimney stacks.

Eve frowned. Crickley Hall's architect either had a limited imagination or was hindered by budgetary constraints.

A rough-edged, sparsely gravelled pathway angled from the end of the bridge towards the house's main entrance, joining with a perimeter walkway which was also a mixture of mud and thinly layered stones. The sheer gorge wall of lush vegetation that towered over the grey building somehow should have cowed it, yet failed to do so: Crickley Hall's brooding presence was unequivocal.

Eve kept the thought to herself: this place was not just grim – it was ugly.

A little way off to the right, with bushes and tree branches on the gorge wall louring over its flat roof, stood a small garden shed whose weather-worn planking was turned dark by the rain.

'Come on, Mummy!' Cally and Gabe were almost at the front door to the house and Cally had called over her shoulder. The two of them waited for Eve and Loren to catch up.

Chester, who was still poised by the gently swaying swing, lingered until they drew level, then trotted alongside.

'Have you got the key ready?' Eve called out to Gabe, a drop of rain spatting against her cheek.

'The key will be in the door. The estate manager had cleaners in this morning to make sure the place is bright and sparkling.'

As they stood together on the two long but low steps, Eve realized that the broad, nail-studded, worn oak door seemed to be from a different era than that of the plain building and she wondered if the wider than usual portal had been designed to accommodate it; the door might well have been reclaimed from some ancient demolished manor house or monastery, with its almost gothic leopard-head iron door knocker. She watched as Gabe made great ceremony of pressing the big china-white doorbell that was surrounded by a ring of discoloured brass between the wall and right-hand pilaster. They all heard a rusty electric brurrr from inside.

'What are you doing?' she asked.

'Just letting the ghosts know we're here, hon.'

'Dad, there's no such thing,' chided Loren, indignant again.

'Sure of that?'

Eve was impatient. 'Come on, Gabe, open up.' She wondered if the inside was as austere as the exterior.

Gabe pushed at the huge central doorknob with his right hand and, without a single creak, the heavy door swung open.

'Cooool.'

It was a drawn-out sound of awe from Loren.

Gabe smiled at Eve. 'Not too shabby, huh?' he asked, giving her a moment or so to be impressed.

'I never expected...' she began. 'It's...' She faltered again.

'Something, right?' Gabe said.

'From the outside I thought it'd be a mean interior. Roomy, but, you know ... kind of skimpy.'

'Yeah, doesn't figure at all, does it?'

No, it didn't figure at all, thought Eve. The entrance had opened onto a vast galleried hall that rose beyond the first floor, which itself was marked by a balustraded landing running round two sides of the room.

'It must take up half the house,' she said, eyes raised to the beamed ceiling high above and the cast-iron chandelier that hung from its centre. The chandelier resembled a black upturned claw.

'The rest of the place isn't as fancy,' Gabe told her. 'To your left there's the kitchen and sitting room; those double doors directly ahead lead to a long drawing room.' He gestured upwards with his chin. 'Bedrooms are off the balcony, left and centre. There's plenty to choose from.'

She pointed to a ground-floor door he had missed. It stood near the kitchen door, an old-fashioned chiffonier between them, and it was slightly ajar. She could see only a thick blackness beyond. 'You didn't say what's through there.'

For some reason – for safety probably, because there was a steep descending staircase just inside – this door opened into the hall, unlike the other doors, and Gabe strode over to it and firmly pushed it shut. 'Leads to the cellar,' he said over his shoulder. 'Cally, you keep away from this door, okay?'

Their daughter stopped swirling round for a moment, her eyes fixed on the chandelier. 'Okay, Daddy,' she said distractedly.

'I mean it. You don't go down there without one of us with you, y'hear?'

'Yes, Daddy.' She swirled on, trying to make herself dizzy, and Eve wondered why Gabe's instruction was so stern.

She ventured further into the hall, Loren following, leaving Cally behind by the open entrance door, now swaying unsteadily. To the right a broad wooden staircase led up to the gallery landing, its lower section turning at right angles towards the hall's centre. From the turn that formed a small square lower landing, there towered an almost ceiling-high drapeless window through which poor daylight entered. Dull though the light was, it nevertheless brightened much of the hall's oak-panelled walls and flagstone floor. Eve allowed her gaze to wander.

A few uninteresting and time-grimed landscape paintings were hung round the room and two carved oak chairs with burgundy upholstery stood on either side of the double doors to the drawing room. Apart from these, though, there was precious little other furniture in evidence – a narrow console table against the wall between the doors to the cellar and the sitting room, a dark-wood sideboard beneath the stairs, a circular torchère with an empty vase on top in the corner of the carpetless lower landing, and that appeared to be it. Oh, and an umbrella stand by the front door.

There was, however, a wide and deep open fireplace, its iron grate filled with dry logs, set into the wall beside the staircase and Eve hoped it would bring some much needed cheer – not to mention warmth – to the huge room when lit. She gave an involuntary shiver and folded her arms across her midriff, hands hugging in her elbows.

Because of the building's unambiguously plain exterior, the hall seemed almost incongruous. It was as if Crickley Hall had had two architects, one for exterior, the other for interior: the architectural dichotomy was puzzling.

Gabe joined her at the centre of the hall. 'I don't want to disappoint you, but it's like I said: the rest isn't so fancy. The drawing room's pretty bleak – it takes up the whole rear part of the ground floor – and it's empty, no furniture at all. The kitchen's no more'n functional, and everything else is just okay. Oh, the sitting room's not too bad.'

'Good. I was worried I'd be overwhelmed by it all. So long as the other rooms are comfortable.' She peered up at the galleried landing. 'You mentioned the bedrooms . . .'

'We can take our pick. I figure the one directly opposite the stairway will suit us – it's a fair size and there's a big four-poster bed that goes with it. No canopy, but it's kinda quaint – you'll love it. The room next door'll be fine for the girls. Close to us and with their own beds from home. But there's other rooms to choose from.' He indicated more doors that were visible through the balustrade on the left-hand side of the landing. 'We can jostle beds around, see what suits.' He raised his eyebrows at her. 'So what d'you think? It'll do?'

She settled his apprehension with a smile; Gabe was trying

*too* hard these days. 'I'm sure it's going to be okay for a short while, Gabe. Thank you for finding the place.'

He took her in his arms and brushed her cheek with his lips. 'It'll give us a chance, Eve. Y'know?'

A chance to forget? No, nothing will ever do that. She remained silent and held on to him. Then she shivered again and pulled away.

He looked at her questioningly. 'You all right?'

It wasn't the chill in the air, she told herself. It was the pressure of all these past months. Too much trying to live a normal life, not for her own sake, but for the girls, for Gabe. Relentless grief and . . . and guilt. It was those spiteful shards that caused her to shiver, spiking her whenever she forgot for a moment.

'I just felt a draught,' she lied.

Unconvinced – it was plain in his expression – Gabe left her to go to the open front door.

'Hey,' she heard him say behind her. 'What's up, fella?' Eve turned to see him squatting down in front of a shivering Chester. The dog stood in the open doorway, his rear legs still on the outside step.

'Come on, Chester, get in here,' Gabe coaxed easily. 'Your butt is gonna get soaked.' It had begun to rain in earnest again.

Cally trotted over to the dog and patted his head. 'You'll catch a cold,' she told Chester, who shuffled his front paws and gave a little whine.

Gabe lifted him gently and stroked the back of his neck. The puling began again but Gabe carried Chester across the threshold and used a foot to nudge the door shut behind them. The trembling dog began to struggle.

'Easy, Chester,' Gabe soothed. 'You gotta get used to the place.'

Chester disagreed. He tried to get free, squirming his wiry body in Gabe's arms, so that Gabe was forced to put him back on the floor. The dog scuttled back to the front door and began to scrabble at it with his paws.

'Hey, quit it.' Gabe pulled him away from the door but did not attempt to pick him up again. Cally and Loren looked on with concern.

'Chester doesn't like it here,' Loren said anxiously.

Eve slipped an arm round her daughter's shoulder. 'It's just a bit strange to him, that's all,' she said. 'You wait, by tonight he'll be treating Crickley Hall like he's lived here all his life.'

Loren looked up at her mother. 'He's afraid of this place,' she announced gravely.

'Oh, Loren, that's nonsense. Chester's always been skittish about new things. He'll soon get used to it.' Eve smiled, but it was forced. Maybe Chester sensed something that she, herself, had sensed the moment she'd set foot inside. The *something* that had made her shiver a few moments ago.

There was something not quite right about Crickley Hall.

The rest of the house was a disappointment. The girls explored with enthusiasm, but Eve followed distractedly when Gabe gave them the full tour. It was as he had said – the other rooms, apart from the drawing room, which was impressive only because of its length (it was once used as a schoolroom according to the estate manager who had first shown Gabe around) – were functional. Certainly the large kitchen fitted that description, with its old-fashioned electric cooker, deep porcelain sinks next to a scarred wooden worktop, plain but deep cupboards, walk-in larder, linoleum floor covering, and the black iron range (a fire had already been laid and Gabe wasted no time in putting a match to it). Gabe had already bought and installed a cheap washing machine and tumble-dryer on his last visit to Hollow Bay, so that was one less problem for them to contend with.

On the first floor there was, as promised, a choice of bedrooms, and she and the girls went along with Gabe's original thought (oddly, Loren did not complain about having to share with Cally and Eve guessed that she, too, was a little intimidated by the very size of Crickley Hall). Although they had not climbed further on this first exploration, their tour guide informed them that the top floor obviously had once been a dormitory: there were still skeletal frames of cotbeds up there, but from the dust that had gathered and the weather-grime on the row of dormer windows along the sloping section of ceiling, the room had not been used for many, many years.

Most of Crickley Hall's furniture was old but not antique and Eve was quietly relieved: children and pet dogs did not go very well with valuable antiquities, so it was another thing less to worry about.

Another area that went unexplored for now was the cellar which, according to Gabe, housed the boiler and generator (apparently the region suffered from frequent power cuts and the generator had been brought in to allow certain circuits, such as those running heating and lighting, to operate independently). Oh, and there was one other thing down there that would surprise them, Gabe had hinted, but that could wait until after they'd settled in.

They had quickly unloaded from the Range Rover the items they'd brought down with them that day, dashing to and fro in the rain, which had developed into a steady drizzle, careful not to slip on the treacherously wet boards of the bridge, the girls laughing with excitement and shrieking when they splashed through puddles, nobody stopping until every last article had been brought into the house. Then Loren had made her way upstairs loaded down with pillows and bed-sheets (it took three trips) to make up her own and Cally's beds, while Gabe had first attended to the fire in the big hall before checking out the boiler in the cellar.

Chester slept fitfully on his favourite blanket in a corner of the kitchen, lured there and finally quietened with a bribe of chicken nuggets, while Cally painted watery pictures at the worn and scored table set against a wall opposite the working surfaces and two large windows.

Eve took wrapped crockery and kitchen utensils from card-board boxes, soaking all in one of the two deep sinks filled with hot (so the boiler seems to be working okay) soapy water. The windows over the sinks and worktops overlooked the front lawn and river. She could see the swing from there, the wooden seat shiny with rain hanging from rusty link chains, the bridge across the busy river just beyond, and as she worked, scrubbing at the plates that were already clean, careless about not wearing the as yet unpacked Marigold gloves (a year ago it would have been impossible even to contemplate dipping her bare hands into hot soapy water), thoughts – the *bad* thoughts – came tumbling in.

It was the image of the swing gently stirring under the weary, almost leafless, oak that pierced the fragile mem-branes of her emotions. Cameron, just five years old, like Cally now, had loved the brightly coloured swings of their local park.

Her shoulders hunched over the sink, her hands locked beneath the water. Her head was bowed. A single teardrop fell and caused a tiny ripple on the water's surface. Cam, her beautiful little boy with bright straw-coloured hair several shades lighter than his father's but with the same stunningly blue eyes. She stiffened. She must stop. She couldn't let the grief overwhelm her yet again. She hadn't wept in front of her family for two months now and today, on this new beginning, she must not weaken. Only strong sedatives and responsibility towards the rest of her family – she could not let *them* down too – had forestalled a complete collapse, although breakdown had threatened repeatedly. Unconditional love from Gabe, Loren and Cally had pulled her through the worst of her misery – at least outwardly it had. How she wished she could be self-contained like Gabe, could keep the grief deep within. Not once throughout their ordeal had she witnessed him shed a tear, although there were times she knew he was close to it; but then, she also knew that his strength was for her and their daughters, that he had withdrawn into himself so that he could help his family bear the pain. Yes, he was strong; but then, unlike her, he was blameless . . .

A shadow fell across the light. Something moved in the water's reflection.

Startled, she looked up, mouth open in surprise.

Something dark in the rain outside. A hooded shape. Eyes hidden in shadow, but watching her through the window.

With a small frightened cry, Eve took a step backwards.

## 3: GABE CALEIGH

Gabe shone the flashlight at the generator, checking the fuel dial. Quarter-full, it told him. He pressed the autostart switch but only received a wheezy retch from the engine.

The damp smell of dust and must almost clogged his nostrils as he studied the machine before him, which was lit by the dim lightbulb overhead and the beam of his own flashlight. He was only giving the generator a preliminary once-over to ascertain what work would be necessary to have it running smoothly. The battery was a little flat, but Gabe didn't think that was the main problem. Maybe the juice had gone stale if the gen had been standing idle over a long period of time; the agent had told him that Gabe and his family would be the first tenants of Crickley Hall for ten years or so. Power cuts were frequent in these parts, the estate manager had informed him, and the generator was supposed to kick in when the main electricity failed. Probably the spark plugs need cleaning also, Gabe mused as he squatted there in the darkness of the basement room, which was next door to the much larger main cellar. Have to check the fuel filter too – probably full of gunge if it hadn't been cleaned for a while. The machine had a thick layer of dust all over, unlike the boiler that fired up happily beside it, which meant the gen had been neglected for some time.

# THE SECRET OF CRICKLEY HALL

By profession, Gabriel Virgil Caleigh – Gabe to his wife, colleagues and friends – was a mechanical engineer who had been shipped over to England sixteen years ago, when he was twenty-one, by the American company that employed him, APCU Engineering Corp, because it had a policy of staff exchange with its British subsidiary company. The corporation felt a change of environment and learning experience would be good for him. His reckless insubordination had played a tall part in the decision for, although merely a junior engineer, Gabe could be full of his own ideas and often difficult to handle; he seemed to have an aggressive resentment towards authority. However, he possessed a superb and natural talent for most areas of engineering (although chemical engineering was a discipline that didn't suit him at all) and his potential was clearly recognized. APCU was loath to lose someone of his ability.

In truth, the idea of sending Gabe abroad to a place where civility and mannerly traditions might temper the young employee's fiery disposition came from the corporation's CEO, who not only saw the British through rose-tinted spectacles, but also saw something of his younger self in Gabe and was aware of his background (it was fortunate for Gabe that he had one of those chief executives who took a genuine interest in all the people under him, especially the younger members who showed flair; any other kind of boss might well have fired such a peppery junior after their third warning). And he had been right. It worked.

Initially, Gabe had been almost overwhelmed by his new surroundings and the friendly welcome of his colleagues: he soon warmed to them both and began to lose much of his abrasiveness.

He attended college one day a week and quickly achieved higher-level exams in engineering, after which he applied for and gained membership of the Institute of Structural Engineering. Through this he attained more qualifications, eventually becoming a chartered member, attending interviews and writing papers on various aspects of his profession, such as the latest technology, improved processes and new materials. And as he climbed the ladder of success he met and quickly married Eve Lockley. Their family started with Loren only six months into the marriage.

Gabe glanced around the rough-bricked chamber as he straightened up, taking in the long black cobwebs that hung between the wooden beams, the coal heaped in one corner and a log pile close by. The boiler abruptly stopped its surge and the distant sound of running water came to his ears.

It came from the cavernous cellar next door at whose centre was a circular well, around ten feet in diameter, the shaft driven down to the subterranean river that coursed beneath the house itself. The lip of the old stone wall round it stood no more than a foot and a half high. When, earlier, he had brought his family down to see the well for themselves – his promised 'surprise' – he had repeated to Cally that she was not to come down here alone. Continuing to look around, he flexed his shoulders, then rubbed the back of his neck with a hand, twisting his head as he did so, loosening muscles made stiff by the long drive from the city. Old lumps of metal, broken chairs and discarded machinery parts lay about in the gloom as if the basement room was the repository for anything busted or no longer useable. In a far corner he could just make out an old blade-sharpener with a stone wheel and foot pedal. The air was not only dank, but it was chilled too, much of the coldness creeping in from the well cellar. When showing Gabe over the property months before, Grainger, the estate manager, had said that the underground river – imaginatively called the Low River – ran from the nearby moors down to the sea at Hollow Bay, paralleling and eventually joining with the upper Bay River near the estuary. No wonder the whole house felt so chilled, he thought.

He double-tapped the side of the dormant gen with the flat of his hand.

'Later,' he promised, wiping dust from his fingers on his jeans as he made his way through the sundry litter to the doorless opening that led into the main cellar.

Gabe loved machinery of any kind. He loved tinkering with anything from car engines to broken clocks. Years before, until Eve had made him give it up for his family's sake, he had enjoyed stripping down the old motorbike he had owned, putting it back together perfectly each time. It was something he did for fun rather than repair. Back at their London home, in the spare room he used as an office, there were shelves full of venerable mechanical tin toys – marching soldiers, brightly coloured train engines, tiny vintage motor-cars and trucks – and clocks bought mainly from junk shops as well as car boot sales, all of which he'd taken apart, then reassembled. Most of them, broken before, were now in working order. He even enjoyed the smell of heavy machinery – the grease, the oil, the aroma of metal itself. He enjoyed the sound of engines at high and low throttle, the purr of a machine idling, the *clunk* of turning cogs or *clicks* of ratchets. In the past he had liked nothing better than on a Saturday morning dragging his children, as young as they were, along to South Kensington's Science Museum to see the giant steam-train engines housed there, climbing up into the cabs with them to explain every wheel and lever it took to get the great machines moving. To his credit, because of his enthusiasm, only Loren had been bored by the fourth visit. Cally, held in her father's arms, was much too young to be impressed, but Cam went rigid with excitement and awe every time he saw the great iron mammoths.

Gabe quickly sidelined the memory: today had to be an 'up' day, a keep-busy day, for Eve's sake as well as his own. It was the first time they'd left their real home, with all its associations, since—

He cursed himself, forcing the lachrymose thoughts away. Eve needed his full support, particularly now that the anniversary of Cam's disappearance was so close. She was afraid the police would be unable to contact them with any news of their missing son, any clues to his whereabouts – and, hopefully, word that he was still alive, that his abductors were merciful and merely keeping their little boy for themselves – but Gabe had assured her that the police had their new temporary address and phone and cell numbers. He and Eve could be back in the city within a few hours if necessary. But when she had argued that Cam might just turn up on the doorstep on his own to find the house empty, Gabe had been at a loss for comforting words because a small part of him – a small hopelessly desperate part of him – held out for the same thing.

Before passing through the opening into the main basement area, he paused to examine an unusual contraption standing in the shadows left of the doorway, his thoughts at least distracted for a moment. He peered closer, squinting in the shadowy gloom.

The object had two solid-looking wooden rollers, one on top of the other, the smallest of gaps between, and on one side there was an iron wheel with a handle, presumably for turning them. Gabe smiled in quiet awe as he recognized the device for what it was: it was an old-fashioned mangle, used for wringing out water from freshly laundered clothes, the wet material passed through the tight rollers so that the water was squeezed from them. He'd seen one in a book once, but never in the flesh as it were. In the olden days it seemed every home had to have one standing out in the yard or garden. The modern tumble-dryer had taken its place.

Delighted, he touched the rusty cog wheel, then gripped the iron handle, but when he tried to turn it the wooden wheels refused to budge. He shone his light closer, examining the rusted parts, and for a while he was lost to all else. Scrape away the surface rust, clean up the metal, a liberal oiling of the cogs, followed by a smearing of industrial grease, and the mangle would be fine again. Useless, of course, in this day and age – he couldn't see Eve coming down to wring out their clothes with it – but an interesting part of household history.

He stood away from the old mangle, shaking his head in amused wonder, then turned to leave the boiler room. As he did so, the tip of his boot hit something hard and sent it scudding a couple of feet across the dusty floor with a sharp grating noise. He stooped to pick it up and discovered it was a two-foot length of hard metal, two inches or so wide with a round hole at its centre and bevelled edges. It looked like some integral part of a machine, but Gabe had no idea what. He hefted it in his free hand, feeling its weight. Maybe it came from some old gardening machinery, he considered, or maybe—

The small cry came from somewhere next door, barely audible over the noise of the rushing underground river at the bottom of the well. Quickly he stepped through the doorway into the main cellar and heard the faint voice again. Most parents are attuned to the sound of their own child's cry and Gabe was no exception. Cally was calling to him and there was something urgent in her voice.

# JAMES HERBERT

'Daddy! Daddy! Mummy says come –' there was a short break while she remembered the last words – 'right away!'

Gabe tossed the metal bar aside and hurried towards the narrow staircase that led from the cellar.

## 4: PERCY JUDD

She was waiting for him at the head of the stairs, a hand holding open the cellar door, her small tousled head poking through, obviously heeding his warning never to go down on her own. Gabe climbed the stairs rapidly, poor light overhead and his flashlight lighting the way, and Cally took a step backwards, frightened by the grimness of his expression.

'What's wrong, Cally?' he asked even before he reached the top step.

'Man,' she told him, pointing towards the kitchen.

Gabe strode past her, touching her head lightly as he went. 'It's okay, Skip,' he reassured her gently and she trotted after him, unable to keep up with his determined stride.

The old man stood on the threshold of the kitchen's outer door to the small piece of garden at the side of the house, rainwater dripping off his hooded stormcoat and muddy Wellington boots onto the rough-bristled welcome mat. Gabe came to a halt just inside the hall doorway, surprised and wondering what the fuss had been about, why he had been called so urgently.

Eve, whose back was to Gabe, quickly half-turned at his approach and said, 'Oh, Gabe, this is Mr . . . Mr Judd, isn't it?' She returned her attention to the stranger for affirmation.

'Judd, missus,' said the man, 'but call me Percy. First name's Percy.'

He spoke with a soft West Country burr that Gabe warmed to immediately.

''Fraid I couldn't stop it, mister, doggie ran right past me.' It came out as *roit pas' me*.

Gabe appraised the visitor as he walked towards him. He was short and thin, his face weather-ruddied, cheeks and nose flushed with broken capillaries. The hood of his three-quarter coat was pushed back, but he wore a tweed flat cap, silver hair springing from the rim to brush the tops of his large and long-lobed ears.

'Hey,' Gabe said in greeting, stretching out a hand, and the other man looked momentarily puzzled. Gabe corrected himself. 'Hello.'

The old boy had a good firm grip, Gabe noted, and his proffered hand was hard with calluses, the knuckles gnarled and bony, evidence of long-time manual labour.

'What's this about Chester?' Gabe asked, looking round at Eve.

'He scooted out as soon as I opened the door,' she told him.

'Won't've gone fer in this rain, missus.' It was *gorn* instead of 'gone'. 'Sorry, but I gave the missus bit of a shock when I looked through the window. Frightened the doggie, too. Shot past me when the door was opened.'

'Percy was telling me he's Crickley Hall's gardener,' Eve said, eyebrows raised at Gabe.

'Gardener and handyman, mister. I looks after Crickley Hall, even when nobody's livin' in the place. 'Specially then. I comes in coupla' times a week this time of year. Jus' enough to keep the house and garden in good order.'

To Gabe, Percy appeared too ancient to be of much use either in the garden or in the house. But then he shouldn't underestimate country folk; this old-timer was probably as hardy as they come, despite his years. He felt himself being surveyed by blue eyes that were faded like washed denim and hoped that in his old jeans, leather boots and sweater, his hands and forearms grimy with dirt from the cellar (he wasn't aware of the smudge across his nose and cheek), he didn't disappoint as the new tenant of Crickley Hall.

'You take care of the gen?' he asked and, on seeing the puzzlement return to Percy's face again, added: 'The generator, I mean.'

'No, mister, but I looks after the boiler. Used to run the old furnace on coal an' wood, but now it's on the oil and 'lectric, so it's easy. Tanker comes out whenever it's runnin' low and stretches its feeder pipe over the bridge to the tank behind the house. Don't know 'bout the gen'rator though. Don't rightly unnerstand the blessed thing.'

'Guess I can fix it myself,' Gabe said. 'The agent told me you get a lot of power cuts in these parts.'

'Always somethin' interferin' with the lines, fallin' trees, ligh'nin' strikes. The gen'rator was installed 'bout fifteen years ago. Crickley Hall's owner got fed up with using candles an' oil lamps all the time, as well as eatin' cold dinners.' Percy gave a dry chuckle at the thought. 'Yer'll be needin' the gen'rator in good workin' order all right.'

'Who *is* the owner of this place? The agent never said.'

Eve was interested in the answer to Gabe's question too, wondering who would choose to live permanently in such a bleak mausoleum. Even though the big hall beyond the kitchen was imposing, there was still a cheerlessness about it.

'Fellah by the name of Templeton. Bought Crickley Hall some twenny years ago. Never stayed long though, weren't happy here.'

That came as no surprise to Eve.

'Would you like some tea or coffee, Percy?' she asked.

'Cuppa tea'll do me.' His smile revealed teeth that resembled a row of old crooked and weathered headstones.

Gabe pulled out a chair from the kitchen table for the old gardener and invited him to sit down. Percy removed his cap as he ambled forward and took his seat. Although his silver hair was full over his ears and round the back of his neck, it was sparse over the top of his head.

'Coffee for you, Gabe?' Eve had moved to the sink and was filling the plastic kettle they'd brought with them.

'Yeah, please.' Gabe pulled out a chair for himself and carefully moved Cally's painting aside. He noticed his daughter had remained in the doorway.

'She's a bonny miss,' observed Percy, giving a small wave of his fingers. She responded by smiling and coyly sidling up to the back of Gabe's chair and hanging on to it.

It was Eve who introduced her. 'This is Cally, our youngest. Her real name is Catherine after my mother, but ever since she understood our surname is Caleigh she's insisted on being called her version of it. Our older daughter, Loren, is busy upstairs at the moment.'

'Hello, missy.' Percy stuck out a gnarled old hand to be shaken and Cally shyly touched it with her fingers, withdrawing them swiftly once she'd done so. Percy chuckled again.

'So tell me, Percy,' said Gabe, leaning his forearms on the table, 'who built the house?'

'Crickley Hall was built at the beginnin' of the last century by a wealthy local man by the name of Charles Crickley. He owned most of the harbour's fishing fleet and all the limekilns hereabouts. Great benefactor to the village, he were, but ended up an unhappy man by all accounts. Wanted to make more of Hollow Bay, make it a tourist attraction, but the locals went agin' him, didn't want no changes, wanted the place peaceful like, holidaymakers be damned. All but broke him in the end. Fishin' stocks dropped, South Wales stopped sendin' limestone 'cross the channel to his kilns, and money he invested smartenin' up Hollow Bay for the tourists came to nothin'. Locals even voted agin' him building a pier for pleasure boats an' such in the bay itself.'

'But Charles Crickley built this place,' Gabe prompted.

'Drew the plans for it hisself, he did. Weren't one for fancy ideas.'

'That explains a lot,' said Eve as she poured boiling water over a tea bag in a cup.

'No one likes the look of Crickley Hall,' commented Percy with a sigh. 'Don't like it much meself, never have done.'

'You've worked here a long time?' Eve was now pouring water over the coffee granules.

'All me life. Here and the parish church, I've looked after 'em both. They gives me help with the churchyard nowadays, but I takes care of Crickley Hall on my own. Like I says, jus' a coupla days a week, I come in. Tend the garden mainly.'

He must be seventy-something if he's a day, thought Gabe, glancing at Eve.

'Only time I didn't,' Percy went on, 'were towards the end of the last world war. Sent abroad then, to fight for me country.'

Yup, Gabe confirmed to himself, definitely in his late seventies or early eighties even, if he'd been old enough to fight the Germans back then. He studied the short, wiry man with interest.

'Ol' Crickley blasted a shelf out of Devil's Cleave with

dynamite,' Percy continued, 'then built his home on it. Then he dug down to the ol' river that runs underground down the Cleave, made hisself a well in Crickley Hall's cellar. Even though the Bay River was only yards from his front door, he must've reckoned he'd have his own fresh water supply inside the house. Maybe he thought it were purer that way. An' he liked things simple, did Crickley, plain like. Only fancy part were the big hall itself.'

'Yeah, we noticed,' agreed Gabe.

'If he liked things simple,' put in Eve, 'and presumably functional, that must be why the kitchen is at the front.'

'The las' of the Crickleys lef' here in '39,' Percy went on unbidden, 'jus' afore the shebang in Europe started. They wanted to avoid the trouble, thought England were doomed. Scarpered off to Canada, while I stayed on to work 'til I got my call-up papers. Be then, gov'mint had requisitioned the place 'cause it were empty an' they thought it'd do for evacuees. Sold coupla times since – Crickleys didn't want it no more – then the Templetons come along an' bought it. Retired early, Mr Templeton sold his business – somethin' to do with packagin' he told me – an lef' the city fer the countryside. Thought him an' his missis would be content, like, down here.'

She handed Percy his tea and he took it with a nod of gratitude. He blew into the cup to cool it as Eve came back to the table with Gabe's steaming coffee.

'I've just spotted Chester out there sitting under the tree with the swing,' she said anxiously. 'He's looking very sorry for himself.'

'Let him sulk for a while,' said Gabe. 'I'll get him in a minute. He's gotta get used to this place.'

Percy carefully put his cup back onto the saucer. He said gravely: 'Pets don't shine to Crickley Hall.'

Eve returned her gaze to the mongrel, feeling sorry for Chester sitting out there all alone, evidently confused by their long journey away from the home he had always known. Even from the kitchen window she could see that Chester was shivering.

She tapped on the glass to get his attention while the two men behind her continued talking. But the dog wouldn't look her way. He seemed rapt on something quite close to him.

The swing. The swing was swaying gently, but more so than before, when they had first arrived: back and forth it went, almost as if someone – a child – were sitting on it. But of course it was empty.

Must be the wind, Eve thought. But then, although it was raining, the leaves and the tree branches were perfectly still, as were the shrubbery and the longer tufts of grass. There was no wind.

## 5: LOREN CALEIGH

Wearing a yellow Fat Face long-sleeved T-shirt and beige fatigues more suited to summer than autumn, Loren pulled up her younger sister's baby-blue bedsheet and plumped up the Shrek and Princess Fiona pillow. She reached for the colourful Shrek, Fiona *and* Donkey duvet at her feet and dragged it up onto the narrow bed, which was twin to her own bed a few feet away. Dad and 'Uncle' Vern had brought them from their real home and put them together a week ago (she and Cally had slept in the spare room until the move). Her long brown hair hung over her face as she tucked the duvet's end and sides under the mattress and when she stood upright there was a frown marring her features.

Loren was at that sensitive, awkward stage of being neither a teenager nor a child, a time when hormones were kicking in and sudden outbreaks of tears were not uncommon. Her thin arms and legs were beginning to develop beyond cuteness. Although she didn't feel it, she was just a normal pre-teenager.

She didn't like Crickley Hall, she didn't like it at all. Away from her friends, having to start a new school on Monday where she would stand out like a freak, a city girl among country bumpkins. It wasn't fair. It was too harsh.

Then she remembered the main reason for the temporary

move. It wasn't just because of Dad's job – he often spent weeks away from home on various engineering assignments. No, this time it was because they had to get Mummy away from their proper house. Loren's eyes glistened as she thought of Cameron; what a lovely little brother he was. Now he was gone and Mummy still hadn't got over it. It hadn't been her fault. Mummy was tired and couldn't help falling asleep on the park bench. Cam had just wandered off and someone bad had taken him. Loren tried to imagine who could *be* that bad, what wicked person would snatch a small boy away and keep him all this time. Why didn't they bring him back, or let him go so that the police or someone kind could find him and bring him home to his family? Who could be that dreadful?

She brushed at her damp eyes with the back of one hand. Dad said they had to be strong for Mummy's sake and she, Loren, had done her best. She rarely cried over Cam any more even though she missed him terribly; she almost had right then because she was in a strange place and was already feeling homesick.

She leaned forward to straighten the duvet and as she did so she caught something moving out of the corner of her eye. Something small had walked past the doorway – no, had *run* past the bedroom door. She hadn't heard footsteps, but she had definitely seen a blur go past.

It must be Cally. It seemed to be her size even if it was rushed.

'Cally?' Loren called out. 'Is that you out there?'

No reply.

She walked to the open door and looked along the balustraded landing that ran round two sides of the big hall.

Nothing. No one there.

Except . . . Loren wasn't sure she'd really heard it. But it came again. It sounded like a whimper.

Loren stepped out onto the landing and looked to her right, towards where she thought the sound had come from. Holding her breath, she listened.

It came again. A quiet little sob. And then again. A small child crying.

'Cally?' she called again. 'What's wrong? What's the matter?'

Loren could hear the low buzz of conversation coming from the kitchen doorway below, but the sound she strained to hear again wasn't from there. She took a few paces along the landing, then stopped when she heard another whimper. It came from a cupboard set in the wall.

'Cally,' she called again, this time somewhat irritated. Why wouldn't her sister answer her?

She went to the closed cupboard. Was Cally playing a game, hiding from her? Now she'd shut herself in the cupboard and had become afraid of the dark. But then why didn't she just come out? Had she locked herself in? But she couldn't have: the key was in the lock.

Another tiny sound of a sob. Definitely from inside the cupboard.

Loren reached out a hand for the key. Her fingers closed around it.

And suddenly she was afraid.

The whimpers, the sobs, hadn't sounded like Cally at all. And Cally wasn't a cry-baby anyway. She was mostly a happy girl. The quiet whimper came again and it seemed much further off than from inside the cupboard. Somehow it was distant now.

With sudden resolve, Loren gripped the key hard, turned it and pulled.

The cupboard door swung open and inside there was only – Loren shivered – inside there was only blackness. A blackness so deep it seemed solid.

## 6: WHITE SHADOW

'Mum! Dad! I heard someone—' Loren all but skidded into the kitchen, her words broken off when she saw the stranger sitting at the kitchen table. All eyes turned to her.

'What is it, Loren?' Eve asked calmly as she leaned back against the sink. There always seemed to be a crisis in her eldest daughter's life these days.

Loren didn't reply immediately, her attention taken up with the visitor, a funny old man with stick-out ears and a red face.

'I heard something ... someone upstairs!' She burst out the news, despite the presence of the stranger.

'This is Mr Judd,' Eve told her, ignoring Loren's agitation for the moment. 'He's Crickley Hall's gardener and handyman. He'll be helping us with the place.'

Percy gave her a quick smile but, sitting close to him, Gabe noticed the curiosity in his stare. Was there something else, too? Something that was close to alarm?

'Now, what are you going on about?' Eve's voice was patient.

'I was in our new bedroom,' Loren said in a rush, 'and I saw something go past the door. I thought it was Cally.'

Her little sister was hanging onto the back of her father's chair and she looked confused. 'Not me,' she said as if anxious that she was being accused of doing something naughty.

'I know it wasn't you, silly.' Loren shook her head at Cally.

'Not silly,' Cally insisted.

Gabe stepped in. 'Who *did* you see, Loren?'

'I . . . I don't know, Dad. It was like . . . it was like a white shadow.'

Gabe raised his eyebrows and glanced at Eve, who went to her daughter and put an arm round her shoulder.

'It's true, Mummy,' Loren insisted. 'It was gone before I could look properly. And then I heard someone crying. It wasn't very loud, but I could still hear it. I thought it was Cally at first, but she's down here with you and it didn't really sound like her when I got closer.'

'Closer to what?' asked Gabe, still at the table with Percy Judd.

'To the cupboard upstairs,' Loren replied. 'I thought someone had shut themselves inside the cupboard.'

By chance, Gabe had looked towards the gardener again and now he saw there *was* alarm in those old faded eyes. Yet Percy said nothing. Gabe swung back to Loren and began to rise. 'Let me take a look. Maybe you heard a mouse or something.'

'It wasn't a mouse. It was a voice, Mummy. It was someone small crying.' She looked up at Eve for support.

'It must have been something else, darling,' said Eve gently. 'Perhaps the wind, a draught whistling through.'

'No, it was a voice. Please believe me, Mummy.'

'I do. It's just that you may have been mistaken.'

'C'mon, Loren, we'll take a look together.' Gabe came towards her, reaching out a hand as he approached.

'I already looked, Dad. There was nothing in the cupboard. It was just . . . *dark*.'

'Well, we'll take a proper look. I'll bring the flashlight. You okay for a minute, Percy?'

The gardener had already risen to his feet and was adjusting the cap on his head. 'That's all right, mister. You best be goin' with your daughter.'

'Gabe. Call me Gabe. My wife is Eve, and now you've met Cally and Loren.'

Loren pulled at her father's hand, impatient to take him upstairs.

'I'll be on my way.' Percy headed for the kitchen's outer door as if keen to be gone. 'I'll see yer Tuesday afternoon 'less yer wants me sooner. Phone number's on this.' He placed a small crinkled piece of brown paper on a worktop as he passed. 'Anythin' at all, just give me a holler.'

With that he was through the door, pulling the hood over his cap as he went. Rain dampened the welcome mat before he closed the door behind him.

'Okay, Slim,' Gabe said to Loren, 'let's see what all the fuss is about.'

'Not much to see,' Gabe announced, shining the light into the deep cupboard. 'Just some cardboard boxes, a mop and a broom, and what looks like a rolled-up rug at the back, nothing much else.'

He had snatched up the flashlight from the narrow chiffonier against the wall in the hall where he'd left it after leaving the cellar earlier, and all four of them, Gabe, Eve and the two girls, had climbed the broad wooden staircase to the first-floor landing.

'It was just dark before,' Loren insisted, looking over his shoulder. 'There was nothing there.' Gabe was crouched so that he could look through the cupboard doorway; the opening itself was about five feet high and three feet wide.

'Sure, but now we got the flashlight. And hey, look back there. The board at the end of the closet is painted black. No wonder it looked so dark in here when you looked before.' The smell of dust wafted from the opening.

'But I heard someone, Dad. I definitely heard someone crying. I thought it was Cally.'

Eve, also crouched, turned to Loren. 'Cally has been with us all the time,' she said softly so that Loren would not feel she was being disbelieved, only mistaken. 'You couldn't have heard her.'

'I know. I mean it sounded like her. A child was crying.'

Gabe moved into the cupboard, going down on one knee. He shifted boxes aside, raising dust. 'Might've been a small animal. Probably a mouse.'

'It wasn't a mouse! Why don't you believe me?'

Eve touched her daughter's shoulder: Loren became distressed all too easily these days. 'We're only saying you might have been mistaken,' she said soothingly.

'But I saw something too. Something went past the door.'

Gabe had moved further into the shadowy space and was pushing more cardboard boxes aside. 'Well, there's nobody in here now,' he said over his shoulder as he began to pull back. 'Coulda been a breeze blowing through the house, as Mummy said. Wind through a crack in the wall can make all kinds of spooky noises.'

'It wasn't the wind,' Loren told him firmly.

Eve could feel no draught or breeze coming from the cupboard. She looked around the landing, then over the balustrade at the hall below.

Gabe backed out and straightened. 'Nothing there, Loren. Guess you imagined it. No big deal.'

Loren turned on her heels and stomped away, disappearing into her new bedroom and closing the door after her.

Gabe and Eve looked at each other and Gabe raised his eyebrows. 'Hormones,' he said.

Eve remained silent.

## 7: FIRST NIGHT

'Gabe.'

'Uh?'

'Gabe, wake up.'

Eve shook his shoulder. Gabe was a heavy sleeper.

'What...?' He stirred, opened his eyes, eyelids sluggish with sleep.

Eve pushed herself into a sitting position and leaned back against the curved wooden headboard. Rain outside pattered against the room's windows.

She shook Gabe's shoulder again, this time more fiercely. 'Gabe, can't you hear him?'

Reluctantly, he dragged himself from sleep and raised his head. 'Hear who?' he said.

'Listen.'

Now he heard it. Chester's howl drifted across the hall and up the stairs from the kitchen.

'He's frightened,' said Eve.

Gabe rested on one elbow and briskly wiped weariness from his face with the flat of his hand. It had been a long, hard day and this he could do without.

'He'll be okay,' he assured Eve. 'Just needs to get used to the place.'

Eve was staring at the dark opening of the doorway, the

door left ajar so that they could hear either of the girls should they wake up in their strange room and be frightened. Their bedroom door had been left open too.

'Gabe!' she said sharply. Something pale had moved into the opening, but it was too dark to see what: so cloudy was the night that the window offered little light. 'There's someone out there.'

Gabe felt the back of his neck go cold, short hairs there stiffening. He sat up in the bed and stared at the doorway and drew in an involuntary breath.

'Mummy? Daddy?'

Both Eve and Gabe felt their bodies relax when they realized Loren had come to their room. The door swung even wider open and the howling below grew more mournful.

'Chester's upset,' Loren said from the doorway.

'It's all right,' Eve soothed. 'He just doesn't like being alone in a new place.'

'He'll settle down soon,' Gabe added.

'But he's crying, Daddy.' In the cold darkness of night he had become 'Daddy' once more.

He pushed the bed's heavy duvet aside, giving in only a tad reluctantly. He was concerned for the mutt too. That afternoon he'd had to venture out in the rain to Chester, who had refused to leave his spot by the oak tree, heedless of their calls and coaxing. He had picked the mongrel up bodily and carried him back into the house; once inside, Chester had shivered in the corner of the kitchen next to the door while Loren wiped him down with an old towel, his eyes bulging so hard that the whites at the sides were visible. Eventually, and with Loren stroking his wiry fur, Chester had fallen into a troubled sleep.

'You go back to bed, Loren, and I'll go down and see to Chester,' Gabe said as he padded over to the door.

'Can't he sleep on my bed?' Loren implored.

'Uh-huh, kid. He's gotta get through the night on his own. We can't have him sleeping upstairs.'

'Just this once, Daddy. He won't disturb me if he's on the end of my bed. I promise he'll be good.'

'Let me see how he is first.'

'Thank you, Daddy.'

'I didn't say I'd bring him up, I said I'll see how he is. And if he does come up, he'll be in this room, not with you. Now get yourself back to bed before you catch cold.'

She disappeared into her own room, but before he could go to the stairs, her head popped out again.

'You won't be cross with him, will you?' she said plaintively.

'Bed.' He used his no-nonsense tone and she disappeared.

He remembered there was a light switch somewhere on the landing and his hand scrabbled against the wall beside the bedroom door. There, found it. He clicked on the landing light, which was dim, hardly strong enough to spill into the hall below. The switch to the iron chandelier was inconveniently somewhere by the front door.

Gabe usually slept in T-shirt and boxers, but because the house was cold, tonight he wore dark pyjama leggings below the T-shirt. The landing's bare floorboards, which had been varnished some time ago, were cool under his bare feet and for once he wished he was the kind of guy who wore slippers. Hand using the wide rail for guidance, he went down the stairs into the hall's shadowy darkness, old boards creaking beneath his tread. Pausing on the small square landing at the turn of the stairs, even the tall window behind him affording scant light, rain pitter-pattering against the glass, he looked across the grand hall towards the closed kitchen door. But it was another door that caught his attention, a deeper blackness among the shadows. The cellar door was open and he swore he'd closed and locked it earlier in the evening, ever fearful of Cally wandering down to look at the well and its dangerously low wall. Now it was open, unlocked. Had Eve gone down there to see the well for herself – they had been too busy for the full tour earlier – and forgotten to close and lock the door after her? Yet he was sure, being the last one to turn in that night, that the cellar door was at least closed if not locked. He mentally shrugged. Okay, if that was the case, maybe a draught from the well below had forced it open. Had to be, there was no other explanation. A river running beneath the house could cause all sorts of air disturbances, a breeze – a wind even – travelling up the shaft, then funnelled up the cellar stairs.

He descended the rest of the stairway and crossed the umbrageous hall, its flagstones even colder than the wood under his feet. He was an idiot not to have taken the flashlight up to the bedroom with him: he could just make out its black barrel standing erect on the chiffonier where he'd left it next to the old-style phone earlier. Padding over to the narrow sideboard, he picked up the heavy flashlight and switched it on. No need to turn on the hall's light when he had his own source.

Just for the sake of it, he swept the beam around the room, chasing shadows away, lighting up the deeper corners. Everything seemed in order apart from the open cellar door, which he swiftly moved towards. He shut it and heard the lock *click* as he turned the key. Foolishly, Gabe had to admit to himself he somehow felt more at ease with the door locked.

From the kitchen came Chester's desperate howl and Gabe realized the dog must have quietened when he heard the creaking of the stairs, although for some reason Gabe hadn't noticed. Now the cry was more urgent than before.

The flashlight's beam providing a path for him, Gabe went to the kitchen door and opened it. The howl broke off midway and Chester's short tail began to thump the floor in nervous agitation. Lit by the strong beam, Gabe saw that Chester's neck was stretched to its limit as he perked up.

'Okay, fellah,' Gabe said soothingly as he approached the tough-haired mongrel. 'No one's gonna harm you. Just tell me what all the fuss is about.'

Without switching on the overhead light, Gabe knelt down in front of the quivering dog and began to stroke his head, then pat his side. In return, Chester endeavoured to lick Gabe's face and, when Gabe pulled back, was content to lick his master's outstretched hand.

'There you go.' Gabe kept his voice soft. 'No spooks around to scare you. Only me. Now settle down so we can all get some sleep.'

But Chester would not lie down. He stood on all fours, his favourite blanket rumpled beneath him, and tried to nuzzle his master's face again. Gabe pulled the dog to him and cradled the trembling body in his arms.

'Hush now, you crazy mutt,' he whispered. 'Nothing to bother you in this place. Momma and the girls are in bed where I oughta be, so just you snuggle down and go to sleep.'

Chester only pushed against him all the more.

A flurry of rain suddenly lashed at the kitchen windows causing Gabe to swing round and almost overbalance.

'Wild out tonight, Chester,' he said to the pet. 'You don't wanna be out there in this weather, do you? Is that what all the fuss is about? You busting to go AWOL again, or maybe you just wanna get busy?' 'Busy' was their code for Chester relieving himself. 'You need go find a nice tree?'

Gabe stood and reached for the key in the kitchen's outer

door, twisted it, then pulled back the top and bottom bolts. He swung the door open just enough for Chester to slip through the gap, but the dog merely shrunk away from the opening as rain gusted through.

'No? Don't want out? Don't blame you, Chester, don't blame you at all. But come on, you gotta stop this wailing. You're keeping us all awake.' Gabe closed the door and locked it again, then squatted down beside the trembling dog.

'What is it? You wanna come upstairs with me, is that it?'

The dog pressed against his knees.

'Can't do it, boy. You gotta get a handle on the place. Toughen up, okay?'

Gabe stood and went to the inner door. 'Now not another peep outa you. Be a pal and go to sleep.'

As soon as Gabe shut the door behind him, the wailing began again, only this time it was even more agitated. He heard Chester scratching at the kitchen's inner door. Gabe went back, threw open the door and scooped the dog up in his arms.

'Just for tonight, Chester,' he told the dog as he headed for the stairs, flashlight shining ahead. 'Tomorrow you're on your own, understand? No more howling, no more looking moon-eyed at me. Tomorrow night you stay down here no matter what ruckus you kick up. I'm serious, mutt, you can caterwaul as much as you like, but you're staying in the kitchen. If I leave you in the hall you'll be up the stairs, so that's just not gonna happen. You hear me, Chester?' He lifted one of the dog's ears when he made the last remark, but Chester only snuggled further against him.

Gabe had kept his voice low as he chastised the mongrel, but firm enough to let him know he meant business. Halfway across the flagstone floor with Chester's head nestling in the crook of one arm, the other supporting the dog's hindquarters as well as directing the flashlight, Gabe suddenly hopped onto one foot.

'What the hell . . .?'

His foot had splashed into a puddle on the floor. He manoeuvred the flashlight so that he could look down at his feet and, sure enough, there was a small puddle of water there. He must have missed it earlier on his way to the kitchen because he'd been diverted towards the cellar. He also became aware of that now-familiar musty, damp odour that was so prevalent in the cellar: it had invaded the hall itself.

Swinging the light beam up towards the high ceiling, he searched for any damp patches, reasoning that the fierce rain outside had found a way into the attic area (which had not yet been inspected) and was dripping through the floor. The great iron chandelier threw eerie shadows onto the ceiling, like a giant spider's legs; but there were no wet patches or stains up there.

Still wondering at its cause, Gabe skirted the small pool of water on the floor and made for the stairs, Chester still shivering in his arms. And when he reached the stairs, he came to a halt again.

There was another tiny puddle in the middle of the third step. Another on the small square landing turn.

Avoiding the first stair puddle, he made his way up, stopping once more at the turn. He shone the flashlight up the second, longer flight of stairs.

There seemed to be small puddles on every second or third step. He wondered how he'd missed them on his way down.

## 8: HOLLOW BAY

They left the dog behind in Crickley Hall because they intended to have lunch in Hollow Bay's pub/restaurant (the previous week, when Gabe and Vern had taken a break from moving furniture and other essential items into Crickley Hall, they had sampled Barnaby Inn's fare and Gabe highly recommended it; he also favoured the local brew) and they didn't know the management's policy regarding customers bringing pets into the establishment.

The inn was certainly quaint, with its white walls, thatched roof, leaded windows and outside hanging lamps that were lit due to the day's dusk-like gloom. It would certainly have been a tourist magnet had the indigenous population not been so stranger-shy; the locals seemed to set more store in privacy than financial gain for, although it was late in the season and the weather was foul, there should have been more people on the two streets of the village than there were today – those few they did meet along the 'promenade' were certainly not holidaymakers, to judge by their sensible if dour attire.

Although the few shops and many of the houses looked pleasant enough in their pastel pinks and blues, the majority of them white-fronted, on closer inspection it could be noticed that the paintwork was flaky and cracked in places, the decoration tired and weather-worn, the woodwork chipped.

Most windows were dark and uninviting, as if concealing their tenants, only one or two orange with the glows of autumn hearth fires. Rainwater gushed along gutters and pooled round overworked drains, sodden October leaves piling into heaps that blocked the gratings. The single teashop – perhaps the village's only deference to the sightseer – that Gabe and his family passed on their journey to the inn seemed dingy and unappealing, its fluorescent lighting too harsh, and drab lace half-curtains hung from a tarnished brass rail across the long window-front as if privacy was more important than invitation.

Fortunately, the Barnaby Inn, with its smoky-yellow walls and broad, sturdy posts rising to a low, beamed ceiling, a roaring log fire in the large inglenook fireplace at one end of the room, had proved a welcome retreat from the dismal mood of the harbour village itself (possibly the downpour negatively influenced their judgement).

Eve had at least tried to convince herself that overcast skies and constant fall of chilled rain, together with the great steel-grey expanse of the Bristol Channel whose waters lapped at the harbour wall, all conspired to render the village joyless and somehow, if it could be said of a place, sullen. Or was her own morbid depression tainting everything she saw and felt?

The only thing that slightly spoilt the pub's welcoming atmosphere was the hard stares they received from the customers inside when the family bustled in, dripping water onto the rubber entrance mat and voicing their relief to be out of the rain. They were boldly watched as Gabe guided Eve and the girls to a cushioned benchseat against a wall, a long wooden table between it and two hard-backed chairs.

'We don't loik strangers 'roind ere,' Gabe whispered to Eve in an awful version of the West Country accent as he pulled out one of the chairs for her. At least she smiled when she shushed him.

The other customers returned to their conversations and brews, little warmth or further interest coming from them.

However, the barmaid, who had short chestnut-coloured hair and a dazzling smile, was courteous and friendly as she reeled off the two specials of the day to them from her position behind the bar, and the food, when it arrived, was both tasty and abundant. Even Loren, who was a picky eater at the best of times and who had groaned when the huge plate of sea bass with chips and peas was placed in front of her, finished nearly every last morsel. The sea air and the long walk down to the village were obviously doing wonders for her appetite, Eve thought to herself, pleased by the transition. Gabe relished the local brew again (he and Vern had sunk several pints of Tawny Bitter between them on their earlier visit, the hard graft of lifting and unloading stuff back at Crickley Hall engendering a special kind of thirst), while Eve stuck to tonic water (she used to enjoy good wines, but hadn't touched alcohol in almost a year), the girls orange and lemonade mixed (Loren's idea of a sophisticated drink, Cally copying her big sister).

When Gabe returned to the bar for a refill and another tonic for Eve, a thickset man with a florid face and greying hair appeared from a doorway behind the counter. He had the air of a landlord or manager and it was he who served Gabe.

'Passin' through, is it?' the man asked conversationally as he drew the pint.

'Uh-uh, I'm working in these parts for a short while, coupla months mebbe,' Gabe replied. 'Staying up at Crickley Hall.'

The beer flowed over the lip of the glass into a hidden sink below the bar as the man stared at him.

*Wait a bit,* Gabe thought. *I've seen this movie. Isn't this where the ruddy-faced local warns him to keep clear of the old house up there on the hill? 'Strange things 'appen up there at the 'all.'*

But the barman merely pushed back the pump and righted the glass. He smiled pleasantly as he placed the ale on the bar mat in front of Gabe and said, 'Dreadful weather we're havin' lately. Must have rained for three weeks solid now. Hope it don't spoil yer stay.'

'We'll be keeping ourselves pretty busy,' Gabe told him as he waited for the tonic. 'My daughter starts at the local school Monday.' The 'local' school was several miles away in the nearest town of Merrybridge.

Pouring half the tonic water into a fresh glass and leaving the rest in the bottle, which he stood beside it, the barman nodded. 'That'll be Merrybridge Middle School, will it? She'll be all right there. Most of the village kids go to the Merry Middle. Picked up by bus from the main street. S'pect the driver will make a stop at Crickley Hall for yer daughter, no problem for him. Frank's one of my regulars so I'll mention it when he comes in tonight. The school will have to make the formal arrangement regarding payment and insurance, but that's easily done.'

'Thanks, I'd be grateful. I'm taking her in myself the first morning but I'll fix it with the school. I need to go into Ilfracombe anyway.'

'And what about the little 'un?'

'She's only five. My wife'll take care of her while we're down here.' Gabe knew Eve would teach Cally the basics of reading and writing far more strictly than any nursery school.

As the other man took the money for the drinks and food from Gabe, he remarked, 'Big place, that Crickley Hall. Yer'll be rattlin' around in it.'

'I bet it'll be cold, too, in this weather.' This came from the attractive chestnut-haired barmaid, who had come back from serving a customer at the far end of the bar. Her Devonian burr was barely noticeable; if anything, her accent was more south London than West Country. 'It'll be damp. All those old places are.'

'Yeah, I found puddles on the stairs last night and I'm not sure how they got there,' Gabe replied. 'Maybe from a loose window frame. There's a big window over the stairs. All gone this morning, though, not even damp patches left behind.'

'You wait 'til there's a proper storm. Then you'll know about it. You've probably got a leaky roof too.' The girl gave a brief mock shiver.

The barman shrugged. 'Owner's not lived there fer years and them that rented it never stayed long.'

*Oh-oh*, Gabe said to himself wryly, here it comes. *Fifty years ago a mad axeman chopped up his family and hid the body parts all over the house, or at the turn of the last century the wealthy owner of Crickley Hall, old Charlie Crickley himself, forbade his daughter to marry the local ratcatcher and she hanged herself in the cellar.*

But the bartender went on: 'That's why the place has been so neglected and why yer gettin' yer leaks.'

'I thought the old guy, Percy – Percy Judd? – took care of the house.'

The other man gave him a rueful grin. 'Percy's a bit ancient to do much upkeep. That's why the estate manager pays two ladies from the village to go in and give it a good dusting once a month. No, Percy can't do a lot on his own nowadays. To be honest wiv yer, he's only kept on out of kindness. Has he been knocking on yer door yet?'

'Yesterday, soon after we arrived. Just how old is he?'

The barman's forehead creased as he took a moment to

think. He scratched his chin. 'Oh, he must be . . . well, I don't know for sure, but he's got to be nearly eighty by now. Served overseas wiv the army at the end of the last world war, so he must be getting on a bit.'

Gabe whistled softly through his teeth. 'And he's still working?'

'Like I say, as a kindness. No one likes to sack him, y'see. He helps out at the church en' all, but nothing too heavy, just tending the churchyard, collectin' hymn books after Mass, that sort of thing. He's a dear old chap, set in his ways, though, determined like. Won't retire no matter how many times it's been suggested. He's harmless – won't give yer no bother.'

'He's sweet,' chimed in the barmaid.

'Customer wants serving, Frannie.' The barman gave a nod towards a customer waiting further down, two empty glasses before him on the counter. Giving Gabe one final smile, Frannie went off to take the customer's order.

The barman leaned one elbow on the bar. 'I'm the landlord of the Barnaby,' he told Gabe, 'and anything yer want to know about the area, just drop by and I'll try to oblige. If I'm not around, my wife, Vera, or our Frannie will be.'

Warmed by the man's friendliness, Gabe smiled. 'That's kind of you. I guess we'll be okay.'

'Well, don't hesitate. We could do with some new faces around 'ere. Good luck to you and yer family, Mr . . .?'

'Gabe Caleigh.' Gabe extended a hand across the beer mat and the landlord shook it.

'Sam Pennelly's me name. Enjoy yer stay, Mr Caleigh. Yer in a beautiful spot up there in the gorge.'

Gabe poured the rest of the tonic into its glass and was about to turn away, both glasses in his hands, when a thought struck him. 'Out of interest, how did Devil's Cleave get its name? It's kinda dark for such a wonderful place.'

Now the landlord had both elbows on the bartop as he leaned forward as if to speak confidentially. 'Centuries ago,' he said, his broad face serious, his voice husky, 'the Devil, hisself, tried to cut his way inland from the sea to flood all the villages hereabouts. First he took a bite out of the cliffs and that's how Hollow Bay came to be. Years of land erosion have widened the bay, of course. Anyway, they say after he took his first bite he attempted to gnaw his way up to the moors, but his teeth eventually got worn down to the gums and he couldn't get no further so, frustrated like, he sloped off back to sea swearing to have his revenge one day. And he did, but I'll leave that for another day, Mr Caleigh.'

The landlord straightened up and Gabe grinned at him, then froze the grin as he realized Pennelly's expression remained serious. For a beat or two there was a silence between the two men and Gabe was bemused.

Then the other man chuckled, his face breaking into a broad, yellow-toothed smile.

'Sorry, didn't mean to get a rise from yer,' the landlord apologized, continuing to smile, 'but that's how the tale goes. There's a lot of nonsense legends in these parts and they make good conversations round a roaring fire on winter nights.' He had one last chuckle before saying, 'Nice to meet you and your family, Mr Caleigh. You're always welcome at the Barnaby, so don't you stay away. You take good care of those girls of yours, now – all three of 'em I mean.'

Pennelly strolled off to talk to some customers at the other end of the bar and Gabe brought the drinks back to the table.

Eve looked up at him as he placed the glass before her.

'You seemed to be having a nice chat,' she said, and it was really a question: what were they talking about?

Gabe took his seat. 'Yeah, nice people. But I think the guy was twisting my head at the end.' He supped his beer.

'How did the guy twist your head, Daddy?' asked Cally, taking her lips from the straw she was using.

'Oh, he was just telling me how Hollow Bay and the ravine were made.'

'Gorge,' corrected Loren, who liked her father to speak proper English on occasion (she did this not out of embarrassment but because she genuinely thought she was being helpful, even though all her friends thought his American accent was cool).

'Tell us how, please,' Cally demanded noisily draining the last of her drink.

Gabe lowered his own voice as he told them the tale of how Hollow Bay and Devil's Cleave got their names.

## 9: THE PROJECT

'See it out there?'

Hunched in his coat against the steady drizzle, Gabe pointed over the stone harbour wall and Eve and the girls followed his direction. Loren and Cally wore yellow, hooded plastic macs while Eve had on her parka, deep blue in colour and drawn in at the waist to give it shape. While she and the girls had the hoods of their coats up, Gabe had stuffed his woollen beanie hat into one of his reefer jacket's pockets, because sometimes he enjoyed the feel of rain or wind on his face and head. His hair was already darkened by the hard rain, but his only concession to the weather was to pull his coat collar up round his neck.

He was pointing at a metal column topped by a square-shaped box that rose from the sea like a sentinel just over two miles from the harbour boundary. A scarcely visible ladder ran down its length into the choppy waters.

'How can you fit in there, Daddy?' asked Cally peering up from beneath her hood. 'It's very tiny.'

Gabe grinned. 'It's bigger than it looks. That's where I'll probably be next week, checking it out.'

'It's too far to swim,' she said, frowning.

What they couldn't see was the important submerged part of the structure, two giant twin rotors resembling aircraft propeller blades attached to either side of a steel monopile which was set into a deep hole drilled into the seabed. Essentially it was a brilliantly conceived device for harnessing power from the sea itself, using tidal flows to turn the rotors.

It was situated where full advantage could be taken of the Bristol Channel's high tidal current velocities; because sea water was eight hundred times more dense than air, quite slow velocities of water could generate significantly more energy than whole crops of surface windmills, and with considerably more regularity and predictability. Gabe's company APCU Engineering (UK) was but one of a consortium of varied companies involved in the production and financing of the prototype, with the UK's DTI and European Commission also partly funding and supporting the enterprise. The parent company, whose invention this was, was aptly named Seapower. The end view was to create whole lines of such marine turbines just off the coast of countries and continents around the world, most of them linked to national grids.

However, as cost efficient and energy productive as these marine current turbines would be, there was a downside, and this was one of the reasons APCU's engineering skills had been sought for the prototype. Maintenance and repairs were, to say the least, challenging, and APCU's engineers had suggested that if the structure's rotors and drive chain could be raised above the waterline when necessary, then maintenance and repair could far more easily be carried out working from a surface vessel. Gabe, who many times in the past had helped design and worked on offshore oil rigs, had been sent to Devon to replace a colleague who had had to resign from the project for health reasons. The temporary assignment was to assist in solving the various but crucial technical problems involved in such an operation.

Loren tugged at his elbow. 'Dad, won't it be awful working out there all day? What if there's a storm?'

'Uh-uh. I only have to visit the actual site now and again. Most of the problems are gonna be worked out on paper. S'why I brought my laptop and printer with me.' The AutoCAD computer program was a boon to the engineering industry, solving problems that used to take hours, if not weeks, in seconds. 'Most of my work time's gonna be spent at the company's local office in Ilfracombe.' Ilfracombe, some ten or twelve miles away, was the nearest big town to Hollow Bay. 'And then a lot of work I can do back at the house, so you'll probably be seeing much more of me than usual.'

'But you brought your laptop too, Mum,' Loren said, turning to Eve. 'Why do you need yours?'

'Oh, just to keep hooked up to a few magazines back in London. You know I still do occasional freelance work.'

'But you haven't for a long, long time.'

'No, and it's time I got back to doing something useful.' God, Eve thought to herself, as if writing trivia for women's magazines was anything useful. At least if some assignments did come up they would keep her mind occupied for a while. She desperately needed distraction and she intended to call some of the mags she'd written for in the past. Perhaps an article on moving to the countryside, or making friends in a completely new environment. Perhaps something on how it feels to lose a beloved child. No, not that – she could never do that.

Cally, who was barely tall enough to see over the harbour wall, tugged at Gabe's hand, impatient to move on. 'Can we go now?' she pleaded. 'Chester will be lonely on his own.'

Feeling wicked, they had locked the whimpering dog in Crickley Hall's kitchen: it would have been even more heartless to leave Chester tied up by his lead in the rain while they had lunch. Besides, they had spoiled him last night when Gabe had brought him up to their bedroom and allowed him to lie at the end of the bed (Gabe had felt Chester continue to shiver in his sleep before he, himself, had dropped off). Leaving the dog alone today might just cure his nervousness. Of course, equally, it might just make him worse. With an inward sigh, Gabe turned away from the sea and led his family back up Hollow Bay's main but narrow thoroughfare.

Towards the end of the street and almost opposite an iron and concrete bridge that crossed the swift-flowing river, they came upon a shop whose broad sign above two large plate-glass windows proclaimed it T. Longmarsh, General Store/ Newsagent, and Eve, her arm linked through Gabe's, brought them to a halt.

'I need to get something for tonight's dinner,' she told Gabe. 'And for tomorrow's lunch.'

Gabe peered through the window. 'Okay, let's see what they got. S'all freezer-packs by the look of it.'

Cally had taken time to stand in the kerbside gutter and stamp her Wellington boots into the stream of water that rushed towards a storm drain further along. Loren jumped away to avoid being splashed.

'Hey, Cally, quit it,' Gabe warned. 'You can look at the books in the store while we shop.'

'Bummer,' Cally complained as she stepped back onto the kerb and Gabe had to hide his grin as Eve frowned at her.

Loren giggled, but knew better than to encourage her sister's take on Bart Simpson, so turned away as if honestly interested in the window display. Eve mounted the step into the store's porched entrance and the wood-framed glass display cabinet next to the door caught her eye. Inside it were cards of various sizes and colours, each bearing handwritten or typed messages advertising second-hand goods or services for purchase or hire. She glanced over them with casual interest. There were plumbers, gardeners and garden tools for hire, a pram, used cars and kittens for sale. There were ads for a veterinary service, estate agents and local dentist on view, and more items for sale such as an 'almost new' Apple computer and a Singer sewing machine, cottages to rent, and a church jumble sale announced for a date long since passed. There were faded cards for a psychic reading, an undertaker, speckled pullets, a lime distributor and a reconditioned tractor.

'We going in, hon?' Gabe prompted from the rain-soaked pavement.

Eve had been lost for a moment – such moments were becoming more and more frequent lately – taking in the cards without registering any in particular. A bell tinkled above the door when she pushed through.

The shop was crowded with small freezer units and shelves loaded with confectionery and tinned food, alongside stationery, the smaller kind of DIY products – glues, picture hooks, nails, saws and hammers – with stand-alone magazine and book racks taking up much of the floor space. Jars of sweets, miniature displays of mints and chewing gums, and local and national newspapers shared space with a cash machine on the counter, behind which a plump woman of middle years and severe countenance had become alert to her new customers.

Eve, Gabe, Loren and Cally piled in, dripping wet, a fresh breeze blowing in with them, carrying rain through the porch and over the threshold. Gabe hastily closed the door behind them to preserve the warmth inside.

'Pretty nasty out there,' he said half apologetically to the woman behind the counter, who merely stared back at them through horn-rimmed glasses. 'Yep,' he answered himself under his breath, 'it's pretty wild.'

Eve nudged him with an elbow and he feigned interest in a bookrack close by. Eve immediately went to one of the two freezer units, smiling hello to the shopkeeper as she passed by her. Shrugging off her hood, Cally trotted over to the shelves of sweets and chocolate bars, while Loren went to the magazine carousel.

Gabe, standing by his own book carousel, glanced around the store and wondered at the cornucopia of goods on offer. Bags of dog food leaned against one wall, the shelves above filled with lemonade, Coke and Fanta bottles; affixed to card displays on the walls were combs, hairgrips, packs of women's tights, hairbrushes and cheap digital watches. More shelves were stacked with soap powders and detergents, dusters and mops, firelighters and sunglasses, loaves and bread rolls. The place seemed to cater for all needs and, judging by the abundance of stock, did a brisk trade, although at that particular moment there were only three other customers: a stockily built old lady wearing a pink see-through ankle-length mac, who was ambling over to the counter clutching a ready-sliced loaf in one arm and a pack of PG Tips in the other, while behind the magazine carousel where Loren was studying teen magazine titles there lurked a girl of about Loren's age and height but stocky, and a taller, older boy. They were taking peeks round the carousel at Loren, ducking back whenever she looked their way.

Shy kids, Gabe thought, browsing himself. One of the titles before him caught his eye. *The Great Hollow Bay Flood* the title said and, curious, he picked out the front copy. It was a slim, soft-covered edition and he flicked through the first few pages. It seemed the harbour village had suffered a devastating flood during the Second World War, when buildings had been destroyed and many lives lost. He became more interested and thumbed through to the pages of black-and-white photographs that showed the village in the flood's aftermath. The images were grim: houses totally demolished, vehicles turned over onto their backs in the main street, workmen clearing rubble, giant boulders in the streets, broken walls, debris of wrecked homes and buildings littering the mud of the foreshore along with overturned fishing boats. Later photographs depicted excavators and cranes clearing the wreckage, military vehicles bringing in troops (as there was a war on at the time, Gabe assumed that these were drawn from the reserves), diggers bearing loads of rubble and wood, and fresh scaffolding being erected. It must have been one hell of a night, he thought.

Loren was aware of the two customers on the other side of the carousel – she'd glimpsed a hefty-looking girl, probably around her own age, but who dressed a lot older, and a taller boy with stick-up hair and a harsh case of acne – and tried to ignore them, even when she felt the magazine rack held firmly from the other side as she tried to turn it. Forced to move round the rack instead of spinning it, she soon came within proper sight of the two and she gave them a hesitant smile of greeting. She had half pulled a *Shout* from its rack between *Cosmogirl* and *Pop Star* when the big-built girl spun the carousel and the bottom corner of the magazine was caught and pulled from Loren's grasp. It fell to the floor, its contents of special offers and other junk literature spilling out.

Loren flushed and immediately went down on her haunches to retrieve the magazine and its colourful detritus, growing even redder when she heard the other girl say, 'Geek.' Sniggers followed.

Feeling embarrassed, humiliated even, such was her

sensitivity, Loren gathered up the gaudy adverts for teenage skincare cream, panty liners and hair gel, and stuffed them back inside the magazine.

Just then, Cally came trotting round a floor shelf clutching a tube of Smarties in one hand (she guessed her mother would refuse to let her have them so, even at that tender age aware that daddies were much easier to manipulate, she was bringing them to Gabe). She came to a stop when she saw the big girl and boy glaring at Loren and heard them call her a silly name. Cally poked her tongue out at them.

'Spazzie,' the big girl called her.

'Bite my shorts,' Cally replied.

Loren put a hand to her mouth to suppress a giggle. She took her sister's hand and led her away. 'It's not *bite* my shorts, Cally,' she whispered, leaning close to Cally's ear. 'Bart always says *eat* my shorts.'

Gabe had witnessed the minor encounter from behind the bookrack, reluctant to interfere: Loren had to learn to stand up for herself. Sure, if the situation had got serious, if the girl and boy had tried physically to bully his daughter, then he would have stepped in, but instead Cally's response had made him wince, then grin. They really had to wean their youngest daughter off *The Simpsons*.

'What are you two up to back there?' came a stern voice from the other side of the shop. It was the shopkeeper, whose broad upper body was angled over the counter as she stood on tiptoe to see round the magazine racks. 'Is that you acting the maggot, Seraphina Blaney? Come on out and bring yer daft brother Quentin with yer. Yer've spent too long already moochin' around. Are yer buyin' or not?'

Reluctantly, the girl sidled out from behind the magazines, the boy, who must have been about fourteen, slouching after her, and Loren got a good look at them both as they deliberately brushed by her.

'Saddo,' the girl slyly said to Loren as she passed; the acne-cursed youth sneered a grin.

'Come on now, what yer got there to buy?' It sounded like *to boiy*. The shopkeeper had evidently lost patience with them, for she added: 'It's taken yer half the day to choose.'

The sturdy-looking girl offered up a can of Diet Coke while the spotty boy grasped a Twix in his fist. Seraphina wore her hair scraped back over her scalp in sink-estate style, a rubber band holding it together at the back of her neck so that it hung down in a lank ponytail. There was a hardness to her features despite the pudginess of her flesh: her eyes were mean and narrow anyway, but were made even meaner and narrower by the surrounding plumpness, and even the shortness of her nose failed to soften her looks, for the lips below were thin, almost a gash in her face.

It would have been hard to tell they were brother and sister, for the boy had large doleful eyes and, although stocky, he was tall as well, with slouched shoulders and a concave chest that made him appear slightly paunchy. His tufty hair was slick with gel and his mouth hung gormlessly half open. His face and neck were tortured by angry-looking pimples and pustules, but such was his bearing – he somehow walked with an arrogant but hunched swagger – it was almost impossible to feel any sympathy.

Both had on brightly coloured anoraks – hers blue, his red – and both wore heavy boots. The girl looked back at Loren, spite in those narrow eyes, as she collected her change.

'Found a mag you want, honey?' Gabe said to distract his daughter, who had brought Cally over to him.

'Oh, it doesn't matter, Dad. I was only looking.'

Although Cally had saved the day and made her giggle, Loren was still skittish, still intimidated, and he wanted to enfold her in his arms. He realized they all – all except Cally, who was a tough little tiger and too young to mourn the loss of her brother after all this time – had the tendency to over-emote given the slightest provocation these days, although they had different ways of expressing it. Loren would verge on the hysterical at times (or was over-reaction the norm for a girl of her age?), whereas Eve gave in to things too easily, almost as if detached from them. And Gabe, himself? Well, he was aware his old aloofness had returned, that he kept his emotions on a tight rein, allowing no one in, afraid of letting go. He was conscious of his own lack of overt emotion, didn't like it in himself, but he was afraid of lowering his defences once more. He tried, oh how he tried, but instead feigned a superficial cheerfulness. Not just for the sake of his family and friends, but for himself also. Inside, he was hurting badly.

'Choose a couple anyway,' he said to Loren, indicating the magazine rack.

'Thanks, Dad.' She picked out the magazine she had dropped only a few moments ago.

The bell over the door tinkled as the hefty girl and her brother left the shop.

'These'll do for tonight and tomorrow's lunch, Gabe.' Eve was holding several packs in her arms: tagliatelles, shepherd's pies, steak and mushroom pies and a vegetable mix.

'They'll do for about a week,' he commented, taking some of the packs from her.

'Hardly. Not with you three gannets. I'll do a proper shop on Monday. There's bound to be a Tesco or, with luck, a Waitrose in one of the local towns.' She had lowered her voice, presumably so as not to offend the shopkeeper who was watching them attentively.

'Bring your magazines, Loren,' Gabe said over his shoulder as he followed Eve over to the cash till. 'Sparky, where you got to?'

Cally's squeaky voice came from behind a display of kitchen utensils. 'Coming, Daddy.' She appeared clutching a jumbo bag of Maltesers in her hands as well as the original Smarties.

Grinning, Gabe shook his head. 'That's too much. Ask your mother.'

'No, Cally, just one thing, just the Smarties, okay?' Eve told her.

'But, Mummy . . .'

'No buts,' Gabe said firmly. 'Put the big pack back.'

Having extorted at least one prize, Cally scooted back to the confectionery shelves.

While the shopkeeper was totting up the bill on the cash register, Gabe returned to the rack and picked out the book he had glanced through before. He also took an Ordnance Survey map of the Hollow Bay area.

'Some flood,' he said as he laid the book on the counter and pointed at the black-and-white photograph of the devastated village on the cover.

The shopkeeper's severe expression had considerably softened now that the evidently troublesome brother and sister had departed and her new customers had made a decent purchase. 'It happened in the night,' she responded as she put the packs in plastic bags marked with the store's name. 'Sixty-eight people crushed or drowned. Don't think Hollow Bay's ever got over it even after all these years.'

*You got that right*, Gabe thought to himself. There was

definitely something brooding about the harbour village, a kind of heaviness in the very air. Then again, maybe it was only due to the constant rain: it'd make anywhere seem miserable. He nodded his head sympathetically at the woman. She took them all in, studying each member of his family individually through horn-rimmed glasses as she continued to pack by instinct alone.

'Yer stayin' local like, are you?' she asked Eve after payment had been made.

'Crickley Hall,' Eve said back and Gabe noticed the shopkeeper's eyes harden for a fraction of a second. 'My husband has business in these parts for a month or two,' Eve continued by way of explanation.

'Yes, I heard it were bein' rented out again. S'been a long time since.' The woman folded her arms and suddenly looked formidable. But once again, she softened when she looked over the counter at Cally and Loren. 'Just you look after the little ones,' she said to Eve and Gabe both.

Eve glanced round at Gabe and he raised and dropped his eyebrows at her.

## 10: THE GRAVES

The rain had thinned and turned into a steady drizzle as they made their way up the hill towards Crickley Hall. There were only a few houses on either side of the great gorge, and all looked solid, thick-walled, but none as austere, nor as big, as Crickley Hall. Gabe carried two plastic bags of groceries, while Eve and Loren held one bag each.

'I'm beginning to have doubts about this place,' Eve said to Gabe, a little out of breath with the climb.

'You mean the village or the Hall?'

'Both.' She looked at him from beneath her hood. 'Hollow Bay is, I don't know – depressing somehow. And it shouldn't be. It's a picturesque village even if jaded by time and wear, but there's something . . .' She was lost for the correct word. Then: 'I don't know . . . mournful about it.'

Keeping his voice low so that the girls, who were several yards ahead, wouldn't hear, Gabe said, 'I felt it too. Nothing you can hit on, but the place is kinda depressing.' He gave a short, forced laugh. 'Maybe it's just the weather getting us down. And well, you know . . .'

He didn't have to say the words for her to understand. Perhaps it was because they were still grieving that everything seemed so joyless to them. It was a new place, yet it had none of the excitement of a new place, nor of a new

73

beginning. Perhaps if they knew for certain that Cam truly was dead, and not just missing, things would at least have some kind of closure.

Eve pushed the worst of those thoughts away and faced her husband. 'I don't think I can stay here too long, Gabe.' Her voice was cold rather than plaintive.

He came to a halt too and leaned into her, finding her eyes beneath the hood. He spoke softly.

'Hey, it's only for a coupla months, probably a lot less if things run smoothly. It'll pass in no time.'

Even in the shadow of the hood he could see the misery in those deep brown eyes of hers.

'Oh Gabe, why did we have to come here?'

He gently shushed her, his face only inches from hers. 'The cops know where to find us. DI Michael said if he found anything new he'd contact us immediately. They're not gonna stop looking 'til they get a result.'

Cam . . . missing . . . no sign of him for nearly a year. Was that good? Or was it bad? Surely if Cameron were dead they'd have found his body by now.

The detective inspector had let them both know he wasn't hopeful, but Eve clung to the belief that if their son had been murdered then they'd have some evidence of it by now – like his body. She could not let go of that thought. And in a way, neither could he, Gabe. There had to be some hope, otherwise . . . otherwise there was *nothing*.

They began walking again, the girls well ahead of them by now. On their left, the gorge's swollen river hurtled down to the bay, its level not far below the grassy, shrub-filled bank; the waters were brown and angry with spume. The thick naked limb of a tree swept by. The sky was leaden, dark cloud masses promising more rain to come. The girls had realized they were walking alone, their parents some way behind. They both turned and waited for Eve and Gabe to catch up.

'Come on, slowcoaches,' Loren complained. Cally was studying the wet shine on her colourful rubber boots, her shoulders drooping; she was growing tired of the hike. As they approached she pointed over her shoulder.

Raising her voice over the rushing noise of the river, she called out, 'Look, Mummy, that old church again.'

They had passed the ancient Norman church on their way down to the harbour earlier and Eve had suggested they visit inside for a few minutes, but the girls were hungry and totally uninterested. Gabe had half promised they'd go in on the way back, but he knew his wife would hold him to it. Since the loss of their son, Eve had attended Mass regularly every Sunday (she had mostly been a Christmas and Easter worshipper before) and often during the week when their local church was usually empty. He was aware of what she prayed for; she still believed.

The church was built with grey, probably local, stone, as was the irregular wall around its boundary. It was a small but solid structure, with a square tower surmounted by a short steeple, a weathervane at the steeple's apex. The escarpment, lush with the deep greenery of trees and thick scrub despite the late season, rose up majestically behind the building and Gabe thought, not for the first time, that Devil's Cleave was more like a deep-sided valley than a gorge. A gravel path from the wall's lychgate led to the porch through a grassy graveyard; headstones dark with age leaned as if wearied, an occasional elm tree breaking up the quiet grimness of the landscape.

Close to the gateway was a mounted wooden board with faded gold lettering announcing that this was THE CHURCH OF ST MARK and the vicar was one REVEREND ANDREW

TREVELLICK and his curate was ERIC RISSEY, all of this in neat capital letters. Underneath, also in faded gold, were times of services, and below this, in caps again but the largest message of all, it said: 'IN GOD WE TRUST'.

*Yeah, right,* Gabe said to himself as he read the comfort legend.

'I want to go inside,' insisted Eve, stepping towards the closed gate, her tone allowing no dissent this time.

Loren pulled a face, while Cally wasn't bothered either way.

'Sure,' agreed Gabe, his spirits sinking.

The gate opened with a squeal and they all passed through. As they trudged along the path, Gabe saw that the gravestones, some larger and more ornate than others, continued round to the side and possibly the back of the church. They crunched their way to the porch, glad of its cover even though the rain was now no more than a light drizzle.

Eve tested the black metal handle and one side of the big door opened easily. She stepped inside and the others followed, Gabe reluctantly. Although it was gloomy in there, stained-glass windows glowed brightly above them despite the poor light of the day. There was only one centre aisle, with pews on either side, that led to the high pulpit and altar. Some of the pews near the front had little doors on them so that the seats were segregated from the rest, and Eve assumed that these were once for the more important families of the community – probably still were. Her footsteps echoed hollowly as she went to an open pew halfway down the aisle. She knelt on the padded knee-rest and bowed her head into her hands.

Loren looked round at Gabe and he gave a short nod of his head. She went to a pew just behind Eve's and Cally followed. Cally sat on the wooden bench while Loren joined her mother in prayer.

# THE SECRET OF CRICKLEY HALL

At the back of the church, Gabe wished that he could have their faith. All he felt was anger, though, anger at a God who could put them through such agony. If there was a God, of course. *If* He did exist, then He seemed to care little for the part of His creation called mankind.

Gabe's fists clenched and his teeth bit into his lower lip. He wanted to pound the stone pillar beside him with his fist. But instead, he turned away and let his anger subside into bitterness. Let Eve and Loren pray for their miracle. As for him, he knew miracles never happened. Not in this life, they didn't. And this was the only life anyone ever had.

Gabe turned away and paced the uneven stone floor, straining to drive these useless thoughts from his mind as he went to the other side of the church. It was then he saw all the names on a polished board mounted on the rear wall of the church. In fact there were two boards, side by side, but it was the first one that made him pause.

The lettering was inscribed in white yellowed by age and it was the heading that had caught his attention:

## IN MEMORY OF THE POOR ORPHANS WHO PERISHED IN THE GREAT STORM OF 1943

Below this there followed a list of all the children who had died in that storm:

| | |
|---|---|
| ARNOLD BROWN – 7 yrs | EUGENE SMITH – 9 yrs |
| MAVIS BORRINGTON – 7 yrs | MAURICE STAFFORD – 12 yrs |
| PATIENCE FROST – 6 yrs | SUSAN TRAINER – 11 yrs |
| BRENDA PROSSER – 10 yrs | MARIGOLD WELCH – 7 yrs |
| GERALD PROSSER – 8 yrs | WILFRED WILTON – 6 yrs |
| STEFAN ROSENBAUM – 5 yrs | |

Reading the names of all these dead children – orphans every one of them – almost broke Gabe right there and then. He had contained his anguish, his debilitating grief, for nearly a year now so that he could be resolute for Eve and their daughters, refusing to break, to weep, to expose the weakness he felt in such adversity, because his family needed his strength, especially Eve, who blamed herself. Now today, inside this small ancient church, absorbing the poignant death list on this board before him, Gabe's self-control wavered. Sixty-eight, the shopkeeper in the village had told them, sixty-eight victims either drowned or crushed. How many other kids had been among that number?

He lowered his gaze, stared sightlessly at the stone floor beneath him, his shoulders slumped.

He was aware enough to realize his sorrow was looking for expression, a release, so that once unmasked the healing might begin. And this plain but emotive memorial to all those lost children was almost the catalyst that bent him, for it confirmed his own despair at the perpetuity of life's unfailing cruelty – happiness was only in the pauses between suffering.

He regretted having entered the church. For two months after Cam had disappeared, Gabe had accompanied Eve and their daughters to Sunday Mass – and only because he wanted to support Eve, not because he had suddenly seen the light and thought miracles might just happen if you prayed hard enough – but when nothing had changed, when there was still no trace of Cam after all that time, he had desisted. And Eve had not urged him to go with her any more, because she understood the bitter anger that was beginning to rage inside him, was aware that, for him, attending Mass was doing more harm than good. When he was a juvenile, Gabe had spent time in the Illinois Institute for Delinquent Boys, where he had been obliged to attend chapel twice a week, but in those days he had been cool about it; it beat working in the sweltering laundry room or raking dirt on the drill yard. Chapel service meant little to him, but at least it gave him the chance to think for an hour – thinking time was at a premium on a campus full of wayward, excitable youths. Sure, in those days he was resentful – he figured he had a right to be – but he never blamed God for his circumstances then. Didn't blame Him because he didn't believe in Him, despite the sermons and the priest's entreaties.

But Eve had mellowed Gabe and, even though she hadn't necessarily been deeply religious herself when they were first married, she had gradually coaxed him to see the goodness around him, and that this spirit of goodness had to come from somewhere. She hadn't made him believe in a Supreme Being, but he no longer dismissed the idea out of hand. And the blessings that were their children opened up his heart even more. There was a period of time when he had *wanted* to believe.

Gabe deliberately trod lightly as he made his way out of St Mark's and it took some effort. It was not that he felt contempt for Eve's so-called 'Supreme Being' – whatever *that* meant – it was just that he had no respect for Him. *If* He existed.

Gabe left the church, closing the door quietly behind him, not wanting to disturb Eve at her devotions – her *pleadings*. Outside, in the light drizzle, for the first time since he'd given them up, he wished for a cigarette. That had been when Eve had become pregnant with their first child, Loren, and that, for him, was reason enough. He needed a smoke now, maybe even a large shot of Jack Daniel's. Cold anger was returning like a winter season and it smothered the grief. He walked round to the other side of St Mark's, where the gorge wall rose sheer and abundant with trees and foliage. In the grassy space between church and gorge were more headstones.

He saw them at once, for they were better tended than the other graves around them. Their small headstones were clean even though over half a century old and their carved inscriptions were clear. The small plots were set out in a tidy row and bunches of wild flowers were in water jars below the headstones. In the rain, the flowers looked fresh, vibrant, and Gabe wondered who had put them there. Perhaps it was a kind of ceremony, the flowers laid out every year in the month of October; Gabe had already glanced at the preface of the book bought in the village store and it had said the Great Storm, as it was called, had occurred in the October of 1943.

He read the names on the neat little headstones and noticed that the Prosser children – obviously brother and sister – had been laid side by side. Arnold Brown, 1936–1943, Patience Frost, 1937–1943, Eugene Smith, 1934–1943, and so on. Gabe felt his eyes moisten, but he would not give in to tears now. His anger became subdued. But there was something wrong about this setting, some small thing that nagged at him.

He walked further into the hidden cemetery, distracting himself by reading the messages on other markers, noticing that all the lives here had ended in 1943. So this was where some of the adult victims of the flood were buried, along with the children. These other graves, though, had not been as well cared for. They were stained, weather-worn, lichen growing on most. It seemed the children were better remembered than the older flood victims. And maybe that's how it should be.

He was almost at the angled rise of the gorge when he spotted the stone hiding in long grass and weeds and, because it was set aside from all the other graves, Gabe was curious.

The American squatted before it and parted the long grass and weeds so that he could read the headstone's inscription. It said:

AUGUSTUS THEOPHILUS CRIBBEN
1901–1943

No other words had been carved into the stone. No RIP, no IN LOVING MEMORY. Nothing. Just the birth and death dates. 1943: the same year as the flood. A flood victim like all the others in this part of the church cemetery? It seemed likely. But then why was this grave set apart from the others? And why so neglected? If the man had no living descendants to tend his resting place, surely St Mark's curate or groundsman would have made sure the stone was not practically obscured by grass and weeds like this; after all, the rest of the grave-yard, front and back, was kept quite orderly. It was almost as if this particular grave had some shame to it.

Gabe stood erect, feeling strangely disturbed without knowing why. Maybe it was because he was still puzzling over whatever nagged him about the children's neat line of graves.

With a shake of his head, he turned away and headed back to the porch, hoping Eve would be waiting for him there; he had no urge to re-enter the church. Before he reached the corner he heard the quiet murmurings of voices.


Eve, Loren and Cally were sheltering from the light rain inside the porch, and as he approached he saw his wife was talking to a man and woman, both of whom were wearing green Barbour jackets. Both also had their trousers tucked into high, green rubber boots, the man sporting a smart flat cap, the woman wearing a colourful blue-and-yellow scarf and carrying an umbrella under which they both sheltered.

'Ah,' the man said as he saw Gabe's approach. 'You'll be Mr Caleigh, then.' He smiled and offered a hand.

Gabe shook it and nodded at the woman. They looked to be a compatible couple in their matching coats, both tall, but the man taller than the woman (and taller than Gabe), their features similar: strong nose, high cheekbones, chin a little weak, trim figures. Their eyes were different, though, his a washed-out blue, hers like a hawk's, sharp and staring, grey in colour. He looked to be in his early forties, she possibly younger, and his smile seemed more genuine than hers: Gabe thought there was reserve in her thin-lipped acknowledgement of him, and her gaze was too intense, as if he were a trespasser, there to steal the church silverware.

'Gabe,' said Eve almost nervously, 'this is the vicar of St Mark's, and his wife.'

'Andrew Trevellick,' the man said, still smiling. 'The Reverend Andrew Trevellick, actually, but please call me Andrew.'

Gabe was surprised that the vicar wore a shirt and knitted tie rather than a white collar.

'Bad weather, huh?' Gabe didn't know what else to say. Besides, the Brits usually referred to the weather after they'd been introduced, didn't they? He'd at least learned something in his sixteen years over here.

'Dreadful, dreadful,' returned the vicar. 'The rain doesn't seem to want to stop, does it? My wife's name is Celia, by the way.' They stood close together under the umbrella, as though joined at the hips.

Again, Gabe nodded his head at her, feeling under scrutiny.

'And your wife, Eve,' the vicar went on, 'tells me you've moved into Crickley Hall.'

'Just for a short spell.' Gabe noticed that the false smile on the vicar's wife had quickly dissolved.

'Splendid,' said Trevellick. 'I hope the place isn't too draughty for you.' Although the vicar had a West Country name, there was nothing parochial about this accent. He was pure Home Counties.

'We'll get by,' Gabe said, and he looked at Eve as though to reassure her. Cally hung on to Eve's sleeve and scuffed the sole of her boot against the porch step, restless and probably bored. Loren paid quiet attention to the adults as she always did.

'Celia and I are so pleased you decided to visit our little church so soon,' said Trevellick.

'It's lovely,' Eve acknowledged. 'Really lovely.'

'Yes, even on a day like today. You'll find it very peaceful inside. Of course, I hope you'll all attend our Sunday service while you're here in Hollow Bay.'

'We intend to,' Eve responded. 'At least, my daughters and I will. I'm not sure about Gabe . . .'

'Not a religious man, Mr Caleigh? Well, that's fine; you're still welcome to our services, or to visit on your own at any time. I rarely lock the church door during the day even though the rectory is further down the hill, nearer to the village. With two young daughters I'm sure you need some quiet time now and again.'

They all chuckled politely, and then Gabe said: 'I was looking around the grounds . . .' He waved an arm loosely as if to indicate where he had just come from.

'Ah, yes,' said Trevellick, a self-satisfied smile on his face. 'Walking among the dead, eh? Are you interested in that kind of thing?'

JAMES HERBERT

'*Andrew.*' Celia Trevellick tugged at her husband's arm indignantly. 'What a macabre thing to say.'

'Oh no, dear. Some of the messages on the more ancient headstones can be quite fascinating. One or two are highly amusing, and others a trifle sinister.'

'I saw the row of children's graves at the back,' said Gabe bluntly, and the vicar's jocularity swiftly vanished.

'Yes,' he replied, 'those poor children, all those years ago. They were taken from us during the war, as you will have seen by the date on their headstones. I believe the shock of the flood and the losses it caused has been passed down from generation to generation in Hollow Bay. Sixty-eight people died in one night, you know, eleven of them just children.'

That was it. That was what had been bothering Gabe when he'd viewed the graves. 'But there's only nine markers back there and there's eleven names mentioned on the board inside the church.' As an engineer Gabe's working life was detail – it was an essential requirement of his profession – and now he wondered how he'd missed it before. Nine kids buried, but eleven names on the remembrance board. Two kids missing.

The vicar spoke with great sadness in his voice. 'Unfortunately, the bodies of two of the children were never recovered. It seems the sea claimed them for its own.'

'They were swept out when the village was flooded?' Gabe, perhaps morbidly, was interested to know.

'Apparently, Mr Caleigh.' It was the vicar's wife, Celia, who answered. 'The children were evacuees, you see, sent down from London to escape the Blitz. All of them had been evacuated to Crickley Hall. That was where most of them drowned.'

84

## 11: IMAGINATION

'I knew I didn't like this place.'

Eve folded her arms and leaned back against a kitchen worktop while she waited for the plastic kettle to boil. They both needed hot coffee after their uphill trek from the harbour village. The girls were upstairs arranging their new bedroom to their liking, prized possessions they had brought with them to Devon finding suitable places to rest.

Gabe sat at the kitchen table, stroking Chester's head to calm him; the dog had become overexcited on their return and was still trembling.

'It was more than sixty years ago,' Gabe told Eve, exasperated. 'Those poor kids've been long gone.'

She came back at him. 'Time has nothing to do with it. Look, even Chester's nervous of this place.'

'He's not used to it yet.'

Eve ignored him. 'It's as if the house has a memory. I can feel it.'

'You're talking crazy.' Gabe's voice was low and even, but he was becoming impatient. 'You're saying the place is haunted, there's ghosts running around? Sure the house is spooky, but there are no ghosts, no such thing.'

'Of course there aren't any ghosts. But somehow some places are forever marked by their own history. Remember

**85**

the first time I took you to the Tower of London, how you actually shuddered when we went into the Bloody Tower? You told me it was because you could *feel* its brutal past, as if the memory of murders and executions still lingered.'

'Ah, c'mon, Eve . . .'

She turned away from him to make the coffee.

'I can sense something bad about Crickley Hall,' she tried to explain, her back towards Gabe.

'It's in your imagination.'

'Those children died in this house. They all died in the flood.'

It was a terrible story, a deeply tragic one, relayed to them by the vicar himself, his wife frowning all the way through the telling of it.

During the Second World War, when the German Luftwaffe was constantly bombing London and other English cities, many young children were evacuated without their mothers – most of the menfolk were overseas fighting for their country – to safer havens in countryside towns and villages. Eleven boys and girls had been sent to Hollow Bay for the duration from a south London orphanage. They came to live in Crickley Hall, which, because it was empty, had been appropriated by the Ministry of Health with the consent of the owner at that time who rarely used it as his personal residence anyway. There they would be cared for and resume their education.

On the night of the Great Storm, as the vicar had called the 1943 flood, and after the high moors had, sponge-like, absorbed six weeks of continuous rainfall so that they could accept no more, they had disgorged their load into the already rising local rivers and streams around them. The Bay River was a natural conduit more or less straight down to the sea.

Debris and fallen trees had been blocked by the bridges along the river's length, and when these finally gave way under the pressure, the floodwaters were disastrously released. Some houses on the riverbank were demolished, others badly damaged, as the floodwaters had poured down to devastate the harbour village. Although Crickley Hall, built so solidly, was left standing, all the evacuees and their guardian perished. Because the children were orphans, there were no relatives to mourn them, not even uncles and aunts, but the surviving villagers took them into their hearts and grieved for them along with their own lost. A special area of the church grounds that had never been used before became the burial plot for the children and the other members of the community who had died on that terrible night.

When Gabe had asked Trevellick who maintained the children's graves so caringly, he had received a surprise. It seemed it was Percy Judd, Crickley Hall's own caretaker and gardener, who tended them, laying pretty wild flowers under each stone in October every year, the anniversary of the orphans' deaths.

At the time, Gabe refrained from asking the vicar about the neglected grave, the one that stood apart from the rest, overgrown with grass and weeds and left unkempt. It could be that Augustus Theophilus Cribben, who was buried there, was just a local who had died of natural causes (although the marker claimed he was only forty-two when he'd passed away) in the same year as the flood. Maybe he had been buried at the back of the cemetery because he wasn't a popular figure among the locals and hadn't anyone to mourn his passing.

'Gabe, your coffee.'

Eve was standing before him, a steaming mug in her hand.

'Sorry, hon. I was thinking on something.'

'About the house, Gabe. I don't want to stay here.' Her voice was soft, not nagging. She was sincere, genuinely troubled.

'Eve, we've only been here one night and a day.' He took the coffee from her and quickly put it down on the table. He blew at his fingers. 'We gotta at least give it a chance to work out. The job's important.'

She leaned into him, a hand going to the back of his neck. 'I'm sorry. I know it seems stupid, but can't you sense it too? There's . . . there's a *mood* about Crickley Hall. Loren said she heard crying coming from the landing cupboard yesterday.'

'She heard a sound *like* crying. Coulda been a trapped animal.'

'But there was no animal inside when you looked.'

'Mouse or, God help us, a rat. Maybe even a squirrel. Found its way out the way it got in.'

'And the shadow she saw.'

'Trick of the light. What else could it be? Whoever heard of a *white* shadow?'

'What if it *was* a memory of someone, a person – a child – who died here in traumatic circumstances? The house has stood empty a long time, we've been told. Don't you wonder why?'

'Yeah, because it's too big, it's too cold, and it smells of damp. I just never realized it when I found the place in the summer. And you're emotionally worn out, Eve.'

She flinched at that, but said nothing, because she knew it was true. Gabe hadn't made her confront it until now. Then: 'Perhaps Loren saw a ghost.'

'I was afraid you were gonna say that. Eve, Loren might

believe in that kinda thing, but we're adults – we should have more sense.'

'Meaning I'm being irrational.'

He didn't want to start anything with her; her emotions were too fraught, she'd been hanging on the edge for too long now.

'Crickley Hall isn't haunted,' he said evenly.

'Isn't it? How do you know?'

'Like I said, there's no such thing as ghosts.'

'Gabe, a few years ago I wrote a piece on celebrities and models who used psychics and clairvoyants, people who wouldn't make an important decision without first consulting their personal oracle. It was one of the psychics I interviewed who told me about houses that sometimes held on to memories, usually when something traumatic has happened in them. Like the Bloody Tower. The psychic told me this was often the cause of hauntings, images released into the atmosphere by the house itself.'

'And I guess your psychic had a direct line to ghosts, huh?'

'You can be cynical, Gabe, but three out of the five I interviewed were totally convincing.'

'So the other two were frauds.'

'Not necessarily. They explained to me that occasionally their powers let them down. It didn't mean they were fakes.'

Gabe suppressed a groan. 'Look,' he said patiently, 'let's give it two weeks and if you're still uneasy I'll find us somewhere else to rent. Deal?'

She did not reply immediately and her fingers slid away from his neck down to his shoulder. 'I don't know . . .' she said eventually.

'Give it a try, Eve.'

'Just two weeks?'

JAMES HERBERT

'Guaranteed.' His own hand slipped round her waist. 'If you're still unhappy living here by then, we move on.'

Chester's muzzle pushed into his lap. The dog whimpered as if displeased with the arrangement.

# 12: SECOND NIGHT

It was night and rain continued to hurl itself against the windows. Heavy clouds concealed a gibbous moon.

Eve lay awake next to Gabe, listening to his gentle snoring, the soft sound reassuring rather than annoying. She would have turned and laid a hand over his hip, but she did not want to disturb him. Gabe was tired; he'd worked hard that morning and afternoon, finishing the unpacking with her, moving furniture so that rooms suited them better, the only break being the trip down into the village. The walk back up the hill in the rain had been pretty tiring. The girls were fast asleep next door, having gone to bed much earlier than usual without complaint.

It was well past midnight and she was restless, even though she, too, was worn out. She hated these nights when her mind would not allow her sleep; she knew she could take a Zopiclone, but she'd been taking the sleeping tablets for too many months now and she wanted to break the habit. But night thoughts tormented her. Haunted her.

Gabe was ever patient, comforting her in her darkest moods, never himself weakening – at least, containing the heartache Eve knew he felt. But then Gabe had learned to repress his emotions at an early age. When she first met him, when he boldly marched up to her in a fashionable bar in

Notting Hill Gate that Eve and her friends from the magazine used, he had seemed breezy, confident, sure of himself. Later, when they got to know each other – when they realized they had fallen in love; so fast, it had happened so fast! – he had revealed to her that he'd been scared witless when he had introduced himself that night, scared of rejection, scared that she would turn her back on him. (Gabe never had been aware of the stunning effect he had on most women. Sometimes in a certain light, or if his face was seen at a certain angle, he was beautiful – with cornflower-blue eyes, sandy hair that was neither blond nor brown, and a compact body that seemed always poised as if ready to pounce.) In those days he had a natural aggression that simmered just below a surface of cool. It came from his upbringing.

He had been raised in the town of Galesburg, Illinois, and had never known his father, a salesman in pharmaceuticals apparently, who hadn't stayed around when his girlfriend had fallen pregnant with Gabe. Jake was his name – that was one of the few things Gabe knew about the man other than his profession. Oh, and Jake was a gambler and a drinker and a scumbag who, Gabe's mother often told her son, had a bitch in every town he visited.

Irene Caleigh, Gabe's mother, was a drinker too. She was also a cheap lay – by the age of eleven, Gabe had come to know the meaning of the word 'lay' – for men called on her at all hours of the night. Sometimes the man – 'uncles' she had told him to call them – and Irene would go out to local bars and return later to the ramshackle apartment that was Gabe's home, but as often as not, the men friends would bring bottles of booze – 'hooch' Gabe called it – with them and the boy would be told to wait on the stairway with a warning not to go 'roaming around'. The one bed he shared with his mother would be 'occupied' for the evening.

Sometimes, when it grew late, Gabe would fall asleep on the stairs only to be woken by heavy feet stepping over him, 'uncles' on their way out. His mother would then come to fetch him, picking him up in her arms, cuddling him and planting wet, sour kisses on his cheeks. She seemed most loving then, most tender, and he would curl up contentedly against her back as they slept in the rumpled bed. This from the age of eight.

By ten he was running wild with other, older, neighbourhood kids, stealing from stores, taking hubcaps from cars, vandalizing property, and more than once Irene was called down to the local cop station where they threatened to lock her boy up for a while if he persisted in his antisocial behaviour. That always frightened him, and Irene would belabour the warning on the way home. Yet Gabe could not remember his mother ever raising a hand to him; sure, she tongue-lashed him and made all kinds of threats in the days that followed, but not once did she strike him in anger or frustration. In later years, he thought it might have been her guilt that always stopped her, the guilt of being a poor single mother. Also, he believed, she truly loved him in her own inadequate way.

When Gabe was just twelve years of age, Irene Caleigh died (cirrhosis of the liver, he reasoned years later, because one of the 'uncles' at the funeral bluntly told him, 'She died of the drink, son'). Gabe had spent a month or so (he could never remember how long exactly) in a care home, until one day an aunt called Ruth, his mother's older sister and who he hardly remembered (she hadn't attended the funeral), came to collect him. Aunt Ruth took her nephew back to her old ramshackle but clean clapboard house on the outskirts of Quincy, where some areas were even rougher than those he had been used to.

Aunt Ruth was kind to him, if somewhat distant, but the wildness was already in him, and he was soon loose in the streets, again joining a gang whose members were mostly older than himself. Cars were his obsession – other people's cars, that is – and he soon learned to hot-wire them. In fact, his skill at breaking into vehicles and quickly getting them running without keys and no matter what model quickly earned him the respect of his elders in the gang – even then, he seemed to have an affinity with machinery of any kind. But when he was fourteen, Gabe's increasing delinquency came to a sudden and tragic end.

The pristine stolen Mercedes saloon in which Gabe and his friends were joyriding went out of control on a bend and crashed into three trees, one after the other. The driver, seventeen years old and gang leader, a tough guy who was good in a rumble, went through the windscreen when the car hit the first tree, to die instantly as his body slammed into the tree trunk, his bowed head snapping at the neck and smashing his own ribcage, while the passenger in the seat next to him broke his spine at the second tree and had his foot turned back to front on the third impact. Gabe and another gang member, who shared the rear seats with him, were thrown to the floor at the first impact, and there they stayed, bounced around but saved from serious injury by the backs of the front seats.

Perhaps it was to deter him from a career of crime that the authorities decided to deal with Gabe firmly. For the auto-theft itself and because of its serious outcome, plus Gabe's past record of minor offences, he was sent to the Illinois Institute for Delinquent Boys for one year, while his companion, who was even younger than Gabe and had a clean sheet as far as the law was concerned, was given a period of probation. The front-seat passenger, who had broken his back and lost a foot, was deemed punished enough.

Because of Gabe's ongoing problem with authority, he served a further three months at the facility. But something worked there. They found he had an aptitude for machinery as well as calculation and they encouraged him to pursue his gift. Because he did not want to serve any further time, those last three months of incarceration had more value than the first twelve months: Gabe knuckled down and began to study for a career as an engineer, a mechanical engineer. When he was released, he returned to Quincy and Aunt Ruth, went back to high school and attended night college to learn as much as he could about engineering. On weekends he worked as a junior mechanic in a garage and car showroom (which meant mainly washing cars and handing tools to real mechanics), watching everything they did to engines, learning fast while he did so. The meagre amount of cash he earned was handed over to Aunt Ruth to help pay towards his own keep.

At seventeen, having achieved good results in both school and night college, he left Quincy for New York City. Unbeknown to him, his aunt had been secretly saving money for precisely this kind of move, which she knew would come sooner or later; she had even put aside the money he had given her from his weekend work. He had spent almost a year of hardship in the Big Apple, living in a one-room attic apartment in the South Bronx, taking any job that came his way – washing dishes in a Harlem bar, short-order cook in a diner, delivering pizzas, shelf-stacking and serving in an all-night Mini-Mart – mostly night-time labour so that he could hunt for work as an engineer during the day (on occasions, he had introduced himself to as many as five engineering companies during the course of one day). Eventually his persistence paid off: he got himself taken on as a junior trainee structural and mechanical engineer in a large, global corporation, APCU Engineering, and he had never looked back. At the age of twenty-one, Gabe had been sent across to England, and there he'd stayed ever since.

And then, he and Eve had met. In that hip bar in pre-film Notting Hill. They had quickly married when she had become pregnant with Loren and neither of them had regretted the union: she loved him now as much as ever – no, perhaps even more than in the early days; she had come to know so much about him – and she was sure Gabe felt exactly the same way about her. It was just that she was so . . . so distracted now, thought too much about their lost son. *If only Cam would . . . would he come back?* she asked herself. There was still a faint, almost elusive, hope in her that one day soon their son would be returned to them. As long as he remained on the missing list there was always that chance . . .

A flurry of rain, driven by a vigorous wind, beat against the bedroom's two windows, making her start. She craned her neck to look towards the sound as the windows rattled in their frames. The night outside was wild, unrelenting, and no friend to slumber. Eve faced the ceiling again, lonely because her partner slept. She tried to clear her mind of everything but, as ever, the misery crept back, staking its claim.

*Oh God, don't let it be so,* her mind pleaded as it had for almost a year. *Missing doesn't have to mean dead. Someone could have taken him for their own, some stranger could be loving him as we love him. Please, please send my innocent child back to me!* In the daytime lately it had become easier to suppress the torment but in the darkness of night, when others slept and she felt so alone, the thoughts were almost impossible to control. Yet even the possibility that Cam might be dead seemed like a betrayal of her son.

The wind suddenly died and the rain's fury went with it. Now the rain pattered against the glass. Low clouds overhead must have parted, for moonlight entered the bedroom.

Then a sound different from the steady soft drum of the rain. It was a tapping and it came from somewhere out on the landing.

Eve listened, tried to determine its source. It was becoming louder, no longer a tapping but a muffled knocking.

She levered herself up on her elbows, looking towards the open doorway, wondering if she should wake Gabe, whose gentle snoring could not drown out the sound coming from the landing.

After last night, the landing light had been left on so that the girls would be able to see should they stir from their sleep and become disorientated. But it was a dim glow, the lightbulb weak, hardly strong enough to govern the area it was supposed to; instead it seemed to create even deeper shadows, shadows that were impenetrable.

The bedroom became almost darker again as the moon was concealed behind another cloud, but there was just enough light from the landing to see the small figure that suddenly appeared in the doorway.

Eve drew in a sharp, startled breath.

'Mummy,' Loren said from the bedroom's threshold, 'I can hear someone knocking.'

Eve let her breath go and relaxed her tensed shoulders.

'I think it's coming from the cupboard again,' Loren said.

'I can hear it, darling.'

They both listened as if for reaffirmation. Loren took a step into the room. 'Mummy?'

The fear in her daughter's voice caused Eve to tense again. She nudged Gabe's shoulder with her elbow.

'Gabe, wake up,' she said in a harsh whisper. 'Gabe.'

Loren was standing by the bottom of the bed now, a hand on one of the corner posts. 'Daddy!' Although urgent, she spoke in a whisper as if she didn't want to be heard by anything outside the room.

Flat on his back, Gabe roused. He lifted his head from the pillow.

'S'going on?' he murmured, not quite awake.

'Listen,' Eve urged him, her voice low.

Gabe listened.

'What the hell is it?' he said after a few moments.

'Loren says it's coming from a cupboard.'

'Which one?' There were more than a few in the big house.

'Somewhere along the landing, Daddy.'

Gabe pulled the duvet aside and his feet touched the cold wood flooring. Fortunately, he was wearing his grey T-shirt and dark boxers, so there was no embarrassment before his daughter. He sat on the edge of the bed to listen again. Although muted, it sounded like knuckles on wood.

Eve left her side of the bed, the hem of her wrinkled nightie falling to her knees. She went to her daughter, putting a comforting arm round her shoulders.

Loren clung to her. 'What is it, Mummy?' she asked in a scared half-moan.

'We'll find out,' Eve assured her. 'Is Cally asleep?'

'Yes, I checked on her.'

Gabe was by the bedroom door and he peeked out cautiously as if expecting a surprise. The knocking came from his right, somewhere past his daughters' open bedroom door. He squinted into the general gloom.

One hand holding the doorframe as if to pull himself back from harm's way, Gabe took a step out onto the landing. Below, the hall looked like a great dark pit, the poor light from above barely touching the flagstones. Even the big window over the stairway failed to offer any light.

Behind him, Eve scrabbled for the bedroom light switch, then flicked it on. A little more light graced the landing.

The knocking became louder, although still muffled, and it wasn't because he was closer to it. Someone or something was beating even louder against the cupboard door.

Gabe cocked his head as if it would help him hear more clearly. The noise seemed to emanate from a cupboard along the landing as Loren had said; it was the same one he'd investigated for her only yesterday. With a puzzled glance back at Eve and Loren, he moved quietly towards the sound, placing each footstep carefully as if trying not to make a sound himself, which was crazy: he should be stomping and hollering to frighten any intruder off. Instead he continued to tread cautiously.

Eve, with Loren clutching her arm, followed, both of them holding their breath.

There was a key in the lock of the cupboard door, as there seemed to be in all the cupboards in Crickley Hall, but Gabe could not remember if he had left it unlocked. As he stood directly outside the cupboard, the knocking became more intense, as though whatever was inside was becoming desperate. Eve and Loren crowded him from behind, and Eve placed a hand on his shoulder.

'What is it?' she almost hissed.

'I got no idea,' he whispered back. Feeling foolish for keeping so quiet he raised his voice. 'Hey!' he said sharply, expecting the noise to stop.

It didn't. It increased in both volume and rapidity.

99

'Goddam—' Gabe cursed and he felt Eve's fingers dig into his shoulder in sudden fright. Loren gave out a sharp squeal.

Now Gabe felt his temper rise. Enough was enough. He reached forward to the small brass doorknob just above the key, ready to yank the cupboard door open. But the knocking became a *pounding* before his fingers could grasp it and the door itself seemed to strain against its frame.

As one, Gabe, Eve and Loren jumped back and Loren gave out a terrified scream. Eve held on to her, squeezing her hard out of her own fear. Still shocked by the loudness of both the pounding and the now frantic clattering of the door, Gabe steeled himself and grabbed at the brass doorknob, determined to put an end to the disturbance.

And, as his fingertips touched metal, the lights went out.

And the knocking stopped.

And a scream came from the nearby bedroom.

## 13: DARKNESS

Total darkness. Impenetrable blackness.

They stood there in shock for several heavy heartbeats, unable to move until parental instinct kicked in. Cally continued to scream.

Although disorientated, Gabe and Eve moved towards their daughters' bedroom together and, because Loren was still clutching at her mother's nightdress, she went with them.

Gabe felt the wall with his hands, working his way along the landing, Eve following his sound. Dim shapes were slowly beginning to reveal themselves – the balcony railings, the tall window below a slightly paler blackness, the doorway to Loren and Cally's bedroom the same.

Gabe had just felt the emptiness of that doorway when the imperfect moon fought clear of the roiling clouds below it and suddenly they could see more clearly. Moonlight flooded through the hall's tall window, brightening a long segment of the flagstone floor, and Eve was able to discern her husband's silhouette in the opening.

'It's all right, Cally,' she heard him say. 'We're here, you're okay, baby.'

Eve pushed into the room behind him, dragging a terrified Loren in her wake. Cally was kneeling on her bed, the duvet bunched up before her.

'Cally, what is it?' Eve made straight for her, arms outstretched.

Cally had stopped screaming, but her shoulders heaved with her sobbing.

'In the corner, Mummy,' she wailed, throwing herself into her mother's arms.

Eve, Gabe and Loren all looked towards the corner that Cally's trembling finger was pointing at. In the semi-darkness they could see it was empty.

'There's nothing there, darling,' Eve soothed as Cally clung to her. 'You've just had a bad dream.'

'No, Mummy, there was someone standing there, all black.'

'No, you just had a fright when the lights went out. We probably disturbed you when we were out on the landing.'

'The banging woke me up,' Cally complained as she cried against Eve's shoulder, the words coming out between sob spasms. 'I sat up and saw someone in the corner. He was – he was looking at me.'

How could she tell if whatever she had imagined watching her was all black? Eve wondered, but quickly dismissed the thought: logic wasn't going to calm Cally down.

Gabe, who had found his way over to the empty corner, turned back towards the bed. 'It was just a bad dream, Cally,' he told her softly. 'Look, there's no one there.'

'But, Daddy—'

'Hush, darling.' Eve hugged her tight. 'It's over now. We're here with you.'

'I left my flashlight beside our bed,' Gabe said. 'I wanna take a look inside that closet.'

At any other time Loren would have amended 'closet' to 'cupboard', but tonight she was too upset. 'Don't, Daddy,' she pleaded. 'Not while it's so dark.' The moon was abruptly hidden again and she sat on the bed with her mother, pressing against Eve's back.

'It's okay, hon. I just need to find out what was making that racket. We don't want it starting up again.'

He was gone before Loren could protest any more, ducking through the doorway, silently cursing the sudden power cut. Nevertheless, by the time he reached his and Eve's bedroom, his eyes had adjusted to the darkness some more. He felt his way along the side of the bed until he found the cold metal of the flashlight standing erect on the floor; there were no bedside cabinets in this stark room, just the bed itself, a tall chest of drawers, a high wardrobe set against one wall, and an oval mirror hung on another. He pressed the switch and the flashlight came on. He shone it towards the landing so that his wife and daughters would see its glow and feel reassured. He quickly padded back to his daughters, shining the light on Loren and Cally's beds first, and then into the suspect corner. It really was clear; no dark man lurked there.

'See?' he said. 'Nothing there at all.'

Leaving the bedroom again he returned to the cupboard out on the landing.

'Okay, you bastard,' Gabe muttered to himself, 'let's find out what the fuss is about.'

But all remained quiet now, although he didn't trust the silence.

He reached for the brass door handle and tugged it. The door did not move. He remembered he *had* locked it previously and he dropped his hand to the key below. Without giving himself time for further thought, he turned it.

Gabe felt the easing of pressure as the unlocked door shifted in its frame. He yanked the door open in one swift movement and shone the light beam into the cupboard's depths. Eve and the two girls joined him as he bent to peer inside. They stared nervously over his shoulder.

He shone the flashlight around the interior, checking the corners, the back and even the cupboard's ceiling. All that was there were the cardboard boxes, the rolled-up rug and the mop and broom that he had already discovered. Moving aside two of the boxes, he noticed there were two thinnish waterpipes running along the left wall an inch or so above the floor and disappearing into the back wall.

'Guess there's the answer.' Gabe's light-hearted tone was forced as he aimed the beam directly at the two copper pipes. He reached down to feel them. 'One of 'em's hot. Might be an airlock in it.'

'Gabe, that can't be it. We saw the door move when the banging got really loud.'

He couldn't explain it and he didn't even try. He was looking for a rational reason for the noise; he didn't want to spook the girls any more than they were spooked already – and that included Eve.

'I'll check it out tomorrow,' he promised. As he straightened up, he kept the light pointing into the cupboard as if expecting an animal of some kind – a trapped bird maybe (although how a bird could have found its way inside, he had no idea), a mouse, a *rat*, or even a squirrel. Nothing stirred, though; nothing appeared from any hole in the skirting board; no bird fluttered out at them.

The overhead light and the one in the bedroom further down flickered, dimmed, came back on for a moment, dimmed once more, almost went off again, then returned to a steady glow.

'Thank God for that,' Eve murmured in a release of breath.

'Percy Judd said there were power cuts here and I think we've just experienced one. I'll take a good look at the gen tomorrow, see if I can fix it. It should kick in when the power goes.'

'This house . . .' Eve allowed her comment on Crickley Hall to peter out, the inflection in those first two words containing the message.

'Yeah, I know. We'll give it just *one* week, okay?'

Once more, Eve gave no response to the time limit set by Gabe even though he'd reduced it by a week. She wasn't sure she could stand as much as another day here. She knew it hadn't been the waterpipes creating that din and so did Gabe; he was only trying to soothe the girls with his unlikely – no, ridiculous – explanation.

'Let's all get back to bed,' he suggested, swinging the cupboard door shut and locking it again.

'Daddy, can we come in with you and Mummy tonight?' It wasn't Cally who asked but Loren, and her voice was plaintive.

'Sure you can.' He hugged his daughter close and Cally raised her arms to be picked up by Eve. But before they could find their way back to the bedroom, a mournful howl came from Chester in the kitchen below. Although the kitchen door was closed, the howl seemed to echo around the great hall.

Not only did the children sleep with Gabe and Eve that night, but the dog also slept on the floor close to Gabe's side of the bed.

## 14: SUNDAY

Gabe had cleaned the generator's spark plugs and reset the gauges. He'd also cleaned the oil filter and made sure that the coolant level was correct. Then he'd washed out the fuel filter and checked the gen's fuse, to find that it had blown, which was probably the sole cause for the machine's malfunction. Luckily he had a selection of different amp fuses in his toolbox, so was able to fit a replacement. Oil level was fine and he tested all the electrical connections to make sure it was not just the fuse that was at fault. The only thing he was concerned about was that if the generator had been standing idle for a long time, then the gas – *petrol*, he reminded himself – might have gone stale, which would mean draining and refilling it with fresh.

However, the latter proved to be no problem, for when he tested the gen by switching off the main fuse to the house's power, the generator sprang into life like a runner taking over the baton. Satisfied, he switched back to mains electricity and returned the generator to standby.

Smiling at the machine as if they had solved the problem together, Gabe wiped his oily hands on a dry cloth he kept in his toolbox.

'Don't let us down, baby,' he said to the generator. 'We don't need any more scares like last night.'

Carrying the long metal toolbox, Gabe left the boiler/generator room and went next door to the well cellar. Like the landing light, the lightbulb down here was far too weak to brighten the place efficiently and the thicker shadows that were created somehow made him feel uneasy.

The rushing of the river at the bottom of the well was loud enough to catch his attention. Downing the toolbox, he went over to the low wall that encircled the pit at the cellar's centre and shone his flashlight into it. The beam of light reflected off the slick mossy wall before revealing the spumy, surging river thirty or so feet below. Anyone unfortunate to fall in wouldn't stand a chance, he mused: there would be no grip on the rough but slimy stonework and the coursing waters would immediately sweep that person away. He reminded himself to make sure the door at the top of the stairs was always locked in case Cally's curiosity got the better of her (he thought he'd locked it yesterday, but this morning he had found the door ajar again). The stone wall round the well was low enough to be dangerous should either one of his daughters lean over it for a look-see.

The noise of the river was amplified by the round wall to a constant, only slightly muffled roar, and the air here was so chilled he could see his own breath vapour.

Gabe checked himself. He had been leaning too far over the wall, almost mesmerized by the black pit he was staring into. He hurriedly stepped back from the brink and drew in a slow breath. Damn right it was dangerous. Loren, too, would be banned from venturing down here alone.

He climbed the cellar stairs and at the top he carefully locked the door behind him, giving it a pull to ensure it was secure. It was loose in its frame but remained shut. Leaving the toolbox on the hall floor, Gabe went into the kitchen.

Chester had dragged his sleeping blanket into the corner

by the kitchen's other door and he looked up expectantly at Gabe.

'Still jumpy, boy?'

Gabe squatted to pat the dog's flank. Although no longer trembling, Chester nevertheless gazed appealingly into his master's eyes.

'Guess you're still not happy with the place, right? But you gotta acclimatize, pal. We *all* do.'

Gabe wondered if they would. He felt that Eve would leave right now if she had her way. And the girls? Last night's incident scared them, but neither of them had complained this morning at breakfast. It was as if Loren was looking to her mother for guidance, and Cally seemed to have forgotten her upset already. The three of them had gone off to the Sunday-morning service at St Mark's – even though it was C of E – without mentioning the episode; but Gabe knew that Eve was waiting to get him alone.

With one last comforting pat on Chester's rump, Gabe rose and went to the sink where he poured tap water into the kettle. While he waited for the water to boil, his thoughts returned to Eve.

She really was creeped out by Crickley Hall. And he wasn't too comfortable with the place himself. When he had gone downstairs during the night to bring Chester back to their room, he had trodden in more small puddles on the broad steps, and there were others across the flagstone floor of the hall. If the dog hadn't been shut away in the kitchen, Gabe might have suspected him of leaving his mark all over the place. But these had no smell: they were plain water. However, it had been windy outside and he supposed that rain might have been blown through cracks in the tall window over the stairs. Had it been windy when he had first noticed the puddles the night before? He couldn't remember. But anyway, that wouldn't explain the ones across the hall.

Maybe they should get out right away, find some other house to rent, something not as weird as Crickley Hall. A place slap-damn in the middle of a village or town, somewhere not so isolated. Or so lonely. He couldn't risk Eve becoming more depressed than she was already. She had been through too much this past year – they *all* had.

But the tragedy had changed Eve more than it had Gabe.

When they had first met, she had been a staff fashion writer for a magazine called *Plenty*, organizing fashion shoots, auditioning and hiring models, choosing photographers, finding suitable locations for background interest, liaising with PR companies, reporting on the main fashion shows in the UK and Europe, interviewing celebrities to discover whose labels they were currently wearing.

She and Gabe were only married six months before Loren came along and Eve went freelance. Her contacts and her reputation were good and before long she was doing work for a number of magazines – *Marie Claire, Vogue, Elle*, among others – and was able to concentrate on writing purely about fashion without the baggage that went with it. But when Cameron was born, and then Catherine (Cally) a year later, Eve put her career on hold for a while so that she could devote more time to her family.

By then, they were living in a largish Victorian property in Canonbury, north London, and Gabe's salary was high enough to cover most of their needs. She still accepted the more interesting assignments, however, and when she did she would put her best efforts into them, which was why her very last freelance job – covering London's Fashion Week – had left her so exhausted. And that exhaustion had led her to falling asleep for a few minutes in the park where Cameron had gone missing . . .

Eve was wrong to blame herself, but how could he convince her? He pushed the thoughts away as he spooned coffee granules into a mug, then poured boiling water over them. There had been too much brooding for way too long. If only for Loren and Cally's sake, Eve had to snap out of it. But how could he help her?

Although Cam was a real boy's boy, a son that a father could really enjoy, Eve seemed to have a special 'connection' with him. No, he wasn't a momma's boy, but there was an affinity between them. They even shared the same trivial abnormality: the little finger of Cam's right hand was shorter than the one on his left, the same as Eve's; they also both had fingerprint whorls on the fleshy mount of their right palm. It was a similarity that they enjoyed, for it wasn't an obvious deformity – hands had to be compared to notice it.

Looking out the window, Gabe saw that the rain had stopped, although only temporarily judging by the ominous clouds that cruised the sky. As he watched, the sun broke out from behind one of those clouds and the lawn glistened with raindrops caught in the grass. The sudden brightness and the green denseness of the grass and foliage lifted some of the heaviness of spirit from him. Whatever the shortcomings of Crickley Hall itself, it couldn't be denied that it was in a beautiful location. From where he stood in the kitchen he could see past the old oak from which the swing dangled to the rushing waters of the Bay River, fallen leaves and small broken branches swept along with its hurried journey down to the Bristol Channel. He watched as a heron landed on the opposite bank close to the wooden bridge; the heavy bird must have decided that this was a poor place to catch passing fish, for its great wings soon flapped and it took off again in an impossibly lumbering rise into the air.

Gabe felt the need for fresh air himself and he carried his mug of coffee into the main hall where he unlocked the big front door to let the breeze, such as it was, circulate and disperse some of the musty odour that permeated the house. He stood on the doorstep and sipped the coffee as grey wagtails, with their black bibs, wheeled and dived over the garden, catching insects and celebrating the rare sunshine.

His thoughts returned to Eve, how she had changed, how she was before that fateful day. She was still beautiful to him – slim, small-breasted, long-legged, with deep-brown eyes that matched her deep-brown hair – but now there were lines on her face that had only appeared during the last few months, and there was a darkness round her eyes that spoke of sleepless nights and sadness of soul. Her hair, once worn so long that its ends cascaded over her shoulders, was now cut short, urchin-style, not because of fashion but because it was easier to manage, nothing to bother over. A psychologist might suggest it was shorn as self-punishment, arising from guilt.

She used to have a sly humour, a sharp wit, but now Eve was subdued, her thoughts – and her feelings – distracted by the loss. To see her this way added to Gabe's own grief, but there was nothing he could do that he hadn't already tried to ease her despair. Even harsh, desperate words, tough love they called it, had failed to draw any positive response because she fully accepted her own condition and refused to be stung by his criticism. Ultimately, he could only love her, not in an indulgent way, but in a way that let her know that he cast no blame on her.

Gabe drew in a deep breath of fresh moist air. A little

sunshine made a difference, he thought. It helped cheer the soul. If only the rain—

His legs almost buckled as Chester brushed by him. The dog scooted across the lawn, past the swing that stirred lazily in the breeze.

*Goddamnit!* He'd forgotten about the mutt, hadn't closed the kitchen door behind him. Chester had seen his chance for freedom and had taken it. Like a bat out of hell, he streaked towards the bridge.

*'Chester! Get back here!'*

The dog hesitated at the bridge, turned briefly to look back at his master, then scooted across it without stopping on the other side. Gabe stepped out of the doorway, coffee in hand, and stared open-mouthed.

*'Chester!'* he tried again. Exasperated, he put the coffee mug on the doorstep, then took off after the runaway. Gabe ran across the bridge, continuing to call the dog's name, but knowing that by the determined way Chester had bolted up the hill he would stop for no one. Gabe stood in the middle of the lane, hoping to see some sign of the dog, but Chester was nowhere in sight.

Gabe called out once more, this time through cupped hands, but it was futile: Chester had vanished.

A shout from behind had Gabe swinging round.

'Daddy!'

Eve and the girls were walking up the hill towards him from the direction of the church.

'What is it, Gabe?' Eve asked as they drew nearer.

'It's that goddamn mongrel.' Gabe shook his head in frustration. 'He's hit the road.'

'*Daddy.*' It was a moan from both girls.

'It's okay. We'll find him. He can't have gone far.'

Cally's face was already screwed up, ready for tears.

'How did he get out?' Eve was a little breathless from the steady climb up the hill.

'Aah, I had the front door open and he hightailed it.' Gabe shook his head once again, angry at himself. *'Goddamnit.'*

Loren's face was full of concern. 'We haven't lost him, have we, Dad?'

'No, honey. We'll find him.' To Eve he said: 'I'll take a walk along the road. If I keep calling him, he might just be obedient for once and come back.'

'I'll go with you, Dad,' Loren said immediately.

'Me too, me too.' Cally raced to him and pulled at his arm.

Gabe leaned down to her. 'You go with your ma, Sparky. We'll find him quicker if it's just me and Loren.' He had chosen his words carefully, leaving no doubt that they would find the wayward pet. He kissed her plump cheek, tasting her tear trail that already stained it.

Eve wasn't convinced. 'Oh Gabe, we haven't lost him, have we? You will get him back . . .?'

'We'll find him, he can't have gone far.' Gabe hoped she would believe him.

## 15: THE DREAM

In Crickley Hall's high-ceilinged sitting room off the great hall, there was a lumpy but comfortable couch and it was on this that Eve relaxed. She was tired. Last night had left her both weary and tense. The lights going out when Cally had started screaming had almost freaked her out. Thank God her daughter was only having a nightmare. But the knocking from the closed cupboard had been no dream and Gabe's explanation that it was an airlock in the waterpipes inside the cupboard wasn't convincing. But what else could the noise have been? Lying sleepless for much of the night with her imagination running wild had left her edgy and skittish this morning, only the service at St Mark's calming her.

In the church, and in the cold light of day, most of the night fears had been vanquished, common sense prevailing. That it had stopped raining and the sun could find periods of cloud breakthrough had helped accommodate logic – it really *had* been the waterpipes causing the disturbance and it really *was* a draught beneath the floorboards that had caused the rattling of the cupboard door – but doubt lingered. There was something strange about Crickley Hall, something dark, Eve could sense it. She could easily believe there were ghosts here.

She leaned sideways and pressed her head into the

embroidered cushion that rested against the couch's arm. She closed her eyes.

Gabe and Loren were still out looking for Chester, having come back for the car – oh God, Eve hoped they hadn't lost him – and Cally was upstairs playing in her bedroom. Lunch wasn't a problem: microwaving a couple of the freezer-packs they'd bought in Hollow Bay yesterday wouldn't take long. Sunday lunch was usually a roast, but Gabe and the girls wouldn't mind missing it for one week.

Her eyelids flickered, opened once more. The sitting room, with its high windows and long beige drapes, was one of the nicer rooms in the house, although there was still an air of austerity about it. The windows were almost filled with the trees and greenery of the gorge slope and riverbank so that they were like natural murals. The wallpaper was old, traditional, but its flowery pattern at least cheered the room a little. The couch itself faced an oakwood and brick fireplace where Gabe had laid and lit a fire that morning to chase away the room's chill. The heat from it did not stretch far, but nevertheless it was making Eve drowsy. She blinked, forced her eyes open.

On a round occasional table opposite the couch were framed family photographs that they had brought with them to Crickley Hall and were among the first things Eve had displayed after the main items had been unpacked. They represented happier times. A wedding shot of Gabe and three-months-pregnant Eve, a large colour group shot of them all taken almost two years ago so it included Cam. To the fore was a small silver-framed picture of a brightly smiling Cam. She pushed away the thoughts, afraid of their conclusion. No body had been found, death *could* not be assumed. In the photograph, his hair, sweeping down almost to touch his eyebrows, was a striking yellow; when he grew it would probably darken, become shades closer to his father's. But the vivacity of those cornflower-blue eyes – so like Gabe's – would remain until old age paled them.

Her eyes moistened.

But her eyelids were heavy and a gentle warmth came from the coal and log fire.

Eve drifted, consciousness waned. She slept. She dreamed.

At the beginning it was bad, for although she slept she was still aware of the brooding house around her. She felt its chill, its shadows. She felt the misery that was in this place, in its memory, in its soul. Eve shivered in her sleep.

There was something wrong inside this house – perhaps it was her subconscious that told her this – some grim secret kept within it. She heard distant whimpers, then quiet sobs. The sounds of misery. Of being lost.

A tear squeezed through the corner of her eye, a silver droplet made red by the fire.

There was something ominous contained – *caged* – within these stone walls. A truth that was unattainable. A secret. The word formed in her mind as though written in stark, unembellished letters.

She stirred on the couch, twisting her neck to push her face into its cushioned back.

In her dream she was being called, but no matter where she looked, the source lay hidden. Faraway though it was, the voice was that of a child and its urgency was muted by the distance.

And suddenly Eve was dreaming of herself: she was looking down at her own sleeping body as though her mind had left it and was floating near the ceiling. Now her physical self was no longer inside the house. Instead, she was somewhere that was full of green space, a place where children played, where her own child, little Cally, slumbered in her buggy close by the bench, while her brother, almost one year older, played in the sandpit not far away.

Something was wrong, though. Something was terribly wrong. Yet still the body below her – her real self – slept on.

Five-year-old Cameron was slowly vanishing as sand ran through his tiny fingers to pile around and over his bent knees. Disappearing as a whole, not bit by bit, but fading as if a white fog was enveloping him. And still Eve dreamed, unaware of this dangerous decline of her son, sleeping as his image weakened, dimmed from sight, smothered by the fog.

Then she became aware of another presence in her dream, although this was so clear, so real, that she wondered – in her dream – if she was no longer asleep. The dark but sharp silhouette of a man loomed over her. The figure had narrow shoulders and a thin physique, and as he leaned towards her, his shadowed face only inches away from hers, there came a smell that was strange yet somehow familiar, an odour that mingled with his own thick rancid breath. She tried to turn her head away, but twin lights from the dark caverns of his deep-set eyes held her there mesmerized and afraid. Eve no longer viewed herself from above – she was back inside herself. She felt a huge pressure on her, weighing her down.

He exhaled and his breath was worse than before: it was stinking, fetid, the scent of a putrid cesspit. Yet still there was that underlying scent, the pungent odour of . . . of *detergent*? She felt scrutinized, inspected; she felt dread. Eve shrank away, but the head, with its gleaming inset pinpoint eyes, followed her. Although still shadowed, the features of the dream-visitor were revealed: he had a sharp, hooked nose, prominent, as his cleft chin was prominent above a thin scrawny neck; she still could not tell the colour of his eyes, she could only see those two gleaming lights that shone from them, reflections only but like searchlights used by him to scour her soul. That this man was wicked, she had no doubt; it was as evident as the malodour that came through his thin lips.

He raised a big-knuckled hand to her cheek, his bony fingers curled. He drew the hand down the skin of her face and, although his touch was weak, his flesh seemed to scratch against her own. In the dream and in the reality she gave out an anguished cry.

A lump of coal on the fire cracked with the heat, but its sound – and the sound of her own cry – failed to rouse her. Still she lay in troubled sleep. She groaned. Her leg flexed, an arm crossed her breasts, hand gripping her shoulder.

The nightmare should have awakened her, as such fantasies do when they become unbearable, but it failed and she dreamt on.

She reared away from the cold touch and just when the terror was at its zenith, she felt the clawed hand withdraw to be replaced by another touch, one that was gentle and soothing. A small soft hand was stroking her cheek and the fear very slowly began to leave her.

Her body relaxed and the touching of this little hand – a child's hand – was healing, driving away both terror ... and guilt. She had the vaguest impression of a child's featureless face under a mop of hair so fair it looked white, but the image was both weak and fleeting. The nightmare faltered, became nebulous, finally left her.

She called out his name, a question.

'Cameron?'

And it was the sound of her own voice that finally woke her.

She stirred, almost reluctantly opening her eyes, not wanting the serenity to end, hoping to find it was real.

But the 'presence' vanished with the awakening.

'Cameron?' she said again, and even though there was no reply, the wonderful peace was not completely gone.

Eve sat up and looked around as if expecting to find her son somewhere in the room with her. But the room was empty of any other person. Nothing had changed.

Except the photograph of Cam on the nearby table had fallen on the floor.

It lay on its side, supported by the strut at the back, and Cam's eyes seemed to be looking directly into her own.

And although his photograph drew her attention, she was aware that there was something else different about the high-ceilinged sitting room. That odd aroma still scented the air and she now recognized the smell. It was the sharp reek of carbolic soap; it was all that was left of the dream.

## 16: CHESTER

'Hold on to Chester while I find something to tie him with.'

Gabe rose to his feet, a dark damp patch on the knees of his jeans where he had been kneeling on the wet grass. He hung on to the dog's collar until Loren took over.

'Good boy,' she said soothingly into the animal's cocked ear. 'Nothing to be frightened of, is there?' She wrapped an arm round Chester's neck.

Gabe shook his head in bemused irritation. He'd tried to coax their pet up to Crickley Hall's front door, but the dog wasn't having it. The more Gabe pulled, the more Chester squatted on his haunches and dug his paws into the turf. Gabe couldn't understand the mutt's fear. Sure, there wasn't much that was homely about the Hall, nothing comfortable about it, but it was just a house, stone, mortar and timber. Maybe Chester was picking up vibes from Eve, who seemed to think Crickley Hall was haunted. Wacky, maybe, but Gabe didn't want to argue with her; his wife was still in an ultra-sensitive state. Which was why he had promised to find somewhere else to rent if she hadn't settled in after two weeks – no, one week now. He was sure she'd change her mind once she got rid of the idea that there were ghosts in the place. But in the meantime, what to do about Chester?

Gabe and Loren had found the runaway half a mile up the

lane, heading for unknown territory. He had stopped by the side of the road when Gabe and Loren drove up, his head high and eyes bright as though he recognized the Range Rover. And there had been no problem in getting him to hop up onto the back seat, his short-haired stumpy tail wagging happily, responding to Loren's hugs and kisses enthusiastically. But when Gabe turned the 4x4 around and began heading back to Crickley Hall, Chester had become agitated again.

Gabe had to pick up the dog and carry his skinny quivering body across the bridge and then he had to drag the mongrel by his collar across the lawn towards the house's solid front door. Chester had protested all the way, his brown eyes bulging. Gabe had reluctantly taken him back to the oak tree where the swing hung, holding down his exasperation more for Loren's sake than for Chester's; the dog's panic was upsetting her.

'Okay, mutt,' Gabe grumbled, 'let's see how you like being outside all day.'

'Dad!' Loren objected. 'We can't do that. What if it starts raining again?'

Gabe glanced up at the troubled sky and saw the clouds had become dark and threatening.

'We'll have to see,' he told Loren. 'You keep him calm while I go look for something to tie him with.'

He left daughter and dog by the oak, Loren's grip on Chester firm but loving – she was whispering sweet nothings in Chester's ear – and strode towards the battered-looking shed that stood some distance away from the house, bushes on the rising gorge behind it brushing its flat roof. There was no padlock on the door's locking arm and it opened with hinges squealing and bottom plank scuffing the ground.

The interior smelt of dust and damp. It was shadowy, its

only window so badly smeared by weather grime it was virtually opaque. He could make out what looked like well-used gardening tools – a rake, hoe, shears and other implements – hanging from the wooden wall opposite the window, and a couple of plastic sacks that may have contained fertilizer or weedkiller, or both, resting on the stone floor, while at the back, behind a lawnmower, an old Flymo hover-mower leaned on its side against the wall, its rotor blade missing. On a shelf above the hooks was a petrol can (gasoline, to Gabe) and a half-sized chainsaw, probably used for trimming tree branches and cutting up logs for Crickley Hall's fires. There were also cobwebs, plenty of cobwebs, dusty nets draped from corners and ledges. The shed needed a good clean-up, which Gabe thought he'd probably do himself rather than ask old Percy who, no doubt, was too used to the dirt to notice. Many gardeners were like that.

Gabe spied what he had been looking for: a length of rope dangled from a shelf hook at the far end of the row. Moving round the lawnmower occupying the centre floor space, he unhooked the rope and carried it back to the daylight coming through the open door. The rope was thin and almost black with dust, but it was long and strong enough to serve his purpose. After scraping the shed door shut and pushing the slot of the locking arm into the metal hasp, he returned to the oak tree where Loren and Chester were waiting.

Loren frowned as Gabe threw one end of the rope round the tree trunk and deftly caught it when it came round the other side. 'It's wicked, Dad,' she complained, holding Chester closer to her.

'Can't be helped, Slim,' Gabe responded, feeling only a little guilty. 'If he won't come into the house, this is all we can do. If we left him untied, he'd scoot again. We don't want to lose him, do we?'

'But we can't leave him out all night.'

Gabe tied a knot so that the rope was looped securely round the tree. He knelt beside Chester and slid the free end through the dog's collar. As he tied another knot, he said, 'He'll wanna play house after he's spent the rest of the day on his own. You hear me, mutt.' He playfully poked Chester's ribs. 'You want company again, you gotta learn to love Crickley Hall.'

'He'll get soaked if it rains.' Loren clung to Chester more fiercely.

'If it rains, I'll haul him inside and if he howls or whines he goes down to the cellar. I don't like it much myself, Loren, but it's the only solution.'

Gabe took his daughter by the elbow and brought her unwillingly to her feet. She stroked Chester's head a few more times before following her father towards the house. When they both looked back, Chester was standing stock-still, his tail in the air, watching them as if expecting their return. Gabe put his arm around Loren's shoulders and gently urged her on.

'Chester's gonna be okay. Wait and see – he'll decide life indoors in comfort and with good company is a lot better than time alone, trussed to a tree.'

'But why doesn't he like Crickley Hall, Dad?' Loren's voice was woeful.

'Well, I guess he'd rather be in his own home, like the rest of us,' he told her. 'Being somewhere strange gives him the jitters. He's a jumpy kind of mutt anyway, always has been.'

If Loren was satisfied with the reply she wasn't saying. She walked alongside Gabe in silence, a troubled look on her young face. He wondered if he'd been wrong in bringing his family down here to Hollow Bay. Hell, even the dog hated it here. But Gabe thought he'd been acting for the best: the anniversary of Cam's disappearance would soon be on them and Gabe hadn't wanted them all – especially Eve – to face it in the house where their son had been born and raised, and where there were so many heart-stabbing memories of him.

Father and daughter bypassed Crickley Hall's main door, Gabe tapping on the kitchen window as they walked past, Eve turning round from the table where she and Cally were setting places for lunch. She gave Gabe and Loren a short wave and a smile.

The door to the kitchen was unlocked, as Gabe knew it would be (irrationally, some impulse deep within Eve caused her constantly to leave the front door of their London house unlocked as if she were afraid that Cam might suddenly appear only to find himself locked out), and they stepped inside, stamping their boots on the thick doormat to shake off loose rainwater and mud. To Gabe's surprise, Eve was still smiling.

'You found him easily enough,' she said, having watched Gabe tether their wayward pet to the tree from the window.

'Yep,' agreed Gabe as he shrugged off his reefer jacket. 'Way up the hill, heading for the city lights.'

To his further surprise Eve gave him a peck on the cheek, and then did the same to Loren. There was a sudden brightness to his wife that had been absent for a long time. Puzzled but pleased, he studied her face with some confusion.

'Daddy, why didn't you bring Chester inside?' Cally looked up at him, a clutch of tablespoons held in one podgy little hand. Eve obviously had lifted her up to the kitchen window so that she could see they'd found Chester.

'Because he told me he wanted to catch some fresh air for a while. He's tired of being cooped up in the house all day long.'

'Chester can't say words, Daddy.'

'Sure he can. You just never seem to be around when he says 'em.'

'Doh,' she said meaningfully.

'You don't believe me? When I was a cowboy back in the States I had a horse that gabbed to me all the time.'

Eve and Loren rolled their eyes at each other.

'Woody hasn't got a talking horse,' Cally responded doubtfully, referring to another favourite cartoon character. Bart and Homer Simpson were not the only guys in town.

'That's because he hasn't even got a horse.'

Eve intervened. 'Gabe, you're going to be in trouble when she wises up to you. You know she believes everything you tell her.'

Gabe only grinned back at her. 'Loren seems to have adjusted well enough.'

'You weren't there, Dad, when my friends laughed at me. I'm still disappointed about Father Christmas.'

Cally's head swung round to her older sister. 'Father Christmas?'

'You're too little to understand, Cally,' Loren informed her patiently. 'Daddy makes up stories.'

Cally's head swivelled back to Gabe.

'Well, look who's all growed up all of a sudden,' he teased Loren.

Eve intervened again before Cally became disillusioned. 'But it seems you haven't,' she said to Gabe, and amazingly her smile was genuine.

Gabe stared at her. Had some of her lustre come back? He felt a lifting of his own spirit.

'You had a good morning?' he asked, probing her. When he and Loren had picked up the car, Eve had looked her usual beaten self. Had something happened while he and

Loren were out? If so, was Eve saving the explanation for when she and Gabe were alone? He would just have to wait and see.

But Eve gave nothing away, even though the sadness that she had worn like a shroud all these months appeared to have lifted – not entirely, it was true, for there was still an unshakeable air of melancholy about her, but this was now subdued, her manner more alert, her voice a little lighter, her movement not quite so leaden. It gave him a glimpse of her real self, the woman he had loved for so many years, and he was afraid to say anything that might change the mood. The difference in her was not great, but to Gabe it seemed significant. Maybe a turning point.

He hadn't even pressed her when they were on their own, the girls off somewhere playing, Loren probably texting her friends on her brand-new cell phone, but at one point he had softly ventured, 'You okay, hon?' and she had merely turned to him and said, 'Yes.' No more than that.

So he let it be. Maybe her mind had taken all the misery – and guilt – it could handle. If so, he guessed the change probably wouldn't last long; but at least it might be a step towards her recovery. He hoped that it was.

# 17: THE DORMITORY

Loren and Cally were in the bathroom, Loren brushing her teeth, anxious about the first day at the new school tomorrow, while her sister sat on the toilet nearby, pyjama leggings bunched round her ankles, squeezing out the last few drops of her pee. Cally hummed a tuneless song while she waited, her eyes roving around the stark black-and-white-tiled room.

A deep porcelain bath supported by ugly clawed metal feet took up much of the length of one wall and the octagonal-shaped sink on its sturdy pedestal was set against the wall opposite beneath a tall mirrored cabinet. The light from a pearled bowl centred in the high ceiling was too harsh and made the wall and diamond-patterned floor tiles look garish and cold, the reflection of Loren in the mirror unflattering. The window above the low toilet cistern was frosted and without curtaining; the door at the room's other end was painted black, its brass doorknob tarnished with wear, no key in the lock beneath it. Even more so than most of the other rooms in Crickley Hall, the bathroom was utilitarian and charmless.

Loren had decided, with no urging from her parents, to have an early night. Perhaps it was only because her sleep had been interrupted the previous night, but she felt very tired. She was anxious to be fresh and bright for the next day.

She would read for a while as Mum or Dad read Cally a bedtime story (Gabe had fixed up a lamp on the small cabinet between Loren and Cally's beds) and when Cally drifted off as she always did before the story's end, she would try to sleep herself. Perhaps she wouldn't even bother to read; sometimes she liked to listen with Cally – even though her younger sister's stories were childish, there was something very comforting about them.

Loren was also frustrated that her cell phone wasn't working; the whole point of having it was so she could keep in touch with her friends back in London while she was away. She had tried for ages to send text messages, but when she switched on the Samsung the screen just said 'Limited service' and each time she persisted in tapping out a message with her thumb and pressing SEND, it said 'Message failed'. In fact, she couldn't even *call* her friends, because 'Limited service' *always* came up. When she'd complained to Dad he'd tried his own cell phone with the same result. He said it was probably because they were in the ravine – 'gorge', she'd corrected him yet again – and most likely there were no masts nearby. Use the land line, he advised her, but she wanted to contact her friends in private and Crickley Hall's 'ancient' phone was in the hall where just *everybody* could overhear everything she said. It was very annoying.

Loren exhaled a yawn as she brushed.

Cally was sure the last drop had been forced out and so she slid off the cold toilet seat. She bent to pull up her pyjama bottoms.

Then both girls stopped what they were doing and looked up at the ceiling.

*

Downstairs in the kitchen, Gabe and Eve were sharing a bottle of Chablis while their two daughters were upstairs in the bathroom preparing for bed. Gabe leaned across the table and topped up Eve's glass with the white wine and she held up a hand in protest.

'You'll get me tipsy,' she complained but with a smile.

'No bad thing,' he replied, grinning back at her and continuing to pour.

Eve had lit four candles and placed them at strategic points around the room before turning off the overhead light, which exposed the room's plainness too much for her liking. One of the candles was between her and Gabe on the table, its glow bringing a soft lustre to Eve's eyes.

'We used to do this a lot,' Gabe remarked in a soft voice, then immediately regretted having said it. *They used to do this a lot before their son went missing.*

But Eve did not react, even if she realized the implication. She sipped the wine.

To move on, Gabe said, 'Not like Loren to go to bed early.'

'She seemed very tired.'

'Yeah, and a little antsy about her cell phone.'

'And your mobile too. Won't you need it?'

'I'll use the regular phone.'

'That old thing.'

'At least it's digital. I'm surprised it's not Bakerlite with letters as well as numbers.'

'It looks first-generation digital.'

'It's a *man's* phone.'

'Yes, completely out-of-date.'

'It'll do. Eve, you seem . . .' He hesitated, then came right out with it. 'You, uh, you seem more relaxed than of late. You know, I've been kinda worried about you.'

She lowered her gaze. Should she tell him what occurred

this afternoon, the dream that wasn't quite a dream? Would he believe Cameron had reached out to her somehow, if only for a few seconds? She was quite sure in herself that it had happened for real, but would Gabe accept it? She had been half asleep, dozing, that was true, and the horrible man with rancid breath and the odd after-smell must have been some kind of waking nightmare, but the presence that could only have been Cam was genuine, she was sure. The undefined vision had come to her. No, she couldn't tell her husband, not yet. Not until she was truly sure that Cam was trying to contact her. Oh, she'd had sight of him before, but these had been in proper dreams, sleep fantasies that quickly faded when she woke. But this afternoon was different. There had always been a uniquely strong bond between her son and herself, and Gabe would never deny it. But would he believe that Cam was now trying to reach her through their psychic link? She doubted it. The idea was too off the wall for someone whose attitude to life had always been pragmatic. No, she would have to prove it to him. But first she had to prove it to *herself*. And there might just be a way of doing that.

Eve smiled inwardly: for the first time in nearly a year she felt hope, and it was a wonderful thing.

'Honey?'

She realized she had been distracted. 'Yes, Gabe?'

'You really do seem a little different today,' Gabe persisted, hunching forward over the tabletop and brushing her hand with his fingertips.

'Perhaps . . .' she began to say, but Chester, lying on his blanket by the kitchen door, suddenly shot to his feet and gave out a sharp yelp.

Surprised, they both turned to the dog as one. Chester's fur was bristling, his short tail erect, his teeth bared. Eyes wide and bright, he was staring at the open doorway to the hall.

'What's wrong, Chester?' Gabe pushed back from the table, the chair legs scuffing the linoleum. 'What is it, boy?'

Then both he and Eve heard it.

A faint scuffling noise coming through the doorway.

As if frozen – they had become wary of Crickley Hall's inexplicable noises by now – they listened.

The distant sound continued and Chester's yelps and barks relapsed to a whining. He cowered, his whole length close to the floor, front paws pushing himself against the door to the garden.

Gabe rose and went to the threshold of the hall. Eve followed.

Behind him, her hands resting on his shoulder, she tried to locate the source of the sound.

They both peered up at the hall's high ceiling.


Loren and Cally were standing outside the bathroom door, also looking upwards, Loren with her hands on the balustrade, Cally peeking through the rails. They were open-mouthed, their upturned faces pale.

Below, in the hall, Eve hissed into Gabe's ear, 'What is it?'

His gaze did not leave the ceiling. After a moment, he whispered back, 'Sounds like footsteps. Lots of 'em.'


They crowded round the door on the landing that led to the attic room – or rooms – the one place that neither Gabe nor Eve had yet visited.

'Is it locked?' Eve asked, for some reason speaking in a half-whisper.

'Don't know,' Gabe replied, his own voice quiet. 'Key's in the lock anyway.' He transferred the unlit flashlight (they couldn't know if the lights beyond the door would work) to his left hand and gripped the doorknob with his right. There was a slight resistance, as if the lock might be rusting inside, but it turned. He pulled, then pushed at the door and it opened inwardly easily enough, although there was an initial squeak of its hinges. Now he clicked on his flashlight.

The sound of numerous soft footsteps from above had faded away (faded as if turned down by a volume control) minutes before and now the family was curious but understandably cautious.

'There's a light switch just inside the door.' Gabe pointed towards it with his beam.

Eve reached past him and flicked the switch. Nothing happened.

She aimed her own small torch up the narrow staircase leading to the attic.

'Look, there's a light connection hanging down, but there's no lightbulb.'

'I'm going up,' Gabe announced.

'We're coming with you,' Eve informed him.

'Not a good idea. There could be, well, you know . . .' He didn't want to say it in front of his daughters.

'Rats,' Loren filled in for him.

'Might be squirrels.' Squirrels sounded more appealing.

'Gabe, we heard *foot*steps,' said Eve. 'They weren't made by animals of *any* kind.'

'Oh yeah? And what's the alternative?'

'Who knows with this house?'

Cally tugged at her waist. 'What is it, Mummy?'

Eve looked down at her, aware that any mention of ghosts would frighten both her daughters.

'Let's go and look,' she said finally.

'All of us.' Cally clutched at her even more tightly.

'All right. All of us.' Eve knew the girls would refuse to stay downstairs by themselves, so she didn't argue.

'You first, Daddy,' Cally insisted anxiously.

'Yep, me first.' Gabe grinned his wide tight-lipped grin, one that was wryly resolute rather than happy.

The wooden steps creaked as he made his way up, his family following close behind, Cally tightly gripping her mother's hand, Loren coming up last and taking each step carefully as if one might break beneath her.

The staircase smelt of rotting wood and dust, and it turned a corner beyond which Gabe found an open hatch. No proper door, just an open hatch.

He poked his head through and paused, shining the light around what was more than just a roof space. The room was long, even though a partition wall appeared to section it off at the far end, but the ceiling was low. Dormer windows were built into its slanting walls and two rough brick chimney stacks disappeared into the roof (there must have been similar stacks out of sight on the other side of the partition, for the house had more than two chimneys on its roof). Bare floorboards ran its length and there was no furniture other than what looked like iron-framed cotbeds piled against one corner.

Dust motes danced crazily in the beams of light as if disturbed by fierce draughts. Yet no windows were open or broken and he felt no breeze on his face. Only faint moonlight shone through the grimed glass, casting dark shadows around the room. He pointed his light at the skeletal cotbeds again and realized that this place must have been the dormitory for the evacuees who had come to Crickley Hall all those years ago.

Eve's voice came from the stairs below. 'What's the hold-up, Gabe?' She still spoke in a half-whisper as if afraid of being heard by someone other than her husband.

'Just checking—' He caught himself whispering his reply and continued in a normal voice. 'Just checking it out. Doesn't appear to be anything much up here 'cept a bunch of old bedsteads.'

He climbed through the hatchway and stood looking around. What had stirred up the dust?

Eve helped Cally through and Loren scrambled up behind them. Eve swung her torch beam from wall to wall, from floor to ceiling.

'Gabe. The dust . . .'

'Yeah, I know. Can't feel or see anything that could've caused it.'

He ran the light the length of the room. Two bare light-bulbs hung from the ceiling.

'Can you see a switch anywhere?'

Eve turned the torch towards the wall nearest to the open hatch. 'Over here,' she said, going to the single light switch that was fixed into the angled wall. She pressed it down, but only one overhead light came on and its power was insufficient, as, it seemed, were most of the lights in Crickley Hall. It was positioned at the far end of the long room and it did manage to reveal a door in the wood partitioning. She shivered. It was very cold in the attic.

Eve spotted the iron cotbeds piled together and taking up most of one corner. There must be a dozen, she thought to herself, or at least eleven. 'Is this where the children slept, d'you think?' she asked Gabe. 'Was this their dormitory when they stayed here during the war?'

'Yeah, it figures.' Gabe ran his lightbeam over the jumbled frames. 'If they'd stayed up here when the flood hit they would've survived. Makes no sense.'

'But it's so bare. Surely they'd have had their toys and other things with them.'

'It was a long time ago, hon. The place would've been cleared out.' He pointed his flashlight towards the partition door at the other end of the room. 'Unless a lot of stuff was stored away.'

He started forward, his footsteps sounding hollow in the room's emptiness.

Eve caught his arm as he went by. 'Have you forgotten why we came up here?'

'Uh?'

'The noises, the footsteps,' she reminded him. 'The footsteps sounded light, like children running around in bare feet.'

He hesitated. Thought for a moment. Then: 'Coulda been anything.'

'No, you know I'm right. It was children we heard. I think this house holds on to its memories.'

'Not that again. Crickley Hall isn't haunted.'

He regretted the words as soon as he'd uttered them.

'Dad?' Loren looked up at him, fear in her wide eyes.

Eve went to her. 'It's all right, Loren. We didn't mean to frighten you.' She put her arm around her daughter's shoulders.

'But you said it was haunted.' Loren was frozen; she did not move into her mother's embrace.

Eve tried to reassure her. 'No, I didn't mean that. I said the house has memories. That doesn't necessarily mean there are ghosts here.'

'I don't like ghosts, Mummy,' Cally piped up.

There was no anger in Gabe's voice, only despair. 'You're spooking 'em,' he said to Eve.

'Then you tell me what made the noise.'

And that was the problem: Gabe had no idea.

'Maybe there's something behind that wall.' He waved the flashlight at the partition and started to walk towards it through the floating dust.

'No, Daddy,' Loren pleaded.

Cally looked at her older sister and her mouth was downturned. She quickly joined Eve and Loren. The three of them stared at the far door as if something horrible might be on the other side.

'I'm just taking a look,' Gabe reassured them as he went.

'Gabe, I don't think . . .' Eve began to say, but stopped. What was there to be afraid of? If it was only memories that haunted the house, then there'd be nothing to fear. Yet she still felt a strong sense of foreboding.

'You stay there with the girls,' Gabe suggested over his shoulder.

Eve recognized his determination. He was cautious, she knew that, but it would take more than unaccountable noises to intimidate him. She ignored his suggestion and, gathering up her daughters, Eve reluctantly followed him through the unexplainable dust storm. The dim overhead light barely lit his head and shoulders.

Gabe halted before the plain hardwood door and examined the doorknob. There was no lock below, only a swivel latch. He pushed the latch with his finger so that it was vertical and he felt the door jolt slightly as it released from pressure. Eve and the girls silently watched as he pulled the door forward.

The utter darkness inside slunk back from the torchlight as if caught unawares.

Gabe poked his head into the opening.

'Junk,' he announced after a moment. 'Nothing but stored-away junk in here.'

He disappeared inside and Eve and the girls filled the open doorway. Eve waved her torch around, more curious than scared now, and although the lights chased shadows away, it caused others that were dense. She saw odd pieces of furniture – chairs with straight backs, boxes piled high on a table with thick rounded legs, more boxes on the littered floor; an old-fashioned two-bar electric fire; rolls of what looked like curtain material; lampshades; a figurine whose head was broken off at the neck; a small statue of Christ with a burning heart, one of its supplicating arms missing; two tall matching vases, both chipped and cracked. There was more: a round hanging clock lying flat on its back and minus a minute hand; a framed landscape painting leaning against a box, its glass cracked; a dented iron bucket; several battered cardboard suitcases with broken handles; other items covered by dirty wrinkled sheets. The partitioned room was filled with Crickley Hall's detritus, oddments of no value or use any more.

Eve moved further in, the girls, clutching each other's hand, following, afraid to be left alone outside. She could see Gabe moving things around in the gloom. The atmosphere was thick with dust and stagnation.

She heard Gabe whistle through his teeth. 'Will you look at this,' he said.

She caught up with him to see what he'd found. 'Toys,' she said almost breathlessly.

'*Old* toys,' he corrected her. 'Look at 'em. Some are still in their boxes. You can make out what they are under the dirt.'

It was true: the images of their contents were partially visible beneath the thick layers of dust. A train set. Snakes and ladders. A farmyard with painted wooden animals. Eve picked up a flattish box and wiped her hand across it. The box apparently contained a jigsaw; the picture was of a park, with illustrated children playing, some of them on swings, others on slides ... a cartoon boy on a roundabout, yellow hair ... like Cam's.

Gabe interrupted her melancholy thoughts. 'And check this out.'

His light revealed an archaic blackboard, its corners rounded, chalk markings just visible underneath the dust. It rested against the angled wall, its easel leaning against it. Crammed close to the blackboard were stacked rectangular trestle-tables, their metal legs housed beneath the flat surfaces.

Gabe went over to a large open cardboard box and dug his hand into it. He brought out a strange rubber contraption with large glass eyeholes and a stubby round nose.

'I'll be damned,' he murmured.

'A gas mask,' Eve said.

'Yeah, from the Second World War. But it's small, meant for kids. There's more in there.'

'Do you think all these things have been stored away since then?'

'Seems likely. Look at those toys. They don't make simple stuff like this these days.' He reached down for something lying at his feet and showed it to her, blowing some of the dust that dulled its brightness. 'Made of tin. Look, it's even got a key to wind up the engine.'

Slipping the flashlight under his armpit, Gabe used thumb and forefinger to wind up the old motorcar but the key stuck on the first turn. 'Must've rusted up inside,' he remarked, gazing at the machine in wonder.

Eve picked up a limp ragdoll lying on top of a carton. 'You won't find many of these around any more,' she said, turning the soft doll over in her hand, the reason for searching the attic lost to her for the moment. 'It's a golliwog. It's just not PC for children to play with anything like this these days. I had one myself when I was very young.'

'You know what's strange?' Gabe, having discarded the tin car, was crouching by a cardboard box and wiping away the covering dust with the palm of his hand. 'Look, this one's never been opened and, from what I can tell, nor have any of the others. These toys have never been played with.'

'But why? It doesn't make sense.'

'Maybe they were being kept hidden in here for Christmas. The flood took the poor kids before they got the chance to be given 'em.'

'You think that was it?'

'Only guessing. But they were out of sight behind other boxes and stuff. I moved that blackboard and easel to get to the toys. Could be that they were forgotten after the disaster and more junk was stashed in here in front of 'em so they couldn't be seen. S'way I figure it, anyhow.'

'Daddy, what's this?'

Gabe and Eve turned and searched out Cally among the shadows. She was squatting on her haunches, a podgy little hand resting on a round object standing on the floor.

'Don't touch it, Cally, it's filthy,' Eve warned her. 'Let Daddy have a look at it first.'

Gabe climbed over boxes and other neglected toys to reach his daughter.

'I think it's a top, Dad,' said Loren, who had become interested in her sister's find. 'You know, one of those spinning tops. I used to have one like it when I was little.'

'Let's see.' He knelt on the floorboards and picked up the toy with his free hand. He wiped it on his sweater sleeve and bright colours sprang into life.

Cally gave out a small squeal of delight.

'Don't get too hopeful, Cally. Doubt it's gonna work after all this time.'

He steadied the spinning top on the floor, then pushed down its spiral plunger. It gave out a rusty growl as it spun one and half revolutions before stopping with an ominous *clonk*.

'Yep, probably rusted inside.'

'Can you mend it, Daddy?' Cally asked hopefully.

'Sure, I can try.'

'Can we take it downstairs? Can I play with it?'

'Lot of other toys here to choose from, Sparky.'

'No, this one, Daddy. Please.'

Gabe straightened. 'Okay, let me carry it 'til we can give it a good wipeover, okay?'

'Yes, please.'

Eve, apart from them in the gloom, felt a sudden shiver run through her. She thought of the sounds they had heard coming through the ceiling when they were downstairs. A scurrying. A rushing of feet. From the attic room that had once been used as a dormitory.

A sound that was loud on the bare floorboards; yet somehow light. As though the sounds belonged to children scampering in bare or stockinged feet.

Running, scattering, children.

## 18: THIRD NIGHT

Yet another night they slept together, the girls snuggled between Gabe and Eve. The only difference this time was that the dog refused to leave the kitchen, the rain having forced Gabe to bring him in. Chester had resisted Gabe's tugging at his collar, whimpering at his master's coaxing, haunches low. Despite Gabe's entreaties, the mongrel had refused to leave his spot beside the garden door; he cowered there, eyes wild with fear that only he could understand.

In the end, Gabe could only shake his head in mystified frustration. Sure, Eve was right – there *was* something weird going on in this place – but last night the mutt had howled to be allowed upstairs with the family; tonight nothing would induce Chester to leave his blanket by the door. The engineer was certain that if he opened the outside door the dog would be through it like the wind and this time, in the dark, they'd never find him.

Exasperated, Gabe had left Chester there, hoping he wouldn't howl in the night.

Naturally, Loren and Cally wanted to know who or what had been running around in the old dormitory earlier (although Cally had seemed more interested in the spinning top she was allowed to bring downstairs) and there was no logical explanation either parent could give them. Gabe had unconvincingly muttered about airlocks and waterpipes once more and the girls were not taken in. They were too tired, though, to be more curious, especially Loren, who, unusually, wanted to go to bed. Gabe and Eve knew their daughters would be too jittery to fall asleep on their own, despite their tiredness, so had retired with them.

Because of this, Gabe and Eve had no opportunity to discuss the phenomenon between themselves, and the truth was, neither of them felt like it that night; they both lacked the energy.

They were all fast asleep within minutes of settling down and the only noise in Crickley Hall, apart from the distressed mewlings of Chester in the kitchen, was the creak of rough floorboards and timbers, and the faint but constant whispering of rushing water that crept up from the bowels of the house and through the open cellar door . . .

## 19: MONDAY

'You nervous, Slim?' Gabe changed up a gear and stole a glance at Loren, who was strapped into the Range Rover's passenger seat beside him.

There was no guile about Loren; she was still young enough to be open and honest and totally without front. She responded without hesitation: 'Yes, Dad.'

'Don't be. You'll soon make new friends.'

'I'm not from around here.'

'It'll make you more interesting.'

He slowed the car, indicated left, and swung out from the narrow lane with its high hedges on either side into a wider and busier road.

'I've spoken to the headteacher, Mr Horkins, a coupla times, once on the phone and once in person when I scouted out the school last time I was down here. Seems an okay guy, runs a tight ship. The kids impressed me when I visited, almost civilized, y'know?'

Gabe was taking Loren to Merrybridge Middle School on her first morning, but the school bus would bring her back in the afternoon. They had all overslept, even Cally, who normally could be relied on to be wide awake and singing loudly or playing with her dolls at the crack of dawn. But it had been a late night for her and a troubling one for them all. Gabe had lamely put the sleep-in down to 'good country air' and there had been no time to discuss the events – the mysterious running footsteps – of the previous night. A quick breakfast of coffee and toast for Gabe, cereals for the girls, and then he and Loren set out for Merrybridge. Chester, who once again had been tied outside to the tree, barked after them as they hurried across the bridge.

Gabe slowed down with the flow of traffic. It seemed even coastal Devon had its rush hour.

'It's horrible not knowing anybody,' whinged Loren, gazing ahead through the windscreen, chewing at her lower lip.

'Hey, you'll find someone to hook up with. You're good at making friends.'

'I really don't want to go to a new school.'

'It's only for a short time. We talked about this.'

'Will Mummy get . . . will she get better?'

'I think being away from our old house might help her come to terms with the situation. New surroundings, new people.' He didn't add that the first anniversary of Cam's disappearance was almost upon them. 'It won't make her forget, but it might divert her attention for a while, maybe help her get a grip.'

'But she's been sad for such a long time.' Loren turned towards her father. 'Mummy still cries when she's alone. I can always tell, even when she pretends she's all right.'

'I know.'

'We're all sad about Cam. I still miss him a lot, but . . .' Her words trailed off.

'But eventually you have to get on with life.' Gabe finished for her. He took a quick look her way. She was pale and troubled and there were faint smudges under her eyes.

'Sometimes I feel guilty because I think of Cam less and less,' she said.

'Don't be. It's natural. You can't grieve for ever, especially not at your age. So long as you remember him from time to time, it's okay. No one expects more of you.'

'I still cry sometimes.'

'Sure, but not so much any more, right? And that's good, Loren, it's part of the healing. But we all have to carry on with our lives, it's the only thing to do.'

'Dad . . .'

Gabe felt her eyes on him again.

'Cam *is* dead, isn't he? He must be, mustn't he? He couldn't just disappear.'

It was the first time Loren had come straight out with it and he had been dreading such a moment. What to tell her? What did he himself believe? What did he *really* believe?

'I don't know,' he answered after a few moments. He couldn't lie to her; yet neither could he affirm what he knew they all thought. There was no other way to say it. 'Until they find his body we can only assume he's been taken away by someone.'

Loren was equally frank. 'If he was alive the police would have found him by now. No one could've hidden him all this time.'

This was the reality but, mostly for Eve's sake, Gabe would not admit it, even to himself.

'Could someone have stolen him because they didn't have a little boy of their own? Perhaps they were lonely. They took him from the park because he looked so nice. Cam was always smiley, even with strangers.'

He blessed Loren for her innocence. A kidnapping was what Eve wanted to believe even now. She'd been in denial from the first day Cam had vanished. Something deep within her refused to accept the worst and it was this faulty reasoning that kept her from complete breakdown. And, in truth, maybe the same unrealistic hope lay within himself – why else had he not wept for his own son?

They had reached the town and the main street was busy with people, among them, in groups of three or four, the blue uniforms of Merrybridge Middle School pupils. Loren watched them apprehensively, hoping they wouldn't treat her as an outsider, praying she wouldn't make a fool of herself on her first day.

Soon the uniforms – navy-blue trousers or skirts, electric-blue jumpers and blazers over white shirts worn with blue-and-grey-striped ties – began to multiply, then mass, so that it seemed the world's predominant colour was blue. Gabe hung a right into the wide side street and there it was, Merrybridge Middle School – or Merrymiddle as it was known – a concrete congestion of two-storey plain stone-and-glass buildings so beloved by misguided architects and cost-conscious town-planners in the Sixties. If the town itself still had a modicum of charm left, it was lost on the solid but drab interjoined buildings.

Gabe pulled up behind another 4x4 whose passengers were being disgorged and set the handbrake. Some of the children passing by gawped in the passenger window at Loren as if already sniffing a stranger in their midst, and she studiously ignored them. She reached over to the back seat for her school bag. Perhaps in a few days, when she herself wore the Merrybridge uniform, she would not be so visible.

'All right,' Gabe smiled reassuringly: he understood her nervousness. 'You want me to come in with you?'

'No, Dad!' She looked alarmed at the very idea.

'Sure?'

She nodded her head vigorously.

'Okay. So just go inside and ask someone where you can find Mr Horkins. He'll see you right.'

They leaned towards each other and Loren gave her father a peck on the cheek. She grabbed her school bag from the back, then pushed the passenger door open. Gabe saw the apprehension on her face and his heart nearly melted.

'Bye, Daddy,' she said, before slamming the door after her.

'See you tonight.' He watched her go through the gate following two uniformed girls, and he pressed the switch to lower the passenger side window.

'Hey, Slim!' he called, stretching across the seat.

Loren turned and looked back at him.

'Don't talk to boys!' He gave her a broad smile.

She rolled her eyes heavenwards and the two girls in front looked over their shoulders and giggled.

Then Loren was gone and Gabe felt a heel.

## 20: THE SPINNING TOP

Eve snatched another look out of the kitchen window, checking on Chester who lay forlornly on the grass, roped to the tall oak tree from whose lowest branch the swing hung. His head was down, muzzle resting between his front paws, and he was looking forlornly towards the house.

She was relieved to see it wasn't raining this morning, although the dark clouds looked threatening, otherwise she would be forced to bring him inside, and the thought of dragging him all the way across the lawn while he fretted and resisted was unappealing.

That morning there had been too much frantic bustle to reflect on the events of the previous night because the whole family had overslept. Hasty breakfasts, Chester taken out on his lead to do his stuff, quick kisses goodbye for Gabe and Loren, Eve especially twitchy for Loren, who was starting her first day at the new school, finally waving to them as they crossed the short bridge, and then the panic was over. Peace returned. Eve helped her youngest wash and dress, then came back down for a second cup of coffee at the kitchen table, while Cally played with her toys upstairs until it was time for her reading lesson.

The house seemed different today, not so dispiriting, not so – not so *joyless*. Perhaps it was because the sun kept breaking through the rainclouds, cheering the air itself as it flooded through the hall's tall window, brightening even the gloomiest corners, its warmth stirring the air so the dust floated in its beams. Still in her white waffle dressing gown, Eve sipped from the mug, holding it to her lips with both hands, the coffee's heat reviving her, yet a calmness seeping through her limbs, her back, her neck. It had been a long time – almost a year – since she had felt this level of relaxation, this lessening of tension, and it was good. No, it was wonderful.

But why? she asked herself. Then she remembered, although it had not truly been forgotten, just temporarily laid aside as life around her continued with its flow. Yesterday, in the sitting room, on the couch. The dream. The *bad* dream. Something – *someone* – horrible, leering over her. The foul smell; then the other smell underlying it: the stinging scent of harsh soap. And the paralysing fear that had gripped her while she dozed.

Then its easing. She had felt – she *knew* she had felt – Cam's presence. She had not seen his face, but then never in her dreams had his features been clearly defined. And with most of those dreams had come a terrible sadness. But not so yesterday. Yesterday there had only been a calmness and a sense of loving. Cam, somehow, had reached out to her.

She had been under threat, she remembered that; threat from something wretched in this house; something horrid; something hidden inside Crickley Hall itself. But then the relief: Cam touching her, unseen fingers soothing her brow and cheek. It hit her then: was it his spirit that had come to her?

*No! No, it couldn't be! If that were true, if it was his spirit, then Cameron must be dead! And that just could not be! She could not allow it to be!*

Besides, there was another conclusion, she told herself, almost slyly, for she could not – *would not!* – accept the death of her little boy.

It wasn't Cam's spirit that appeared to her, not his *soul*. No, it was his *mind*. There had always been a telepathic link between them, between mother and child, but it had never been anything to wonder at, nothing so strong that it demanded anything more than casual interest. Neither was it particularly odd: many mothers had intuitions about their offspring, knew instinctively when their child was in pain or disturbed in some way when they were in different rooms, or even miles apart. Mothers could understand their baby's incoherent cry, mothers could sense their child's moods and ills. But her psychic connection with Cam was stronger than just that. Three out of the five clairvoyants she had interviewed some years ago had virtually convinced her of supernatural power, but she had never followed through, had lost interest once the feature had been written. Yet afterwards, she could never again deny there was something more than mere physical existence.

Hadn't she, herself, sensed the strangely sombre ambience of Crickley Hall? She had felt it even before she set foot inside, when she had studied it from across the bridge. Was it haunted, then? No, she couldn't quite buy that. But it seemed susceptible to paranormal activity. Was that the same as being haunted? Eve had no idea, although she was vaguely aware that paranormal didn't always mean supernatural. She needed guidance.

Leaning against the counter and putting her mug down, Eve brought her hands to her face and pressed the fingertips against her closed eyelids.

What did it mean? Had Cam subconsciously contacted her from another place? Was it possible? *Was it really possible?*

She lowered her hands again and turned from the window, intending to finish her half-drunk coffee, when something caught her eye.

The old-fashioned tin spinning top that Cally had found in the upstairs storeroom last night was standing nearby on the work surface where she had left it. Attractive colours gleamed from the section Gabe had wiped with the palm of his hand; she moved closer.

Those colours were primary and vivid. Curious to see more of the toy's pattern, Eve reached into a drawer and took out a soft duster. Cally was anxious to play with the top for reasons only a child would understand and that morning Gabe had promised to check out the mechanism when he returned from work. 'Drop of oil is probably all it needs,' he had reassured his daughter.

Eve picked up the toy by its plunger and began wiping the metal surface with the duster, soon revealing glorious colours and patterns. She could not help but smile at its gaiety. Running round its bulging circumference were dancing children, their tiny hands joined and their knees bent in frozen motion. Their depiction was simple and quaintly archaic in style, but wonderfully rendered. They played under a bright blue sky, with gentle but radiant green hills on the horizon, a deeper and no less pleasant green beneath their feet.

She blew away dust from her face and continued to clean the toy. There were coloured rings top and bottom, with small stars in the bands of red and yellow. It was a joy to look at and Eve could only wonder why it appeared never to have been used – nor even touched. There were no blemishes or scratches, no dents in the tin, nor any chipped paint. The spiral plunger was not rusted, although it refused to sink into the ball when she pushed at it. Perhaps the turning wheel inside was locked with lack of use.

She was about to call Cally to come down and see it, but had another thought. She put the spinning top back on the work surface and went to the cupboard beneath the sink where Gabe had stored his toolbox. Drawing the scuffed and grimy metal box out and planting it on the floor, she opened up its flaps, then pulled it open wider to reveal all its sections. There was a small can of light machinery oil lying on its side, pointed plastic cap firmly in place.

Taking out the can, Eve returned to the pristine spinning top. She uncapped the oil nozzle and pushed it against the tiny gap where the top's spiral drive rod entered the tin body. She squeezed drops of oil into the gap, the rod's spiral shape helping the fluid to sink down into the interior workings of the top itself. For good measure, Eve lubricated the visible part of the spiral rod. Satisfied, she put down the oil can, wrapped her fingers round the handle at the top of the rod, and plunged down.

The ball began to turn and then the plunger rod stalled, became stuck. She drew it up once more, counted to three, and tried again. This time the rod went all the way down and the top began to spin. She pulled it up again, then pushed down, working up a rhythm, the ball spinning faster and faster, the dancers moving swiftly, catching more speed as Eve plunged, lifted, plunged again. The colours began to flow into each other, began to meld, the dancers becoming a blur, Eve holding her breath as she worked, a humming noise now rising from the toy, soaring higher in tone with each spin, the colours beginning to fade, to become white, absent of any design, and Eve, as she pushed and pulled, remembered that the absence of colour was not black but white, white like the spinning top, its whiteness capturing her attention, the humming somehow hypnotic, the gyration mesmerizing, so that she could feel herself sinking into a void . . .

The top spun faster, faster, the humming pitched higher, higher . . .

And then she experienced a blissful peace, a consuming warmth that could only be described as spiritual, its catalyst the spinning toy.

She moaned as in the whirling bleached brightness she saw the dancing children reappear but without colour, only in subtle shades of ghostly grey. Eve's head felt light and giddy, but her gaze never abandoned the soft spinning images before her. The humming transcended into voices and they belonged to children at play a long distance away. She searched for Cam's voice among them, but there were too many to distinguish just one.

The spinning top began to lose speed and the voices reverted to the high-pitched humming, which now dropped to a softer *thrumming*, which then sank into a drone, which sank to a dissonant groan. The colours returned, the patterns reappeared, the painted children continued their dance. The top rocked on its base, then came to a gradual stop.

There was a stillness in the kitchen until Eve blinked and swayed against the counter.

Outside, the sun still shone intermittently through breaks in the scudding clouds.

Inside the house, there was only quietness.

Until a child's voice called out to her.

## 21: DANCING DUST

It was neither excited nor urgent; just a small voice calling from a distance.

*'Mummy.'*

At first, Eve had to dissociate it from the other voices she had heard while entranced by the bright whirling toy. It was a little cry, but at the top of its range and it entered the kitchen from across the cavernous hall.

*'Mummy,'* it came again and Eve, still lost in her imaginings, languidly stirred. Instinctively she moved towards the sound, a mother's natural response to the call of her child. Dazed, expectant, she hoped beyond all realistic hope that it was her son's voice she heard. Her heart beat faster; her breath was caught in her throat.

She stopped in the kitchen's open doorway and stared across the broad expanse of flagstones at her daughter, who stood at the turn of the stairway opposite. Sunlight flooded through the tall window behind her, transforming a drab mausoleum into a room of antiquated charm. Dark wood panelling blazed intricate grains of brown and honey, the stone slabs of the floor had mellowed to a soft yellow, and old pieces of furniture were given fresh grandeur.

'Look, Mummy.' Cally, with her pink teddy bear tucked under her arm, pointed at the middle ground between them.

Eve looked, but all she could see was thousands – *millions* – of golden dust motes drifting in the air as if disturbed by the warm rays from outside mingling with the cold draughts of the hall itself to generate lively breezes that carried glittering particles which wheeled and turned and dazzled like a galaxy of minute, shifting stars.

Eve gasped at the splendour, but she did not yet see as her daughter saw. She remembered the dust storm in the attic dormitory yesterday, how it had risen and whirled in the glare of their torches, but it had been nothing like this, nowhere near as thick and fast moving. These radiant particles seemed to be forming definite patterns.

Cally giggled. 'See them, Mummy, you see them dancing?'

And that was when Eve began to discern shapes among the tiny purling dust motes. It was like staring into one of those illusory picture puzzles where hidden in repetitious patterns were individual objects, persons or animals; unfocused eyes had to be used until, usually quite suddenly, the main image appeared in 3-dimensional effect. The same kind of thing seemed to be happening to Eve right now. The figures inside and also made of swirling dust became clear in a rush. They were still part of the great mass filling the sunlight in the hall, but they suddenly took on individuality, images emerging from the whole while still remaining part of it. The closest of the children had their backs to her as they danced past, holding hands, moving from right to left in a circle so that she could now make out the children facing her on the other side. The spinning top! They were like the children on the spinning top! Dancing in a ring, holding hands, their legs bending and straightening as they skipped along, as if they were *real* children, not just colourful illustrations. And now she heard their happy chants, distant as before, but nevertheless voices raised in happy union.

The same warmth as before came back to her – that *spiritual* warmth – and she wanted to weep because there was a sadness mixed with the joy, a longing, a yearning, for something that could not yet be.

She became lost in the vision. Fantasy or revelation, what was it meant to be? Cally saw them too; she jumped up and down on the small square landing at the turn of the stairs and she pointed at the dancing children, crying out at the fun of it. Because of that, Eve knew that it was real, it was no hallucination: she shared the sight with her daughter.

She could not see their faces clearly, but she could at least make out their attire, the boys in short trousers and braces, the girls in frocks and some with plaits in their hair. Shoes were not visible, but Eve could see socks on the boys, most rumpled down round ankles. She tried desperately to distinguish their features, but it was like watching a moving stippled painting, the dust motes representing the stippling. But she could count them as they passed by. There were nine of them. Nine children. Nine little headstones down at the church graveyard. Nine out of the eleven child victims that had been taken by the flood more than half a century ago.

Why were their ghosts still here?

What could be here for them at Crickley Hall?

It was as though the questions had broken the vision.

For everything changed.

The sunlight disappeared, the sun obscured by an immense roiling raincloud, and the great hall was once more thrown into gloom and shadow. Rain pattered on the tall window and Cally's figure on the landing was suddenly shaded.

Eve felt her heart lurch, as if fear itself had entered the

hall. Before her, the swirling specks of dust that had glittered so brilliantly but a moment ago dispersed, then disappeared. Eve either heard, or imagined she heard, a faraway wail that swiftly faded to a barren silence broken only by the rain on the windowpanes.

'*No, wait*—' Eve began to plead but almost instantly there was nothing left of the dancing wraiths or the dust that had constructed them.

Eve's body sagged as if a peculiar despair had hit her, and she almost sank to her knees. But she soon stiffened when she heard a new sound. Cally had heard it too and she was looking wide-eyed up at the landing above her. Eve slowly turned her head, following her daughter's gaze, her eyes lifting.

*Swish-thwack!* The sound came. Again: *swish-thwack!* A pause, again: *swish-thwack.* It seemed to be moving along the landing, although there was no one there to be seen.

*Swish-thwack! Swish-thwack!* Moving towards the stairway.

To Eve it sounded like something smacking leather ... no, like something smacking against flesh. The *swish* of its fall, the *thwack* when it hit.

*Swish-thwack!*

The loudest of all, at the top of the stairs.

Then, nothing more.

Only the rain continuing to beat against the window.

## 22: THE CARD

They trudged down the lane, Eve and Cally with their hoods pulled over their heads against the soft rain, Chester trotting alongside them, restrained by his leash which was gripped by Cally. The tufty-haired dog was mindless of the wet, only happy to be free of that cold old house that wasn't his proper home. Occasionally, he would peer up at his mistresses as if to ask where they were going, but they both just made encouraging noises at him.

The river beside the lane rushed by, journeying in the same direction, towards the sea, its flow much swifter than their pace; white spume washed against the leafy banks and broke over embedded boulders; debris of leaves, small branches and stones were carried in the flux and water spray cast a thin mist over the river's rough bubbling surface. Trees that edged the lane and the opposite riverbank glistened with silvery raindrops, while the steep verdant cliffs behind them were darkly lush, which somehow made the gorge seem narrower, more enclosed, than it really was.

As they passed the small Norman church of St Mark's on their left, Eve made a surreptitious sign of the cross over her left breast, offering up a short silent prayer as she did so. Cally barely gave the church a glance; she was too busy trying to keep Chester from running ahead of them.

'Is it far now, Mummy?' she asked after bringing the dog to heel with a sharp tug on the leash.

'You know it isn't, silly,' Eve told her, smiling down at Cally and taking pleasure in the rosiness that had appeared in her daughter's cheeks. 'You can see the village from here. Look, there's the big bridge and the shops are just beyond it.'

'I like walking downhill,' Cally announced, 'but I don't like walking up. It makes my legs sleepy.'

Eve chuckled. God, it was good to be out in the fresh air, rain or not. Good for both of them. And good exercise for Chester, too. He'd almost gone into hysteria when she attached the leash to his collar and he realized they were going for a walk. He couldn't get away from Crickley Hall fast enough. Before the vision, she had felt the same way.

She wondered at what she and Cally had really witnessed in the sunny, dust-filled hall.

For a brief time, the sunshine pouring through the big window over the stairs had altered the whole atmosphere of Crickley Hall, changing this one room at least from a sombre, dispiriting chamber into an imposing open space, whose panelled walls and flagstone floor embraced the light, became warm, radiated their own glow. (Had this been the original architect's intention? Had he specifically designed the great hall with its high, south-facing window to catch the sunlight and reveal the room's true grandeur? If so, it was the only redeeming feature in a house that had all the charm of a large neglected tomb.) It was the sun's rays that had made the dust visible, draughts and heated air causing the particles to rise and float. And it was the dust that had made the dancing spectres visible; and it was when the sun had been obscured by rain clouds and Crickley Hall was once again cast in shadow and gloom that they had disappeared.

Eve knew in her heart that those visions were the ghosts

– if not ghosts, then remembered or recorded images – of the boys and girls who had once lived in Crickley Hall. The poor orphans who had drowned. Eve also knew in her heart, though reason told her otherwise, that there was a link between these spirits, these images, and her son, Cam, whose presence she had felt only yesterday.

It was a mystery – that frightening *smacking* sound alone was a mystery – and Eve needed help. But not from Gabe, whose pragmatism – and yes, his cynicism – would make him dismiss the whole idea. Certainly, he would be sympathetic, but he would tell her that her grief was 'messing with her head'. He wouldn't accept the notion of ghosts.

Eve shivered and it was not because of the rain.

She ushered Cally and Chester onto the grass verge at the side of the lane as a white van approached from the village. The van's wheels sent up a spray of water that spattered Eve's ankle boots and Cally's colourful Wellingtons as it passed by. Chester dodged behind Eve to avoid further drenching. A red Almera followed close behind the van and its two passengers stared at them rudely.

Once the traffic was safely by, Eve, Cally and Chester continued their walk down to the village. The wide bay, filled with the gunmetal-grey waters of the Bristol Channel, spread out below them, the rocky cliffs on either side filled with dampened vegetation. On a bright day, Eve thought, it would have been a magnificent sight, but today the constant chilly rain had muted the scenery to lacklustre hues.

Twice more Eve and Cally had to step onto the lane's verge for safety as more vehicles going in either direction passed them by, but soon they were at the long iron and concrete bridge which joined the lane to a wider and busier road that also led away from the village but in a different direction. They reached the row of shops lining one side of the harbour road, which ended abruptly at the cliff face.

It was one of the first shops that interested Eve. She stepped into the small porch of Hollow Bay's general store, gently pulling Cally in behind her. Chester hopped onto the step and busied himself sniffing at a corner by the entrance door.

'Are we going in the sweetshop?' Cally asked expectantly, her eyes beneath the hood lighting up. 'Can I have some Smarties? Please, Mummy?'

Eve had pushed her hood back onto her shoulders and was scanning the cards in the display cabinet fixed to the porch wall.

'We'll see,' she answered distractedly.

She caught her breath, her heart beginning to sink. She recognized some of the business cards and personal ads that had been pinned inside on Saturday, but most of the older-looking faded ones were missing. The particular card she was searching for had gone. Eve gave a little inward groan of disappointment.

Cally was already reaching up and tugging at the shop's door handle, eager to get inside where the goodies were, and Chester was trying to push by her, just as eager. The bell tinkled as the door opened a few inches and, with a rush, girl and dog had entered. Eve took another quick scrutiny of the cabinet's contents, then followed her daughter and the dog into the shop.

There were two other customers, both at the cash register counter, one of them sifting through her purse to pay for her goods, the second woman waiting patiently behind her holding a wire basket filled with household items and packets of food. Cally made straight for the sweet shelves, Chester trotting beside her, stubby tail wagging, while Eve pretended to be interested in the magazine carousel. She took one out and flicked through the pages but, even though it was a fashion magazine, it failed to gain her interest.

Behind the counter was the same broad-looking woman who had served Eve two days ago – green apron over blue-spotted dress, horn-rimmed spectacles, short greying hair permed rigid, severe expression – and she was just giving change to the first customer. Eve remembered she was supposed to do a proper week's shop today and had intended to catch the bus she knew ran from the village to the nearest town, where hopefully she would find a good supermarket. Well, change of plans. More frozen dinners for the next day or two. Gabe would survive as long as there was quantity, and the girls wouldn't be fussed either way. Besides, shopping here would help underplay her enquiry.

She slipped the *Cosmopolitan* back in its rack and went to the corner by the door where the wire baskets were stacked, one on top of the other. Taking the first, she moved to the freezer cabinet and loaded the basket without paying too much notice of what she was choosing; really, she was waiting for the second customer to leave so that she could make her enquiry with as little embarrassment as possible.

At last, the bell over the door rang and the customer was gone. Eve quickly closed the freezer lid and went to the counter.

The shopkeeper frowned at her at first, then looked at her quizzically; some of the hardness left her features.

'You were 'ere Saturday' – Sat'day, it was pronounced – 'wasn't you? Yer've moved into Crickley Hall for a spell, that's right, isn't it?'

'Yes, we're here for a while,' Eve replied.

'Thought as much. Recognized the pretty little girl.'

The shopkeeper smiled down at Cally, who had joined her mother with a tube of Smarties clutched in one hand and holding Chester's leash in the other.

'Helped yerself, have yer? Well, I'm sure Mummy don't mind.'

Eve placed the full wire basket on the counter and took the Smarties from Cally to lay next to it. The tube started to roll away, but the shopkeeper snatched it up and stood it on its flat end.

'Right then, we'll ring the sweeties first, shall we? Then little missy can start on them right away.'

Eve returned the smile as the shopkeeper registered the purchase and handed the tube back over the counter to Cally, who took them gratefully.

'What's yer name, if yer don't mind me askin'?' The shopkeeper took a moment to look directly at Eve.

'Oh. Caleigh. Eve Caleigh, and this is my daughter Cally.'

'An' the other pretty girl with yer on Saturday, the older one . . .?'

'That was Loren. She's at school today.'

'Charmin' girls,' the shopkeeper remarked. 'An' everything's okay up at Crickley Hall, is it?'

Eve hesitated before answering, wondering why the woman had asked. 'Yes, everything's fine.'

The shopkeeper never took her eyes from the foodstuff she was taking out of the basket and ringing up on the till. 'That's all right, then,' she murmured absently.

Soon, everything was accounted for and Eve, checking the green-lit figures on the machine's cash window, delved into her purse. When she had passed over the money and was waiting for change, she said: 'I was, uh, I was wondering what happened to the cards that were in the display cabinet outside.'

The shopkeeper ignored the question while she counted out the correct change into Eve's outstretched hand.

'Now, then, what's that you was askin'?' she said, leaning her stomach against her side of the counter.

'The, the cards outside. Some seem to be missing.'

'Oh them. Lots of them've been there two years or more. My husband had a good clearout over the weekend. Was there one in particular you was lookin' for?' The woman's eyebrows rose above the top of her glasses.

Eve reddened a little, but decided to come straight out with it. 'Yes, there was. The one advertising a psychic. Psychic readings, I think it said.'

'Ah.' The shopkeeper straightened. 'That one. Yers, that was in the window a couple of years or more. Young lady paid for it to be put in, if I remember right, an' I haven't seen hide nor hair of her since. Should've taken it out a year ago, that card. Long past its rent date.'

'You've thrown it away?' Eve hid her frustration.

'Well, that may not necessarily be so. Bin men don't come 'til Tuesday, so the card yer want will be with the other rubbish out back. Here, let me jus' go an' ask Mr Longmarsh. He'll know what he's done with it.'

The shopkeeper went to the far end of the counter where there was a closed door that probably led to the back storeroom or living quarters. She opened the door and put her perm-hard head through the gap. 'Ted, you got a minute? Customer here's got a query 'bout one of them cards you took out of the window yesterday.'

The woman – Mrs Longmarsh, Eve assumed – came back, her expression a mixture of curiosity and suspicion. 'He won't be a minute, dear, he's jus' puttin' his shoes on.' From behind thick lenses, her eyes bored into Eve's. 'So it's a psychic – one of them clairvoyants – you'll be needin', is it?' Her voice had lowered itself with the question as if any reply would be in confidence.

'No, no, nothing like that,' Eve quickly insisted. She could imagine rumours about Crickley Hall and problems with the new folk being passed around the village. 'It's just that I'm a freelance writer, you see. I've been commissioned to do an article on mediums, mind reading, that sort of thing. I thought the person who placed the ad might be willing to be interviewed.'

Mrs Longmarsh squinted at her for a few moments, suspicion now dominant in her narrowed eyes.

A gruff voice came from the other end of the counter and Eve turned her head to see a portly man had emerged from the back room. 'What's that yer sayin', May? What blessed card you on about?'

He was short as well as portly and wore a brown sleeveless cardigan over a plain white shirt. Oddly, his hair was full and crinkly on the top of his head, but straight at the sides over his ears. He had heavy, thread-veined cheeks and jowls, and his eyes were small, deep-set over an equally small podgy nose.

'Ted, this is Mrs Caleigh, moved into Crickley Hall for a while. D'yer know what yer did with them out-of-date cards from the shopfront?'

The West Country burr of his accent matched the woman's perfectly, except his voice had a harsher, no-nonsense ring to it, a brusqueness that made him sound cross, although Eve couldn't think why. Perhaps he was irritated at being disturbed while he toasted his feet by the fire; Mrs Longmarsh had said he was putting his shoes on.

'What card are you lookin' fer exactly, missus?' he growled.

By now Cally had opened the Smarties and was dropping

them one at a time into Chester's open and appreciative mouth, feeding herself at the same time.

Eve ignored her for the moment. 'I think it was a yellow card, quite old,' she told Longmarsh.

'Well, that don't tell us much, do it?'

'No, of course. It was for psychic readings; I can't remember the name now.'

'Yers, I know the one. Looked at it myself only yesterday. Don't know if the woman will still be in business after all this time. Peel, her name is. I know 'cause I noticed when I took the card down. Lillian, or just plain Lili, I think it was. Yers, spelt funny L-I-L-I. Remember thinkin' it were a nice name. Lili Peel, that's right.'

He rocked back on his heels and scrutinized Eve in a way that made her uncomfortable.

'As a matter of fact,' he went on after a pause, 'I think yer in luck. I put all the old cards in a plastic bag, then into the wheely-bin with the other rubbish. Luckily, the bag was the last thing in so it's at the top. I could get it fer yer.'

Again he paused, studying her, and Eve wondered if she was supposed to offer him a bribe for the effort.

'Now you go an' fetch it, Ted,' said his wife, 'while I'm puttin' Mrs Caleigh's shopping in the bags.'

Longmarsh frowned at her as if about to argue, but Mrs Longmarsh had already turned away and was bringing out two plastic bags from under the counter. Her husband gave a long-suffering sigh and ambled back to the open door, through which Eve could now see a blazing fire in the hearth, a comfortable-looking armchair in front of it. Yes, Eve thought, Ted Longmarsh had obviously been toasting his feet.

\*

The long wet hike up the hill was naturally more tiring than the downward trip and Cally was complaining about her 'sleepy' legs well before they reached the short bridge to Crickley Hall; even Chester had his head down and his tongue hanging out as he panted. Eve, carrying the shopping, did not feel much better: the walk back somehow seemed a mile longer. Yet it wasn't so on their first trip to the harbour village and back again, but perhaps that was because they'd broken their return journey visiting the church and chatting to the vicar, Trevellick, and his wife; or perhaps the interrupted nights recently had taken more out of them than she'd realized. Then again, it could be just that they were 'townies', worn down by strenuous exercise.

Eve waited by the bridge for Cally and Chester to catch up. They weren't very far behind – Eve was too wary of passing traffic to leave her daughter out of grasping distance, even though Cally knew her road drill.

'Come on, slowcoaches,' she called out, but now saw that Chester was dragging at his leash, holding Cally back. The dog seemed agitated, almost desperate to get away. Was it because they were close to Crickley Hall? Chester certainly didn't like the house, he made that clear enough. But then, neither did she. That is, not until now for, although she still had reservations about the place, she was drawn to its mystery – and the small hope it had given her.

She heard Cally chastising the dog: 'Chester, you're being a very bad boy.'

Eve put the shopping bags on the bridge and strode back to them, taking the leash from Cally's hand. She wrapped it round her knuckles a few times to shorten its length. 'You behave, Chester,' she warned the dog. 'We're nearly home and we're tired, so let's get inside and then we can all flake out.'

JAMES HERBERT

The dog whimpered and tried to pull away from Eve, who tugged impatiently, bringing him to heel. She half dragged him towards the bridge, his haunches inches from the ground, front paws digging in. It took some effort, but she finally got him to the beginning of the bridge. Eve was tired and frustrated, and just a little angry. What was wrong with Chester? She bent down to stroke him, to calm him, because by now he was shivering. His eyes were bulging, staring across the river, and he strained against his leash, front paws hopping off the ground, head pulled to one side as he tried to escape.

'Chester, will you please stop it!' Eve had become really exasperated. She jerked the leash harder, but it only made the dog more desperate.

'Mummy, look!'

Eve, too busy with her struggle to control Chester, ignored her daughter.

But Cally tugged at her mother's free arm and insisted. 'Mummy, look at the children!'

Startled, Eve immediately straightened and swung round towards Cally, who was pointing across the bridge up at Crickley Hall's dormer windows. A smile was on her daughter's upturned face.

Eve's eyes followed the direction of Cally's finger and she saw the pale blurs that could only be faces at three of the rooftop's four small grimy windows.

'The children, Mummy!' Cally repeated and Eve felt her jaw drop.

Chester used this moment of distraction to make his break. The leash in Eve's hand loosened, unwound, and with a final yank the dog was free. He scooted up the hill, the leash dragging along the ground, before Eve realized he was gone.

# THE SECRET OF CRICKLEY HALL

'*Chester, no!*' she called sharply. '*Stop!*'

But the dog took no notice and continued his bid for freedom, racing up the hill as if there was a wind behind him.

Confused, angry, perplexed, Eve turned back to Crickley Hall.

The pale blurs at the rooftop windows were gone.

## 23: DECISIONS

Eve's hand hovered over the phone – the digital phone that must have been one of the first of its kind: heavy and solid-looking, with big numbered press-keys – but something stopped her from picking it up.

She had been about to ring Gabe at the Ilfracombe office, the number of which he'd written down for her and left beside the phone on the chiffonier, but now realized it would be foolish to do so: what could he do about a missing dog when he was miles away and probably trying to make some kind of impression on his new colleagues?

Chester had vanished somewhere along the winding lane that followed the river and even though Eve and Cally had spent more than an hour searching for him, calling his name over and over, it looked as if this time he was gone for good.

Oddly, Cally, who was in the kitchen finishing her lunch, had not taken it as badly as Eve would have expected. Certainly she'd bawled her eyes out for the first five minutes after Chester had broken free and disappeared into the distance, but then, after the initial excitement of the search, she got tired and hungry (not to mention wet), and complained to Eve about her state of hunger. Eve took her back to Crickley Hall, keeping an eye out for their errant dog along the way.

As she stood by the phone, undecided, the receiver still in

170

her hand, a deep disquieting physical chill crept up her spine and seeped under her hair to cool the flesh at the back of her neck. She shivered and slowly – slowly because she suspected someone was standing behind her and she really did not want to see who it was – turned round.

She exhaled a breath when she saw the partially open cellar door. It was obvious that the draught of cold air had come from there. Because the door was only half open with very little light entering, the shadows within were peculiarly deep, as black as jet, and there was something strangely inviting about them, tantalizing almost. In some way it was like standing on top of a high cliff or building, when the space you're looking down on seems to be inviting you to jump. Eve gave a small shake of her head – it might have been a shudder – and, phone still clutched in one hand, took a bold step towards the door and slammed it shut. Its key fell from the lock to the stone floor with a heavy clink.

The coiled telephone cord was stretched to its limit as Eve bent to pick up the long key. When she replaced it in the lock and turned it she felt relieved. She would have to get Gabe to fix the lock or fit a new one, perhaps even add a bolt high enough to be out of Cally's reach. Eve looked at the receiver in her hand and, decision made, returned it to its cradle. No, she wouldn't worry Gabe about the missing dog, nor anything else for the moment. But now she vacillated over another number she should ring.

For Eve, it was a difficult decision to make. That same morning she had set out determined to contact the psychic whose address and phone number were on the card she'd obtained from the village shop. She remembered the tingle in her hand when she had taken it from Ted Longmarsh, the anticipation she felt when she slipped the faded card into her pocket. Now she was unsure.

What good could a psychic do; what could she tell such a person? That she thought she was living in a haunted house? That her own missing son's psyche had been drawn to the place because there were unknown forces at work in Crickley Hall, things that were supernatural, things that were hard to understand for normal people? What would a psychic make of noises in the night that could not properly be explained, of mysterious footsteps, of Cameron coming to Eve in a dream, filling her with hope? What would Lili Peel think when she was told of the dust ghosts playing ring-a-ring-o'-roses here in the hall, of little pale faces looking down from roof windows? Would she think Eve insane, or a neurotic woman driven mad by grief? Or would the psychic humour Eve, go along with her 'visions' as some charlatans might just to fleece her of money? What was the use? Eve asked herself. But then, what did she have to lose by contacting Lili Peel? At worst it might help Eve just to talk about it to a perfect stranger. Gabe couldn't help her, although he had tried, had tried desperately; his sympathy was limited, worn by time and his own early life. He already thought she was heading for a breakdown; she suspected he expected it. Why else had he brought her to this 'sanctuary' so many miles from their proper home at such a significant time? The new location was to help her forget.

Even though he had himself heard the strange night noises and discovered unexplainable puddles in the hall and on the stairs, and even though he knew how afraid Chester was of the place, he still would not believe Crickley Hall was haunted. His life had no room for such preternatural ideologies. She was not sure he even believed in God; he had always walked away from or changed the subject whenever she brought up the idea of a Supreme Being or religious inclinations. It didn't mean he lacked imagination; it only meant he was averse to such things. No, there would be no point in telling Gabe that she had sensed the presence of their missing son right here in Crickley Hall and that she had also witnessed ghostly apparitions in the house. Perhaps there was something special about this place that engendered supernatural activity, a peculiarity that enhanced or was a catalyst to certain psychic energies. If she told him this he might finally lose patience with her and dismiss it all as 'horseshit'. She loved him and trusted him with her very life, but she didn't need that kind of negativity right now: she wanted so much to believe. Eve doubted he would be convinced that she had seen little faces watching her from Crickley Hall's roof windows on her return from the harbour village, even though Cally had observed them too.

When they had come back after their fruitless hunt for Chester, Eve and Cally had gone up to the attic room together – she couldn't have left her daughter alone downstairs in the big house, and besides, Cally showed not an ounce of trepidation at the prospect of meeting the 'phantom' children – to find the long-disused dormitory completely empty without an ethereal body in sight. 'What did you expect?' would be Gabe's reaction. 'The dormer windows are filthy with grime, rain was on them, you could have seen anything you wanted – whatever you expected – in them.'

No, only a genuine psychic or clairvoyant would understand and Eve had almost decided on Sunday after her 'contact' with Cam that she would seek out the one advertised in the village shop's display cabinet. This morning's events had strengthened her intention.

Nevertheless, Eve still hesitated.

*

Gabe stood by the window, a plastic mug of coffee in one hand, a sandwich with a great bite taken out of it in the other. Laid out on a desk behind him were the design plans for the prototype of the first marine current turbine, a smaller detailed sketch showing the turbine's rotor and drive chain on top of this. He had declined the invitation from his three colleagues, who were employed by the parent company, Seapower, to join them for lunch, because he knew discussions would continue while they were eating and he needed to take time out to assess all the information he'd absorbed during the morning.

The Seapower project was important globally, because the system would be able to use the limitless energy of the sea currents. A submerged machine could generate a maximum of three hundred kilowatts in a current of only five and a half knots, which eventually could be linked with a land power grid by a marine cable that would emerge from the base of the pile and lie out of sight on the seabed. Environmentally the submerged turbines would have very little impact and they would cause no pollution whatsoever; they would be installed beneath the sea at places with high tidal current velocities. Locations like Hollow Bay, Gabe thought.

He took another bite from the sandwich that the team's one and only secretary had nipped out to buy him before she went to lunch herself. Hollow Bay.

Gabe continued to gaze out at the dismal view of the backs of office blocks, the rain adding its own dreariness to the grey scene. The sun had broken through the clouds earlier that day and its warmth had hinted at an Indian summer, but that hadn't lasted very long – the clouds had closed up and the endless drizzle had resumed. His thoughts meandered from the harbour village to the house to which he had brought his family.

Crickley Hall was a seriously weird place, no question. And although Eve seemed in better shape yesterday, he knew her nerves were already frazzled. And more trauma could tip her over the edge.

'Fuck it,' he said aloud.

Suddenly his mind was made up. They were moving out of Crickley Hall. They would find somewhere smaller, a cottage maybe, anywhere that was warm and without puddles that had no cause, or strange noises in the night, or doors that kept opening by themselves. Although he had no belief in ghosts, there was definitely something eerie about the old house. Neither he, nor his family, needed it; Loren especially was becoming more and more frightened, though for her mother's sake she managed to hide it well. Hell, even the mutt was scared.

He felt a weight lift from his shoulders and he smiled to himself. Yeah, he'd drop by the realtor's office some time tomorrow.

## 24: THE EVACUEES' TALE

Percy Judd sat at the kitchen table as he had three days ago when the Caleighs had first moved into Crickley Hall. His hands dangled the flat cap between his knees, his storm coat hung on a hook beside the kitchen door. For such an elderly man his faded blue eyes were watchful and alert. Like last time, Eve was brewing him a cup of tea.

Cally had been sent to her room to play or read one of her picture books; Eve had questions she wished to put to Percy, but not in front of her daughter.

He shifted awkwardly in his seat. 'Don't mean to disturb yer none, missus. Been workin' down at the church all mornin', but I'm finished there fer today.'

'It's okay, Percy, you're not disturbing me. Besides, you can't work outside in this weather – that's why I called you in. But call me Eve, won't you? You already know my husband's name is Gabe.'

'If it's all the same to yer, I'll stick to mister and missus. It's only proper. Yer my employers, y'see?'

'Well, it seems you come with the house,' Eve agreed. 'But you don't mind us calling you Percy, do you?'

He chuckled and shook his head. 'That'd be fine, Missus Caleigh.'

She smiled at him. There was something she really liked

about this old man, even though she hardly knew him. He seemed simple in a good way, a special way, without complications.

'Actually,' she said, 'I'm sort of glad to see you today.'

He looked at her quizzically.

'There are things I'd like to ask about Crickley Hall.' She paused. Had his face momentarily darkened when she said that?

'There's a lot to do in the garden this time of year,' he said, as if he couldn't spare the time for idle chat.

'Really? I thought with winter on the way there wouldn't be much for you to do out there, especially in the rain.'

'Oh no. In some ways this is the most important part of the year. Have to get things ready for the cold weather.'

She brought his tea over as he enthused on what was obviously his favourite topic. Percy placed his cap on the table and took the proffered cup.

'Not that yer got much of a garden, apart from the lawn, but what there is still needs tendin'. There's prunin' to be done an' the tyin' back of the plants, mulch to be spread over the beds to save 'em from the frost. Then there's the trimmin' of the trees, cuttin' out the dead wood. Then yer apples want collectin' an' the fallen ones picked up – yer got a coupla healthy apple trees roun' back. Make lovely jam with 'em, yer could, if yer've a mind to. There's more plantin' of bulbs needed – daffodils, tulips, snowdrops – which've gotta go in now if they're gonna come through by next year's spring.'

He blew into his cup to cool the steaming liquid.

'Then there's yer logs yer'll want choppin',' he resumed. 'I've already put a fair amount down in the boiler room, but if yer gonna keep all yer fires burnin', bedrooms an' all – there's a particular damp cold about Crickley Hall that radiators can't best – yer'll soon be runnin' out of wood to burn.'

'We don't expect you to do that, Percy.' Eve took a chair opposite him. 'Gabe will be only too willing to chop wood. In fact, he'll enjoy the exercise.'

'It's choppin' the right wood that's important. Some'll only make a lot of smoke, others yer won't even be able to light. Yer gotta know the right kind to axe.'

Eve nodded. 'You can show him which are better to use.' She leaned her elbows on the table. 'How long have you worked at Crickley Hall, Percy?' she asked, looking directly into his eyes as if the question was of some importance.

'Most of my life, missus. Since I were twelve years old. Never got on with school, an' in them days t'weren't unusual for a lad to start work at that age. Not down in these parts, anyway.'

He sipped the hot tea and smacked his thin lips in appreciation. 'I likes it strong,' he remarked appreciatively. 'Proper cuppa tea, this.'

Eve was still staggered that Percy, who must be in his late seventies if not early eighties, had spent so many years in the one job. She quickly gathered her thoughts.

'You said you look after St Mark's cemetery too?' she asked.

'The graveyard, yers. I make sure it's kept neat an' tidy, 'specially roun' the back, even though it don't get many visitors.'

'That's where the children are buried, isn't it? My husband saw the small graves.'

Percy fell silent. He looked down into his tea, the cup in one hand, saucer in the other and held under the cup as if to catch any drips.

Eve persisted. 'The children came from here, didn't they? They were all staying at Crickley Hall when they drowned, weren't they?'

Percy's face became grim, set like stone. His eyes pierced Eve's suspiciously and she instinctively pulled back an inch in surprise.

But those old faded eyes soon softened again; now they were full of sadness.

'The poor little mites were sent down to Devon durin' the last world war. 1943 they come here. Late summer. People in London thought the Blitz were over, didn't wanna send their kids away, split up the families, like. But the authorities knew better. They knew the bombin' weren't over yet and they wanted the young 'uns out of harm's way. The evacuees that came to Crickley Hall had no choice anyway – they was all orphans, y'see.'

He fell into silence once more and a distant look came into his eyes. Eve thought tears might appear in them, but the old man was made of sterner stuff. His eyes refocused on her.

'What makes yer ask about the kiddies, Missus Caleigh?'

There was more than just curiosity in the question: Percy seemed anxious.

'I . . . I just thought it was so sad,' she answered. 'All those poor children . . . drowned. I wanted to know more about them.'

What else could she tell Percy? That she – and Cally, Cally saw them too – had seen the children's ghosts? That they were haunting Crickley Hall? Surely he would only scoff, think her mad. Eve could imagine the word spreading round the harbour village – there was a madwoman living up at the Hall, thought the place was haunted. It seemed a close-set community, one where all kinds of rumour might start. It had been bad enough that morning in the shop, asking for a psychic's card, the odd looks that the shopkeeper and her husband had given her when she took it from them. The locals would think her eccentric, at the least. And who could blame them.

He drank more tea, then seemed to come to a decision. 'If yer wants to hear about it, then all right, I'll tell yer.'

And so Percy Judd told Eve the heartbreaking story of the evacuees from London who had come to Crickley Hall in the late summer of 1943.

'A course the Blitz were over by then,' Percy told Eve, 'but as I says, the gov'mint knew better. They knew the Germans weren't finished with their bombings yet an' the gov'mint wanted to get as many children outa London as possible. Lotta parents wouldn't hear of it though – they thought the worst was gone – but kiddies in orphanages had no say in the matter. Those that came to Crickley Hall shoulda got away from the city long afore, but I s'pose the authorities had trouble findin' 'ccommodation for 'em until this place come up.

'Gov'mint were right, en' all. Krauts sent over them doodle-bugs in '44 – "buzz bombs" some people called 'em, but V-1s was their proper name – an' they created havoc in London an' along the Kent flypath. But our eleven evacuees came afore that happened, much good it did 'em in the long run.

'There were six boys an' five girls, only two of them related: Gerald and Brenda Prosser were brother and sister. The eldest boy were twelve years old, though he were big for his age an' looked older too. His name were Maurice Stafford, a gawky unlikable lad, an' the eldest girl, eleven years old, were Susan Trainer. She played mother to 'em all, but especially to Stefan Rosenbaum, who were only five, the youngest of the lot. He were from Poland and didn't understand much English.

'Poor little mites, they was,' said Percy. 'All they come with was the clothes on their backs, cardboard suitcases with a change of clothes, I suppose, an' their gas-mask boxes hangin' roun' their necks. They looked happy enough when they arrived, chatterin' an' excited as they got off the bus that'd brought 'em from the station. Didn't last long though, that happiness.'

Eve listened intently as the story went on . . .

Percy told her that the children's guardians and teachers, who were also from London and new to the area themselves, were brother and sister, Augustus and Magda Cribben.

He was in his early forties, a cold hard man, a religious zealot and disciplinarian, who ruled the children with a rod of iron. His sister, a plain, stone-faced woman of thirty-one – 'Looked older,' remarked Percy, 'looked much older than her years' – was equally harsh with the children.

Augustus Cribben, whose middle name was Theophilus, had been deputy headmaster of a London school for boys that had been closed because most of its pupils had been evacuated to other parts of the country. Magda had been one of his teachers. Other than that, very little else was known about the couple and the only person in Hollow Bay that Cribben engaged with was the vicar of St Mark's, the Reverend Horace Rossbridger, who admired the guardian for his dedication to the Lord and the firm control he had over the children in his charge.

Percy, who as a lad was the gardener-cum-handyman to Crickley Hall, even then taking care of the house and grounds whether it was occupied or not, had tried to befriend the children when his daily duties took him inside the house, but

181

Cribben had soon forbidden any fraternization between Percy and the children lest they be distracted from their own duties. That hadn't prevented Percy from observing, though.

Within a matter of days the children had changed from happy, vociferous youngsters into wary and quiet creatures, afraid to do anything that might incur Cribben's or Magda's wrath. They had come to live in a regime so strict that it seemed to have broken their spirit. Punishment for anything Cribben deemed misbehaviour was severe, Percy learned. Their daily diet was porridge and a cup of water for breakfast, mincemeat, boiled potatoes and cabbage for lunch, cheese and an apple for their supper, all of which might have been fine, if limited, but Percy had seen for himself the meagre portions each child received. While they were not conspicuously undernourished, they soon lost any ounce of fat they might have had before, and their robustness was drained from them.

Inside the house they had to go about in bare or stockinged feet despite the damp coldness that always clung to the rooms no matter what the season. As well as saving on shoe leather, this also avoided 'excessive' noise. Augustus Cribben apparently suffered mightily from migraine headaches.

Nor were the evacuees allowed to play with toys that were sent by the various charitable organizations that regularly supplied orphanages and schools in poorer areas with clothes and books as well as playthings. Toys were put away in the attic storeroom next to the children's dormitory, almost as if their proximity was meant to torment – or test – the boys and girls.

'We found them,' Eve informed Percy, glancing at the old-fashioned spinning top that sat between them near the edge of the kitchen table. 'Gabe discovered it in the attic. As you said – hidden away in the storeroom next to the dormitory. My God, they've been there all those years.'

Percy studied the colourful toy, and there was sorrow in his gaze. A moment or two passed before he said, 'S'been no proper family here since to take any interest. No kiddies who might've had fun with things like that.' He sighed, and to Eve he seemed to shrink a little. The old man went on with his story.

'I remember seein' all the evacuees together once, marchin' down to St Mark's for Sunday service. September, it were, and the weather had turned cold. They was in pairs, holdin' hands like, the little 'uns trottin' along to keep up, girls in brown berets, the boys wearin' overcoats either too small or too large, none fittin' properly. All of 'em had gas masks hangin' across their chests, even though there were little chance of gas bombs in Hollow Bay. I still recall how quiet they was, not like ordinary kids who'd be laughin' an' chattin', some of 'em skippin' mebbe. Like they was when they first arrived. No, they was all silent as the grave, sort of ... sort of ...' He searched for the right word. '... cowed, if yer know my meanin'. Like they was afraid to enjoy themselves.'

Percy shook his head sadly at the memory. 'Cribben were up front, leadin' 'em, Magda fetchin' up the rear, watchin' out for any mischief the kids might get up to along the way. Maurice Stafford marched with her at the back, a tall boy, like I say, who looked older than he were. For some reason he was treated different from the others by the Cribbens. A tattle-tell, he were, I found out later. Told on the other kids if they did anythin' wrong. A big kid all right, but skinny, awkward-lookin'. I remember him grinnin' at me as he passed by, cocky with it, a great black gap in his grin where a tooth should've been. He weren't liked by the other kiddies an' there were a reason for that. Teacher's pet, he were. An' sly, very sly. A sneak. I found out about that when Nancy came to teach at Crickley Hall.'

He came to a stop again and Eve wondered if he were picturing this Nancy in his mind. He seemed far away, lost to another time.

'Tell me about her,' Eve gently prompted and the old gardener collected himself, clearing his throat, stiffening his shoulders.

'Nancy – Linnet were her surname, Linnet like the little bird – Nancy were nineteen years of age. Pretty thing, she were, delicate like, but strong in herself, if yer knows my meanin' . . .'

Like the eleven evacuees at Crickley Hall, Nancy Linnet was also an orphan who had been raised in an institutional home in the suburbs of London. She had left the home at the age of sixteen to dedicate her life to teaching and aspiring to educate underprivileged children, especially those who were orphans like herself. She had jumped at the opportunity to teach the orphans at Hollow Bay.

'Nancy had ringlets that shone like bright copper down to her shoulders,' Percy told Eve, 'an' merry hazel eyes, an' she had freckles on her cheeks that made her look like a twelve-year-old. Well, we sort of took a shine to one another, me an' Nancy. Oh, I knew she were too good fer me an' I used to think the only reason I stood a chance with her were 'cause she had a withered arm. That didn't spoil her beauty fer me, not one little bit, but other lads in them days . . . Well, there were a different attitude towards disfigurement then, only by the time the war were over an' all them pilots an' sailors an' soldiers come back with burnt-off faces an' missin' limbs, people started to get used to such things. Not entirely, though

– some people nowadays still can't abide other people's afflictions, but I s'pose there's no changin' that.'

He gave a mournful shake of his head. 'Anyway, we struck up a friendship – a courtship yer might say – an' through her I got to know more about what was goin' on in Crickley Hall, things I hadn't seen fer myself . . .'

The children's routine was stringent as it was inflexible. They rose at six every morning, weekends included, and made their own beds before washing and dressing; they had breakfast, then attended assembly in the hall where Cribben led them in prayer; by eight o'clock they began lessons in the large drawing room (it was also their dining room), which had been furnished with desks that had fold-up benches attached, a teacher's table with drawers, a coloured tin globe of the world that stood on a sideboard, and a blackboard and easel. Their lunch was at twelve o'clock and only lasted twenty minutes, after which they were each given chores to do around the house: sweeping, dusting and polishing (scrubbing floors on Saturdays), cleaning out the fire grate and re-laying the fire in the sitting room and for the Cribbens alone (despite the constant chill that hugged the house because of the underground river it was built over, the boiler was never used to heat the big iron radiators). Lessons resumed at two and finished at six. They were free to read books in the dormitory until seven (no games were allowed), when they had supper. Bathtime after supper, each of the children bathing on alternate evenings, more assembly prayers in their nightclothes, then bed, lights out by 8 p.m.

Nancy herself lodged in the harbour village, and she arrived at Crickley Hall promptly at 7.45 a.m. every day for lessons, leaving at six each evening.

'It were the punishment dealt out to the kiddies that upset Nancy so much, the beatin's Cribben gave 'em, sometimes with a leather belt but more often with a stick. Nancy was a quiet little thing, but it distressed her the way the orphans was treated. She remonstrated with Cribben more 'n once, but she were frightened to go too far in case she got sacked – couldn't bear to leave the children, she couldn't, in case they was treated worse when she were gone. One time she did go see the vicar, old Horace Rossbridger, to complain about the Cribbens, but he were too much an admirer of Augustus Cribben to listen to her. Told Nancy to go back to work an' mind her business. But I think Nancy resolved to do more about it, but I don't know what.'

Eve regarded Percy. 'What do you mean? Surely—'

He waved a hand at her as if in despair. 'I was conscripted into the army roun' that time. I'd turned eighteen an' the Forces needed every man and lad they could get.'

(Eve quickly did the maths. My God! Percy was eighty-one!)

'We kep' in touch by letter, Nancy an' me, but her letters stopped comin'. Las' one I got from her said she'd made up her mind an' were goin' to the authorities to tell 'em what were goin' on at Crickley Hall. I carried on writin' to her, but nothin' ever came back after that. So I got in touch with her landlady at the lodgings an' she wrote back tellin' me Nancy had quit her job and gone away. Magda Cribben turned up one day at the lodgings and informed the landlady that Nancy was returnin' to London that very afternoon an' needed the rest of her things. Magda didn't explain any more, jus' collected Nancy's few clothes and left with 'em. Nobody heard from Nancy agin'. She were hardly known down in the village anyway and it were wartime – people comin' an' goin' all the time. Nobody bothered to ask questions.'

'But didn't you find Nancy after the war?' asked Eve, touched by Percy and Nancy's romance.

'Oh, I tried, Missus Caleigh, believe me, I tried, but I weren't demobbed 'til late '46 an' by then . . . well, by then the trail'd gone cold. People went missin' durin' war an' more went missin' after. It was all the confusion, y'see, the country was a mess, gov'mint an' people tryin' to get back to normal. The authorities had no record of Nancy after '43 an' there were too much goin' on for them to care much. Said she probably returned to London and were mebbe killed in the bombing – it was them doodlebugs, them flying bombs that were doing the damage in '44. Bigger ones after that – V-2s they called 'em . . .'

Percy Judd had searched for but never found Nancy Linnet. After the flood in October 1943, Crickley Hall remained empty and almost derelict for several years. He was kept on as gardener and handyman by the managing agents who looked after the property for the owners, the direct descendants of Charles Crickley, who had moved to Canada at the beginning of the Second World War and had lost interest in the house (which was soon requisitioned by the government for official wartime use). Percy confessed to Eve that he stayed with the place in the foolish hope that Nancy might some day return, or at least make contact with him there. But it was not to be: it was as if his sweetheart had disappeared off the face of the earth itself.

Eventually the house was restored to its former condition – Percy could not force himself to say it was restored to its former *glory*, because he had never found anything remotely glorious about the place – by successive owners, the last of whom were the Templetons. But rumours about the Hall had spread among the villagers. Rumours that the children had been deliberately trapped in Crickley Hall's cellar on the night of the flood. Rumours that had never entirely gone away.

'Only nine bodies was found inside the house, all of 'em in

the cellar,' said Percy, a mistiness in his eyes now. 'It were reckoned the other two'd been washed into the well by the floodwater an' the underground river had carried them out to the bay. Maurice Stafford and the little Polish boy, Stefan, that were. Their bodies were never recovered. The question at the time were why was the children down there when Cribben coulda taken 'em up to the top of the house, or even the landing, which was high enough.

'Augustus Cribben's body were found dead in the big hall, his neck an' back broken, his body cut to pieces when the floodwaters smashed through the window over the stairs. They said he were discovered naked.'

Eve frowned and suddenly felt colder.

'Magda Cribben,' Percy continued after a moment, 'were found next mornin', waitin' alone on the platform of the railway station at Merrybridge. No one knew how she got there. She were only in her usual black dress and brogues – no coat an' no hat – an' she couldn't answer no questions, couldn't speak at all. Never spoke another word.'

'Good God,' said Eve. 'What happened to her?'

'She were put in what they used to call an asylum.'

'She was mad?'

'Mad an' dumb. Couldn't or wouldn't say a word. When she got too old they put her in a nursing home.'

Percy drained his tea, which was cold by then. He placed the cup and saucer on the table and rose to his feet.

'I best be goin', missus. That's all I can tell you 'bout the evacuees who came to Crickley Hall, poor souls.'

'But there must have been an investigation of some kind into why the children were in the cellar. It doesn't make sense.'

'If there were, the outcome were kept quiet. Yer have to remember there were a war goin' on. People had enough to worry about. An' parents wouldna let their kiddies be evacuated at all any more if they thought bad things was goin' to happen to 'em. No, I think the gov'mint in them days didn't want to cause no fuss, morale of the country an' all that. An' there were no proper evidence agin' Augustus Cribben anyway. Even the vicar, old Rossbridger, still spoke highly of the man. The only person left who knew what'd been goin' on at Crickley Hall was Magda Cribben an' she weren't sayin'. But y'know, I think Rossbridger were in league with the authorities who wanted things hushed up, 'cause Cribben were buried without ceremony an' his grave were right at the back of the graveyard.'

Percy managed a faint smile for Eve, but the melancholy remained in his faded eyes.

'I'll be gettin' on with the garden. I've given yer enough to think on.'

Eve stood too. 'Thank you, Percy,' was all she could think of to say; her head was reeling by now.

Donning his cap and adjusting it on his head, he walked to the door and turned back to her before opening it.

'Are things all right fer yer here, Missus Caleigh?' he asked.

Eve wondered what she could tell him, what he would believe. 'Yes, Percy. Everything's fine.'

'You'd let me know . . .?' He did not complete the sentence.

Know what? That Crickley Hall was haunted? That the spirits of the children who had died here were somehow making her aware of their presence? That there might possibly be a connection between them and her own missing son? It was too soon to tell. Besides, she could scarcely believe it herself.

'Everything's fine,' she repeated. And her mind was suddenly made up: she knew what she should do.

## 25: BULLY

Now it was not in Loren Caleigh's nature to hit anybody; in fact, never in her life had she raised a hand or fist in anger, let alone physically struck someone. She abhorred violence in any form and she hated confrontation almost as much. She didn't like it when Dad and little Cam used to play-wrestle on the carpet, Dad allowing her tiny brother to think he'd pinned him down before Dad reared up and held him high over his head until Cam, who loved it when that happened, 'squealed' for mercy, both of them ending up giggling and rolling around the floor again. It always made Mummy laugh too (Mummy laughed a lot in those days), but Loren herself had only smiled, pretending to enjoy the game.

Then one day, Loren had returned home from school and burst into tears. It turned out that a particularly nasty girl in a class a year above Loren's had been picking on her for several weeks, for no other reason, it seemed, than Loren had an American father, someone who 'talked funny'. (Gabe and Eve suspected there were probably other reasons, such as their daughter's own shyness and her quiet personality.) Eve had wanted to complain to the school's headmistress, but Loren had begged her not to. 'It will only make matters worse,' she had wailed. So Dad, much to Mummy's protests, had shown Loren what to do when you were picked on by a bully who was not only older but bigger too. This, of course, was if you'd been pushed to the limit and there was no other way to settle things.

The trick was to get in the first blow. Once you knew there was only one way for the situation to go and it was bound to get physical, you had to strike first. But – 'this is important, this is very important' – aim for the bridge of the nose. Not the tip of the nose, nor any other place like the jaw, and never the chest (belly if you just wanted to wind them, but it was not advised). Just that spot at the bridge of the nose, 'smack-down between the peepers'. That should do enough damage to finish it right there and then – 'And if it doesn't, get the hell out.'

Warming to the subject – and to Mummy's further chagrin – Dad had told her: 'If your opponent is much bigger than you, or there's more of 'em, never, but *never*, take it outside. In a room you got furniture to throw, chairs to use as a shield or to whack their heads with, walls to back up against, tables you can push 'em over, and even bits and pieces – say like vases or ornaments – you can throw at the other guy, make 'em back off.'

Mummy realized Dad was half fooling around, but she was angry anyway. Violence could never be an answer, she'd said, and Dad had winked at Loren.

As it happened, the bully girl in question was removed from the school after it was discovered that she was forcing girls even younger than Loren to hand over their dinner money and pocket money. Also, a supply teacher's purse had gone missing from her handbag and the bully girl was discovered in the girls' toilets counting out the change by another teacher. So, much to Loren's relief (and her parents'), the problem was resolved. Whether or not she would have had the courage to 'punch the bully's lights out', as Gabe would have it, was another matter entirely.

But two years later, on a damp Monday afternoon in October, she had certainly used the tactic on Seraphina Blaney. To her dismay, Loren had found herself in the same class at Merrybridge Middle School as the girl she had met – acrimoniously – just before. She remembered her in the store at Hollow Bay, a big girl, stocky, with a face that might have been pretty had the jaw not been too heavy, the forehead too bulbous and the thin lips too scowling.

The moment they set eyes on each other, which was when Loren was being introduced to the class by the teacher, Loren knew she was in for a hard time. Her eyes had locked with Seraphina's, and Loren had recognized the girl who had stared at her with such spite on Saturday. Seraphina had whispered something to the girl sitting next to her and they had both sniggered into their hands. It had turned into a bad day.

Loren had been subjected to mean stares and flicked elastic bands to the back of her neck throughout lessons. At lunchtime, Seraphina, seated at a table, had deliberately stuck out a foot as Loren passed by with her tray of food; Loren had stumbled, tipped the tray, and the full plate on it had skittered across the floor. Losing the macaroni with cheese and jacket potato wasn't the worst part: it was the humiliation that turned her face beet-red in front of the school that Loren hated.

It hadn't ended there. Throughout the rest of the afternoon Loren had been subjected to hissed name-calling, masticated paper pellets aimed at her whenever the teacher's back was turned and pathetic take-offs of her London accent. Fortunately, Seraphina appeared only to have a small coterie of friends to enjoy the tormenting; most of the other pupils were friendly and curious about her in a good way.

She managed to make a friend of another girl from Hollow Bay, a shy little thing whose name was Tessa Windle. They had connected when Tessa had helped Loren pick up the remains of her lunch after Seraphina had tripped her. She was the same age as Loren, but seemed a year younger; her Devonian accent was slight and her manner gentle. By the end of the school day, she and Loren had become firm friends.

With an exaggerated flourish the driver drew back the blue people-carrier's passenger door.

'All aboard who's goin' aboard,' he called out to the mass of blue-uniformed pupils spilling out of the school gates. Members of his boarding party broke off from the main crowd, skirting round waiting mothers and fathers, arriving at the minibus in groups of two and three, eight of them in all for the journey home to Hollow Bay. Loren, with her new friend Tessa, waited as three boys ahead of them climbed into the vehicle, while the driver looked her over with an unattractive grin. His teeth were yellow, each one isolated from its neighbour by a discernible gap that emphasized their crookedness. Long, lank hair fell to his narrow dandruffy shoulders and he scratched an unshaven chin as he appraised the unfamiliar passenger.

'You'll be the new 'un, will yer?' He scrutinized Loren's face as if suspecting her of carrying some contagious disease that might infect his regulars. 'Laura Caleigh, 'ennit? I was told to expect an extra passenger this afternoon.'

'Loren.'

'Eh?'

'My name's Loren.'

'Laura, Loren. Same thing.'

She wanted to tell him it wasn't – her name was Loren,

not Laura; there was a difference, but she didn't like the smell of his rank breath so didn't want to open up a dialogue.

She made to move past him but he said, 'My name's Frank. You can call me Mr Mulley, all right?' *Awroit.* 'In yer get then. No messin' about when I'm drivin', okay?'

Loren was about to follow Tessa into the bus when a stocky arm blocked her way. Seraphina Blaney glared at her.

'After me, grockle.' She gave Loren a shove.

Grockle, Loren knew, was a derogatory term for tourist or outsider. The girl with Seraphina gave a chortling snort, while Seraphina herself gave Loren a tight-lipped contemptuous smile. Loren chose not to respond and waited as the big girl and her friend climbed aboard. She followed them in, another breathless, older girl arriving and climbing in behind her.

The minibus was not full: the three boys took up the back seats, an empty double-seat in front of them where the last girl to arrive sat; Seraphina and her friend occupied the next seats right behind Tessa. Loren took the seat next to her. Nobody, apparently, wanted the seat closest to the driver. Loren and Tessa balanced their school bags on their knees, Loren glad that the school day was over; it would almost be a relief to get back to Crickley Hall.

Frank Mulley pushed the passenger door shut with a loud sliding thud, then walked round to the driver's side and got in. Wrists resting over the top of the steering wheel, he craned his head round and silently counted off his passengers, lips mouthing each number. When his eyes met with Loren's, he gave her a smirky wink and, although she shuddered inside, she returned a polite smile. He engaged gear and the people-carrier pulled away from the kerb and soon turned into the town's main thoroughfare.

'What yer sittin' next to her for?' Seraphina dug stiff

fingers into Tessa's shoulder. 'She yer new best friend? Like grockles, do yer?'

Tessa shrugged her shoulder away from the other girl's touch as Loren glanced round.

'What yer lookin' at, skanky?' This time the fingers jabbed at Loren's shoulder. 'Think yer better than us, do yer?'

Tessa leaned into Loren and whispered, 'Take no notice. She's even worse when her brother's with her. Quentin's on suspension for two weeks for fighting. It's usually Seraphina who gets him into trouble.'

They both giggled together, more out of nervousness than pleasure.

Seraphina wasn't pleased about that. 'You laughin' at me?' She dug into Tessa again, harder this time, using her knuckles.

Tessa shrugged her shoulder away once more, but the girl behind persisted, this time punching Loren's shoulder.

'Please don't do that,' Loren said, half afraid, half annoyed.

'*Please don't do that,*' Seraphina mimicked in a whining voice. 'Why?' *Woy?* 'What yer gonna do about it?' Her head did the Bombay shuffle, her neck flexing first to the right, then to the left and then to the right again, head held upright throughout.

Loren turned her back on her and stared ahead. They were passing through the outskirts of the town now, leaving shops and offices behind, many of the dwellings on either side of the road made of flint or quarry stone. Loren feigned interest in the landscape, which was beginning to open up, fields of heather and bracken glimpsed between breaks in the high hedges, with low sullen hills and clouded skies brooding above it all. Raindrops spattered the windows, but there was not much force to them. Throughout the day the rain had seemed to tease, falling in thick flurries one minute, drizzling lightly the next. The gloom that came with the inclement weather somehow nurtured the despondency she felt. It had been a rotten day, even more rotten that she had expected it to be, and it was Seraphina Blaney who had made it worse.

Loren clutched her bag and tried to ignore her tormentor. Those in the bus were aware of what was going on – the taunting of this newcomer, an outsider, a grockle – and some, namely the boys on the back seat and the girl sitting along-side the bully, laughed along with Seraphina's snide remarks; others, though – Tessa and the girl who had entered the minibus behind Loren – looked out of the windows and tried to ignore what was happening. As for Loren, she wanted to cry.

She felt more nudging on her back, each nudge harder than the one before, but she refused to retaliate. She calmed herself with the thought that it was only a short journey, no more than fifteen minutes or so, and soon it would be over and she'd be back with her family ... in Crickley Hall. The thought of the cold, shadowy house failed to elevate her mood: it depressed her even more. But she felt the mood turning to anger. The bully's jibes were now including a fresh victim, Loren's 'spazzie' little sister. Loren began to burn.

But it was her new friend, Tessa, who snapped.

'Just stop it, Seraphina Blaney. Leave Loren alone. She's done nothing to you.'

The boys on the back seat laughed aloud and for a moment the tormentor was stunned into silence. Then she rose from her seat, stretched herself over Tessa's shoulder, grabbed Tessa's school bag and emptied the contents into the bus's narrow side aisle. The books spilled out onto the floor and under the seats, pages flapping and pens and pencils clattering, then rolling. Tessa was aghast – and frightened.

And now it was Loren who snapped.

There was no need to remind herself of her father's advice regarding bullies – what took place seemed to happen naturally (and if she'd taken time to think, then probably it wouldn't have happened at all).

Seraphina was still standing between seats, a broad gloating grin on her face, her friend beside her snickering into her hand, the boys behind uncertain and quiet. Her head had just began to turn towards Loren, her small, deep-set eyes glittering with malice, when Loren's balled fist, thumb on the outside, bent level with the knuckles, smashed into the pudgy part of Seraphina's nose.

Loren was disappointed, because she'd been aiming at the bridge of the big girl's nose, right between the eyes as advised; nevertheless, the blow had more effect than she ever would have dreamed. Blood immediately spurted out of Seraphina's nostrils, two bright red jets that splattered her mouth and jaw. Tears sprung into her eyes as she rocked back, the contact between the seat and the back of her knees forcing her legs to buckle so that she had no other choice but to sit. In shock, she stayed down, her fleshy hand cupping the blood that poured from her nose.

The friend next to her stared in horrified awe. One of the boys on the back seat breathlessly said, 'Wow.' Apart from that, there was no other sound inside the minibus. Until the boys started to applaud.

# 26: CONVERSATIONS

'You did *what*?' Gabe stared at Loren in disbelief and there was a hint of amusement in his open-mouthed gape.

He had returned home from work and barely had time to discard his coat before Loren came into the hall from the kitchen, followed by Eve, who had told her what she had to do: own up to Dad.

'I didn't mean to.' Loren shook her head as though her actions earlier on the school bus were a mystery even to herself. 'It just happened.'

'You whacked her?' He was incredulous; he had never known his elder daughter to use violence before.

'She knocked Tessa's school bag to the floor.'

'And Tessa is . . .?'

'She's my new friend at school. She lives in the village and we sat next to each other on the bus coming home. Seraphina deliberately tipped Tessa's bag out so that everything fell on the floor.'

Gabe looked over Loren's shoulder at Eve, who stood grim-faced, arms folded, behind her. He thought he might find a suggestion of a smile, but Eve had no intention of encouraging him or Loren.

'I couldn't help it, Dad,' Loren went on. 'I just did what you taught me without thinking.'

THE SECRET OF CRICKLEY HALL

Eve gave a disapproving shake of her head, her eyes glaring at Gabe, as if it was entirely his fault that Loren had punched Seraphina Blaney on the nose.

'Hey, wait a minute,' he said indignantly, his blue eyes wide as he returned Eve's accusatory glare. 'You can't pin this on me. Sounds to me if anyone's to blame it's this other kid, Seraphina.' He remembered where he had first heard the unsuitable name. 'Isn't she the big girl who was in the store the other day with her brother?'

Loren looked ashamedly down at the stone floor. She slowly nodded her head. 'Tessa said Quentin's been suspended for two weeks for fighting in school. Dad, Seraphina was picking on me all day.'

'Then you did good.'

'Gabe!' Eve was in despair.

'The other kid had it coming. Loren did right to defend herself and her friend.'

'Violence is never an answer,' Eve huffed.

'No, you're right,' Gabe agreed sheepishly, at the same time giving Loren a surreptitious wink.

Eve wasn't fooled. 'I saw that. I mean it. Punching someone – especially another girl – doesn't solve anything. Loren will only have to deal with the situation again tomorrow.'

'I'm guessing not,' asserted Gabe. 'Seraphina will have had enough.'

'You don't know that. Hitting her might only have made matters worse.'

Gabe saw that it would be pointless to continue defending his daughter. And he certainly didn't want it to sound like he was countenancing what she'd done (Eve would kill him if he did).

'How's your hand?' he asked Loren.

She held up her right hand so that he could see. 'I

199

thought I'd broken some bones, but it's all right now, just a bit sore.'

Gabe couldn't help chuckling as he examined her knuckles. 'That must've been some punch.'

'I made her nose bleed.'

'You kept your thumb on the outside like I told you? You didn't tuck it inside your fist?'

'Gabe, will you stop this.' There was no humour whatsoever in Eve's expression. 'You shouldn't be giving her boxing lessons.'

'Hey, I'm making sure Loren doesn't break any of her own bones.'

'She's a girl. She's not supposed to fight. And if it comes to that, nor should boys. It's uncivilized.'

Gabe held up both hands in submission. 'Okay, you win. It was a bad thing and Loren won't do it again. Right, Slim?'

Loren nodded her head and Eve softened. 'But you'll let us know if this girl tries to bully you again, you hear me?'

Again, Loren nodded. 'Yes, Mum,' she said. But she and her father exchanged a secret smile.

Gabe stamped his feet on the rough mat just inside the kitchen door, shedding wet mud from his boots. Loren, who had accompanied him in the search for Chester, was already hanging her coat on the rack by the door.

Eve appraised Gabe anxiously and he shook his head. 'No luck,' he told her. 'No sign of him anywhere.'

Cally looked distraught and Loren went to Eve for a hug. Arms round Loren's shoulders, Eve said: 'What are we going to do?'

Gabe slipped off his coat and hung it beside Loren's. 'He

might turn up on his own, either tonight or some time tomorrow. I'll make another search in the morning, a better one in the daylight.'

'Our London telephone number is on his collar. If someone finds Chester they won't be able to reach us.'

'I'll ring the local police if I don't find him in the morning. And we'll tell Percy to keep a lookout. I'm sure he'll pass the word on to the locals, so there'll be plenty keeping an eye out for the mutt. We'll get Chester back, don't you worry.'

'What's changed your mind?' Gabe was bewildered. 'A coupla days ago you didn't like Crickley Hall, you couldn't wait for us to pack our bags and leave.'

Gabe and Eve were in the sitting room. A fire blazed in the hearth, but Gabe had to lean forward in his armchair to catch any warmth. Eve sat opposite him on the couch and she, too, leaned forward, a mug of coffee in her hands, elbows resting on her knees. His coffee mug stood on a coaster close by his foot.

She did not know how to respond to Gabe's question. Blurting out that she'd seen ghosts here wouldn't do at all, because he would demand some kind of evidence of their existence and how could you prove something that wasn't real? He had not been witness to the dancing children; he had not felt Cam's hand soothing his brow.

'Come on, Eve, something must've changed your mind, so help me, tell me what it is.' He couldn't conceal his exasperation.

'I'm sorry, Gabe. It's difficult to explain.'

'Try me.'

'I just feel we need time to get used to the place.'

'That's what I said the other day and you wouldn't listen. It's cold and it's damp, and we keep hearing strange noises. And don't forget Chester – something here scared the hell out of the poor mutt. We don't need this kind of thing at this point in our lives. We got enough to worry about.' His tone changed, dropped in pitch. 'Look, I could see the agent tomorrow, see what else he's got on his books. We could probably be out by the end of the week. What d'you say?'

'Let's give it more time.' What she meant was give *her* more time, time to discover the meaning of the haunting, time to find out if it had anything to do with their missing son. She thought of a compromise. 'Let's wait just a few more days. If you still feel the same by then we'll move.'

'I can't help thinking that it should be me arguing with you to stay. That's how it was before. Why can't you tell me what's happened to change your mind?'

He was no fool; but then, she already knew that. 'Go with me on this, Gabe,' she pleaded and said no more.

With a sigh, he leaned back in his chair. 'Okay, you win,' he said reluctantly, not quite sure now why he wanted to leave Crickley Hall. Viewing more properties, packing, then unpacking again – he sure as hell didn't need it. But the compromise was fair. Sure, the house was uncomfortable – although it was almost *cosy* sitting here in front of a roaring fire, even if the heat did not extend too far beyond the hearth. Maybe they did need more time to settle in. Maybe Chester just hadn't liked the strangeness of the house – he was too used to their home in London. Maybe there were odd noises, puddles on the floor, doors that would not stay locked, but there was probably a logical reason for all those things. Wasn't there?

Anyway, what could happen to them here? It was just a cranky old house that, now it had new occupants, was creaking back to life.

He smiled at his wife, who looked even more beautiful in the warm glow of the firelight, a colour back in her cheeks and lively little flames reflected in her eyes.

'Okay, Eve,' he said. 'We'll give it another try.'

After all, what *could* happen to them here? A house was just a house.

It was as if Crickley Hall had paused to take a breath.

There were no incidents that night, no rappings, no sounds of running feet, no 'whimpering' from closed closets. Nothing untoward occurred during that night and the Caleigh family slept peacefully. Even Eve rested, although her mind was filled with ethereal images of spinning tops and dancing children.

Loren and Cally fretted over their missing pet for a short while, but sleepy tiredness soon overcame them both. Gabe was out almost as soon as his head hit the pillow.

The wind that rushed through Devil's Cleave to the bay below died away and the rain became a light patter.

All was still and silent in Crickley Hall, save for the creaking of the cellar door as it opened a few inches.

Not for the first time Gabe strode across the hall to close the open cellar door. He examined the lock first, though, turning its long key backwards and forwards, having only to use slight pressure to move the locking bolt in and out. There appeared to be no reason for the door to keep unlocking itself and straying open a few inches, enough for a breeze to rise up from the cellar below and escape into the hall. The breeze, he realized, must come from the well down there, rushing waters creating strong draughts of air. But strong enough to push a locked door open? It seemed unlikely, but it also seemed to be the case.

Opening the door even wider, he peered into the inky gloom. The dismal daylight from the hall itself did not travel far into the stairway: it was as if the blackness was pushing back the light, rather than the other way round. Without a candle or flashlight, he ruminated, a person would be swallowed up by it. As if for reassurance, Gabe reached in and flipped down the light switch. The light that came on at the bottom of the stairs was barely fit for the job, for its dusty glow had only a limited effect on the darkness. The smell that wafted up was dank and unpleasant and the low, muffled roar of the underground river was somehow disturbing, as if it were boasting its threat, bragging its danger.

Gabe closed the door and the river's sound diminished, could only be heard if he really listened. He twisted the key again so that the door was locked, and he wondered how long it would remain so. Eve had suggested that he fix a bolt to it, high enough to be out of Cally's reach, and he resolved to visit a hardware store when he was next in town.

It was early, just after 6 a.m., and Eve and the girls were still in bed waiting for their alarms to go off. Gabe was wide awake, though, and full of repressed vigour after a decent night's sleep, finally. Despite the chill, he wore only a pale grey sweatshirt with the arms cut off at the elbows, slim black joggers and his usual sturdy ankle boots. Back at home in London, he managed at least twenty minutes pounding the pavement every weekday before work and he felt he needed to get back to a similar routine. The air should be better and the scenery was certainly much more pleasant.

Still puzzled by the wayward cellar door, he went to the hall's front door, which did have bolts top and bottom, although so far they had relied only on its key lock. This was deep countryside where houses were not meant to be vulnerable to late-night intruders – or so the theory went, he told himself, as he unlocked the door. Maybe no home was safe from burglars any more, country, town or city.

He swung the door wide and fresh air seemed to throw itself at him, immediately cleansing his nostrils of the cellar's lingering odour. The sun had not quite risen above the gorge wall and the trees and shrubbery across the river appeared black and a little forbidding; in the city even the darkest of mornings were lit by street lamps and early-opening shops. Nevertheless, the day would quickly grow brighter as he ran and at least there would not be hazardous junctions to cross, traffic to dodge. He'd keep a lookout for Chester and call his name while he ran: maybe the mongrel hadn't travelled too far and was only keeping clear of the house itself. He would ring the local police station later that morning to report their missing pet, but that was in Merrybridge and they were hardly likely to send out a task force to look for Chester.

Gabe drew in great lungfuls of air, priming himself for the run, and when he bent low to stretch his spine, he saw something lying on the doorstep. He frowned, then knelt beside it. Only one of its wings was splayed, the other lying half beneath the bird's body and, although the light was poor, Gabe saw no wounds or any other reason for its demise. It looked like a wood pigeon to him, and when he picked it up, the head hung loose and the released wing fell open. He examined it further and still could find no gashes or death-causing breaks. It seemed the bird had died of old age rather than anything else. It had probably crashed to the ground mid-flight during the night and had just happened to land on their doorstep.

Gabe was glad he had found it first before Loren or Cally set eyes on it: they would have been distressed. He stood and with his free hand he closed the front door behind him. He trotted past the swing hanging from the old oak and stopped by the bridge. Rather than throw the dead pigeon, he leaned over the rushing waters, one hand hanging onto a rail and, as gently as possible, dropped the feathery corpse into the swollen river where it was swiftly washed away by the current.

Pulvington was easy to find on the map and Eve made the journey in less than twenty minutes. Mostly the roads were good, although several times she had to slow the Range Rover to walking pace in order to squeeze past oncoming traffic. Gabe working at home today gave her the perfect opportunity to use their car. It was a shopping expedition, she had told him, the chance to find a supermarket and a decent range of shops. Pulvington appeared to be one of the larger local towns.

Although he would be working in the room off the L-shaped first-floor landing, which he had turned into a make-shift office, he'd be able to keep an eye on Cally, whose bedroom/playroom was only a few doors away on the other arm of the landing. It wouldn't be a hassle for Gabe, because Cally was good at playing on her own, her lively imagination creating all kinds of scenarios for her and her dollies, or the little plastic play people she was so fond of, to act out. Gabe would be within easy hearing distance of her and Cally knew she could go along to his 'office' whenever she liked or wanted something; even though he would be working on the complex operation of the marine turbine, Eve knew that Gabe would be only too glad of interruptions as long as there were not too many, and Cally had promised she would disturb Daddy only when it was absolutely necessary. Eve had used the excuse that she could get a big shop done in half the time without Cally in tow and Gabe had readily agreed to have their daughter with him for a couple of hours, despite his work load. 'Not a problem,' he had told Eve.

Eve parked the Range Rover in the town's small busy carpark and then walked round to the high street, looking for the address on the card she held in her hand. It was a cold autumnal day, but at least it wasn't raining yet.

Eve had thought of ringing ahead, but Crickley Hall oddly only had that one telephone, despite the size of the house, and it was in the hall, which was not at all private. She hadn't wanted Gabe to overhear her. Also, the phone was not the ideal medium for telling a complete stranger the story of her missing son and how she thought the house she was presently living in was haunted.

No, the only course of action was to go to the psychic reader's address and speak to her directly. Telephones were too impersonal for a story such as hers. Of course, it might be that the psychic, this Lili Peel, had moved on – Eve knew that the faded card she clutched in her left hand was two years old, but she was prepared to take the chance. At the least, it provided an opportunity for some required shopping (as she walked she noticed there was a supermarket, albeit a smallish one, along the high street).

She noted the numbers on houses and shops that she passed, once or twice almost bumping into other pedestrians because her attention was mainly on door numbers, which on her side of the road were even. 96, 98, 100 went by, and soon she found what she was looking for. Number 116 High Street, Pulvington, came as a surprise.

It was a tiny crafts shop squeezed between a florist's and a dry cleaner's. The narrow half-glassed door was painted apple green, as was the frame around the window next to it, and the sign stretched above both simply declared in elegant, white script: Craftworks. Displayed in the show window were pots and vases of various sizes painted in either bright or soothing colours. There were also little figurines and statues on display with glass animals and clay dishes, along with pendants and metal earrings, brooches and bracelets, all carefully set out yet nonetheless crammed together. The hanging sign on the glass part of the door said OPEN.

With a short intake of breath, Eve went in.

*

Gabe sat perched on a stool at his drawing board and easel, chewing on the end of an HB pencil. He was none too happy. He didn't know why, but finding the dead bird on the doorstep that morning had spoilt his day. It was unfortunate that it had fallen at Crickley Hall's door.

There had been no sign of Chester when Gabe was on his run. He'd called the dog's name every hundred yards or so, but there'd been no response. The mongrel had well and truly got himself lost. The whole family, but especially Loren and Cally, was upset and, although Chester was only a dog, his disappearance so close to the date of Cam's disappearance nearly a year ago was particularly distressing. The engineer resolved to search a wider area once Eve was back with the car. He had reported the missing pet to the local police but, as expected, they didn't seem very interested.

Before him on a sheet of A4 paper was his rudimentary sketch of the improved machinery that would raise and lower Seapower's marine turbine rotor and drive chain, a much simpler arrangement than they had at the moment, so there was less to go wrong. He'd also suggested a mechanical device that would relieve the system of much of the strain when lifting machinery from the water in strong tides. He would ink in a more detailed specification, sign it, and have a copy sent to APCU's head office for checking by his principal engineer.

Gabe quickly checked out some measurement figures on his laptop, which sat on a small wooden side table that he had brought in from another room. It was at right angles to the board and easel and held items such as set squares, pens, pencils and paper, as well as a couple of engineering manuals. He was pleased with his morning's work, but would go over every detail two or three times to make sure the operation was viable before submitting it. It was only when he was jotting down numbers in a half-filled notebook that he heard the muted sound coming from along the landing.

He smiled to himself. Its source was Cally, playing in her bedroom. She was singing or talking to herself, a common enough trait of kids around her age. He strained to hear what she was saying or singing, but her voice was no more than a muffled drone.

Gabe suddenly had the urge to see her, a response that was not unusual for him, or for any other father of a five-year-old. Resting his pencil on the edge of the drawing board's movable plastic ruler, he slipped from his stool and went to the door of the makeshift office. He listened again and Cally's voice was a little louder.

She was both singing and holding a conversation, probably with one of her dolls, or Jumper, the pink teddy bear. Once in a while he and Eve eavesdropped on Cally's dialogue with her 'friends' and it always filled them with wonder at their daughter's conviction that she truly was conversing with a real person. She would say something in her little girl way, then become silent as if listening to a reply, and then she would respond to that. It made Gabe and Eve chuckle on occasions until they had to creep away, hands over mouths, lest they be heard. Not that it would have made much difference to Cally: she believed what she believed.

Evidently, his daughter was having a fine old time with her imaginary playmates, for giggles interspersed the chatter and songs. Gabe moved out onto the landing and leaned over the balustrade, trying to peer into her room from that angle. He couldn't see her through the open doorway, but her voice was clearer. Where many young children might answer themselves by assuming another voice, Cally never did. Replies were always inside her head.

Intrigued as always, Gabe pulled back from the balcony

and tiptoed along the carpetless landing, quietly taking the turn, slowing his pace as he drew nearer to her bedroom because he didn't want to interrupt her.

When he was within a step of the doorway, a floorboard creaked beneath his foot and it was loud enough to announce his presence.

Cally stopped talking.

Discovered, Gabe stepped into the doorway, a smile on his face, a greeting on his lips.

His jaw stayed open but no sound came out. He blinked in surprise. And in that blink, the tiny bright lights that hovered around his daughter vanished.


As was to be expected, the inside of the crafts shop was narrow, but the ceiling was high and two switched-off paper-ball pendant lights hung low from it. A lamp on the small desk at the far end of the shop was on, though, and its glow brightened the blonde hair of the woman whose head was bowed as she worked on something sparkly on her desk.

Like the display window, shelves and solo stands in the long room were crowded with things to buy. Original paintings adorned the walls, most of them watercolours and all of landscapes or fishing boats; some were excellent, others merely adequate. Sheer but colourful scarves were draped round the necks of white headless busts on the shelves, while more clay and stone figurines along with bric-a-brac and glass vases filled the spaces around them. There were two hat trees, both with straw hats and straw baskets hanging from them. On the solo display stands were pendants, bracelets and brooches, most made of plain or coloured metals; there were rings and more bracelets of coral and seashells, as well as copper and pewter emblems fashioned into signs of the zodiac.

Without even pretending to be interested in the goods on show, Eve walked the length of the shop to where the blonde woman was absorbed in her intricate labour. Eve saw that she was working on a crystal necklace, passing thin black thread through minute silver links pressed into the tops of the stones, all of which were of soft, various-coloured hues. The lamplight glinted off the crystals.

The blonde woman raised her head as Eve approached. She was strikingly pretty, Eve thought at once, her yellow hair shortish but flicked out at the sides, her fringe tethered by a thin leather thong she wore as a headband. Even sitting, she appeared petite, almost fragile, her shoulders narrow, her neck long and finely curved. Her face was pale, her nose small but nicely defined, and her lips were a delicate pink. But it was her eyes that struck Eve most of all, for they were of the palest green flecked with brown, with full dark eyelashes framing them. As interesting as those eyes were, they stared up at Eve impassively, as if deliberately guarded.

Her voice was soft but direct when she spoke. 'Can I help you?'

Eve could not help but feel it was not a sincere offer. She held out the small card she still had in her hand. 'I'm looking for this person,' she said. 'Ms Lili Peel.'

Those lovely but somehow brittle green eyes went to the card. 'That's old.' She looked up at Eve again. 'It's out of date.'

'I know,' Eve replied. 'It's been in a shop window for the past two years.'

She noticed that the woman at the desk wore wide wristbands of small different-coloured beads on both wrists, the sleeves of the soft-knit top she wore only reaching her elbows.

'Are you Lili Peel?' Eve asked.

The green eyes hardened. 'I don't do psychic readings any more.'

Eve felt the disappointment drag at her. 'I'm willing to pay more than your usual fee,' she tried.

'No. I mean it. I don't do readings.' Lili Peel picked up the crystal necklace and resumed threading it as if Eve had already gone.

But Eve knew the blonde woman was still conscious of her; her hands shook a little as she drew the thread through its link. 'Ms Peel, I really need your help. Something is happening and I have nobody else to turn to.'

Still not looking up, Lili Peel said, 'Try the local weekend newspaper, you'll find small ads for spiritualists, clairvoyants, whatever you need.'

'This can't wait 'til the weekend. I have to do something now. Won't you at least listen to me and then decide?'

Lili laid the necklace down and regarded Eve, the hardness still there in her eyes, a lack of compassion that seemed so wrong for such a pretty girl.

'I'm sorry, but I can't do anything for you.'

'You're no longer psychic?' Eve only asked the question because she wanted at least to engage Lili Peel in conversation, take it past the stranger-on-stranger stage.

'You don't choose to be psychic,' Lili said, her voice softening only a little. 'Neither do you choose not to be.'

'But if you can help people . . .?' Eve let the question hang.

'It doesn't always work that way. Sometimes it does more harm than good. Please, I don't mean to be rude, but there really isn't anything I can assist you with.'

'Hear me out, that's all I ask. If you still can't help me – if you don't *want* to help me – then fine, I'll leave your shop and

JAMES HERBERT

won't bother you again.' Tears blurred Eve's eyes and she
tried to control the tremble in her voice. 'I'm so ... I'm so
desperate. Perhaps it will help me just to talk about it.'

She couldn't stop them. Eve had tried to stay in control,
but the tears just came unbidden. She had put too much hope
into something that might only have been a dream or illusion.
She dug into her pocket for a handkerchief.

'I'm sorry,' she said, at least containing her sobs. 'I didn't
mean to ...'

Lili Peel still eyed her coolly, but said: 'There's a chair by
the wall. Why don't you bring it over to the desk.'


Gabe didn't want to frighten Cally; he kept his tone light.
'Hey, how y'doing, Sparky?'

''Lo Daddy.' She went on positioning her little plastic
people around the little plastic house. A yellow Bart Simpson
was somewhere among them.

*She seems calm enough*, thought Gabe. But then, nothing
seemed to faze Cally much. Surely he must have imagined
the lights? Or it was a trick of the light, the sun shining
through remaining raindrops on the window. But then, why
had the lights disappeared almost as soon as he laid eyes on
them?

He went over to his daughter and squatted by her. 'You
having a good time there, honey? Is ol' Bart in trouble again?'

'He's bin good.'

Gabe watched her as she manoeuvred the teeny plastic
people around the miniature house whose whole front wall
was swung open.

'Who were you talking to, Cally?' he ventured cautiously.

'To these guys?' He motioned towards the plastic Lilliputian figures.

'Nowah.' The negative had two syllables, rising at the end as though she was impatient with his dumb question.

'Really? Oh, who then?'

She shrugged. 'My friends.'

'Your friends? The ones you make up?'

'Nowah.' Two impatient syllables again, now uttered with disinterest.

'Well, who then? I can't see anybody.'

'They've gone now. Gone away.'

'Who are they?'

'You know – the children.'

He studied her bowed head for a moment.

'Why can't I see them?' he asked.

She became even more impatient with him. ''Cos you can't, Daddy. I told you, they've gone away.'

'But why didn't I see them before they went, you know, when I came into the room?'

'I 'unno.'

Bart Simpson was becoming a regular pain. 'Tell me properly, Squirt. Why didn't *I* see the kids?'

''Cos they're a secret,' she answered, finally looking up at him.

'I think I saw the lights, those little floating lights. But they went away as soon as I came in. Is that what you mean, are the lights the children?'

'Children are jus' children, Daddy,' she explained as if he were the child and she the adult.

'Uh, do you see them a lot? The children, I mean.'

She shook her head.

'What d'you do when they come?'

'We play.'

He rose to his feet, knowing he was not going to get any more from her. *What is it about this goddamn place?* he asked himself. 'Okay, Sparky –' he began to say, but whirled towards the door when a great banging started up outside on the landing.

Cally stared after him in alarm as he rushed through the doorway.

## 28: CAM

'My son Cameron disappeared a year ago,' Eve began to tell Lili Peel. 'Almost a year ago' – she corrected herself. 'I'd taken Cam, as we always called him, and his sister, Cally – she was four years old then, a year younger than my son – I'd taken them to a local park. Our home is in London, but we're here in Devon while my husband conducts some business with a Devon-based company.' She didn't feel details were necessary at this stage, but the psychic asked a question.

'Where are you living while you're here?'

Eve dabbed at her eyes, the tears all but dried out now, while the misery lingered as always; there was no relief in tears for her.

'Near Hollow Bay. Do you know it?'

'I've visited once or twice.' Lili Peel didn't add that she had never liked the place, even though the harbour village was pretty enough. It was the atmosphere she didn't care for, the unsettling gloom that somehow shadowed the place. She supposed that, as a sensitive, she picked up vibes more easily than other 'normal' people. 'Two years ago I left my card in the shop there.'

'Yes. Of course you know Hollow Bay.' Eve crumpled the handkerchief into a ball in her fist. 'You have no Devon accent, though. You're not from the county.'

'No, I come from Surrey. I moved here seven years ago.'
She'd answered curtly as if reluctant to talk about herself.

Lili Peel must have come to Devon in her early twenties –
she could be no more than twenty-eight, twenty-nine.

'Have you always had the gift?' Eve nevertheless enquired.

'If you can call it that,' the psychic replied. 'I realized I was
different, that I seemed to know things I shouldn't, from the
age of seven. If my parents ever mislaid something – anything
from a sewing needle to the car keys – I always knew where
it was.' She said no more, expecting Eve to continue.

Eve gathered herself, resolving to tell the story of her
missing son without too much emotion. It wouldn't be easy,
not even after all this time.

'Cally was asleep in her buggy, while I watched Cam from
a bench close to the park's play area. He was on the swings,
then at the climbing frame – he seemed to be all over the
place at once. I kept my eyes on him all the time and it was
only later when he wanted to play in the sandpit that I relaxed.
Although the weather was cold and the sand was damp, Cam
insisted on playing in there, so I let him. I thought at least he
could come to no harm; there wasn't any way he could injure
himself. And so, yes, I relaxed for a few moments.'

It was painful for Eve to relive that horrendous day, but
she managed to maintain control. Months and months of guilt
and sorrow had worn her down; going over and over that
crisply cold day in October time and time again in her mind
until she was exhausted with it, tortured by it. Perhaps it was
emotional fatigue that stemmed her tears now.

'I was a freelance writer for fashion magazines back then,'
she went on, even now hating herself for having such a time-
consuming and wearing job, on a freelance basis or not. 'I'd
worked 'til three in the morning to meet a copy date, and I
was very tired. I'd promised Cam and Cally – we have another

daughter, Loren, who's now twelve years old – I'd promised I'd take them to the park the previous day if they left me alone long enough to write my piece.' She smiled wanly. 'As it was, I never really got into the article during the day – too many phone calls, too many other things going on – which is why I ended up working late into the night and the following morning.'

She paused and Lili Peel at least nodded sympathetically.

'I fell asleep on the park bench. I don't know how long for – it felt like seconds, but it must have been minutes, several minutes. There were lots of other children with their mothers in the play area, so I thought he'd be all right. Even so, I didn't deliberately go to sleep; it just happened, sleep just overcame me.'

Eve cast her eyes downwards, away from the psychic's stare.

'When I woke up, Cam was gone. Cally was wide awake and howling to be let out of her buggy so she could play too. It must have been her crying that roused me. I looked towards the sandpit – it was only a few yards away – and Cam wasn't there any more. I looked everywhere in the play area and rushed up to other mothers and older children to ask them if they'd seen Cam anywhere. I asked them if they'd seen anyone take my son away. I was frantic, close to hysteria, and some of the mothers were kind enough to help me look further afield. We split up, each of us going in different directions into the main park, searching, asking people if they'd seen a blond-haired little boy wandering on his own or being led away by some person, man or woman.'

Eve's upper body sagged in the chair as she experienced – yet again – the nightmare.

'But it was hopeless. Cam had vanished. I rang the police on my mobile and they sent a WPC over; together, Cally very quiet in her buggy as if she sensed something was terribly wrong, we covered every inch of the park. The policewoman did her best to calm me down while we looked, but by then I was completely strung out. Because it was October, dusk came quickly, and by then there was a whole team of policemen and women searching for Cam in the park and the area around it. They even drove me back to my own home and scoured it from top to bottom. My son went on the missing persons' list right away, and I believe the police did their best to find him, but we never saw our little boy again.'

Lili Peel's voice had softened only slightly. 'Did you – did the police – suspect he'd been snatched?'

'Eventually a kidnapping was my only hope. And although we never received a ransom note or call – not that we're wealthy anyway – and known paedophiles in the neighbourhood were questioned, the police never found Cam, nor any trace of him – a piece of clothing, a lost shoe. Nothing.'

The psychic's next question was put awkwardly. 'Mrs Caleigh – Eve, are you asking me to contact your dead son for you?'

Eve sat rigid in the chair. '*No*,' she almost shouted. Then, softer: 'No, Cam isn't dead, don't you see? That's why I don't care if you're not a clairvoyant or spiritualist, a medium, whatever they call themselves. I'm certain my son is alive and that's why I'm asking you to use your psychic ability to reach him.'

'Eve ... Eve, *why* do you think Cam is still alive after all this time? It's a hard thing for me to say, but you have no evidence that he's alive. How can you be so sure?'

'Because I would *know* if he were dead, I would *feel* he wasn't here any more. A mother just knows these things. Call it intuition, or – or telepathy, but I truly sense Cameron is still here, still alive.'

She stumbled over her words as she tried to explain, tried to *convince* this person that her son wasn't dead. 'Cam ... Cam ... and I ... we were so, so close. Some of the time – no, *most* of the time we even knew – we even knew what the other one was thinking, something I don't share with my daughters.'

Eve raised her left hand, her fingers straight and joined together. Then she lifted the right one, putting both hands together, palms facing inwards towards herself.

Lili Peel looked at them, mystified.

'You see the little finger on my right hand?' Eve said, jabbing that hand forward an inch. 'You see? It's much, much shorter than the little finger of my left hand.' She joined both hands again, both little fingers side by side.

The psychic saw that Eve was correct: there was a marked difference in the sizes of the smallest fingers, the one on the right far shorter than the one on the left. But she shook her head, not understanding.

Eve dropped her hands into her lap. 'A medium, a credible one I interviewed a long time ago, noticed how my right little finger was shorter than usual and it was she who told me to compare both hands. I suppose I'd never really thought about it before; I'd noticed, but had just accepted the difference, it was of no consequence. But the medium, who'd impressed me during the interview, told me it was a sign that I had the capacity for psychic ability, but that I'd never bothered to use it.'

She briefly showed her right hand again. 'When I informed her my very young son's hands were the same, she said it was a sign that we shared a telepathic link. And it made sense to me. That was why we often knew what the other was thinking, how Cam was always aware when I'd been hurt, even if it was only a stubbed toe. He could be at playschool or somewhere off with his father and he'd know it and would ask me about it when he got home. He was only a toddler, but he would know my moods instantly, whether I was happy or sad, and he'd act appropriately. I didn't sense things in quite the same way he did; his ability, maybe because he's just a child and his mind is still clear and open to such things, has always been stronger than mine. I'd always considered my own sensing of him to be just maternal instinct anyway, even though it wasn't the same between my daughters and me.'

The other woman attempted to calm Eve, who had become quite agitated again. 'Wait, wait a minute.' She held up her own hand to stop her and dropped it again. 'If you both share this extrasensory gift, then why hasn't your son contacted you by now? You might feel within *yourself* that he's alive – and I'm sorry to be so harsh – but why hasn't he let you know?'

'But he has, don't you see? True, I haven't received what you might call a clear "mental message" from him, but I think he's been trying to let me know he's alive ever since he disappeared.'

'You're sure of this?'

'No, I can't be sure! How could I be? I've had my doubts since he's been gone, but that's only natural. I've always come back to the feeling – the *sensing* – that Cam is still here, though. What's more, something happened on Sunday that confirmed those feelings, something that prompted me to come to you.'

One hand clutching the edge of the small desk, Eve went on to describe the events of two days ago, that early Sunday afternoon when she had dozed on the couch in Crickley Hall's sitting room: how Cam – she was certain it was Cam even if she hadn't actually *seen* him; her deepest inner feelings couldn't be wrong – had touched and soothed her after she had been frightened by something dark ... something *evil* that was somehow connected to the house itself. And then waking to find Cam's photograph had fallen onto the floor. She stared earnestly into the psychic's green eyes.

'I *knew* it was my son who made the bad thing go away,' she insisted. 'I couldn't have imagined it all.'

Behind her, Eve heard the shop door open, followed by the heavy trudge of boots on wood flooring. Lili Peel had already looked towards the entrance and Eve swivelled on the chair to see the customer who had entered. It was a woman, middle-aged, portly, a scarf round her head, a closed umbrella in one hand. She was wearing hiking boots, baggy corduroys tucked into the ankles.

The customer frowned back at the two figures sitting at the desk and something must have been conveyed to her, a feeling that she'd interrupted something important and private, for she quickly picked up a stone ornament on a shelf, turned it over in her hand, perhaps to find the price sticker on the bottom, and just as quickly returned it to the shelf. Without inspecting another thing, the woman left the shop, closing the door quietly as she went.

Lili Peel jumped in first before Eve could say another word. She rested her elbows on the desktop, clasping her hands together, and said: 'Because someone has the psychic gift, it doesn't necessarily follow that that person believes in ghosts.'

She lifted a hand again, palm towards Eve, who was about to interrupt.

'As it happens,' Lili Peel went on, 'I do believe in ghosts and the afterlife. So what I want to know is, what makes you so sure that what you saw or sensed wasn't, in fact, your son's spirit, his ghost? It would sound more reasonable to me.

Spirits have been known to move material objects, so why not the photograph? Why do you think it was telepathy rather than contact with your dead son's ethereal spirit?'

Her eyes bore into Eve's with a coldness to them, a kind of brittle hardness that could not be easily broken.

'Because Cam gave me hope again,' Eve responded immediately. 'I had almost given up, almost come to believe Cameron *was* dead, I just couldn't find it within myself to accept it. My doubts have been steadily growing stronger these last few months; but on Sunday, after what happened, the feeling it left me with, I knew, just knew, Cam was alive and trying to contact me through his mind. He's trying to tell me where I can find him.'

The psychic was silent for a few moments, as if she didn't know how to react. Then those green eyes hardened once again. 'I'm sorry,' she said, 'but that's not enough.' Her tone was still curt, as if she were determined not to accept Eve's conviction. 'It doesn't mean your son is alive. The opposite, if anything.'

Eve's own voice became curt. 'What if I told you he was being helped by others?'

'What do you mean by that?'

Eve, undaunted by the younger woman's attitude and without a trace of self-doubt, went on to explain what had been happening in the house they were renting, the rappings, the small pools of water, the cellar door that refused to stay shut. She told the psychic about the running footsteps she and her family had heard coming from the attic dormitory. She told Lili Peel about the spinning top and the dancing children that she *and* Cally had witnessed, the small faces at the dormer windows. Eve told her that eleven children had perished in the house, drowned in the great flood of 1943.

'This house,' said Lili Peel. 'What's it called? It has a name, doesn't it, not a number?'

Eve was surprised by the question. 'Yes. It's called Crickley Hall. Do you know of it?'

A shadow seemed to pass over the psychic's face. She stared intently at Eve. 'I was told about the floods when I was last in Hollow Bay. When I gave my card to the shopkeeper to put in her window, she read it and said if I was a psychic I should go up to Crickley Hall. Plenty of ghosts up there, she said, then she told me about the flood and the children, and that nobody had ever stayed at Crickley Hall for long. It was an unhappy house, she said, and I thought that in a strange way she enjoyed telling me about it. I remember passing the place – across a short wooden bridge, the shopkeeper said, a mile or so up the lane – and I remember I shivered when I saw it. There was a terrible depression about the place, not unlike the depression that hangs over the village itself, only this was stronger, more concentrated.'

'Then you do think it could be haunted? Haunted by those poor children.'

'I didn't say that. I've never been inside, so I wouldn't know.'

'But you said there was an atmosphere – a depression – about it, which you felt even though you were only passing by.'

'Some houses are affected by the tragic things that happen in them. It's as if the walls retain the memory. It doesn't mean they're haunted, though.'

Lili Peel was silent for a few moments. Then, abruptly: 'No, I won't – I can't – help you.'

Eve was dismayed. After all she had told the psychic, how she'd poured out her heart to her and had thought she was being believed. Despite her curtness, Eve had thought Lili Peel was sympathetic. Now she was refusing to help her.

'Haven't I convinced you?' she asked at last, almost pleadingly.

'It isn't that, although I wonder why, if as you say your son and you have always shared a telepathic link, he hasn't let you know his whereabouts psychically.'

'Because our mutual ability, *especially* mine, isn't strong enough. That's why I need you.'

'But what can I do?'

'You can help me find my son. If I do have any power it's too weak to strengthen the psychic link with Cameron. If you're genuinely psychic, it shouldn't be too difficult for you. I'm not interested in ghosts, I don't care if Crickley Hall is haunted or not; all I want you to do is talk to Cam. I know you can succeed where I've failed.'

Lili Peel was suddenly suspicious. 'What does your husband feel about this?' She had leaned back in her chair, one hand remaining on the desk, the other falling to her lap.

'He . . . he doesn't know about Cam coming to me.'

'That's curious. You haven't told him?'

'Gabe is awkward about this kind of thing. He doesn't really believe in it.'

'He's heard noises, has seen some kind of evidence, as you have, hasn't he?'

Eve gave a shake of her head as if dismissing her husband's part in the matter. 'He has heard noises, yes, and he was the one who discovered the puddles that appeared from nowhere. Gabe thinks there's a natural explanation for it all. But then he hasn't experienced what I have.'

The psychic exhaled a short but heavy breath, perhaps one of annoyance, Eve couldn't be sure.

'How do I know you haven't imagined these ghosts?' the

psychic said. 'You seem distraught, you're obviously still in deep grief over your loss. Depression mixed with hope and anxiety can do a lot to the mind, can make you believe in the impossible. Perhaps even cause you to hallucinate. I think a doctor might help you better than I'm able.'

'I'm not mad, I'm not imagining.' Despair was provoking anger in Eve. 'I'm not hallucinating.'

'I'm not suggesting you're mad. But you are overwrought and that can—'

'*Please, won't you help me?*'

Lili Peel was startled by the fierceness of the outburst. When she spoke again, it was calmly, but determinedly. 'I no longer use my gift, Mrs Caleigh. Not deliberately, that is – I can't stop sensing some things, but I no longer practise as a psychic.'

'But why?' Tears had again formed in Eve's eyes.

'I'm sorry, but I want you to leave now. Your problems aren't mine, and I don't want them to be. I can't help you.'

Eve was defeated. There was nothing more she could say to change Lili Peel's mind and she knew it. The expression on the other woman's face was resolute. Eve was beaten.

She slowly rose to her feet, gave one last look of appeal to the psychic, who refused to meet her gaze, and left the shop.

Eve couldn't quite understand how – or why – the meeting with Lili Peel had ended so abruptly.

# 29: HIDDEN

Gabe shifted the cardboard boxes, dumping them unceremoniously outside on the landing. Cally watched as he ducked back inside the cupboard, her first finger crooked over her short little nose, the thumb of the same hand lodged between her milk teeth. Daddy looked very serious.

The knocking he and Cally had heard coming from the landing cupboard again stopped even before Gabe touched the doorknob, but he was determined to find its cause this time.

The boxes were not heavy and through the open lid of one Gabe saw it contained cleaning utensils and liquids – a bottle of Jif and another half-filled bottle of green detergent, bleach, a scrubbing brush and one or two pieces of wrinkled rag, as well as a duster. This was obviously where Crickley Hall's regular cleaners stowed their gear for the upper floor; he had already removed the mop and broom.

Only the rolled-up rug remained inside the cupboard and Gabe snatched it up and threw it out onto the landing. *'Okay, you son-of-a-bitch,'* he muttered under his breath, *'let's see what you're hiding.'*

But all he could make out at the back of the cupboard was the wall that for some reason had been painted black. The two thin waterpipes that were low to the floor disappeared through a small hole cut out of the wall's left-hand corner and Gabe bent low to study it. No animal, mouse-size or otherwise, could have squeezed through the space between the pipes and the edge of the cutout. He ran his fingers along the floor, feeling for any other holes at the base of the wall, but there were none.

Carefully, he backed out, rising as he went, making sure he didn't bump into Cally, who was watching from the doorway.

'Have you found somethink, Daddy?' she asked, staring up at him as he loomed over her.

'Not yet, honey,' he replied. 'Gonna need more light.'

He took his daughter by the hand and led her to the top of the stairs.

'Wait right here, Sparky,' he instructed her, 'while I go get me the flashlight.' He held up a finger in front of her face as if the gesture would augment the command, then hurried down the broad staircase, taking two steps at a time, too agile to miss a step. The flashlight had been left by the telephone on the chiffonier and he quickly grabbed it, switching it on in advance as he mounted the stairs again. Cally was waiting right where he had left her, thumb in her mouth, eyes wide with curiosity and just a little nervousness. He gave her a reassuring smile and tousled her hair as he passed. Striding back to the open landing cupboard, he realized he should have also brought his toolbox with him; he might need a long screwdriver or claw hammer to prise up a floorboard or two.

Gabe stooped to enter the cupboard again and Cally peered round the doorframe. Once through the door, he was able to straighten, although not to his full height; the interior ceiling wasn't high enough for that and it slanted downwards towards the back. Shining the torch beam around, he examined walls, floor and ceiling more thoroughly, checking for openings that rodents might use. There weren't any.

He briefly wondered why anyone would bother to paint the back wall black, and that made him curious. He moved further into the cupboard, stooping low, and the circle of light from the torch became smaller, more concentrated, on the rear wall's pitchy surface.

Looking at the edges all around, he noticed that the paint slightly overlapped the surrounding walls and floor, as if whoever had done the painting had been a little slapdash. Whatever the reason for the colour, it made the cupboard look deeper than it really was, the slope of the ceiling adding to the illusion. He pressed the black wall with his fingertips, testing its solidity, then rapped on it with his knuckles. It sounded hollow.

A false wall? Now that could be interesting. The wall sounded and felt like it was made of thin wood. When he had pressed the surface it seemed to give slightly.

Going down on both knees, Gabe inspected the edges once again, this time more carefully, seeking any flaws or breaks that could be used for leverage. But the black paint had been laid on so thickly that all four sides were sealed.

*Shoulda brought the toolbox up with me*, he admonished himself again. *Coulda sliced through the paint with a blade or screwdriver, used either one to pull out the whole partition.*

He hunched, stretching himself forward to examine the corner where the waterpipes passed through the wooden wall.

'Whatcha doin', Daddy?'

He looked over his shoulder to see Cally cautiously poking her head into the cupboard.

'Gonna try something. You just hang on out there.'

''Kay.'

Gabe dug the index finger of his left hand beneath the lowest pipe and felt the hole beneath it. The bottom corner of the black-painted board had been cut away to allow the pipes access so that there was a small space underneath the lower pipe.

'Might work,' he told himself as he hooked his finger around the edge of the wall. Gabe gave the wood a tentative tug and was surprised when the rear wall moved a fraction with a loud *crack*. He renewed his efforts, pulling harder this time, no longer testing the board's strength, and the crack was as sharp as a starter pistol when the wood came away a few inches. In the beam of his flashlight and through the curls of disturbed dust, Gabe saw that all the sealing paint along the floor and part of one wall had split. Encouraged, and with more space for a better grip, he wrapped his fingers around the edge of the wood and pulled as hard as he could.

The wooden board that served as the cupboard's rear wall suddenly came away with an even fiercer cracking and he realized that it had only been nailed at the sides to long thin stanchions, the nail heads covered by the black paint, making them invisible to the eye.

Cally expelled a frightened cry at the sound and jerked away from the cupboard doorway, her hands flying to her face. Gabe hadn't noticed; he was too busy shining the light through the gap he had made. The partition was still partly attached to the right-hand stanchion, but by holding back the bottom edge and crouching even lower he could see there was something behind the false wall. Something that obviously had been *hidden* back there.

## 30: THE PUNISHMENT BOOK

Eve gathered up the two plastic bags full of shopping from the back seat of the Range Rover. She hadn't bought much from the supermarket in Pulvington, but enough to justify her visit to the town. She had been too distracted to concentrate on a full shop, so had bought only essentials that would get her family through the rest of the week. She would tell Gabe the supermarket was too busy and too noisy for her to stay long.

Overhead the sky had clouded up again, dulling the afternoon and promising an early dusk.

She closed the car door with an elbow and, logoed shopping bags in either hand, she made her way across the bridge towards Crickley Hall. There was a thin green slime on some of the damp boards, which made the bridge slippery, and she went with care. The river below looked angry and brown with loose soil that had broken off from the riverbanks further upstream and she wondered how much more rain it would take to make it overflow; she was sure the level had risen since that morning. Halfway across she glanced up at the Hall's rooftop windows as if expecting to see small colourless faces peering down at her. There was nothing there, though; nobody was watching her. Nevertheless, she felt exposed.

Dejected because her visit to the psychic's crafts shop had

proved so disappointing, Eve took the path leading across the muddy lawn to the house's front door, her boots crunching on the sparse gravel. Her head was bowed, not with the physical burden of her load, but with the mental burden of her despair. She was helpless, powerless on her own to make the vital contact that she knew her lost son was seeking, unable to complete the telepathic link between them by herself. What could she do now? Consult another psychic? That would take time and there was an urgency in her that she herself did not quite understand. Somehow she knew it was important to find Cam soon, before . . . before it was too late . . . She would have to look for another psychic, then.

Perhaps irrationally, she could not face having to explain herself to Gabe. She was only too aware of his frustration with her, no matter how well he concealed it, and she feared that her endeavours now would finally end his patience with her for not coming to terms with their loss. But she would never accept it, not while there was still a chance, not when there were signs . . .

Eve went past the front door, making for the kitchen door instead, so deep in her own thoughts that she failed to notice Gabe standing by the table through the window. She turned the corner and laid one of the shopping bags on the step so that she could use her key, but Gabe beat her to it.

'Hey,' he greeted, reaching for the shopping bag in her hand. He took it from her, then stooped to collect the other one.

'Hi,' she returned as she stepped inside. 'Has Cally been okay? She didn't bother you while you were working?'

'She's the best, no problem at all. She's taking a nap right now.' Gabe frowned. Eve seemed to be avoiding his eyes as she unzipped her coat and hung it on the rack by the door.

'Chester?' she queried over her shoulder. 'Anything?'

'Uh-uh. Still missing.' He silently cursed himself for using the wrong word: too many connotations. 'I rang the police again, but no stray dog's been spotted or turned in,' he said quickly, to move from the 'missing' word. 'Told me they'd get their patrolman for this area to keep a lookout.'

For the first time she noticed the old gardener sitting quietly and unobtrusively on the other side of the kitchen table. She was feeling too low to be surprised.

Eve greeted him with little enthusiasm. 'Hello, Percy.'

'Missus.' He nodded his head without smiling at her. His cap was in his hands on his lap, but he hadn't removed his storm coat.

'Percy was outside working on the flowerbeds,' said Gabe, 'so I called him in to take a look at this stuff.'

Now Eve saw what was on the kitchen table. Curious, she moved closer.

A book of about the size and proportions of an account-ant's ledger lay next to a long wooden stick. Its stiff black cover was dusty – someone, probably Gabe, had obviously wiped it with his hand, for there were streaks across the surface where the black was more intense. The cover's cor-ners were wrinkled, as if battered by wear, and a label, yellow with age, had been glued onto it. Written on the label in neat capital letters that, although faded, were still legible, were the words:

PUNISHMENT BOOK

Eve realized then that the wooden stick lying next to the book was a thin bamboo cane, one end of which was split into even thinner slivers of at least six inches in length. It was the type of cane that, in a different era, some teachers used to beat disobedient or unruly schoolchildren. And just in front of Percy, as if he had been studying it before Eve came in, was a creased black and white photograph. But it was the Punishment Book that really drew her attention.

'My God,' she said, 'what *is* this?'

Gabe waved a hand that took in all the items laid out on the otherwise unoccupied kitchen table. 'It's some interesting stuff I found earlier. Know where they were?' The question was rhetorical; he went on. 'Behind a phoney wall inside the landing closet.'

He told Eve about the now familiar noises he and Cally had heard coming from the upstairs cupboard, the loud knocking sounds, and how he had discovered the black-painted false wall that some time in the past had been used as a hideaway. 'It wasn't very deep, just enough space for the book and cane. Oh, and the photograph over there by Percy.'

Gabe picked up the cane with the split end and sliced it through the air, bringing it down hard on the black-covered book.

*Swish–thwack!*

Eve flinched at the harsh sound it made. Dust billowed up from the book.

Gabe lifted the bamboo cane again and this time brought it down gently onto the palm of his hand. 'See how the ends splay out when they hit. Now imagine it hard against a kid's hand, or leg, or butt. You'd have to be a sadist to use it.' There was no humour in Gabe's tight-lipped grin.

'Cribben?'

'Yeah, Augustus Theophilus Cribben. Cribben, custodian and headmaster to those evacuees back in '43. This place was supposed to be a safe haven for 'em, out of reach from those German bombs that were blitzing the big cities in the last world war. Huh! Some haven.' Gabe indicated again, this time pointing the cane at the big black book. 'S'all in there, written up, all the things he did to those kids, everything recorded in detail, dates and all.'

Percy spoke up and there was a bitterness to his words. 'The man was evil, cruel. Oh, a good Christian all right, an' highly thought of by some in these parts. But they didn't know, not the authorities, nor our own vicar, who wouldn't listen to me, wouldn't take notice, always insisted Cribben were a God-fearing man who believed in strict discipline for children. Well, Cribben might've been God-fearing, but he were no good! Wrong in the head, to my thinking, righteous but wicked underneath. Him an' his sister both. Magda Cribben was a cold-hearted woman, in her way just as cruel as her brother.'

Percy's pale watery eyes had become moist and they stared straight ahead, looking neither at Eve or Gabe as he remembered the past.

'Nancy told me about the things that went on in Crickley Hall behind closed doors, but I don't think she knew the half of it. Otherwise she'd have done something about the situation. Instead she just up an' left. Or so we was told.'

Now he did look directly at Eve, his eyes troubled. She remembered his tale of Nancy Linnet, the young teacher who had become his sweetheart all those years ago, and Eve couldn't tell if the regret in his eyes was for Nancy and their doomed relationship, or for the children who had suffered so much in this place. She picked up the black book from the table and opened it.

God, Gabe was right, she thought, staring at the neat, rigid handwriting: there were names and dates, punishments accorded as well as the reasons for them, all written down in dulled-by-time blue ink. The reason for punishment was the same in every case: misbehaviour. And as far as Eve could tell, none of the children appeared to have escaped it, for all the names she remembered from the church's memorial board were mentioned, some more than others. And the dates started around late August 1943, apparently soon after the evacuees had arrived at Crickley Hall.

Eve turned several pages, glancing at the names and punishments, the latter of which were marked down 4, 6 or 10, presumably denoting the number of strokes of the cane that were dealt out each time.

'It goes on page after page,' remarked Gabe as he returned the cane to the table. 'Seems not a day went by without some of the kids being disciplined. Percy tells me there were other kinds of penalties for misbehaviour too, like making the kids stand on one spot in the hall all day, wearing nothing but their underwear.'

'Nancy tol' me about the punishments.' Percy shifted awkwardly in his seat. 'She said the children often went without food for the day, or was forced to take cold baths. Sometimes, when Cribben were in a rage, he laid about them with the thick leather belt he always wore, but mostly he used the stick. Nancy tried to put a stop to it, but the Cribbens wouldn't listen, said the kiddies was being purified, atonin' for their sins, like.'

Eve considered the page she had stopped at. 'This boy Stefan Rosenbaum is mentioned more than most; he seems to be on nearly every page. Didn't you tell me he was Polish and could hardly speak any English? Wasn't he just five years old?'

The old gardener nodded. 'Five years.' *Foive yers*, it sounded like.

'But why was he punished so much? Was he that naughty?'

'None of 'em was, Missus Caleigh. They was all good kiddies. Bit lively when they first arrived, but that were soon knocked out of 'em. No, Cribben had a special dislikin' for the little Polish boy.'

'Turn towards the middle of the book,' Gabe advised Eve and she did so.

The handwriting had changed: it was looser, sometimes a scrawl, sometimes too big, sometimes almost illegible. Still it went on, though, and she turned more pages, the handwriting changing dramatically as if the author was gradually becoming deranged, the punishments becoming more severe and more frequent. Soon it seemed like the hand of a lunatic. Ten strokes of the cane, fifteen, twenty. And Stefan Rosenbaum's name came up consistently. A five-year-old boy being beaten like this! Why Stefan, why so cruel to him in particular?

As if reading her mind, Gabe said, 'Now move on to some of the later pages. You'll see Cribben's handwriting gets even worse, like he's totally flipped. And you'll see why he picked on this kid Stefan so much.'

Eve leafed through the pages faster, no longer reading each individual record, absorbing the pages as a whole. And then she got to it. The true reason for punishing the same boy over and over again.

The scrawl had descended to an erratic scratching by now. But the word that stunned Eve was clear enough, for it was in spiky capital letters and gave the reason why Stefan Rosenbaum had been constantly punished. It simply said:

# 31: THE PHOTOGRAPH

The word had been written crudely, almost brutally, as if its author was enraged – no, was *disturbed, mentally disturbed* – and the contempt it revealed was so unequivocal that Eve was shocked. She actually gasped.

'How could he . . .?' The words petered out.

Percy leaned towards her, one bony and callused hand resting on the table between them. 'There's some people, them what went through the last world war, who like to forget it, don't like to be reminded of how the Jews was hated in them days. Lotsa people even blamed the war on the Jews, thought Hitler had the right idea when he tried to rid Germany an' other countries of 'em. An' that kind of bigotry ran through all classes, rich or poor. Even some royalty shook hands with Hitler afore the war got started.'

'But . . . but Augustus Cribben was a teacher,' Eve protested. 'And he was a guardian of the children. How could he be a bigot? His background must have been checked by the Ministry of Education and whoever was in charge of evacuation. Surely his sentiments would have been discovered.'

'How?' argued Gabe. 'They'd hardly ask him if he had a thing against Jews, would they? And even if they did, he only had to lie.'

'Oh, Cribben and his sister knew how to play the part, all

right,' put in Percy. 'They was admired an' respected when they first came to Hollow Bay. They was looked upon as righteous folk; a little bit unsociable, mind, a little bit standoffish, but otherwise upstanding people as fer as the locals was concerned. Our vicar in them days were certainly impressed with 'em, like I told yer afore, missus. The Cribbens could do no wrong as fer as old Reverend Rossbridger were concerned. That's what broke him when the rumours went about after the flood.'

Eve shook her head in dismay. 'But to victimize this young boy just because he was Jewish. How did Cribben get away with it?'

'Things that went on inside these walls was kep' secret. Who would the kiddies tell? They was kep' away from outsiders an' when they was seen – like goin' to church Sunday mornin's – they was always behaved, never spoke to no one. But they couldn't help the way they looked, couldn't hide the misery on their faces. Course, people hereabouts jus' thought the orphans was well disciplined an' didn't look any further than that. Folks didn't want to, the war brought 'em problems of their own.'

Percy's hand dropped to his lap again and he wrung his cap out as if in regret.

'Cribben and his sister, Magda, had the kiddies trained, y'see. Nobody could tell if there were anythin' wrong with 'em, save they was quieter than the local children would ever be. Cribben even had me rig up the swing that's still in the garden today so anyone passin' by would see the kiddies enjoyin' 'emselves. He only let them out there two at a time, mind, an' that were only at weekends. My Nancy told me it were Magda Cribben's idea, lettin' the kids play outside. She knew the things goin' on inside Crickley Hall weren't right, but she supported her brother. Afraid of him too. But her heart were stone. In her own way she were worse then him, 'cause she were a woman an' should've had more compassion for the orphans. Well, she pushed 'em on that swing, only it were like another punishment for 'em when nobody were passin' by. She pushed 'em too hard an' too high, so in the end they was terrified. An' Magda, she liked that, liked to see 'em cryin' 'cause they was terrified.'

Eve closed the Punishment Book and put it back on the table. Gabe slipped a hand round her waist, aware of her distress.

'So, they were all badly treated,' she said grimly, 'but little Stefan suffered most of all just because of his race.'

Percy nodded, then picked up the photograph that had been lying on the table in front of him. He held it out to Eve. 'You only had to see Cribben an' his sister to know they was wicked. This were took afore Nancy left Crickley Hall. You can see fer yourself how unhappy the orphans was.'

Eve was almost reluctant to take the photograph; she already had enough grief of her own without looking for more. Her hand trembled slightly as she examined the old creased black-and-white picture, and she realized her heart was racing. It had been a traumatic and disappointing morning, and now this.

Percy came round the table to stand beside her so that he, too, could look at the photograph. Gabe dropped his hand from Eve's waist, although he remained close to her. He had seen the photograph earlier, but he was still drawn towards its images.

It was an eight-by-six print, probably taken with an old-fashioned glass-plate camera, the negative as large as the picture itself, and it showed two rows of children, the taller ones at the back, with two adults sitting on chairs in the centre of the front row. The orphans and their guardians were outside on the lawn, Crickley Hall's big front door plainly visible behind them. The images were extremely sharp and the contrast stark, the black areas quite dense.

Eve suppressed a shudder when she gazed at Augustus Cribben and his sister Magda.

The man could have been anywhere between forty and sixty years of age. His hair, which was bushy on top, but apparently razor-shaved at the sides, was completely white, while his bushy eyebrows were dark. He sat ramrod-straight on his chair, a lean man with high cheekbones that emphasized hollow cheeks. Large ears, accentuated by his cropped hair, stood at right-angles from a severe face. His nose was prominent above a grim slash of a mouth. Beneath those bushy eyebrows were deep-set black eyes that stared stonily at the camera. There was no humour in that harsh, sober face and no softness, and perhaps because of what she already knew of the guardian, there appeared to be no pity.

Cribben wore a tight-fitting tweed suit, one button done up at the chest so that the sides of the jacket fell away to reveal the shiny buckle of a thick leather belt. His shoulders were narrow and the hands that rested over his knees were big-knuckled, arthritic-looking. The tidy knot of his plain tie did not quite reach the stud of the high, white, detachable collar of his striped shirt; the jaw above the collar was strong and square, although the little that could be seen of his neck was thin and scrawny.

Next to this slight yet formidable figure sat a hard-faced woman, who presumably was Cribben's sister, Magda. There was a resemblance between them, for the eyes were black and deep-set, and seemed to regard the camera with suspicion. Like her brother's, Magda's nose was prominent, as was her chin, and her lips were thin and severe. High cheekbones and rigidity of posture completed the similarity.

Her matt black hair was parted in the middle and scraped back over her ears, presumably into a bun at the back of her neck. She wore a long black dress that was gathered at the waist, and hemmed just above black lace-up ankle boots.

Eve allowed her eyes to roam away from Augustus Cribben and his sister, both of whom seemed to dominate the assemblage, and they fell upon the girl – the young *woman* – at the end of the back row.

'Is this the teacher you told me about?' she asked Percy, her thumb indicating. 'You called her Nancy . . .'

'Aye, that's Nancy Linnet, may her poor soul rest in peace.'

'You think she *is* dead?'

'I know she is.'

Eve looked at the girl whose shiny hair fell in tumbling locks round a sweet childlike face. Over her shoulders she wore a shawl, the ends of which covered her forearms, and Eve remembered Percy telling her that the teacher, his sweetheart, had a withered arm: was Nancy deliberately covering up the deformity? The teacher's eyes were large and pale and, although she wasn't smiling, there was no meanness in them – but no joy either.

In fact, no one in the photograph was smiling. All the children were like little waifs, solemn before the camera, no spirit to their expressions or their stance. But wait – there was one boy with not a smile but a grin on his long face that revealed a missing front tooth. He stood at the back near the middle of the line and was taller than all the other children, as tall as Nancy Linnet.

Eve pointed as she angled the photograph towards the old gardener. 'Is this the boy called . . .' She tried to recall the name Percy had mentioned.

'Maurice Stafford,' Percy replied. 'Yers, he could afford to smile, that boy.'

'He's the only one who looks happy,' observed Gabe, leaning over Eve's shoulder.

Percy nodded. 'His is the only name yer won't find in that Punishment Book. He were old for his age, he were, and the only one that Nancy never liked, said he were a sneak and a bully. Maurice were treated different from the others. I don't say he had it easy, but fer some reason Cribben an' his sister favoured him.'

'Which one is the Jewish boy Stefan?' Eve asked, although she was sure she had already spotted him.

Percy confirmed her choice. 'Right there in the front row, the smallest of 'em all. He's standin' in front of the tall girl, Susan Trainer, who looked out for the boy, sorta took him under her wing, like. See, she's got her hand on his shoulder.'

Stefan Rosenbaum wore baggy short trousers that covered his knees, his socks round his ankles. He was a thin child and his jacket, which was done up at the front with three buttons, was at least two sizes too big for him. His thick dark hair hung low over his brow and his eyes were wonderfully deep but melancholy. He had an elfin look. Like the other orphans, his face was solemn, yet there was a beauty about him that reminded Eve of her lost son, Cameron. Even though this boy was dark in looks where Cam was fair – yellow hair, bright blue eyes – they both possessed the same kind of innocence. As renewed despair struck her, she quickly gave the photograph back to Percy. She turned towards Gabe who, although taken aback, held her gently.

To Percy, he said: 'Those two kids – what was it, Maurice . . .?'

'Stafford,' the aged gardener filled in for him.

'Right. Maurice Stafford. I don't remember seeing his name, nor Stefan Rosenbaum's, among the headstones down at the cemetery.'

'No, yer wouldn't. It's 'cause they was the two whose bodies was never found. It's reckoned they were swept out to sea by the river that runs underneath Crickley Hall. The Low River.' Percy shook his head gravely. 'They jus' disappeared,' he said. 'The sea never gave 'em up.'

Lili brought the glass to her lips and swallowed the wine rather than sipped. Its fruity sweetness failed to elevate her mood.

The room in which she sat was lit by only a single corner lamp, so that shadows filled the other corners. Her living quarters were above the crafts shop: three main rooms, one of them a bedroom, another, the smallest, used as a stockroom for goods not yet displayed in the shop downstairs; the third was her living/dining room where she relaxed or worked on delicate stone, shell or crystal jewellery and trinkets, using the dining table as a workbench. Both the kitchen and bathroom were tiny, the latter accommodating a small sink, toilet and shower basin (there was no room for a bath). The walls throughout were painted in soft pastel shades, and oddly, given Lili's profession, there were no pictures adorning them, nor ornaments or statuary on shelves to take away from the plainness of it all.

Listlessly, she rested the stem of the wine glass on the arm of the brown leather chair she occupied and closed her eyes for a moment.

Why did this woman have to come to her? she silently asked herself with a bitter kind of anger.

Lili had curbed her psychic abilities eighteen months ago,

frightened by her own powers and their consequences. Some things were best left well alone; some things could bite back. How strange that the woman, this Eve Caleigh, should come from the same house that Lili had stopped to observe on her way out of Hollow Bay two years ago. Crickley Hall. People in these parts maintained it was haunted, the woman in the village shop had confided. The two women who cleaned and dusted the place every month would only work the rooms together; neither one was willing to be alone in any part of the house. They claimed that Crickley Hall had an 'atmosphere', a creepy mood to it that made a person feel jittery. That was why no tenants had ever stayed long in it over the years. The house didn't welcome people.

At the time, Lili had mentally rolled her eyes. It seemed to her that every community postulated its own haunted house and it was usually for no other reason than that something tragic or traumatic had once occurred within its walls (often a cruel murder or a dramatic suicide) and now a ghost roamed its corridors. In truth, Lili did believe in ghosts because of her own experiences with the supernatural, but she also knew that many people exaggerated or embellished such phenomena for the vicarious thrill that came with the telling.

Nonetheless, Lili had not just noticed Crickley Hall when she left the harbour village, as she had told Eve Caleigh. No, she had parked her car and studied the house across the bridge for several minutes. She had sensed its chill.

It was not merely the ugliness of the building itself that weighed upon her, but it was because there seemed to be – or at least, she sensed – something bad at its very core. The unease remained with her for some time afterwards.

That was one of the more unpleasant sides of being psychic: the inability to prevent bad vibes from penetrating one's own psyche. It was an affliction she had borne since childhood.

Lili first became aware of her sixth sense when she was seven years old, although there may well have been earlier psychic occurrences that she regarded as perfectly natural when she was even younger. She had moved with her family into a large Victorian house in Reigate, Surrey, and her bedroom had been at the very top of the three-floor building. Soon after moving in, the spirit of a girl, no more than nine or ten years old in appearance, had manifested itself as Lili played with her dolls in her bedroom. Although so young – or perhaps *because* she was so young – Lili had immediately, and without any fear, accepted that the girl, who wore old-fashioned clothing, was neither of Lili's own world, nor of her own time. It was all perfectly reasonable to her, even though she could not recall any similar event in her past. Being an only child, she welcomed this new playmate into her home. The stranger never touched anything of Lili's, but would sit attentively on her heels while Lili showed and named every one of her dolls and cuddly fur animals and related little stories about them. Sometimes Lili sang her ethereal friend a short song and then the other girl would sing one of her own. Some of these Lili had heard before, for many nursery rhymes are timeless.

The girl informed Lili that she was called Agnes and that she had died in this same room from something they called diphtheria a long time ago, and ever since she'd been dead, she hadn't known where she was supposed to go. Her death had been sudden after only four days of the illness and she had risen from her proper body to see her mother wailing on her knees beside the bed as her father stood stiffly by with just one teardrop running down his cheek. Agnes had been con-fused and frightened for a long while afterwards and she had not dared to leave the house for fear of becoming lost. She had gradually come to accept her condition and, although no longer afraid, she still preferred to keep within the walls of the only home she had ever known.

Eventually, her parents went away and other families lived there for long intervals at a time. But none had ever noticed her, even though she had done her best to make them aware. Lili was the only person Agnes had been able to talk to and be seen by, and she was pleased finally to have a companion.

Lili's parents had often heard her talking to an invisible friend in her room and they questioned their daughter about it. In her innocence, Lili had told the truth. Her mother and father, however, assumed the girl wearing old-fashioned clothing was inside Lili's own head, a figment of her lively imagination, and had left it at that, believing she would soon grow out of it. After all, lots of little children had imaginary friends, didn't they?

For at least six weeks the ghost of the Victorian girl continued to appear to Lili, always when she was by herself and in the same upstairs room. They played and giggled together, enjoying each other's company, although Lili sometimes became frustrated because Agnes could never catch a ball, or use a skipping rope, or pick up a toy. Apart from that, they got along fine.

It was only when Lili told her spectral friend about a place called Heaven that there came about a subtle change in Agnes. Lili's daddy had told her this was where the angels lived and where good people who had died went to. Agnes's image began to falter; she was not so clearly defined any more. Still they continued to play together, until one day, soon after she had learned about Heaven, Agnes declared she had two important questions to ask Lili: 'Shouldn't I be in Heaven too? Am I a bad person?'

JAMES HERBERT

Lili had readily assured Agnes that she was a *good* person, otherwise Lili wouldn't have liked her. And yes, probably she should go up to Heaven, although Lili would miss her terribly.

The Victorian girl came back to Lili only once more after that and Lili could barely see her, so transparent had Agnes become. She told Lili that she kept hearing someone calling her and that she could feel herself slipping away. She implored Lili not to be sorrowful if she left because Agnes would always remember her. She said she had the same sort of feeling when Father used to tell her that they were all going on a journey; she felt happy because she knew they would travel to somewhere that was different and exciting, but sorry because she always hated leaving her lovely home. So she felt happy and sad at the same time. But she wasn't afraid any more, not since Lili had told her about Heaven.

The voice she heard calling her had become very strong, though oddly never loud, and she felt a presence, as if someone were waiting for her in the same house but in another room.

At first, Lili had asked Agnes not to leave, because they were friends and she would be lonely without her. But soon she realized that Agnes wanted with all her heart to go to the place she felt sure was Heaven. Even that young, Lili knew it would be selfish of her to beg Agnes to stay and she truly wanted what was best for her friend.

The apparition of the young girl from another era dimmed even more before Lili's eyes, and then something wonderful happened.

A tiny, brilliantly radiant light, round and no bigger than a marble, entered the room through the closed door. Swiftly the remnants of Agnes's fading form became nothing but a radiant light too. The little brightly glowing ball of light that was now Agnes hovered in front of Lili for a few seconds, and

250

then it glided towards the other light; they joined, fused together, became incandescent. For a brief moment their shine was dazzling, lighting up the whole room with their effulgence and causing Lili to blink. When her eyes opened again, the coalescent glow was gone. And curiously, although Lili would miss Agnes, she felt nothing but joy for her.

Lili Peel had never forgotten that first experience of the supernatural. Certainly, she had seen other ghosts since then, but nothing compared to the beautiful fusion she had witnessed, or the deep sense of calming peace she had felt that day. She would never forget her friend Agnes.

Over the years, Lili's extrasensory capabilities revealed themselves and developed, much to her parents' amazement and concern. How she had acquired such a gift was a mystery to them for, to their knowledge, nobody in their families' history had ever possessed these kinds of powers.

One night at the age of twelve she had burst into the kitchen in floods of tears, alarming her mother and father, who were having a late-night snack. Through her sobs she managed to tell them that Uncle Peter, who was abroad at the time, had just died. Nothing could console her – certainly not common sense – but in the early hours of the following morning her father received a phone call from South Africa informing him that his brother had been killed in a car accident the previous night.

At thirteen, Lili had a talent for finding lost or forgotten household articles and for knowing the exact location of neighbourhood dogs and cats that had strayed from their homes. By fifteen, she had the weird ability to discover facts about a person merely by touching or holding inanimate objects associated with them. When she was seventeen and attending art college, she had become adept at telepathy, psychometry and clairvoyancy, and her reputation as a psychic had grown. Soon she was giving 'readings' not only for friends and family, but also for perfect strangers who had heard of her reputation.

She did not often communicate with the deceased, but when she did, the results could sometimes be startling. Because the bereaved took comfort in such sessions, Lili continued with them, but limited her sittings to just once a week, for they also left her totally drained afterwards. However, if distraught parents begged her to contact their recently demised son or daughter, she would invariably oblige. Because of Agnes, Lili could never refuse to help where a spirit-child was involved.

But all that was long before the *incident*. It was before she was frightened of what she might conjure when calling on the dead.

Crickley Hall. A tomb of a place. A mausoleum. Unwelcoming, somehow hostile.

It may have just been the chill of her sitting room, but Lili gave a little shiver. Driven raindrops tapped on the window behind her like a thousand fingernails.

Again she asked herself why Eve Caleigh had come to her for help. Why now when Lili was still struggling to make herself immune from the past? It had been eighteen months since the *incident* and still she had not recovered, had not been able to close her mind to it. Why wouldn't the woman understand that Lili no longer wanted to use her psychic powers? Why had she persisted so? And why did she have to tell her of the child spirits trapped inside Crickley Hall? For that was what they were – trapped souls that could not move on. All ghosts that lingered in places they had known when alive were just souls that had lost their way, or were tied to the earthly plane by incompleteness, or by some traumatic experience, that left them shocked, even in death.

But Eve Caleigh was only interested in finding her missing son, a boy who had been gone for a whole year. Why did she believe her son was alive when there was no evidence to prove it? No sightings, no ransom notes, and from what Lili could gather, no suspects either. Yet she maintained that he was trying to communicate with her in some telepathic way. Could that really be so? It was not unusual for many mothers to have a special intuition where their children were concerned, there was nothing too peculiar about that. But then, even if the boy were still alive, could Lili find him?

Perhaps if she had an article of his clothing, or a favourite toy, something – anything – he was familiar with. No! Stop it! It would be plain stupid of her to deliberately start using her extrasensory abilities again. Often it couldn't be controlled, sometimes thoughts just entered her mind, feelings arrived unbidden, but now she knew there could be danger in just that. Opening herself to the spirit world could leave her vulnerable and she had vowed never to let that happen again. Not after last time.

Yet there were still the other children to consider, the orphans Eve Caleigh said had drowned in Crickley Hall all those years ago. It was no wonder that the old house exuded such a negative aura, such a dreadful gloom. It was obvious to Lili that the children were bound to the house by something awful that had happened to them there. That is, of course, *if* what Eve Caleigh had told her was true. Not that she would have lied – what would be the point? – but if she was still so distressed over the loss of her son – overwrought and close to hysteria, it seemed to Lili – then what might be going on in her imagination?

# JAMES HERBERT

But ... Lili bit into the corner of her lower lip. But alive or dead, there was a child involved. And just maybe other children too, young orphans who, according to Eve Caleigh, were haunting the house. Something must be preventing them from passing over. Something about Crickley Hall was stopping them from resting in peace.

When she had paused to look at the big house across the river two years ago she had sensed a conflict within its solid walls, for something seemed to reach out and touch her, something indefinable that called without voice but whose beckoning left her shaking with fear. She had watched Crickley Hall – yes, *watched* it as if it would suddenly disclose the dark secrets she *knew* it held – and the tension that gripped her stayed with her for days.

Now Eve Caleigh wanted her to go back there, to return to a place that had made her tremble. But could she deny the woman her help? And if she did help her, would Lili be inviting back the horror that had manifested during her last séance? The psychic never wanted that to happen again.

## 33: FIFTH NIGHT

It had been a good day for Loren.

Now she was tucked up in bed reading her new Philip Pullman, Cally fast asleep in the bed next to her. Loren laid the book down on her lap for a moment and smiled to herself.

The news was all around school. The new girl had bopped Seraphina Blaney on the nose. Loren had become something of a celebrity, because nobody in their year, all eleven- and twelve-year-olds, had ever had the courage to stand up to the bully before, and certainly no one had ever punched her! A lot of the girls had chatted to Loren today, plying her with questions about the incident on the bus, which Tessa Windle had duly reported to her classmates, who had spread the word so that by the end of breaktime most years knew about it. At lunch, some of the older girls and boys even said 'Hi' to Loren. In truth, she had been nervous of coming in to school today, because she'd had a whole night to think about what she had done. What if Seraphina intended to get her own back? What if she were waiting for Loren on the bus when it picked her up on the way to Merrybridge? Loren wasn't kidding herself that it was anything more than a lucky punch yesterday; Seraphina would be well over her shock by now and might be looking for revenge. Loren wasn't sure she had the nerve to do the same thing again.

Fortunately, something good had happened: Seraphina hadn't turned up for school that morning. Loren had been so relieved that she'd felt light-headed for most of the day. Perhaps she'd broken the big girl's nose. If so, would her parents complain to Mr Horkins, the headmaster, or go straight to Crickley Hall and make a fuss? Even worse, they might have gone to the police and made a complaint. Loren had half-expected a policeman to turn up at school to arrest her! As the day went by though, nothing had happened and Loren's nerves had begun to settle. Everyone had been so nice to her, with Tessa being particularly friendly, and Loren thought she might start to like Merrymiddle.

Yawning, Loren closed her book, first marking her page with a Post-it, then putting it aside on the bedside cabinet. Eyelids already drooping, she reached up and switched off the lamp Dad had put there, and lay flat on her back. She pulled the duvet up over her chin and around her ears, and stared at the ceiling, the only illumination coming through the half-open door from the dull landing light.

Her weary eyes remained open for a short while as she wondered why she always felt so tired in the evenings nowadays. She even woke up tired, but was okay once she got to school and mixed with the other pupils. And she'd be fine for the rest of the day; it was only when she got home that she began to feel worn out.

It was this house. This house made her tired, with its chill and its draughts, and its weirdness. Just thinking about how tired she was caused her to yawn once more.

Rain lightly struck the window. She liked hearing the rain when she was all snuggled up in a warm bed. Why was Crickley Hall always cold despite the radiators and the fires Dad lit in different rooms?

Loren turned onto her side and shut her eyes. She could hear Cally's gentle snores.

As she fell asleep she was thinking of Chester. She hoped he wasn't out in the rain somewhere. She hoped someone had found him and taken him into their nice warm home. Don't worry about Chester, Dad had said. He's a smart cookie, he'll have found somewhere cosy . . .

Loren slept.

It was long past midnight when Loren stirred. Someone was tugging at the duvet.

'Cally . . . stop it . . .' she muttered in her sleep.

But the tugging continued. Through a half-conscious haze she realized that someone was pulling the duvet off her. Still not quite awake, she tried to draw the bedcover back over her shoulder, but it resisted. Loren suddenly became aware of being very cold, and this rapidly brought her to her senses.

The duvet resumed its slide off her body, pausing and moving in stages. Loren felt a prickling at the back of her neck, as if the cold were causing goosebumps. The hair on her head stiffened.

She was awake, eyes open wide. The room was dark save for the muted light coming through the doorway. She could just make out Cally's small shape in the bed opposite.

Loren became aware of an odd smell. It was like . . . it was like detergent, something Mummy might use cleaning the house. Or was it just strong soap? If it was, it was like no other soap she'd smelled before. It was so strong . . .

Loren tried to lift her head from the pillow and found she couldn't. It was as if she were paralysed. Paralysed with fear.

For there was something at the end of the bed. She could sense its presence.

In the periphery of her vision she could make out a shape at the foot of the bed. A hunched shape. The dark shape of a body leaning over her feet. Pulling at the duvet.

Loren managed to open her mouth to scream, but no sound came. It was as if her voice were paralysed too. She attempted to rise, but still couldn't move: fright held her pinned to the bed.

Lying there on her side, she felt the cold on her bare arm, then down her side, penetrating the sleeveless cotton nightie she wore. Her flesh crept.

The duvet slithered over her hip, down her bent legs, left leg over the right; the hem of her nightdress had risen as she slept, and now her thigh and calf were stippled with goose-bumps. She fought against the fear that bound her there, desperately tried to raise her head – she needed to see what lurked at the end of the bed. Her head lifted, came off the pillow, just a little, only a bare inch; and then, Loren fighting all the way, it gained two inches, three, more. And now she endeavoured to twist her neck so that she could confront her tormentor.

Who could it be there pulling, dragging, her bedcover? Not Cally – she was too small, so much smaller than the figure hunched over her. Besides, Cally was opposite her, fast asleep, unaware of what was happening. And not Mummy and Daddy – they wouldn't do such a thing, they wouldn't frighten her so! Who then? That smell, that horrible smell of nasty soap.

Now her head moved, but her shoulders were stuck to the bed as if a heavy weight pressed them there. Her face came round to the dim light.

And she saw the figure rising from its bent position,

standing erect. It was silhouetted by the light behind so that she could see no features, nothing she could recognize. And it was raising an arm into the air, over its head. And the arm was holding something long and thin whose tip nearly touched the ceiling. It seemed to vibrate at its zenith.

Loren heard the *swish* as it came down, but she didn't hear the *thwack*! as it lashed her naked thigh.

The blinding, scorching pain released her voice because it overrode all else – all fear, all confusion, all thoughts of fright.

Loren screamed and the sound ripped through the night.

Again the stick came down and again she was jolted by excruciating pain. Now she did not even hear the *swish* as it swept through the air.

She screamed each time the cruel stick, with its splayed end, cut into the flesh of her legs, marking them, the agony streaking through her whole body.

And then, it stopped. Although the terrible pain lingered. And when, through tear-soaked eyes, through her hysteria, she looked towards the light again, the figure had gone and Cally, awakened by her sister's tortured cries, had started screaming too.

## 34: SCREAMS

Gabe was roused from his slumber as soon as the first scream came from his daughters' room. Eve, who had got into the bad habit of sometimes taking a Zopiclone to help her sleep at night, was slower to wake. She grabbed Gabe's arm as he scrambled to get out of bed.

'What is it?' she asked as the last dregs of sleep were banished by alarm.

'Loren,' he said urgently, throwing back the bedclothes. 'Something's wrong.' In bare feet he rushed to the bedroom door, Loren's agonized screams almost causing his limbs to lock and freeze. He was along the landing and tearing into Loren and Cally's room before Eve had even left their bed.

Although consumed by fear for his daughter, he could not help but register the deep iciness of the room – it was like plunging into a mountain lake or stepping inside a freezer storage unit – and it almost stopped him dead. In sheer reaction, he flicked on the light switch by the side of the door and saw Loren lying uncovered on her bed in a foetal position, her shoulders curled inwards, her arms round her legs. As she screamed, billows of breath vapour were expelled from her open mouth.

Cally was sitting up in bed, rubbing her eyes as if just

awakened, and her cries were not as forceful, nor as shrill, as her sister's.

Before going to Loren, Gabe quickly checked out the bedroom, looking for an intruder. It took but a second to see there was none. He ran to his daughter, Eve coming through the door behind him, and went down on one knee beside the bed.

Loren's eyes were closed and her pale face was drenched in tears. He reached out a hand to her shoulder and she flinched away, her eyes snapping open, a wild hysteria in her glare.

'Loren, it's me, Daddy. What's wrong, what happened?' He pulled her close and comforted her as Eve moved round to the other side of the narrow bed to reach her.

'He-he-hit-me!' Loren cried through chest-heaving sobs. Gabe did his best to calm her.

'Easy, Loren, easy now,' he soothed. 'You've had a bad dream.'

'N-no, Daddy. He hit me. He hit me.'

Eve moved nearer and when Loren felt her presence, she turned and buried her face into her mother's chest.

'There's no one here, Loren,' Eve told her gently. 'There's no one who could have hurt you.'

Gabe grabbed Cally from her bed and held her in the crook of one arm. She stopped screeching immediately, intuitively aware that it was her sister who needed attention.

'What is it, baby?' Eve was saying quietly to Loren. 'What frightened you? Did you see something?'

Loren's panted sobs went on.

'It must've been a nightmare,' said Gabe, his voice equally quiet. 'There's nothing in the room.' Just to make sure, he ducked his head under both beds. 'And nothing could've got past me in the hallway.'

Loren gave a great shudder as if the frigid air had got into her flesh. But Gabe felt it was no longer as cold as a moment before. The room was still chilled, as was the rest of the house, but when he breathed out there was no misty vapour.

Eve hugged Loren tight against her and began a soft rocking motion. 'It's okay, Loren. You're safe now. Mummy and Daddy are here. Tell us what you dreamt.'

Loren suddenly jerked away from her mother, although she stayed in Eve's comforting arms. 'It wasn't a dream, Mummy,' she implored, wanting to be believed. 'Someone hit me. Hard. With a stick.'

She buried her head back against her mother again, and Gabe and Eve's eyes met, both thinking the same thing.

*It couldn't be*, thought Gabe. *That would be crazy.* He gave Eve a little shake of his head. He'd left the bamboo cane he had found earlier that day locked up in a downstairs cupboard, along with the Punishment Book.

Eve stroked Loren's hair. 'But there's no one else here, baby. Nobody could have hit you.'

Loren yanked herself away again, her tears held for a moment. She twisted round to Gabe as if for support. 'He hit me across the legs, Daddy. He hit me really hard.'

'Who did, honey?' he asked. 'Who hurt you?'

'The man. He was standing at the end of the bed. He was holding a stick and he hit me with it, on my legs. I think he made me bleed!'

As one, Gabe and Eve looked down at Loren's bare legs. There wasn't a mark on them.

Loren followed their gaze and searched her own skin for the wounds the long stick should have inflicted. 'But he hit me, he did hit me! It was as if the stick was scalding hot and the pain spread out, like he was hitting me with a lot of sticks.'

Both Gabe and Eve remembered the cane they had examined that afternoon was split several times at one end so that it would act as a flail when struck against anything.

It was Eve who asked, 'Does it hurt you now, Loren?'

The twelve-year-old stifled her sobs once more as she stared at her own body. Slowly she turned to her mother, and then to Gabe.

'No,' she said. 'It doesn't hurt at all any more. I'm not even sore.'

She broke down and Eve took her back into her arms.

## 35: WEDNESDAY

They left the house just before 7.30 a.m. the next morning, Loren protesting, insisting she was all right now, she didn't need to see a doctor. The sun was shining, but leaves were heavy with raindrops that had fallen in the night. The family crossed the bridge and climbed into the Range Rover.

Gabe had phoned one of his new work colleagues who lived in the area, apologizing for the early-morning call before asking him the whereabouts and the phone number of the closest GP's surgery or clinic. Then Gabe rang the latter, which was a health centre, but only got a taped message advising that the centre opened at 8 a.m.; it also gave the number of an emergency doctor if required.

The night before, Gabe had wanted to rush Loren to the A and E department of the nearest hospital, but she had pleaded with him, she was okay, she didn't want doctors and nurses poking her and asking questions. Surprisingly, Eve had agreed with her daughter. There were no marks or weals on Loren's body, no signs at all that she had been beaten with a stick. Wait 'til morning, she had suggested, see how Loren felt then. Their daughter certainly wasn't suffering any pain now.

Gabe had argued that there had to be *something* wrong.

Loren's screams were not just because she was frightened, but because she was being hurt too. Even if it was only a terrible nightmare, there had to be something not right because dreams couldn't cause genuine pain. If she'd imagined the whole thing, that also meant something was wrong with her. Dreamt or imagined, it had been *real* to Loren. She needed to be medically examined in case there really was something physically wrong inside her body, even if it was only severe night cramps.

In the end, they had agreed on a compromise: Loren would see a doctor first thing in the morning. They had left for the health centre early so that they would arrive before the first scheduled patients, giving Loren a better chance to be seen right away.

Gabe was angry and frustrated, a father who had no answers for his distraught daughter. Loren maintained that there had been a man in the bedroom, a man holding a stick. Like the stick – the cane – he had found hidden away behind the false wall in the closet? he wondered. She hadn't been able to describe the intruder because he was in shadow, the light coming from behind. It must have been imagined! Or dreamt! It was this goddamn house. There was something peculiar going on inside Crickley Hall, something that caused hallucinations. Some houses had personalities, didn't they? That's what some people believed and maybe they were right. A house that fucked with the mind. Eve had been affected by it, become a little weird, wanting to stay whereas before she couldn't wait to get out of there. Now Loren had been touched by it. And Cally. Could they have been sunspots he'd seen floating round her yesterday? Or something else, something unreal?

They had to leave, find a different place to rent. It would take a day or two to arrange – no, it would take at least a week, probably more – to organize. But he'd get on with it. They were moving out.

Gabe switched on ignition, shifted into gear, and three-point-turned the Range Rover so that it was pointing uphill. They headed for Merrybridge.

# 36: INTRUDERS

The sister and brother with the impossibly ambitious names tramped along the road. Although the sun shone brightly enough, the air was damp and their anoraks, one blue, the other red, were zipped up to their chins.

A green van passed them heading uphill, as were they, the driver giving a short blast of the horn as he went by. Neither the girl nor the boy bothered to wave back.

'You sure?' Seraphina asked of Quentin.

Her swollen nose was a different colour to the rest of her podgy face: red and sore-looking, its yellowish bridge merging with the purple-yellow at the inner corners of her deep-set eyes.

Quentin, tall and stocky, looked back at her – his sister had a hard job keeping up with him on the steep road. 'Course I'm sure. I saw them driving off when I was doing my egg round.'

His hardworking mother, besides cleaning other people's homes for a living, kept a chicken hutch in their backyard. It was her son's job to collect eggs in the morning before school (from which he was temporarily suspended) and deliver them to various customers in the area. Fresh eggs for breakfast brought a good price and Trisha Blaney needed the extra money. Cleaning did not pay particularly well, despite all the

hours she put in with her friend and neighbour Megan, and
since Trisha's husband Roy had walked out on her and the
kids six years ago, any money she did earn was already spent.
Not that her estranged husband had ever done much to bring
home the bread when he was around. Idle and dim-witted he
was – their son Quentin was of the same mould, had to be
pushed into doing anything – and if truth be told, she had
been glad to see the back of him.

Seraphina, not being one for climbing, nor even for walking far, puffed and wheezed as she straggled behind.

'Yeah, but you sure they won't come back?' she said to
her brother.

Quentin slowed his pace to let her catch up. He was used
to the hill road because of his morning rounds. 'Won't take a
minute to leave it on the doorstep.' He held up the plastic bin-
liner he carried, something heavy bulging at the bottom of it,
and waggled it in the air. 'Be a nice surprise for 'em.' *Noice
sorproise for 'em.*

Seraphina drew level with him. 'No,' she said breathlessly.
'I don't wanta leave this one outside like the pigeon. This
present is going inside the house. Right into her bed.'

'Don't be daft, you can't do that. What if they catch us?'

'Look, I got the key from Mum's drawer so we could do
it. I'm not gonna waste the chance.'

'She'll go demented if she finds out.'

'Mum only cleans the place once a month. She don't need
the key for a coupla weeks yet. She won't notice it's gone.'

'I dunno, Seph. It's dodgy.'

'Don't be such a minger. We'll be in and out, no problem.'

'You don't know where her bedroom is.'

'We'll easy find it. She'll have Barbie Dolls and things,
little girly stuff.'

'You only wanta get your own back, just 'cause she punched your lights out.'

'Shut up, Quenty. You weren't there, you don't know what happened. I wasn't looking and I fell over.'

'She decked you, you mean. Anyway, it got you a few days off school.'

'I weren't going in and letting everybody see what she done.'

'You're lucky Mum's so soft on you. She'da packed me off to school all right if I come home with a busted snout.'

'It ain't busted.'

'Good as.'

'No it's not. It's just swelled up a bit.'

'And red. Like one of them baboon's bottoms.'

'Shut up or I'll make you go into the house on your own.'

Quentin stayed silent. His younger sister could bully him because she was a lot smarter. And she knew things about him that she could tell. Mum wouldn't like him stealing. Or smoking. Or throwing stones through windows when no one else was around. A lot of the time, Sephy put him up to it – she was always winding him up – but Mum wouldn't believe that Sephy could be cruel; much better to do what she said and keep her sweet.

'Let me have another look at it,' his sister called out as she lagged behind again.

'What for?'

''Cause I like looking at it. She won't, though. She'll throw a hissy fit. She'll go to bed tonight, all nice and innocent like, and she'll pull back the blankets and she'll see a bloody great rat lying there. Wish I could be around to see it!'

Seraphina gave a little snigger, an unpleasant sound. Her brother joined in and ran a hand through his spiky hair.

'Why don't you shove it right down in the bed so she don't see it at first? She'd jump in, put her feet down and feel something furry and sticky.'

The stickiness would be the rat's blood. He had cornered it in the chicken hutch, where it was after the feed, and Quentin had thrown the loose brick at it, the brick that helped keep the wire door shut. It had stunned the rat, stopped it getting away, and he had bashed it until it squealed like a baby, and then was dead.

He held the top of the bin-liner for his sister, and she peered in. Like Quentin, she also enjoyed seeing the blood.

'It stinks!' she complained.

'Yeah, it's a rat,' said Quentin drily.

Seraphina raised her head and smirked. 'Fancy-knickers is gonna wet herself.'

Her brother smirked back.

They resumed walking, and though the exercise puffed her out, Seraphina could not stop smiling.

Soon they reached the bridge leading across the river to their destination.

Crickley Hall.

Seraphina didn't like the way the water tumbled over itself to reach the bay. It frothed with impatience.

At least the rain had stopped. Mum said a lot of local folk were anxious about the rainfall lately. It might bring another flood like the big one sixty-odd years ago, some said. The big flood of '43 was a major part of Hollow Bay history and there were even a few in the village who remembered it first-hand. If the high moors could not soak up all the extra rain, then a tragedy might well happen again. That's what some predicted, but Mum had told her it would never be like last time. Higher bridges had been built to prevent blockages, and the river had been widened where it entered the bay, so don't you worry, my pet, the village could never be flooded like before. That's what Mum told her, and Seraphina believed her. Still, she was glad it had stopped raining today.

She stared across the river at the horrible old building. Who would want to live in a house like that? She felt spooked just looking at it. So did Quentin.

'Let's just leave the rat on the doorstep. Like the bird,' he whined.

Seraphina scowled at him. 'I already told you, it's going in her bed.'

'I don't like this place. It gives me the creeps. What if we put it in the kitchen? That wouldn't take a sec, and we wouldn't have to go right inside.'

'No! Stop being such a wuss.'

In truth, Seraphina was a lot more nervous now they were confronted by the house itself, but she wouldn't let her dim brother know it. She was always the leader, and Quentin was always the follower. She couldn't wimp out. Besides, she wanted her revenge.

She jiggled the key in her anorak pocket and felt a thrill at its touch.

'Come on, Quenty,' she said abruptly, hyped up to do the deed.

Quentin took one last, long look up the road before following his sister. He slipped on a plank's greasy surface, but caught himself.

They crossed the wet lawn together, the tall boy close behind the heavy girl, passing by the motionless swing on the way, its wooden seat dark, sodden with rainwater. Just to be sure there was no one at home, Seraphina rang the doorbell, then used the huge gothic door knocker itself, making an attention-grabbing din. If someone did come to the door, she would say her mum had sent her to ask if they wanted any eggs delivered in the mornings. But nobody came and Seraphina grinned at Quentin, a hissed *'Yes!'* steaming from the thin-lipped mouth.

They entered through the kitchen door, using their mother's key. Trisha Blaney had a key because Crickley Hall had been unoccupied a long time now and it was more convenient for the estate manager, who had no desire to visit the property every month just to let the cleaners in.

Seraphina carefully closed the door behind them and they both crept across the kitchen on tiptoe, even though they were certain the big old house was empty. They paused at the kitchen's inner door, which was shut. They glanced at each other for reassurance before Seraphina quietly turned the doorknob.

They sneaked through and found themselves on the threshold of the grand hall. Seraphina was not surprised by its vastness, because her mother had described it to her once.

'Hello?' she called out cautiously, ready to scoot back the way they had come if there was a response. But all was silent. As the grave.

She closed the kitchen door noiselessly, then took in their surroundings.

'Look at all them puddles,' said Quentin, pointing generally at the hall's flagstone floor.

His sister eyed the puddles in surprise. Quentin was right – small pools of water were spread all around the room, mostly in the shallow indents of the worn stone. Then she remembered. When Mum had told her about the hall she had said that sometimes, when she and Megan came in to clean the house, the floor was spotted with little pools of rainwater. She said that Mr Grainger, the estate manager, had had the roof checked out for leaks by one of the builders he regularly dealt with, but there weren't any holes in the roof that they could find. Mum and Megan would mop up, but when they came down again from doing the upstairs, the puddles would be back. It didn't happen very often, but it was a mystery how it happened at all.

Quentin strolled to the centre of the hall and spun round, arms outstretched, face lifted towards the high ceiling, the weighed-down bin-liner in one hand.

'*Hyah!*' he bellowed before coming to a halt and chortling at Seraphina. 'No one here, Seph. Place all to ourselves.'

As she went to join him, she noticed there was one door open in the hall. Well, half open. A musty smell drifted from it and she could feel a draught. She shivered. The house was very cold. She could see Quentin's breath coming out of his mouth, hardly there but still visible.

His shoulders suddenly hunched up to his ears as if the cold had hit him too. Her brother's mood changed.

'Don't like it here, Seph. Gives me the creeps.'

Although the sun shone brightly through the great window over the stairs, there were shadows in all the corners of the room, and the wood panelling of the walls contrived to make the hall seem darker than it really was. Millions of dust motes floated in the sunbeams.

'Let's split, Seph. Look, I'll put the rat on the floor here. They'll see it as soon as they come home.' He bent over, resting the plastic bin-liner on a wet flagstone; he poked in a hand to bring out the stiff, dead animal.

'No!' his sister said sharply, but her voice still low for some reason. 'We're going upstairs.'

Her brother moaned. 'I don't like it.' Something made him frightened and he didn't know what. He needed the toilet. 'Everyone says this place is haunted.' He had straightened, the rat remaining in the bag. He twisted his neck, looked all around, at the closed doors, at the half-open door nearby, up at the galleried landing – *bloodyell, it was dark up there.* 'Come on, Sephy, let's go,' he persisted.

'You can stay down here if you want, but I'm gonna find her bedroom.' Seraphina stepped towards him, splashing through a puddle as she did so. 'Gimme the bag,' she demanded, reaching out for it.

Quentin swung it behind his back, keeping it away from her. 'Don't think you should go up there.'

She huffed irritably, a white mist rolling from her mouth and quickly dissolving. '*Give it me,*' she whispered fiercely.

'Okay, but I'm not staying.' He handed over the bin-liner and Seraphina was surprised at its weight. Dead rats were heavy. She wrinkled her sore nose at the stink that came from the bag. Was it stronger than before?

'You wait for me,' she ordered her brother.

'No way. I'm pissing off. You're welcome to the place.'

Quentin made as if to walk towards the kitchen door, but his sister put the flat of her hand against his chest.

'I mean it, you fucking spazzo,' she said, her mouth shaping into a snarl. 'You just fucking wait – *What was that?*'

Quentin gawped at her. 'What was what?'

'There was a noise.'

'Didn't hear it.'

They looked around, both silent, listening hard.

Seraphina jumped. 'There it was again.'

'Think I heard it that time,' whispered Quentin, his eyes bulging in alarm.

'Where'd it come from?'

'Dunno. Up there, I think.' He lifted his chin, indicating the stairway.

They remained motionless for a full minute. But there were no other sounds.

Seraphina finally let go of a breath that briefly clouded. 'Probably just the house,' she remarked in a murmur.

'Or ghosts.' Despite his fright, Quentin leered at her.

'Shut up, Quenty.'

'You shut up.'

Seraphina made up her mind. 'I'm gonna find her bedroom. You coming or not?'

'Not.'

Carrying the bin-liner in one hand, fingers wrapped tightly round the top to confine the smell, Seraphina strode purposefully towards the broad oak staircase. She muttered something to herself when she trod in another puddle. When she was at the first stair, her foot lifting to take it, the sound came again.

She immediately became still, her foot poised. It had been a kind of swishing noise that ended loudly.

*Swish-thwack!*

It *was* coming from upstairs.

As she craned her neck to see, a shape moved in the darkness of a doorway. It must have been the door to a windowless room, because it was completely black beyond the threshold. No, not completely black: the shape was blacker and it was still moving.

It was the next *swish-thwack!* that galvanized her. She hurried away from the stairs, not bothering to avoid the little pools of water but treading as softly as she could.

'*Quick,*' she hissed to her dumbstruck brother. '*Someone's coming!*'

'*Let's get out,*' he whispered back, at least appreciating the need to speak quietly.

'*No time. Look, in there.*' Seraphina was pointing at the open door she had noticed earlier. It was the nearest exit to them, somewhere to hide. She just hoped the person upstairs hadn't seen them yet.

She pushed her brother towards the opening, both of them treading carefully even though in haste. The sound from the landing above was getting louder.

*Swish-thwack!*

Every few seconds now.

They scuttled through the gap, as quietly as possible, Seraphina tight behind Quentin as though they were playing spoons. By the light that stretched across the hall from the tall window, they could see a stairway leading down to a basement area. Quentin had to descend two steps so that his sister could squeeze in after him.

*Swish-thwack!*

Almost one sound.

Footsteps now. Soft footsteps that made the boards of the stairs under the window creak.

Seraphina pulled the door they hid behind closed; mercifully the hinges did not squeak. She was very careful not to make a noise when the door shut completely. They were in darkness. When their eyes adjusted, they could only make out a line of light from beneath the door. They waited, trying to control their panicky breaths in case they were overheard.

A pungent, musty, dank smell and a soft rushing sound came from below. Seraphina soon realized its source. Her mother had also told her of the well in Crickley Hall's cellar; it dropped to the underground river that eventually joined the

Bay River before reaching the sea. Mum and Megan never went down there, not even out of curiosity. Neither of them liked the idea, but couldn't say why exactly.

Cold draughts came up the cellar steps to chill the girl and her brother even more. Seraphina felt Quentin shivering next to her as they crouched in the darkness and she became aware that she was shivering too. And it wasn't because of the cold.

'Can you hear it any more?' Quentin whispered close to her ear.

She thought she could, but the background sound of rushing water and the closed door itself muted it.

*Swish-thwack!*

Distant.

And then there was a noise behind them. They turned their heads and stared into the pitch-black below, straining their eyes to see and their ears to listen.

It was faint. At first. But it grew slightly louder. A shuffling. Like a shoe scraping stone, underneath the noise of the underground river but audible nevertheless.

*'Oh fuck, there's someone down there!'* Quentin blurted out, his voice shrill, but still a whisper. A very frightened whisper.

*'Can't be,'* Seraphina hissed back. She had caught Quentin's fear. *'The house is supposed to be empty. You saw them leave. We rang the bell and knocked on the door. No one came. There can't be anyone at home.'* She was rambling, trying to calm herself with her own logic.

*Swish-thwack!*

That sounded louder, as if someone were coming down the hall's stairway.

But again, that *thud*-scraping noise from the cellar behind them.

Quentin was scrabbling around for something in the dark;

his elbow kept prodding her. He was looking for something in his anorak pockets.

The boy bit his lower lip. It wasn't in the right-hand pocket. It had to be in the left. A gasp of relief as his shaky fingers closed around the mini-torch he always kept in his anorak. The mornings were growing gloomier as winter approached and he carried the little plastic torch with him on the egg round so that he wouldn't trip over anything in the dark. He brought the torch out now, but his sister caught his attention by swearing under her breath.

*'What?'* he demanded, keeping his voice low.

*'There's water coming in,'* she replied.

Seraphina had been kneeling on the top step, her ear pressed against the door. But she had jerked away when water from the hall oozed under it like slick oil. It had soaked the knees of her blue joggers and was beginning to trickle down the stairs. She stood, careful not to lose her balance and topple backwards. Quentin startled her by switching on the torch.

Its beam was poor, the batteries weak, but a circle of light appeared on the door they hid behind. He lowered the angle so the light went to the bottom of the door.

They saw a broad stream of water seeping through the gap at the bottom, spreading and slowly flowing over onto the first step. The water crept forward until it overflowed onto the second step.

*Swish-thwack!*

Louder than before, but still muffled by the constant flow of the underground river.

*Thud.* Followed by the scraping.

That came from downstairs, from the pitch-black cellar.

His hand trembling wildly, Quentin turned the torch so that its limited beam shone down the steps. They heard the *thud* again. Followed by the scraping on stone, like something being dragged. A leg perhaps, the first sound a heavy footstep.

They barely noticed that the water from outside had reached the third step and was beginning to flow like spring water.

Although the torchlight was feeble, Seraphina and Quentin could make out a small area of the cellar. Something was coming into view.

'*Seph!*' Quentin screeched when he saw what that something was. Most of it was in shadow, but the sight was enough to loosen his bladder so that pee ran down his leg and joined the stream of water that was now flowing like a brook over stones.

Seraphina also screeched at the umbrageous form that stood near the foot of the steps. The shadows emphasized its undefined horror rather than concealed it.

Almost hysterical, Seraphina pushed open the door so hard that it swung wide, the handle smashing into the wall behind. Despite her terror, she halted in the doorway and Quentin, scrambling to get out behind her, gawped over her shoulder.

The hall was flooded as if all the small puddles had expanded into one great lake. The water was shallow, but it completely covered the flagstones. The bigger shock, though, was the figure standing at the turn of the stairs, blinding light shining through the window at its back so that the front was in shade. But not so shaded that Seraphina and Quentin could not see it was a naked man.

The man was skinny and sunlight behind created a halo effect with his white hair. But the image kept fluctuating, fading in and out so that it had no substance. One moment it looked solid, the next it was transparent and they could see the stairs and circular torchère through it. He held something in his right hand – a stick, a long stick of some kind – and as the sister and brother watched, the man raised it high over his head, then brought it down so swiftly it became a blur. The cane smacked against his own thigh, its end splaying over the flesh.

*Swish-thwack!*

Again, almost one sound.

Now Seraphina and Quentin shrieked in terror.

Hand in hand they ran, splashing through the water as they went, their shrieks filling the great hall and echoing off its thick walls.

# 37: GHOST

The plan had been to get Loren to a doctor first thing, have her checked out and, if there was nothing physically wrong with her (she seemed fine this morning, if a little tired – but then with four in a bed again, none of them got a good night's sleep) and her pain last night was not a portent or symptom of serious illness (growing pains couldn't be that violent), they would drop her off in time for school; he would return to Crickley Hall with Eve and Cally, then take himself off to Ilfracombe and get on with the job for which he was being paid. That was the plan. It didn't work out that way, though.

At the health centre, despite the Caleighs' early arrival, all three doctors had eight o'clock appointments. In fact, they had scheduled surgeries running right through the morning to midday. As Loren appeared to be perfectly fine, the clinic's receptionist said she would try to fit their daughter in between legitimate appointments. As it happened, there was a ten-thirty cancellation and Eve and Loren were ushered in to see a doctor while Gabe kept an eye on Cally in the waiting room.

According to Eve later, the congenial doctor, a handsome, short-bearded, middle-aged man who treated Loren with easy-going respect, had carried out a thorough examination of their daughter, prodding her tummy and other places with gentle fingers, pressing hard, though, into the muscles of her legs because she had told him that was where it hurt last night. He listened to her heartbeat and lungs and enquired about her health in general; he also asked if she suffered from depression or if she was hyperactive at all. Did she have mood swings (what girl approaching her 'teens' didn't?) and was she menstruating yet? He asked a score of other questions at the end of which he announced that he could find nothing wrong with Loren, although from the slight pouches under her eyes she looked as if she could do with a good night's sleep. But if Eve wanted, he could send Loren to hospital for further and more extensive tests. Seeing her daughter's negative expression, Eve had declined.

Sometimes, the doctor had gone on to explain, and contradictory to what Gabe had said the previous night, troubled sleepers could have such vivid dreams of punishment that they honestly felt they were experiencing the pain. There certainly were no marks on Loren's legs, no weals, no bruises, not even any redness, so it could only have been a severely traumatic dream experience. Should such dreams continue, then he knew an excellent child psychiatrist to whom he could refer Loren.

Eve told him they would keep it in mind if it happened again.

They left the centre just before 11 a.m. and Gabe rang Seapower's Ilfracombe office on his cell phone (which worked fine in Merrybridge) to let his colleagues know he would be in later. Loren was left at school after Eve had had a word with Horkins, the headteacher. From there the three of them returned to Crickley Hall, where Gabe intended to drop off Eve and Cally before going on to work.

But when they got back to the house, they found a police patrol car in the parking area close to the bridge.

The uniformed policeman was waiting on Crickley Hall's doorsteps, the front door open wide behind him.

'Mr and Mrs Caleigh?' the officer said as they approached.

'What's going on?' Gabe asked, a worried frown creasing his forehead.

'You are Mr Caleigh?'

Gabe nodded. 'This is my wife, Eve.'

The policeman took out a small notebook from his breast pocket and flipped it open. 'Your full name, sir.'

'Gabriel Caleigh.'

'Gabriel?'

'Gabriel.'

The policeman scribbled in his book.

'D'you mind telling us why you're here?' Gabe asked.

'There were more of us earlier,' the policeman responded, stepping off the doorsteps. 'I'm PC Kenrick. I was left to wait for you, sir. Can you tell me what time you left the house this morning?'

'What's this about?'

Eve glanced at Gabe, concern drawing her features.

'If you would just answer the question.' The policeman was eye to eye with Gabe.

'About seven thirty, perhaps a bit later,' Eve said quickly. 'We took our daughter to the health centre in Merrybridge.'

'This little girl?' PC Kenrick indicated Cally, who sidled up behind her mother's legs at the attention. She peeked out at the policeman.

'No, our other daughter, Loren,' replied Eve. 'We dropped her off at school on the way back.'

'And this is the first time you've returned?' He directed the question at Gabe again.

'Uh-huh. We left the centre about eleven. Took Loren to Merrybridge Middle School and came straight back here.'

'Who else occupies the house apart from yourselves?'

Gabe was perplexed. 'No one else, just us. Look, can you tell us what this is all about? And how did you open the front door?'

The officer had decided to consult his notebook at that moment. 'Uh, yes, sir. Sorry. The outer kitchen door was already open when we arrived, although we also had its key. We unlocked the front door from the inside.'

'Who's we and how did you get the key to the kitchen?'

'My sergeant and two other officers. We obtained the key from someone who'd already been inside the house. That was the, uh, complainant.'

'The complainant? Who the hell is that?'

'If you'll let me ask the questions, sir.'

'Well, what's the complaint?'

'Better that you let me ask the questions for now, sir.' There was no West Country in the PC's voice. 'I will inform you as to what this concerns in due course.'

Gabe looked at Eve, then shrugged resignedly. 'Go ahead,' he said to the policeman.

Although PC Kenrick was watching him closely, it was an indifferent stare. *He must be all of twelve years old*, thought Gabe. *Okay, maybe in his early twenties. Young and keen, polite but breakable. Stay cool*, Gabe advised himself; Kenrick was only doing his job, but his guardedness was a little irritating.

'Were you alone in your house some time this morning, Mr Caleigh?' the policeman asked.

'It isn't my house. We're only renting the place for a while.'

'Yes, we were informed of that.'

'Informed by who?' questioned Eve.

'The victims' mother. The mother is actually the complainant.'

'Victims' mother?' Gabe was becoming more intrigued by the minute.

'She and another lady are Crickley Hall's regular cleaners. Now, if we can continue with the questions?'

'The answer is no, I haven't been on my own in the house this morning. I told you – we took our other daughter to see a doctor.' He couldn't tell if the policeman was satisfied or not.

'You're saying the place was empty after you left at around seven thirty? No one else has been staying with you, a relative, or a friend?'

Gabe shook his head. 'No one.'

Kenrick considered this for a moment. He said: 'Does anyone else have a key to the property, anyone other than yourselves?'

'The realtor—' Gabe caught the policeman's frown. 'Sorry, the estate agent would obviously have a set. I guess the cleaners must have a set too.'

'They only have the kitchen-door key. Which is how the victims gained entry. The girl stole her mother's key, the mother being one of the cleaners.'

'I don't get this "victims" thing.'

Eve butted in. 'Officer, it's time you told us what this is all about. If there have been trespassers in the house, then it would seem we're the victims.'

'I was coming to that, Mrs Caleigh.' PC Kenrick slipped his notebook into the breast pocket of his uniform jacket.

'Earlier this morning while, it appears, you were out, two children – well, the boy is a youth, thirteen or fourteen years of age – say that a man exposed himself to them inside Crickley Hall.'

Eyebrows raised in astonishment, Gabe and Eve looked at one another again. Gabe turned back to Kenrick.

'Say what?' he said incredulously.

'A naked man came down the hall stairs and frightened them. They said he was carrying a thin stick that he beat himself with.'

The same thought whirled around inside both Gabe and Eve's head. The punishment cane. It couldn't be: Gabe had stashed it away in a kitchen cupboard along with the book and the photograph. But what man could have got into Crickley Hall? Eve's face paled.

'Hey, wait a sec,' Gabe suddenly said. 'There is another person who I'm sure will have a key, maybe the whole set.'

'Who might that be, Mr Caleigh?' The policeman was interested.

'Percy Judd. He's Crickley Hall's gardener and handyman.'

'Gabe!' Eve was shocked.

'Yeah, I know. It's unlikely.' Gabe addressed the constable: 'Look, he's in his eighties and I don't think he's the kinda guy who'd wander around without any clothes on.'

'Do you have an address for this Mr Judd?'

'No. He lives further up the hill, I think, somewhere off the road. I'm sure anyone down in the village would know – it's a pretty tight community. Or try the local vicar; Percy works around the church.'

'I'll follow it up.'

'You'd be wasting your time,' commented Eve. 'I'm certain he'd never do anything like that.'

'You know him well, Mrs Caleigh?'

'No, not well. But he's a harmless old man. A nice man. It's just not possible.'

'As I said, I'll follow it up. Can you think of anyone else who might have got inside the house in your absence?'

Gabe and Eve shook their heads.

'Nobody,' affirmed Gabe. 'Have you searched the place?'

'Yes, we've done that, sir. We found the house empty.'

'You looked everywhere?' Gabe was worrying about the safety of his own family.

'Top to bottom. Basement too. By the way, have you had any flooding in the house recently?'

Gabe immediately thought of the pools of water he'd found around the hall and stairs on their first night at Crickley Hall. But he wouldn't call that flooding.

'We've had some leaks,' he replied, 'but nothing serious.'

The policeman looked puzzled. 'Well, we found no evidence of flooding actually, but the boy and girl told us the whole ground floor was covered in water.'

'That's crazy.' Gabe rubbed the back of his neck. 'This is all crazy. Is the house flooded now?' He peered past the policeman into the hall and his own question was answered.

Nevertheless, PC Kenrick replied, 'No, sir. Like I said, we didn't find a drop of water anywhere it shouldn't be, not even in the basement where the well is located.'

'Did you find anything when you searched?' asked Eve.

'No. All we did discover that was peculiar was a dead rat inside a plastic bag in the middle of the hall. But the kids owned up to that. Some kind of practical joke, apparently.'

Gabe remembered the dead wood pigeon on the doorstep; he'd mentioned it to Eve.

Eve spoke: 'One of these children wasn't called Seraphina, was she?' Loren had told her mother the unusual name of the bully she'd punched.

PC Kenrick thought before he answered. They had to be informed sooner or later. 'Er, yes, Mrs Caleigh. Seraphina Blaney. The youth is her older brother, Quentin. Their mother is Patricia Blaney; she was the one who called us after her kids came home in a terrible state. They told her they'd seen a naked man in Crickley Hall. They also said the place was flooded. And oh yes, there was something nasty in the cellar.'

'I'm losing this,' said Gabe.

'What did they mean by something nasty?' Eve had gripped her husband's arm. Cally was no longer hiding but had squeezed between her mother and father to gaze up at the blue-uniformed stranger.

'Well . . . they couldn't describe it, actually. They said that something – a figure, an animal, we don't know yet – came out of the dark; the kids were too upset to get much sense from them. Anyway, it scared them enough to make them leave the cellar.'

'They were in the cellar?' asked Gabe, still trying to take it all in.

'Not down in the cellar; they were hiding behind the cellar door, they told us. Whatever it was – and my sergeant thinks it's only their imagination running wild – it scared them so much it drove them from their hiding place.'

'But what were they hiding from?' Eve was as mystified as her husband.

'Someone they heard upstairs. This was the naked man.'

'With a cane,' said Gabe.

'Holding a stick,' replied the constable.

'And then what?'

'They ran. They left Crickley Hall and scooted back home. According to their mother, both were crying hysterically, and she was so alarmed she rang us. What she did get out of them was that a naked man was involved. Because of that we considered it a significant incident.'

'Significant?'

'Not a major one, but an incident that required immediate investigation. We pay special attention where children are concerned. Unfortunately, the boy and girl were difficult to interview because they were both still in shock.'

'Could they identify the person they saw?' asked Eve.

'Yeah,' muttered Gabe. 'Maybe it was a local . . .'

'I wish it were that simple. You see, the kids said it wasn't really a man at all.'

'I don't get it.' Gabe was frowning again, his blue eyes fixed on the policeman.

PC Kenrick looked slightly embarrassed. 'They said he wasn't clear. He appeared to, uh, to fade in and out. Of course, we didn't search the house on that basis – we were looking for a man who had deliberately exposed himself to children. But according to them, what they saw on the stairway wasn't real. They claimed it was a ghost.'

## 38: THE SWING

Eve finished washing Cally's lunch plate (Eve hadn't felt like eating) and laid it on the draining board where it could dry itself. As she pulled off the yellow Marigolds she looked out of the window with blank eyes, observing the narrow river that swept under the bridge and past the brief expanse of lawn with its oak tree near its centre. There was no breeze today to stir the swing that hung from a stout limb of the oak, but her thoughts were introspective, her gaze inwards, so that she did not notice.

Gabe had gone off to Ilfracombe shortly after the policeman had left and she had not felt comfortable alone in the house with just Cally for company. At that moment, her youngest daughter was in the grand hall, playing with her dolls on the stairs. Eve could hear her small voice as Cally talked to, and for, her eternally smiling, glazy-eyed 'friends' and the sound, distant though it was, was somehow reassuring. The word 'ghost' meant nothing much to Cally because she had only seen the cartoon kind, the Caspers and the rather stupid phantoms Scooby-Doo had to deal with on a regular basis. She was too young to wonder how and why dead people might haunt the living; she merely accepted it as an actuality of no particular importance.

How wonderful to be so undemanding, thought Eve, not

to be in the least disturbed by phenomena that mystified and often terrified older people. Cally seemed to have even forgotten about the 'black' man she had seen in the corner of her bedroom the other night.

'Mummy?'

Eve snapped back to the moment. She turned from the window to see Cally in the kitchen doorway.

'Yes, baby?'

'Can I go outside and play? The sun *is* shining.'

'It's still very damp out there; the grass is wet.' And the unfenced river was too near, Eve warned herself.

'Please, Mummy. Can I go on the swing, will you push me?' Cally tucked one ankle behind the other and gripped her hands together.

Eve felt they both needed fresh air and after all that had happened that morning, Cally deserved some special attention. 'All right, let me get a tea towel to wipe the swing's seat. Just ten minutes, okay? Then we're going to do some reading together.'

'Can I choose the book?'

'No, I don't think so. I want you to try something a little bit harder today.'

Cally pulled a face, but it was gone in an instant.

'You'll need your wellies,' Eve instructed her. 'I'll get your coat; it's still chilly out there.'

'Okay, Mummy.'

Cally ran to the hall rack where coats and hats were hung, walking boots on the floor beneath them; she pulled out a pair of Wellingtons that were bright green and dotted with white spots.

In a couple of minutes they were ready to go outside.

\*

Eve contemplated the frothy river. The water was a murky brown, as if the riverbank further upstream was gradually being eaten away. Even though it hadn't rained that day, the river still looked swollen and enraged. If it should spill over its banks, would it flood Crickley Hall again as it had all those years ago? The two children, the trespassers, had told the police that the hall was flooded, but there had been no sign of it later, not even any puddles or wet patches. Did the house itself trigger such images, did its thick walls remember how the house was once deluged by floodwater? Was it possible for stone and mortar to store memories? It seemed impossible, yet so many strange things had happened since the family's arrival. Eve had always been unsure of her own feelings regarding the paranormal, whether or not events that defied natural comprehension could really occur. Now she was even more uncertain. If her lost son could contact her using telepathy, then why not other phenomena? Accept one instance, accept them all? Her beliefs were being stretched to their limits.

It was good to feel the sun on her back, even though it was a weak warmth, the sun itself watery, as if dampened by the incessant rain of the past week. Behind her, Cally swung back and forth on the now-dried swing, her tiny hands grasped round the rusted chain links, her voice exuberant with the rush of it. Eve had started her off, pulling the swing seat with Cally on it as far back as possible, then letting it go with a firm push, pushing again on its return, using just the right pressure to generate a momentum. Her daughter leaned back, kicking out her legs to keep the rhythm going. It was nice for Eve to hear Cally's hoots and chuckles as the swing reached its zenith, then began its journey back.

'Push harder, Mummy!' came the cry, but Eve used only enough force to keep the swing going. Satisfied that Cally could keep up the momentum herself, Eve stepped back, smiling at her daughter's squeals of delight. Then, diverted by her own thoughts, Eve turned away and strolled towards the river.

Her gaze wandered beyond the tumbling waters and up at the high gorge wall, which was lush with vegetation and full of trees that were either deep green in colour or just turning a golden brown. Crickley Hall was splendidly positioned but, because of its structural plainness – its ugliness, would be more apt – it failed to blend in with the natural surroundings. Which was a shame, a waste. Eve drew in a deep breath, relishing the scented air, refreshing both mind and body, cleansing her thoughts so that for a moment, a moment only, she felt uplifted. She almost felt hopeful once again.

Eve caught something moving in the periphery of her vision. Looking downstream, she saw a large grey heron had landed on a glistening stone embedded in the bank at the water's edge and now its long pointed bill was poised above the flow. It was a long-legged cumbersome-looking bird that might have waded out a little way had the river not been so fierce; all it could do was wait until a fish presented itself close to the bank. It was fascinating to watch, for there was a tension in the air as the bird's S-shaped neck hovered snake-like over the water, its beak almost touching the roiling surface, ready to strike. The heron's neck twitched and then—

And then, a high-pitched scream had Eve whirling round to see what had frightened Cally.

Again, just in the periphery of her vision, Eve glimpsed movement; or thought she glimpsed movement, for there was nothing . . . only a white shadow . . . that might not have been there at all. Cally continued to scream and Eve saw her daughter high in the air, the swing's chains almost parallel to the ground, the swing arcing back again, the pendulum movement fast, too fast, Cally gripping the chains hard, her cries becoming one long screech.

Eve dashed forward as the swing reached its highest point on the other side of the oak's bough. Cally's back was to Eve, her hair whipped up behind her, her short legs kicking at empty air as if to control her flight. Now the swing began its return journey and Eve waited, her arms outstretched, ready to catch it and bring its wild oscillation to a halt. But it came at her with a force so much harder than she expected.

Her arms were easily pushed back by the heavy wooden seat, which hit her beneath the chin, sending her reeling backwards. Her legs gave way and she fell to the ground, the swing with Cally on it rising above her. Eve caught sight of her daughter's white frightened face. The swing began its return journey and Eve, trying to regain her feet, had to duck low to avoid being hit again. So high did it go that Cally almost slipped backwards off the seat, only her tight grip on the chains preventing her from doing so.

It was as if the swing were being pushed by strong invisible hands, sending it too high and too fast.

Eve straightened and readied herself this time, backing away from the swing's flight path, raising her arms, her fingers slightly curled to catch the seat as it flew back at her. It smacked into the palms of her hands, Cally screeching all the while, her pale face sodden with tears, but Eve did not try to hold on to it; she merely slowed its pace.

The next time it came her way she applied the same technique, slowing the swing's ascent so that it lost momentum. On the next swing back she managed to slip her arm round Cally's waist, her other hand grabbing one of the chains. It worked. The swing angled, the chain links almost crossing, but it was blocked by Eve's body. She teetered there for a moment, then dragged Cally off the seat, both of them falling backwards onto the soft wet grass.

Eve lay there, momentarily winded, and Cally sprawled over her.

'Why did you push me so hard, Mummy?' Cally wailed as Eve fought for breath. Through her tears, her daughter repeated the question.

'But . . . but I didn't push you,' Eve managed to say as she struggled to sit upright so that Cally was in her lap. 'I stopped the swing.'

'No, before. You pushed me before. I went too high, Mummy. I was frightened.'

Eve drew her daughter close and looked at the dangling swing that now swayed gently as if all the life had gone from it.

Startled, Eve looked across the kitchen to the window.

The man outside who had tapped on the window smiled and pressed a small card against the glass.

'Andy Pierson,' Eve heard him say, his voice distant. '*North Devon Dispatch*. Can I have a word?'

She lifted Cally from her lap, laying the colourful book on the table.

'Who's the man, Mummy?' Cally demanded.

'I'm not sure.' For Cally's sake she didn't want to say she didn't know. 'You carry on reading or looking at the pictures while I find out what he wants.'

As Cally went back to the book, Eve leaned over the sink to read the card this Andy Pierson was holding flat against the glass. It bore out the man's claim: NORTH DEVON DISPATCH it said with the name 'Andrew Pierson' below in smaller type.

'If I could just have a word with you,' the man called out. 'It's Mrs Caleigh, isn't it? Mrs Eve Caleigh?'

Eve was still feeling a little shaky from the incident with the swing earlier and she definitely didn't feel like talking to a journalist right now, whatever it was about. She was convinced that some malign invisible force had pushed Cally on the swing and the thought frightened her. She was no longer sure she wanted to stay at Crickley Hall.

'Mrs Caleigh?' The reporter still held his press card against the window.

'What did you want to talk to me about?' Eve asked, her voice loud enough for him to hear outside.

'Can I come round to the door, Mrs Caleigh?' At last he slipped the card into the breast pocket of his grey suit.

Eve didn't know what to do. Why was the reporter here? Could it have anything to do with what happened at Crickley Hall early that morning? Surely not. How would he have known about it? Then Eve remembered her time mixing with feature writers and journos when her career had been flourishing. A crime reporter had once told her that he gathered news by ringing round various London police stations – all crime journalists did the same – to find out if anything particularly noteworthy was going on that day or night. Duty officers were always good sources of information, especially if there was a 'drink' in it for them; sometimes the officer rang the journalist first if the crime was exciting enough. Eve wondered exactly what this *North Devon Dispatch* reporter had been told by the local police.

She pointed at the kitchen's outer door and he grinned and nodded his head. He quickly disappeared round the corner of the house to present himself at the door. Eve noticed another man, who must have been standing out of sight, following him, camera hanging from his neck. Oh no, she thought, this was going too far. She didn't want the children's ridiculous story appearing in the local rag. (Yes, but *was* it ridiculous? a sly interior voice asked. Was it any more ridiculous than the other strange occurrences at Crickley Hall?)

When she opened the door, the photographer had caught

up with his companion and was pointing his lens straight at her. He reeled off three shots before she even had time to protest.

Too late, she put up her hand and said, 'Please don't do that.'

'It's all right, Mrs Caleigh, we'll choose a good one,' the journalist assured her silkily. 'Now it is Mrs Caleigh, isn't it? I've got that right?'

'Yes,' Eve was too flustered to say anything else.

'And is Mr Caleigh about? It'd be useful to talk to him as well.'

'My husband's at work.'

'No matter. You'll do fine.'

'We couldn't take a picture of you on the front doorstep, could we?' put in the photographer. 'We could get in most of the house that way.'

'In a minute, Doug.' Pierson waved an arm over the photographer's camera as if to ward it off. 'Give Mrs Caleigh a chance to catch her breath. 'D'you mind if I call you Eve?'

The reporter was a slimmish individual in a TOPMAN suit, his age around thirty, thirty-five. His prematurely balding head was an embarrassment to the thick black growth of hair beneath his nose; the circle of hair above his ears was also darkly lush.

'What is it you want?' asked Eve, one hand behind the open door, ready to slam it shut.

'My paper was informed there was an incident here this morning and the police had to be called.'

'It was nothing, just a mistake.'

'Not according to our source.'

There was very little West Country in his accent. In fact, Andy Pierson had been studiously trying to lose any hint of it for the past ten years, because his ambition was to become a

London reporter on one of the nationals, not with the *Times* or *Telegraph* or anything grand like that, but a red-top, the *Mirror* or the *Sun*, either one would do. Unfortunately, he was not getting any younger and he was still only on the second step of his career ladder, cub reporter and obituary writer being the first.

'Actually, Mrs Caleigh,' the journalist went on as he held up a micro-cassette recorder between himself and Eve, 'I've already spoken to the boy and girl involved, as well as their mother who, I believe, cleans this very house on a regular basis.'

'I don't know what they've told you,' Eve quickly said, 'but what they said happened to them is impossible. I think they're both overimaginative, or they made up the story for their own reasons.'

'They told me – and the police, of course – that they were confronted by a naked man . . .'

'As I said, it's impossible. The house was empty; my family and I were in Merrybridge this morning. There was no one here for them to see.'

'Ah yes, but they claimed it was a ghost, they could see through it, and their mother, Trisha Blaney, told me that folk hereabouts—' he gritted his teeth; he hadn't meant to say 'folk', too Devonshire – 'local people, I mean, believe the house is haunted. Have you got anything to say about that, Mrs Caleigh, have you seen any ghosts in Crickley Hall yourself? You're new to the area, aren't you? Mrs Blaney tells me you've hardly been here a week. But even so, you must've seen or heard something that's puzzled you, maybe even frightened you? You know the kind of thing: bumps in the night, footsteps when there's nobody there, furniture moving by itself, stuff like that. Our readers would be very interested.' He held the mini-recorder almost up to her chin.

'It's utter nonsense,' Eve replied with a conviction she
hardly felt. She turned aside slightly to avoid the recorder,
but it followed her.

'Well, the house does have a history, doesn't it? S'what
I've been told. People – children – died here in the Forties,
didn't they? All drowned, I believe. D'you think what happened today is anything to do with that?' He gave a glance at
the photographer. 'Doug, why don't you go round to the front
of the house and take some pics. Maybe from the bridge, eh?
You'll get a nice backdrop. Make it look sinister, though,
right?'

'It already does,' Doug replied without much enthusiasm.

'Well, you know, use one of them funny lenses of yours.'

Doug, an untidy-looking person with long lank hair and a
drooping moustache, grunted something, then slouched away,
Pentax held before him in one hand, finger on the clicker as
though he would be taking pictures on the way.

'Come on, Mrs Caleigh – Eve,' Pierson said, leaning closer
as if in confidence. 'There must be something a little bit scary
about Crickley Hall, with its history. I mean, you only have
to look at the place to feel creeped-out. Give me something to
tell the readers.'

The truth was, it was another slow night and day for the
*Dispatch*, as it often was midweek. Why do the really juicy
murders always happen at weekends? the reporter wondered
to himself. What was it about Saturday nights that appealed
to killers? Too much weekend booze and disappointment?
And Sunday evenings; they often brought out the worst in
people. Depression, he supposed; the drudgery of work the
next day, the thought of another week's grind ahead. Monday
mornings accounted for a lot of suicides.

'The Blaney kids said the place was flooded.' Now he
leaned even closer to Eve and lowered his voice as though

the conversation was only between himself and Eve and not for general consumption. 'Also . . .' Because she was looking to the side, her head tilted downwards, he ducked a little to make eye contact. 'Also, they told the police there was someone – no, some*thing*, they said – in the cellar that scared the – that frightened them very much.'

'It's nonsense, Mr . . .?'

'Pierson. But call me Andy, Eve, everybody does.'

It came out fast, as if she were deliberately not giving herself time to think. 'They must be on drugs, or sniffing glue, doing something to give themselves hallucinations. You can see for yourself.' She waved her free arm at the kitchen behind her (her other was still on the back of the door ready to close it at any moment). 'No flooding, see? The only water is in the sink. As for something in the cellar, well, the police searched the house from top to bottom and found nothing.'

'So you're saying the kids were on drugs, have I got that right?'

Eve could already see the newspaper headline. 'No, I'm only suggesting that what the boy and girl saw – while they were trespassing, by the way – all they saw was in their own minds. The house is big, and it's dark, and yes, it is rather spooky if I'm to be perfectly honest, but . . .'

She had run out of words; she did not know what more she could say to this man.

'Look, Mr Pierson—'

'Andy, call me Andy.'

'Look, all I know is what the policeman told me when I arrived back here with my husband and daughter this morning.'

'You've got two little girls, haven't you? One's called Laura, but I don't have the other one's name . . .?'

'Cally. And my older daughter is Loren, not Laura.' She

knew the reporter would probably get the spelling wrong, calling her Lauren instead, but she couldn't be bothered to explain it to him. Obviously, Seraphina Blaney and her brother had told the journo enough already. But if she herself played dumb, the story might go away due to lack of detail. It would just be something the brother and sister had made up between them.

Andy Pierson was not about to give up, though. 'Now come on, Eve, tell me something that's happened to you or any other member of your family in the house, you know, something spooky, something for our readers. The public likes a good ghost story now and again.'

'There's nothing to tell,' Eve lied, her voice rising in anger. She remembered Cally was still at the kitchen table, no doubt taking everything in and Eve didn't want her to be upset again. She forced herself to be calm. 'I've got nothing more to say,' she told the reporter and began to close the door on him.

'Wait, Mrs Caleigh, Eve. Give me a proper statement.'

The door was shut in his face.

But he was grinning.

# 40: THE VISITOR

Eve was tucking Cally into bed for her afternoon nap when the doorbell went. It was loud and an ugly sound, an electronic *croak* rather than a musical ring.

Cally's eyelids were already flickering with tiredness and she took no notice of the interruption. Her soft Bart Simpson doll peered over the edge of the duvet close to Cally's face and she sleepily hugged him even closer, her nose pressed into Bart's cheek. Eve bent over to kiss her young daughter's curled hair but straightened when the doorbell sounded again.

She wondered who could be at the front door in the middle of the afternoon. Had the reporter from the *North Devon Dispatch* returned to nag her with more unanswerable questions? What if it was the Blaney children's mother come to remonstrate with her? Eve couldn't face that; she hadn't the energy left to deal with irate mothers. But she would certainly ask how Seraphina and her brother had got hold of a door key to Crickley Hall and why they had brought a dead rat into the house! Gabe told her he had found a dead wood pigeon on the doorstep yesterday morning when he was about to go on his regular jog. Had the children planted the bird there? Was it Seraphina's way of getting back at the family because Loren had stood up for herself on the bus? Perhaps they'd intended to leave some poor dead animal every day just out of spite.

*Brurrrr – brurrrr* . . .

The doorbell made its irritating *croak*, the kind of sound whose repetition could put a person on edge. Nothing melodic, nothing galvanizing about it. Instead, it filled the house with a dull dread.

Tiptoeing out to the landing, she looked over the rail down at Crickley Hall's big front door as if it might provide some clues as to who was outside.

*Brurrrr – brurrrr* . . .

It echoed round the stone-floored hall, the acoustics making it louder than it should have been. Whoever was out there was persistent. Why not just knock on the kitchen window? Eve asked herself. Everybody else seemed to do that. She was reluctant to open the door, and she didn't know why. Perhaps she was on emotional overload; it had been a rough day so far. Then again, she had been on emotional overload for almost a year now.

*Brurrrr – brurrrr* . . .

All right, all right, I'm coming. I don't want to know who you are, I don't want to talk to you, but I'm coming down because I know I have to.

She went to the stairs and descended, glancing out of the tall window as she went by. The sky was clouding over again and the sun, on its downward journey, reddened the clouds' craggy edges. Their dark bulk was laden with rain.

The doorbell grouched yet again and Eve quickened her pace, both annoyed and anxious. Perhaps another local newspaper had got hold of the story – she knew the county had more than one daily journal – and this time she would make no comment, she would politely but firmly close the door on any nosy reporter or photographer who stood outside. A new thought entered her head, causing her to pause at the foot of the staircase. Perhaps the policeman had come back with more inquiries. What could she tell him? Why yes, of course Crickley Hall is haunted, I've seen the discarnate spirits of children myself and we've all heard unaccountable noises, and my daughter, Loren, was thrashed in her sleep last night by something I think might have been the evil ghost of a man called Augustus Cribben, who lived here over sixty years ago. Could she say all that? Could she say it and expect to be believed? She could scarcely believe it herself.

Eve crossed the hall – the perfectly *dry* hall – but took a diversion towards the cellar door. Bloody thing! Why wouldn't it stay shut?

*Brurrrr – brurrrr.*

Okay!

Eve pushed the cellar door closed and even turned the key in the lock for all the good it would do. Gabe really had to fix it; it was driving her to distraction.

She finally got to the front door, slid back the floor bolt and twisted the long key. Angrily, she pulled open the door and stared at the visitor on the doorstep.

Lili Peel's smile was weak, hardly a smile at all. She seemed nervous, uncertain. As if she were afraid.

'I was beginning to think you weren't in,' she said by way of an opening. 'I kept ringing the bell . . .'

'Yes. I'm sorry – I was upstairs.' Eve's heart was pounding: she hadn't expected to see the psychic again.

'I'm . . . I'm sorry too. About yesterday.' Lili looked down at the doorstep for a moment as though truly contrite. 'I know I was a bit brusque with you. I didn't mean to be. I've had time to think about what you told me.'

'You mean you'll help me – us?'

'You didn't leave your phone number, but of course I remembered the house. Wednesday is half-day closing in Pulvington, so I was able to get away from the shop.'

She hadn't answered Eve's question. Eve asked it again.

Lili's blonde hair was turned reddish gold by the setting sun. It also gave her face more colour than Eve recalled, but she knew the psychic's skin was pale, almost washed-out looking. Her green eyes were serious.

'I'm willing to try, Mrs Caleigh,' she said at last. 'I'll help you if I can.'

Eve was curious. 'What made you change your mind?'

'You told me you'd seen the spirits of children. There must be a reason for that. When we spoke yesterday, I could feel something was wrong, not just about you and your own suffering, but wrong with whatever it is that surrounds you. It has to come from this house.'

'Sorry, I don't understand.'

'There has to be a reason why the children who died here haven't passed over, why they're still attached to this place. They need to go on; they shouldn't be lingering here. I felt their misery in your own aura and I want to help them. Psychics, clairvoyants, spiritualists have a duty towards the dead.'

Eve was confused. 'And my own child?'

'I don't know. Once, when I was very young, I communicated with a boy who'd been in a coma for three months. They thought he was going to die and, if they'd turned off the life-support machines, he would have.'

There was a deep sadness in the psychic's manner that

touched Eve. Perhaps she'd got Lili Peel all wrong; perhaps the psychic cared *too* much. Rejecting Eve was her way of protecting herself. It was a sudden insight that Eve intuitively knew was correct, and it made her warm to this young woman who had been so cold towards her yesterday. Standing outside under the darkening sky, Lili looked small and vulnerable; frail even. Completely different to how she had appeared before.

'Please, come in,' Eve invited.

But the moment Lili Peel stepped over the threshold and entered the great hall something seemed to happen to her. She went deathly white and swayed on her feet as if about to faint. She reached out to Eve for support and Eve quickly took the psychic's arm and allowed her to lean against her.

'Are you all right?' Eve was perplexed. 'What's wrong?'

'I . . . I don't . . . the presence is so strong. Can't you feel them here?'

'I don't know what you mean.'

'Their spirits – all around, everywhere.'

'The children?'

'Yes. But there's something terribly wrong. There's something else here . . . something, *someone*, wicked. Dark. Evil.'

She swooned and Eve held her tight.

'I must . . . must sit down. They're draining me. So strong, so strong. But they don't have enough power yet. They're waiting . . .'

'Let me take you into the sitting room,' Eve urged. 'You can rest there.'

She began to lead the psychic across the stone floor, supporting her as much as she could, but as they neared the cellar door, Lili drew back, horror on her face.

Eve had gone out of her way to close and lock the cellar door, but now it was half open again. The darkness inside seemed almost solid, a physical thing. Lili backed away and Eve clung to her, moved with her.

'That's where the children were found,' the psychic murmured almost to herself. She began to take sharp, rapid breaths as though hyperventilating and Eve, concerned for her, led her in a semicircular route towards the sitting room. For such a petite person, Lili was surprisingly heavy; it was as if something more than her own body was weighing her down.

At last Eve got her to the couch in the sitting room and gently lowered her on to it.

'I'm sorry, I'm so sorry,' Lili said between short breaths. Eve sat next to her and watched the psychic's drawn features anxiously, not knowing quite what she could do to help. But gradually Lili's breathing calmed and a smidgeon of colour returned to her pale face. She closed her eyes and rested her head back against the couch.

Eve fretted. 'Can I get you anything? Tea, coffee, something stronger?'

The faintest, drained smile appeared on the psychic's face and she opened her eyes again. She turned her head to look at Eve. 'No, thank you,' she said. 'I think I'm okay now. It was just the . . . the oppression inside this house. It's overwhelming. I think I can deal with it now. I hope so.'

For want of anything better to say, Eve ventured: 'Before you spoke of a boy who was in a coma; you said you were able to communicate with him. Will you tell me what happened?'

Lili took in a long, deep breath, perhaps to chase away the smaller breaths, and it seemed to work. Her green eyes studied Eve's for a few moments, searching for some kind of empathy. Many people thought psychics were a little mad, but there was no suspicion, no challenge and no distrust in Eve's expression; only hope.

There was a fire blazing in the room's hearth, but Lili felt chilled; she often did when there was a strong sense of spirit. Incorporeal energies tended to sap warmth from the atmosphere. Nevertheless, she asked Eve if she could take off her coat.

When Eve nodded and said, 'Of course,' Lili stood and removed her brown suede jacket. Underneath, she wore a tight, beige, long-sleeved sweater that emphasized her small breasts, and a loose wine-coloured skirt that ended just below the top of her knee-length burgundy boots. A pretty pink coral necklace adorned her neck and Eve noticed she still wore the wide wristbands from yesterday.

Lili folded her arms but it seemed more like a defensive gesture than a 'don't mess with me' one, because her hands clutched her upper arms. Today she did not wear the thin leather headband; her hair fell over her forehead in a natural fringe. Her light green eyes checked Eve's before she began.

'The parents of the boy who was in a coma didn't know me personally – I was seventeen at the time – but they had heard of my ability through a neighbour of ours.'

Now she unfolded her arms and leaned forward on the couch, wrists resting on her knees, her hands clasped together.

'The boy – Howard was his name – was only eleven years old and he'd been knocked down by a car that failed to stop. It was found later, abandoned; police thought kids had stolen it for a joyride.'

She was gazing at the fire, tiny flames reflected in her eyes.

'Howard was on life-support and the doctors didn't think

he'd pull through. They thought his brain might have been too severely damaged, although they detected some signs of activity through their machines. They advised his parents it would be more merciful to turn off the systems keeping him alive so that he could go without more suffering. That's when Howard's parents contacted me on the chance I could reach him telepathically. They weren't true believers, but they'd heard about my psychic gift and they were desperate. They came to my house and asked me – no, they begged me – to try and make contact with their son. They weren't convinced Howard was all but brain-dead.'

She paused and looked away from the fire as if the flames were burning her pupils.

'Please go on,' Eve urged quietly.

'I agreed willingly. I have this thing about children even though I've never been a parent myself.' Lili did not relate the story of the first ghost she had ever seen, Agnes, whom she'd befriended and helped to move on; how that early experience had encouraged Lili to develop her extrasensory powers.

'I went to the hospital with the parents and was allowed into the intensive care unit. As soon as I saw Howard I felt he was far from death. Our minds made contact almost immediately. Inside his body was a lively, mischievous little boy, who missed his mother and father and wondered where they were and why they hadn't come to take him home.

'The mother broke down when I told her I was talking to her son, but the father, quite naturally, wanted to test me. He asked me questions that only Howard and his parents could know the answer to, and I put the questions to Howard. He thought it was a brilliant game because he was bored lying in the same place day after day with no one to talk or play with. He gave me all the answers, which I passed on to the parents. They were shocked, amazed. And so happy that even the father broke down in tears. They wouldn't allow the hospital to stop the life-support and eventually they were proved to be right. I visited Howard every few days and talked with him telepathically. It took another two months for Howard to regain consciousness.'

'He recovered?' Eve asked in awe. If the psychic could do this, contact a boy who was nearly dead and in a coma, then surely she could reach Cam.

'Completely,' Lili replied. 'Within another six months Howard was running around like any other healthy boy of his age. Could I have a glass of water?'

'Yes, of course. Are you sure you don't want something stronger?' Eve rose to her feet.

'No thank you. I had too much wine last night. Besides, I never drink alcohol when I use my psychic sense. For some reason it interferes with the process.'

'Then you will help us find our son?'

'I'll try. I'm not always successful. I'm also out of practice.'

'Surely it's a gift that's with you all the time.'

Lili shook her head, a single movement. 'Like any other ability, you have to keep at it. You have to develop the skill. We'll see how it goes – just don't expect too much.'

Eve hurried out to the kitchen, excited, more hopeful than ever before, already convinced the psychic would succeed. She took a glass from the cupboard and filled it with tap water, eager to get back to her visitor.

When she returned to the sitting room, Lili Peel was standing next to the round occasional table by the armchair. In her hands she held the photograph of Cam.

'This is Cameron, your missing son,' Lili said as Eve proffered the glass of water.

'Yes. We always called him Cam. That picture was taken on his fifth birthday.'

Eve's eyes fell upon the small silver-framed photograph of her beloved son. A rush of unbound love swept over her and, of course, with it came unrelenting anguish.

'Does ... does the picture tell you anything?' she asked tentatively, her hopes rising because Lili was staring at the photograph so intently. To Eve's regret the interruption seemed to break the psychic's concentration.

'Only that he was a beautiful-looking boy,' Lili replied, her attention now on Eve. 'D'you have anything that belonged to him, a favourite toy, an old jumper or shirt? Anything he was familiar with, or close to.'

'I kept everything of his, I didn't throw anything away. I felt it would have been wrong to, even if he's grown out of his old clothes by now. But we left his clothes and toys behind when we came here to Devon.'

'This photo will have to do, then.' Still holding onto the silver-framed picture, she took the glass of water from Eve.

The psychic sat down in the high-backed armchair next to the round table, keeping Cam's photograph with her. Eve sat on the edge of the couch opposite and leaned forward anxiously.

'Mrs Caleigh—' Lili began to say.

'Please call me Eve.'

'Eve, I don't want you to expect too much.'

'I won't,' Eve said unconvincingly. Lili seemed different today, so much softer than when they first met yesterday. The hardness was gone from those green eyes, which made her even prettier. Inwardly, Eve prayed that the woman really had telepathic powers and could reach Cam with her mind. She was glad Gabe wasn't there, because he wouldn't have approved of this – he was too grounded to believe in such things, and that was why Eve hadn't told him of her visit to the crafts shop in Pulvington. He might even be angry with her for going down such a path. But she had nothing to lose: she would use *anything* that might bring their son back.

Lili Peel placed the glass on the table, then, holding Cam's picture at almost arm's length away from her, she stared at it for a full minute. Eve saw that the psychic's forehead was furrowed with concentration and she held her breath, her own body tensing, thinking only of Cam as if that might help the psychic. Eve had to blink away the tears that threatened.

Lili slowly drew the photograph towards herself and pressed it between her small breasts. She closed her eyes and her wrinkled brow smoothed out as though she was no longer concentrating quite so intensely. Eve could not know this, but Lili was allowing her thoughts to roam free. She had filled her consciousness with images of the boy and was now attempting to 'tune in' to his psyche, even though she could not yet know whether he was alive or dead.

Her breathing became shallow, faster, and her eyelids flickered but did not open.

Eve was alarmed, worried that the psychic might hyperventilate, but Lili's breaths gradually became calm once more and one hand fell away to grip the arm of the chair she was sitting on. Her fingers clenched, then settled round the cushioned arm. Her breathing was deep now, the photograph against her chest rising and falling with the rhythm.

Eve wondered if the psychic was in a trance.

But Lili was only in a semi-trance. She was aware of the room around her, aware of Eve's presence on the couch opposite and aware of the house itself. Again aware of the deep oppression here.

Her head dropped forward, chin resting on her upper chest. She murmured something that Eve did not catch. Perhaps it was only a moan.

Lili's body became agitated, her shoulders giving little shrugs, the fingers resting on the chair's arm twitching. Her head rolled slightly, but remained dropped. Her eyelids flickered once more, then shut completely. The disturbing pallor returned to her face.

Eventually, her body relaxed and became very still. Her breathing was normal and, at first, Eve thought the psychic had fallen asleep; either that or she really was in a deep trance.

Then Lili's head slowly raised itself, her eyes remaining closed. Initially, her voice was but a whisper and Eve leaned even further forward to listen.

'I can ... sense ... some ... someone,' Lili said quietly and Eve strained to hear. 'Yes, someone ... very young ... a boy, a very young boy ...'

Eve's heart leapt. Could the psychic have reached Cam so soon, and so easily? Was it possible? Or was it a trick? Was Lili Peel a charlatan like many so-called mediums? But then, why should she try to deceive Eve? There had been no mention of a fee, so what would be the purpose? If Lili were genuine, Eve would gladly pay any charge she might demand; no price would be too high. Please, God, let this be real.

Lili's delicate lips moved again. 'The boy ... he's so lost. He's calling ... calling for help. He wants ... he wants somebody to find him. He's in darkness ... so alone ...'

'Lili,' Eve tried, 'ask the boy who he is. Is it Cam? Please find out.'

'It ... isn't clear. The connection between us is weak ...'

'Ask him, Lili, please,' Eve implored. 'Is it my son?'

Lili opened her eyes and turned them towards Eve and her gaze seemed to come back from somewhere distant. 'I – I don't know,' she stammered. 'The voice is so faint. The ... the contact between us isn't strong enough. Let me keep trying. But please, Eve, you've got to be quiet. Don't ask any questions, not yet.'

'I'm sorry ...' Eve pressed her lips together, determined not to distract the woman again. The psychic had reached her son, she was sure of that. But Lili's next words stunned her.

'I can't tell if I'm in touch with his spirit or his mind. It just isn't clear enough ...'

Despite her resolution, Eve had to speak out. 'You said the boy was lost. Cam is lost to us, you know that. It has to be him.'

Lili raised her hand to stop Eve. 'The thoughts I'm receiving are fragile. He's afraid.'

'Of course he is! He doesn't like where he is, he wants to be back with me, with his family, don't you see?' Eve could no longer stem the flow of tears. Her hands were clasped together in her lap, their grip so fierce her knuckles were white.

'I can't tell why he's afraid,' said Lili helplessly. 'Nothing is right. He's too far away.'

Eve was desperate. 'Please,' she urged, 'please ...'

Lili's eyes closed again and she leaned back in the armchair. Her face was tight, drawn, the mental struggle reflected in her pained features.

And then something changed.

Lili's eyes snapped open. She twisted in the chair, cowering, her arms up before her face. She groaned and her head turned from one side to the other. It was as if she were in agony.

Eve was startled by the transformation. Lili's mouth yawned open as if in horror and her eyes were wide, gaping up at the ceiling. Dropping the photograph of Cam, she clawed at her own neck with fevered hands.

And Eve shivered as she felt the dark oppression that had infiltrated the room; it weighed upon her like a dense but unseen mantle. Light seemed to be forced from the room, which was now filled with onerous gloom. Even the fire in the hearth seemed to wither under the presence, the flames dying, losing any warmth.

Lili's arms and shoulders shivered, but Eve couldn't tell if it was because of the room's coldness or because the psychic was terrified. Vapour clouds were expelled from her open mouth in short gasps and Eve attempted to rise from the couch to go to her, but she found herself transfixed, frozen, unable even to lift a hand. She was temporarily paralysed.

Meanwhile, Lili Peel's shivers ran through her whole body, from head to toe, her shoulders shuddering against the back of the armchair. Her neck and spine arched in some sort of spasm and her lips quivered; both of her hands clutched at the ends of the armrests.

She moaned, then cried out, '*Go away, leave me alone! You don't belong here any more!*'

Eve wondered at whom or what the words were directed. She and Lili were the only persons in the room, even though she could feel a potent and intimidating presence. And the smell, a malodour that stung the nostrils.

Lili Peel appeared to be having some kind of seizure: her back remained arched and her jaw had dropped so that her mouth was gaping even more; her eyes stared but they were glazed, unseeing. She began to rise from the armchair, still gripping its arms, her stomach pushed forward, head tilted backwards as far as it could go.

Eve felt suddenly nauseous and she fought against it, swallowing hard, breathing through her mouth rather than her nose. It hardly helped. She struggled inwardly to leave the couch, but still couldn't rise. Her spine felt locked, and her flesh prickled. Why couldn't she move?

The answer came to her as a mental taunt: it was sheer *terror* that held her there; she was too afraid to move. All she could do was watch the psychic, whose body now writhed violently in the armchair. Despite her own fear, Eve was concerned for Lili, afraid that in her paroxysms she would hurt herself. Once more, Eve strained to move and this time she was able to raise her arms. Her trembling fingers reached out to the distressed psychic.

But Lili abruptly collapsed in the armchair and became still. Her head sank to her chest again and her eyes closed. Every second or two an arm, or a leg, or a shoulder, twitched, but she remained slumped in the cushioned chair.

There came a stillness to the room.

And it became even colder.

In the hearth the flames almost died.

Eve's eyes stayed fixed on Lili, who lay in the armchair as limp as a rag doll.

And the room was dark not just because it was a late-October evening, but because something more had weakened the already fading light. Shadows grew, seemed to live.

Opposite Eve, Lili Peel lay loosely in the armchair until her left arm twitched once, twice, then once again. Finally it fell slack against her thigh.

Her head slowly rose from her chest and even her light green eyes looked dark in the room's poor light. Perhaps it was because her pupils had dilated, the irises no more than thin rings round them.

At first, Eve thought the psychic was staring at her. But then she realized that Lili's horrified eyes were looking at something over Eve's shoulder.

## 42: DARKNESS

Gabe pulled up behind the people-carrier that served as Merrymiddle's school bus. Because of the narrowness of the lane, it was blocking his access to the short parking space on the right-hand side. As he waited for the bus to move on, he glanced up at the clouded evening sky. Dusk was always early this time of year, but the heavily laden clouds easily smothered any last rays the dying sun could throw out.

Loren alighted from the left side of the bus and Gabe watched her wave goodbye to a friend as the vehicle moved away, heading downhill to the harbour village. He steered towards his parking spot and was surprised to see a small blue two-door Citroën had taken up much of the space in the short lay-by. Wondering who owned the car, and if whoever did was visiting Crickley Hall, he squeezed in behind it, a rear corner of the Range Rover protruding slightly into the roadway.

Loren waved to him as she crossed the lane and Gabe climbed from his vehicle, retrieving the large slim portfolio that carried his design drawings and sketches from the back seat as he did so.

'Hey, Slugger,' he greeted Loren as she skipped the last steps towards him. She kissed his proffered cheek and gave him a smile that told him all had gone well at school today.

''Lo, Dad.'

'You been okay?' Her nightmare last night and her pain, imaginary or not, that came with it had been on his mind all day long.

'Fine, Dad.'

'Really?'

'Honest. It was a dream, that's all.'

'Well, I know the doc thought that, but you were in a pretty bad way last night.' He threw an arm round her shoulders as they strolled to the bridge. *Kids get over things so fast*, he thought. *Let's see how she faces bedtime.*

'How was the injured party today?' His tone was light, but he kept the smile off his face.

Loren was happy to shake her head. Seraphina had to come to school eventually and Loren wondered if the bad feelings would continue. She hoped not, because she doubted she could punch the big girl again, and certainly not as effectively as the first time when surprise was on her side. She didn't think she could summon up the courage or the anger to do it again. However, despite the trepidation, she was enjoying Merrymiddle; she seemed to be making new friends every day and Tessa had definitely become one of her best.

The dull square shape of the house loomed up across the river and her mood changed. 'Dad, I don't like Crickley Hall,' she said, looking up at him.

He noted that she hadn't said 'I don't like it *here* at Crickley Hall'; she'd implied that she didn't like the house itself. He felt the same.

'S'why I left work early,' he told her. 'We gotta talk about this place. It's got bad vibes.' If someone else had said that to him just a few days ago, he would have laughed in their face. How could a house have vibes of any kind?

'Are we leaving?' Loren's eyes searched his in the gloom.

'Let's say it's a strong possibility. We'll see what your ma has to say.' After last night and all the trouble that morning, he felt sure that Eve would want to pack up and go as quickly as possible. And as much as he hated the idea of a mere house defeating him, he would happily do the packing.

They crossed the bridge, the rushing waters gurgling beneath them. Loren almost slipped on the wet boards, but Gabe held her tight against him.

'Why are there no lights on, Dad?'

He followed her gaze and saw that she was right. The building ahead was in darkness, not a single window lit, despite the early-evening dusk. It gave Gabe a bad feeling.

To reassure Loren he said: 'Maybe Mummy joined Cally for her afternoon nap and they've both overslept. None of us got much sleep last night.'

They hurried their pace, Loren moving slightly ahead of her father, passing by the front door – the family generally used the kitchen door for exit and entry now, because the front-door key was too long and cumbersome to carry comfortably. By the time Gabe turned the corner of the house, she was inserting her key into the lock. She waited for him before pushing the door open.

From behind her, Gabe reached in and flicked on the light switch. They blinked at the sudden brightness, then both headed for the open doorway into the hall, Gabe leaving the portfolio propped up against a kitchen table leg.

'Mum!' Loren called out from the hall's threshold. There was no answer.

Quickly becoming aware of the vast room's deep coolness, they stopped in their tracks.

'Hell,' Gabe muttered, perplexed. By now, he was used to the house's chill despite the working radiators and the fires he lit in various rooms, but this was something else. This was like stepping into a deep-freeze again.

'Daddy, look.' Loren was standing perfectly still in front of him, but her head was upturned as she looked at the galleried landing above. He caught sight of them, but oddly he couldn't focus on any.

They sped along the landing, fleeting wisps of – of what? Small stringy smoke clouds, hazy drifts of fog? *White shadows?* On their first day here, Loren had claimed to have seen what she called a white shadow outside her bedroom door – was this what she meant? But now there were several, streaking, *gliding* along the landing, separate entities like – like *spectres* – in a rush. As Gabe and Loren's eyes grew accustomed to the poor light and the depthless shadows it seemed to induce, they saw more of these vaporous moving shrouds on the broad stairway, so faint they were scarcely visible. They darted down to the hall itself to scatter this way and that as if confused.

It was an impossible sight, all the more implausible because of the vagueness of the shapes; nevertheless, Gabe felt the skin at the back of his neck stiffen, the iciness there sharp, almost stinging.

He moved in front of Loren as if to shield her, but incredibly there was no fear on her face, only a kind of astonished awe. Without further thought, he took a step back to the side of the kitchen doorway, where a row of brown light switches was situated, and pushed all three of them down with the edge of his hand.

The light – mainly from the ironwork chandelier high overhead, but also from two single, shaded hanging lights along the L-shaped landing – was ungenerous, but it at least cleared the air of the phantasms. Gabe was relieved, but still mystified.

'Eve!' he called out. 'Eve, where are you?'

He and Loren heard the low cry at the same time and both looked towards the open sitting-room door. Despite the overhead illumination, the darkness beyond the doorway was hardly softened; it was almost as if a solid black barrier barred entry. Gabe and Loren hurried towards it, passing the open cellar door on the way, and they reached the room together.

Without thought, Gabe leaned in, his fingers scrabbling round for the wall light switch, and it was like dipping his hand into thick ink so intense was the blackness there. He nearly pulled back from the awful stench that seemed to saturate the air, but he resisted the impulse, guessing his wife was somewhere there in the darkness.

Even as he sought the switch, which was at least a foot further along than he remembered, he heard Loren gasp beside him. Then he saw it too, by the dismal glow thrown out by the almost extinguished fire in the hearth. There were two figures sitting there in the dark, one in the room's armchair, the other – he knew by instinct this was Eve – on the couch, face half-turned towards something – something even blacker than the room's dense umbra – that stooped over her.

His urgent fingers finally found the light switch and struck it down. The light almost seemed reluctant to fulfil its role, for it came on dimly at first, increasing in power in slow, progressive stages, taking seconds to glow brightly. It was as if the darkness itself had fought against it.

Only Eve and an unfamiliar fair-haired woman occupied the sitting room and both sat like pale statues, perfectly still as if scared rigid.

Only then did the fire flame back into life.

Gabe let his anger rip.

'Tell me again what happened a few minutes ago. You say there was a ghost standing over Eve, but it disappeared when I came in the room with Loren and switched on the light.'

'I don't know that it was a ghost,' Lili replied evenly, avoiding the engineer's fierce gaze. 'It was an entity of some sort, that's all I can tell you, and it wished us harm. We both saw it, a . . . a black shape that was reaching for Eve until you disturbed it. Somehow it lost its power and faded. Maybe it was the lights that did it, I just don't know.'

'But you say the place *is* haunted.' Gabe glared at the psychic, concerned that Eve was being too easily influenced by her.

'Eleven children were drowned in this house over sixty years ago, Mr Caleigh. Now something is preventing their spirits from passing over. We have to help them, we have to find out what's blocking their progress, we have to help them go to where they're meant to be.'

Gabe stopped his pacing to look down at her.

If Lili felt intimidated, she did not show it. She went on: 'I also think your daughter is some kind of catalyst for the spirit children.'

'Come on . . .' Gabe groaned.

'It's not uncommon for astral spirits to use the pure psychic energy of young people – especially teenage or pre-teenage girls for some reason. The darkness and smell that was in this room went away when the light was turned on and Loren came in.'

Before he could interrupt, Lili asked a question. 'Has Loren felt unusually tired recently?'

'Why yes,' responded Eve, surprised. 'We all have, but especially Loren. She's complained of tiredness since we arrived here. We thought it was because of change of environment, or anxiety over starting at a new school. Or just, you know, part of the process of growing up.'

'She's at an age when her psychic energy is strong but all over the place. It's easily tapped into.'

Gabe's voice was incredulous. 'Are you saying our daughter is possessed?'

Lili shook her head vigorously. 'No, no, nothing like that. It's just a phenomenon that nobody can explain. You must've felt how cold it was in here earlier. It's because the spirits drain energy from the atmosphere itself. But their greatest source of power is from living people, particularly young people whose open minds have yet to be dulled by cynicism. That's why I turned towards spiritualism myself; I was used by a child ghost when I was a little girl – that was when I realized I had a special gift that no one else around me seemed to have.'

Gabe regarded Loren with concern. She had been allowed to remain in the room while her mother and the psychic related what had happened earlier because both he and Eve considered her mature enough to hear their discussion – after all, she had experienced some weird stuff herself in this place. Now he was beginning to regret the decision. Loren was sitting on the couch close to her mother and her eyes were intent on the psychic. Most kids believed in ghosts, he thought, but then many also believed in fairies. He returned his attention to the young blonde woman in the armchair.

'Listen, lady—'

'Her name's Lili,' Eve quickly interjected, annoyed at his rudeness – and his blunt refusal to accept what he was being told. 'Lili Peel.'

'Okay, sorry. I don't know what game you're playing, what interest you've got in all this, but you're twisting my wife's head. You got her believing everything you say.'

Eve was about to protest, but he held up a hand as if to ward her off.

'Now it so happens I don't believe in ghosts, never have, probably never will, but I admit something's going on here that isn't normal, so I guess you'd call it the paranormal. The house has certainly got bad vibes that I can't account for. But I do know you can't talk to the dead, not for real. Don't get me wrong, I'm not saying you're a phoney, I honestly believe you're sincere in what you say. I just don't go along with it and I don't want my wife and daughter to either. We got enough problems without this.'

'Then *you* explain the paranormal activity that's been going on since you got here,' Lili came back at him, 'all the things Eve has told me about.'

At last Lili was showing some defiance, thought Eve, secretly glad. Before, Lili had seemed a little cowed by Gabe's verbal disdain. Now she delivered her words with the same brittle coldness that she'd used when Eve had visited the shop yesterday.

'I can't,' said Gabe, shaking his head in frustration. 'I don't know. But I don't want it to be my family's problem.'

'You can't just walk away from it.'

'Watch us.'

'There are young children involved, lost children.'

'But not real kids.'

'They need our help.'

'Your help. We don't have that psychic thing.' The last two words were derisory.

'And if I can find your missing son at the same time?'

Gabe's mouth shut tight. His fists clenched.

'Lili spoke to Cam,' Eve said as if daring her husband to disbelieve. 'He knows we're here.'

Lili faltered. 'I ... I didn't speak to him. Somehow our minds connected, that was all. It was as if he was searching and had finally found what he was looking for. It wasn't very clear, I couldn't be certain it was him. But I can try again. Not now – I feel as if I've been drained dry – but soon, maybe even tomorrow?'

'Forgive my cynicism' – he didn't sound in the least bit sorry – 'but is that how you get your kicks, stringing gullible people along with your talk of contacting lost souls by mind-power?'

Eve was almost out of her seat. 'That's unfair! I went to Lili, not the other way round.'

'Okay, okay.' He held up a penitent hand. 'I'm just saying maybe she's even deluding herself, thinking she can talk to dead people or that she has telepathic powers. Look, I don't know how or why, but I think this house musters up halluci-nations, even in sceptics like me.'

Eve shook her head in dismay. 'You think all this is our imagination? The footsteps in the attic, the knocking behind the empty cupboard doors? Gabe, I saw the spirits of those poor little children myself out there in the hall only two days ago. You think it's all self-delusion?'

# JAMES HERBERT

'I've never been into this kinda stuff, so I don't know what it is. But something's going on here and we're not hanging around to find out what. It's none of our business, right?'

'How can you be—' Eve stopped in mid-sentence. Both Lili and Gabe had turned their attention to the open doorway behind her. She twisted round on the couch to see for herself, Loren following suit.

Cally stood in the opening, spongy Bart Simpson cuddled in one arm, the knuckles of her other hand rubbing at her sleepy eyes. With everything that had happened, Eve had completely forgotten about her youngest daughter napping upstairs. Cally had slept for a long time, far longer than usual.

'Mummy,' the five-year-old said plaintively. 'Why are the children so frightened?'

Outside, the clouds began to shed their load and rain drummed against the windows.

## 44: SIXTH NIGHT

It had been a difficult evening, Gabe and Eve barely speaking to one another for much of it. There was no shouting match (although in some ways that might have been better – it would have at least cleared the air), there was just a brooding awkwardness left between them following a brief argument after Lili Peel had departed. Even this was kept low-level, for they hadn't wanted to upset Loren and Cally any further with talk of ghosts, real or otherwise. But when their daughters had gone to bed, Eve had told him of the incident with the garden swing that morning, how some invisible force had pushed the swing too high, terrifying Cally and frightening herself, how she, Eve, had been knocked to the ground, showing Gabe the small mark on her chin where she'd been hit by the wooden seat. She also spoke of the children's spirits that she – *and* Cally – had seen dancing in the hall. He had been dumbfounded and only made more determined to get his family away from Crickley Hall. Although he wouldn't admit it to them, he was becoming afraid for his wife and daughters. But Eve wouldn't listen, she just wouldn't hear him out. Frustrated, Gabe had retreated into a cool silence, the way he always did when events and emotions seemed to spin out of his control. Tomorrow would be different.

Tomorrow, in the new light of day, he'd get Eve to change her mind.

Gabe turned in his sleep and his eyes suddenly opened. He stared up at the ceiling where the glow from the landing light outside spread through the open doorway, and he wondered what had awakened him.

He was in Loren's bed; the girls had planted themselves in his and Eve's four-poster without seeking permission and both were sound asleep when he and Eve had turned in for the night. They hadn't the heart to disturb their daughters and Gabe, mindful of the previous uncomfortable nights in the crowded bed, had elected to sleep alone next door. Eve had not tried to dissuade him.

Rain lashed the window and he thought a sudden gust of wind might have rattled the frame hard enough to disturb him. He lay there for a full minute listening for any sounds but, despite the heavy bullets of rain that continued to punish the glass, the window itself was still.

Yet something had roused him, he was sure. A noise? A movement? He peered into the room's shadows, into the dark corners, seeking an answer, his imagination held in check for the moment. Nothing there, as far as he could tell.

Lifting his head from the pillow, he looked through the open doorway. There was nothing to see.

Gabe rested his head again, his eyes remaining wide open, and listened to the ceaseless rain. He had become used to England's general dampness whatever the season, but this was beyond usual. Apart from an occasional break, the rain had hardly let up for weeks now. He had a mental image of the river beneath the house, coursing through its subterranean channel, fed by the waters from the high moors. What damage had been done to Crickley Hall's foundations over the decades? How long could stone and cement withstand constant pressure? It was a discomforting thought.

He closed his eyes, wanting to sleep, *needing* to sleep. Crickley Hall had not offered the respite he'd hoped for. There was no peace here for his family, no let-up from their anguish.

His eyes blinked open.

There was no one else in the room, but suddenly it didn't feel that way. He searched the shadowy corners again and still there was nothing to cause concern. Yet . . . yet he could feel eyes watching him. It was an uncanny sensation, but it felt very real. Eerie. As if something malevolent were obser-ving – no, *scrutinizing* – him from somewhere in the room.

He looked towards the open doorway again. Rain, driven by a sudden wind, clattered against the window, causing him to start. A hell of a night out there. But it was a minor distraction, for the sense of being watched was impossible to ignore. The muscles in his neck became taut as he stretched them.

Then he saw it.

But it was only in the periphery of his vision, for his attention had been elsewhere.

He thought a small ragged mist had passed by on the landing outside. Like a shadow. Like a *white* shadow. Now he felt the skin of his entire body tighten as a deep chill enwrapped him. Gabe realized he was very scared.

Of course he had known fear before, but never quite like this. This fear was filled with a dread that almost immobilized him. He had to force himself to sit up in the bed.

Perversely, the dread of something unknown made Gabe angry with himself. He wasn't a child and didn't believe in ghosts. With a muttered curse, he forced himself to whip back the duvet and go to the door. Although dressed only in T-shirt and shorts, he was already too cold to feel any worse as he padded across the wooden flooring. His spine felt rigid, as though it were gripped by an icy brace, and he rolled his shoulders to loosen it. Still he felt as if he were being observed by something in the room with him; something invisible, but nevertheless there, lurking, hiding, where it couldn't be seen.

As he reached the door he caught a whiff of something nasty mixed with the weaker scent of . . .? Of soap? But not a pleasant brand of soap. But the extraneous odours seemed to have nothing to do with whatever had passed by the room a moment or two ago, because the air, such as it was, was purer on the landing. The unpleasant reek was from behind him. Outside the door he paused, then saw the mist again at the top of the stairs. It lingered there, as if waiting for him. A ridiculous notion, it was true, but one he couldn't shake.

Gabe was reminded of the skittering images he and Loren had witnessed earlier that day and the description came to him again: white shadow. This thing looked as insubstantial as that.

As he took a tentative step towards the small immobile mist, it began to descend the stairway. He peered over the balustrade to follow its progress.

The landing light barely infringed upon the gloom of the grand hall below; it was like an umbrageous arena filled with deep blacks and murky greys among which anything might skulk. Yet the sinking mist was clearly visible, as though illuminated from within.

Curiosity overrode Gabe's trepidation. He headed towards the stairway, careful to tread softly as he passed the room in which his wife and daughters slept. He would have liked to have retrieved the flashlight he now kept beside the four-poster bed, but that would risk waking Eve or one of the girls and they deserved at least one night of uninterrupted sleep. Reaching the stairway, he paused again to search the space below.

His eyes had become accustomed to the poor light and he caught sight of the white shadow floating across the hall towards the cellar door.

Gabe hurried down the stairs, a hand on the banister to feel his way, his senses acutely alert, dread countered by rushing adrenaline. He stopped once again on the stairway's square turn, his feet suddenly wet. He was standing in a puddle.

Rain beat at the tall window and it was hardly surprising that water had leaked through the worn window frames. As he stood there, the sense of being observed was powerful enough to make him spin round and search the stairs and landing behind him. There was nothing there, though. At least, nothing that he could see.

Ignoring the feeling of being prey to something unseen, he descended the rest of the stairs, then made his way across the flagstone floor towards the cellar on the other side of the hall. Despite his apprehension, he felt he was meant to follow this mist, this shadow; somehow it was irresistible, as if he were being lured. And he had put reason aside for the moment, allowing himself to be drawn.

He splashed through more puddles on the flagstones, but hardly noticed them now as he moved through the darkness, the light on the landing above too feeble to provide much guidance. He was tempted to find the main light switch by the kitchen door, but if the chandelier came on it would shine through the doorway to where his family slept; he still didn't want to wake them, no point, Loren might freak.

# JAMES HERBERT

Gabe could just make out the solid blackness that was the open cellar door and as he watched, the white shadow slipped through and disappeared down the steps. Reluctant to lose sight of it completely, he quickened his pace, bare feet now slapping on dry stone. As he went, he swung his head round as if to catch whoever was observing him unawares, but there was nobody on the stairway or on the landing above. Nobody that he could see, that is. Still the feeling of being scrutinized persisted, although he seemed to have left the smell of corruption and soap behind.

As he approached the cellar door (which he remembered having locked yet again before turning in for the night), a different smell wafted out to him. This was of dampness and mould, of cobwebs and dust. He could hear the busy rush of the river beneath the house rising from the well below. Cautiously, he peeked through the opening.

Although the darkness was complete at the bottom of the steps, he just caught sight of the lighter shadow moving into it. Gabe reached in and turned on the narrow stairway's light, a naked low-wattage bulb covered in grime. The journey down into the cellar looked uninviting, for the blackness there had hardly receded; instead it seemed to be pushing against the lowest step like a threatening tenebrous tide.

Without giving himself time for further reflection, the engineer began to descend, one hand brushing the wall as he went. He was soon on the last stair and the pitchy blackness spread out before him. Breathing in stale air, he reached round the wall on his right, fingers searching for the light switch. Found it, flicked it on.

Just in time to see the nebulous white shadow flow over the well's low circular wall and drop out of sight.

The cellar was by no means well-lit, for the naked hanging lightbulb, like the one over the steps, was dimmed by years of dust; there were corners and niches that were impenetrable. The opening to the boiler and generator room next door was a black void.

Gabe returned his attention to the well, anxious not to lose sight of the thing he'd followed. Wary of debris scattered around the cellar's floor, he went to the well's low stone wall and peered into its depths. Although he heard the endless roar of the river below – its noise was amplified by the acoustics of the circular shaft – it was like looking into a bottomless pit. Of the white shadow he had followed there was no trace: it seemed to have been absorbed into the umbra. Unconsciously, he leaned further over the lip, his shins pressing against the wall, and stared into the dense blackness below. Gabe had never before suffered from vertigo, but a sudden dizziness came upon him; it was as if the blackness was sucking him in. An iciness seemed to reach up for him, freezing his very bones, and his breath was released in vaporous clouds. He almost toppled, but caught himself just in time, and staggered backwards, away from the opening.

Gabe stood there, a foot or two away from the wall, and he inhaled a deep breath of musty air in an effort to calm himself.

He heard a noise that had nothing to do with the pounding of the river beneath the house. It was a scuffling noise and it had come from somewhere in the spacious underground chamber. Something dragging.

Gabe squinted his eyes, trying to discern anything that might be concealed by the shadows there. It was too dark, though. Someone was using the shadows as a cloak. Just as he had been certain he was being watched upstairs, he was sure that somebody lurked just out of sight.

'Someone there?' he barked with a gruffness he hardly felt.

JAMES HERBERT

Only the sound of rushing water came back to him.

Moving slowly, Gabe edged round the wall of the well, a path that took him closer to the source of the scuffling. There it was again! He hadn't been mistaken. Someone – an intruder – was hiding from him. Maybe they'd seen him come out onto the landing earlier and ducked through the open cellar door before he came downstairs. But then Gabe had gone straight to the cellar, so the intruder must have escaped down the steps, any noise they might have made covered by the sound of the river rising from the well.

Again! Feet scraping on concrete. From right there, inside the opening to the boiler room where the weak overhead light couldn't reach. His eyes might have been playing tricks on him, but he was sure something had moved in the darkness. Dark upon dark.

Gabe wasn't sure what to do. His instinct was to get the hell out of there, lock and barricade the cellar door and call the police. But he couldn't be sure there *was* someone there. Maybe the quiet scuffling he heard was nothing more than dirt falling from the cellar wall or ceiling, the house itself settling. Maybe the intruder was no more than a mouse or a rat. Yet, just as he'd felt eyes on him minutes before, he could *feel* a presence lurking there, hidden in the darkness. And it wasn't a mouse or a rat. This was something bigger. He was certain of that too.

His mouth felt dry and adrenaline pounded through his body. 'Okay,' he muttered to himself, talking up his courage, 'let's see what you got to offer.'

He half crouched, his muscles tensed, fists clenched, and prepared to rush the shadows and drag out whoever was there. He felt the energy surge.

'*Right!*' he yelled, but just as he lunged forward a fierce light came on from behind him.

'Gabe!' It was Eve's voice. 'What are you doing?'

Almost thrown off balance, he wheeled round. He raised a hand to shield his eyes against the bright glare and waited for his heart to stop pounding.

'Gabe, why are you down here?' Her voice was full of concern, bewilderment too.

'Eve,' he managed to utter, 'shine the light through the doorway.' Gabe pointed as he half turned away from her.

'What?' She was even more bewildered.

*'Quick, shine it through the doorway!'*

She did as she was told, even though mystified. 'What's the matter with you, Gabe? There's nothing there.'

Gabe snatched the torch from her and crossed to the opening. The beam lit up the next-door room, revealing the boiler and generator, the old mangle and blade sharpener, the pile of logs and the coal heap, odd pieces of junk that littered the dusty floor; but no one hid here, it was plain to see.

He finally let go of his breath.

It was morning and Gabe sat at the kitchen table, on his second cup of coffee after breakfast and wishing he hadn't given up smoking. Loren had left for school and Cally was at the table with him, enthusiastically crayoning in a horse he had sketched for her (being an engineer, his version of the animal was more mechanical than it was graceful), telling her it was the horse he used to ride in his cowboy days. Cally was colouring it a bright shade of purple.

Eve tapped on the window to get the attention of Percy, who was working outside on one of the garden's flowerbeds, hood pulled up over his cap against the steady downbeat of rain. The gardener straightened and looked her way. She mimed drinking a cup of tea and he gave her a thumbs-up before making his way to the kitchen door.

Gabe was hunched over his coffee, both hands wrapped round the mug as if for warmth, and he appraised Percy silently as the old man stamped his wet boots on the doormat. Shrugging back his hood and removing the flat cap, the gardener nodded respectfully at him.

'Hey, Percy,' Gabe greeted in a low but friendly growl.

'Yup,' Percy replied.

He immediately seemed to sense the frosty atmosphere

between Gabe and Eve, taking them both in as he stood awkwardly on the rough mat.

'Sit down, Percy, and I'll bring your tea over,' Eve told him and the old man mumbled something incoherent as he pulled out a chair from the table. 'Would you like some toast?' she pressed him.

'No, missus, I'm all right.' *Orlroit.* He smiled at Cally and touched the top of her head gently, but she was more interested in giving her purple horse a yellow mane. Eve put the cup and saucer before him on the table.

'Nasty weather, huh?' said Gabe by way of making conversation. He and Eve had barely spoken a word to each other that morning and had not even mentioned his excursion into the cellar last night. Down there, he had explained that he had followed a 'white shadow' and she had seemed to take some satisfaction in the fact that at last he was treating the strange phenomena in Crickley Hall seriously. As for something hiding in the boiler room, he himself had eventually surmised it had probably been a small animal, a rodent, whose scuffling was made louder and more sinister by the bare brick walls and concrete floor and ceiling. Eve had told him something had disturbed her sleep – a noise, instinct, she didn't know what – and when she had gone out onto the landing she had seen the light from the open cellar door below. She had gone next door to rouse Gabe and, on seeing the bed was empty, had assumed it was he who was downstairs. She had grabbed the flashlight from their bedroom and followed.

They had both returned to their separate beds, too weary – the comedown after the high adrenaline flow – to discuss whether Crickley Hall was truly haunted, should they stay or leave, and what did it all mean. Neither of them slept much that night.

'Folks is gettin' fretful,' said Percy in response to Gabe's remark on the weather.

'Oh?' The engineer's thoughts had already drifted.

'Worried 'bout what the rain's doin' to the moors.'

'Has there been a flood warning?' Eve asked anxiously.

'No, not yet there ain't.'

'But they've taken precautions should it ever happen again, haven't they, Percy? I read about it in a book I got from the village store. A flood could never do the same damage as last time.'

'So they reckons, missus. Sometimes, though, nature has its own ideas.'

Gabe didn't like the subject; there were more immediate things to worry about. 'Percy,' he said more casually than he felt, 'tell us a little about the guy who owns Crickley Hall. You said Temple or something like that was his name.'

'Templeton. Mr Templeton.'

'Okay. You told us he was never happy here . . .?' It ended as a question.

'No, he never were. S'why they up and left. But I think that were more to do with his wife, Mary, than anythin' else.'

'Yeah?'

'Had no kiddies, there were jus' the two of 'em an' Crickley Hall's too big for jus' a couple on their own. Needs a family, like yours.'

Percy blew into his teacup, then sipped from it, the saucer held below to catch any drips as usual. He looked directly at the American.

'What makes yer ask, Mr Caleigh?'

Somehow Gabe knew it wasn't an idle question. But it was Eve who replied.

'We wondered why the Templetons no longer used Crickley Hall themselves nowadays. Is there a reason?'

Percy placed the cup back into its saucer and then both on the table.

'Mr Templeton's wife became poorly almost as soon as they moved in all them years ago. She never took to the place, an' I think he didn't either 'cause of her.'

'D'you know why she didn't like it here?' asked Gabe, more than interested.

Percy gave it some thought. 'Mr Templeton, he told me his wife felt there was a bad atmosphere 'bout the house an' it made her depressed, like. She'd heard the rumours, y'see, 'bout Crickley Hall bein' haunted an' all, an' mebbe she took it too serious. Anyways, t'weren't long afore she took to her bed. Small things at first – colds, headaches, backaches, them sort of problems. Then they discovered she had cancer, bad cancer – if there's any of the good kind.'

'What happened?'

'They left. Moved out. Mr Templeton took his wife to London for specialist treatment, but she died anyways, only weeks later, we heard. An' Mr Templeton, well he never came back 'cept fer one day months later. Wouldn't sell the place though.'

'Oh?' said Gabe. 'Why was that?'

'I asked him that very same question the day he returned to sort out things with the estate agent who he wanted to take charge of the prop'ty. After his good lady died, that were.' Percy nodded to himself as if remembering that very day. 'I were workin' in the garden as usual an' Mr Templeton, he came out to see me, mostly to let me know I were bein' kep' on as gardener an' maintenance even though he wouldn't be livin' here no more, but also 'cause he often like to jus' stop an' chat with me awhile. Always had done, said it took his mind off other worries jus' chattin' 'bout the garden an' what needed doin', 'bout the weather or local people, any old thing that weren't important like. When he told me he weren't comin' back to Crickley Hall no more an' that the estate agent feller – a Mr Cardew it were at that time – he had instructions to let the prop'ty whenever there were any interest, I says to him, why don't you sell up an' forget 'bout the place. I knew him an' his wife had never been happy here, y'see, so I were wonderin' why he didn't just get shot of it.'

He looked first at Gabe, and then at Eve, as if to make sure they were paying attention.

'An' he told me,' Percy continued, 'lookin' back at the house as he says it, "Percy, livin' in Crickley Hall fer too long will destroy a person's mind. The house's got a secret that'll forever haunt it." That were the word he used, *haunt*. And he were haunted by it, I could tell. I thought of them poor little mites who had died here years afore, an' I knew he were right. The secret is what really happened to 'em. How could they all've drowned in a buildin' as solid as Crickley Hall? What was the authorities, who came after the flood, what was they hidin' from the local people? An' I, like I told your missus t'other day, think they were terrified if what really happened to them kiddies that night of the flood became known, people in the cities would never allow their children to be evacuated, even though the war were still goin' on. They might figure the children safer at home with their mums and dads.'

Percy gave a sigh, his gaze introspective.

'Mr Templeton told me I still had my job fer as long as I wanted. Much as he didn't like Crickley Hall, he didn't want the place to go to ruin. Cleaners were paid to come in once a month, keep it liveable, like. Mr Templeton didn't like to see anythin' rot away, even if he didn't care for it hisself.'

'Did Mr Templeton ever tell you things had happened here he couldn't explain?' Eve asked quietly.

The gardener turned in his seat to face her. It was a moment or two before he responded.

'Not sure what yer mean, missus.'

'He told you Crickley Hall could destroy a person's mind. He must have had a reason for saying that.'

Percy pondered and Gabe groaned inwardly. Surely she wasn't going to tell the old man about the things that had been happening to them since they'd arrived here? But the doorbell startled them all, so intrusive was its ring.

Eve glanced at Gabe and he rose from the table. 'On it,' he said, glad of the interruption.

He went out into the hall and to the front door, opening it. A woman whose face was vaguely familiar was on the doorstep, an umbrella held low over her head. She was wearing a stern expression and a bright scarf; it was the blue-and-yellow scarf that he remembered.

'Mr Caleigh. We met on Saturday. I was with my husband.' The words were spoken quickly and brusquely.

'Sure,' he said, recognizing the vicar's wife. 'Mrs, uh, Trevellick.'

Her piercing eyes regarded him sharply, her thin unrouged lips set in a straight line across her face.

'Can you tell me the meaning of this?' she snapped at him, slapping the folded newspaper she carried in her free hand against his chest.

Surprised, he took the newspaper from her and unfolded it. The banner told him it was the *North Devon Dispatch* and the front page headline said in caps: COUNCILLOR RESIGNS OVER EXPENSES.

'Sorry, I—' Gabe began to say, but she snatched the journal back impatiently.

'Page five.' Awkwardly using both hands, umbrella resting

JAMES HERBERT

on a shoulder, she pulled open the newspaper. Rain spattered its pages as she thrust it back at him.

On page five was a photograph of a surprised-looking Eve standing in the kitchen doorway. It was inset against a larger shot of Crickley Hall itself, which must have been taken from somewhere near the bridge. Gabe quickly read the headline beneath: CHILDREN CLAIM SEEING GHOST IN MANOR.

His jaw dropped. So much had happened when he'd arrived home yesterday that Eve hadn't mentioned any journalist and photographer having been to the house. Surely she hadn't given them an interview.

Before he could read on, the vicar's wife was berating him again. 'Do you *realize* how irresponsible you're being?'

'Look, I don't know anything about—' he began, but once more she interrupted him.

'Police called to the house, children making up stories about Crickley Hall. A ghost, indeed! And you have to blab it all to the newspapers!'

'Now wait a minute—'

'Do you realize they'll probably track down a poor sick old lady just to dredge up stories that should have been laid to rest years ago! You've started up all the silly rumours again. The whole county will have a field day. There's nothing people like more than a ludicrous haunted-house story. Crackpots will come from miles around just to see the place and take photographs for themselves. Those children the article mentions were drowned in the flood, there's nothing more to it than that!' She was almost spitting at him.

He skimmed through the story: *Seraphina, 12, and Quentin Blaney, 14, while visiting* – visiting? – *an old manor house called Crickley Hall, near the harbour village of Hollow Bay, had been confronted by the ghost of a nude man ... house flooded, water everywhere ... another ghost in the cellar ...*

344

*hadn't seen this one clearly but knew it was there* ... Gabe remembered last night and the fear he'd felt himself because he thought there was something there in the cellar with him, out of sight in the shadows of the room next door. In the light of day he had questioned his own susceptibility, wondering if the noises he'd heard had merely whipped up his own imagination, causing him to *think* he was not alone. But then, he *had* followed the mist from upstairs, the thing he called the 'white shadow', so what was that all about?

Celia Trevellick was still ranting at him – something about letting the dead rest in peace, ruining someone's good name with outrageous rumours, pandering to the press with wicked lies – but he wasn't taking it in. He read on: *Mrs Eve Caleigh and her husband Gabriel ... currently renting the property ... neither confirmed nor denied reports that Crickley Hall is haunted ... police called to investigate disturbances ... two young daughters Laura and Kaley* ... Surely Eve hadn't told the paper all this?

'Are you listening to me, Mr Caleigh?' The vicar's wife's face was taut with indignation, a blue vein clearly throbbing in her left temple.

'I wasn't here at the time,' Gabe explained firmly, 'but I'm sure my wife wouldn't have given a story like this to a reporter. She'd've slammed the door in their face.'

'Well they got it from somewhere.'

'Yeah, from the two kids who broke in most likely. But hey, I don't get it. Why are you blaming us for something we didn't do?'

For a moment she seemed lost for words, but she soon rallied. 'Because you're outsiders here and you've stirred up gossip and whispers about past events that weren't true in the first place. You're tarnishing the reputations of good people who are no longer able to defend themselves.'

'Who exactly?'

'Never mind that. Just stop this nonsense about Crickley Hall being haunted.'

'Lady, we didn't start it in the first place. You think we want crazies turning up on our doorstep asking to see the ghosts? We got better things to do. Now excuse me while I get on with one of those better things.'

He began to close the door, but she held a hand against it.

'I can make a complaint to the owner, you know,' she said fiercely. 'My husband knows the estate manager, Mr Grainger, very well. We could have your lease revoked.'

'You're kidding, right?'

'I can assure you I'm not. People who cause trouble should expect trouble back.'

Gabe felt himself beginning to burn.

'So long, Mrs Trevellick,' he said evenly, keeping his temper in check. 'Go ride your broomstick someplace else.' He forced the door shut, his last sight of the irate woman at least satisfying: she stood as stiff as a rod, her mouth agape, her eyes wide with shock. If he'd given her the chance, he was sure she would have poked him with the sharp end of the umbrella.

He turned to see Eve by the kitchen door, obviously reluctant to have become involved in the altercation. Realizing he still had the newspaper in his hand, he offered it up to her.

'Page five, great picture,' he said.

Eve took it from him and quickly leafed through to the relevant feature.

'Oh God,' she said when she saw the photographs and read the headline. She went through the story, shaking her head at parts of it. 'The reporter makes it sound like I gave a full interview and that I knew Crickley Hall was haunted. I swear, Gabe, I said none of this.'

'Okay, hon, I know.' He shrugged as if to dismiss the article.

'I refused to speak to him. And the photographer took the picture before I could close the door.'

'Don't worry. It couldn't be helped. They just run stories to fill up space.'

'So this is why Mrs Trevellick was so cross?'

'Uh-huh. You heard?'

'Most of it.'

'You did the right thing, not getting involved. She's nuts.'

They went back into the kitchen together, Eve still reading the piece.

'Seems like Seraphina and her brother enjoyed the attention,' she commented, looking up from the newspaper. 'Probably disappointed they didn't get to have a picture too.'

Percy regarded Gabe and Eve curiously. 'Sounded like the vicar's wife out there.'

'That's who it was, Percy,' said Gabe. 'Celia Trevellick. Can't get my head round why she was so mad. Said something about dredging up old rumours. Damage to the community, apparently.'

'I heard her from here. Little 'un was anxious like.' The gardener smiled at Cally, who was watching her parents.

'S'll right, Sparky,' Gabe told her. 'The angry lady's gone now.'

With that reassurance, Cally went back to her colouring, the tip of her tongue protruding from the corner of her mouth as she drew a tree behind the purple and yellow horse.

Gabe waved a hand at the newspaper that Eve still held open. 'I don't get it. We should be the ones to get upset.

Using a picture of Eve without her permission, showing everyone the house.'

'And virtually giving out the address,' Eve put in. 'I just hope we don't start getting daytrippers and loonies looking us up. I can't understand why Mrs Trevellick got so upset though.'

Percy's jaw jutted as he scratched his neck. 'The vicar's wife is an important person in Hollow Bay. She's on the parish council an' the church committee, as well as bein' in charge of the Women's Guild hereabouts. An' her family goes way back, it's part of local history.'

'Oh yeah?' said Gabe, still baffled as to why the newspaper story had rattled her cage.

Percy nodded. 'Expects her husband to be bishop one day, so her reputation is important to her.'

'But what's that got to do with this?' Gabe indicated the journal, which Eve had closed and left on the table.

'Scandals never really fade away in these parts. Rumours don't ever die, an' reputations go back generations.'

Gabe shrugged again. 'I still don't get it.'

'Her grandpa were Hollow Bay's vicar durin' the war an' long afore.'

'So?'

'He were a great chum of Augustus Cribben. Stood by the man, admired Cribben for his pious ways an' discipline. It were the vicar, Rossbridger, who recommended Augustus Cribben for the post of guardian in the first place. Knew him of old, y'see. Not exactly pals, but they both had respect for one another.'

Eve was dismayed. 'But Cribben treated the evacuees appallingly. You told us that yourself and it's all there in the book Gabe found.'

'Yers, but nobody knew that at the time. Nobody 'cept Nancy, of course, an' she weren't able to do anythin' 'bout it in the end.'

Gabe sat back down at the table, giving Cally a faint smile when she peeked up at him. To Percy, he said: 'Why should any of this matter to Rossbridger's granddaughter after all these years?'

'Like I says, it's a dark part of her family history. She don't want it dug up again – might tarnish her an' the vicar's good name.'

'That's ridiculous. How could it matter now? It's in the past.'

'An' as I says, family history is important in these parts, 'specially when yer be fine upstandin' members of the community like the Trevellicks an' yer expects yer husband to become bishop.'

Gabe was confounded, Eve dismayed.

'Old Rossbridger, he were right behind Cribben in those days an' it were him that persuaded the authorities not to look too fer into what went on in Crickley Hall. Seems like they agreed to that – bad fer the morale of the country in time of war an' all that. 'Cause more an' more parents was refusin' to send their young 'uns away to strange parts. Didn't trust the authorities, an' in some cases they was right not to.'

'Wait a minute.' Something had occurred to Gabe. 'Mrs Trevellick said something about an old lady being tracked down by the press. Who did she mean?'

Percy avoided Gabe's questioning gaze for a moment, tilting his head downwards, then bringing it up again.

'No, I didn't tell yer, did I?' he said. 'Didn't think it were important no more.'

Gabe and Eve glanced at each other before Percy went on.

'She's still alive, y'see. Old, in her nineties, but still alive.'

'Who is, Percy?' Eve asked patiently.

'Augustus Cribben's sister,' he told them. 'Magda.'

## 46: MAGDA CRIBBEN

Gabe wrinkled his nose as he followed the plump blue-uniformed nurse down the long corridor. The nursing home smelt of boiled cabbage, detergent and stale pee, all underlined by the more subtle odour of human decay, the slow rotting of living flesh.

'She doesn't get any visitors at all,' the nurse said, glancing back over her shoulder at the engineer, 'so it'll be a nice surprise for her. We thought all her relatives must be deceased by now – that is, if she had any.'

'My folks are distant cousins living in the States,' he lied easily. 'I promised 'em I'd try and look her up while I was on my tour of Europe.' It was the same story he'd given to the receptionist when he'd first arrived at the old people's nursing home. Percy had told him the location of the Denesdown Nursing Home for the Elderly and Eve had begged Gabe to look in on Magda Cribben on his way to Seapower's Ilfracombe office – the home was on the outskirts of the large sprawling seaside town. He had resisted the idea at first. What good could it do? They had both assumed that Magda was long gone by now and if she was still alive she'd be somewhere in her nineties. Percy had repeated to Gabe how the woman had been hospitalized after being found on a station platform in a catatonic state and suffering apparent

351

amnesia. From there she'd been transferred to a mental asylum where countless psychiatrists had endeavoured to unlock her mind over the years, none of them having any success. In her seventies, and regarded as a lost cause, she had been moved to this nursing home and here she remained, speechless and without memory. She was no danger to anyone, not even to herself, and she showed no interest in the world around her. The last Percy had heard, Magda Cribben sat silently in her room every day, unwilling, despite the gentle coaxing of nurses and staff, to join other elderly residents in the common room where they watched television, played board and card games, and conversed about distant times.

To Gabe, the visit seemed pointless – what could he do that medics hadn't already tried to make her communicate? But Eve had been adamant: if he wouldn't go, then she would, taking Cally along with her. Somehow she had got it into her head that the old lady must have the key to the evacuees' mysterious deaths back in 1943, that only Magda Cribben could know why the children had drowned so needlessly in Crickley Hall's cellar. Rightly or wrongly, Eve – strongly influenced by the psychic, Lili Peel – thought that the answer might help the troubled spirits of the children who haunted Crickley Hall pass on peacefully It was all nonsense to him, but what harm could visiting Magda do? It would at least appease Eve to know – or to *think* – he took the matter seriously. Gabe mentally shrugged: no harm at all, he told himself.

The nurse he was following interrupted his thoughts. 'You have been informed of her condition, haven't you? You understand she won't speak to you?'

'Uh, yeah. I just figured it would be nice to see her. Family thing, y'know?'

The nurse, whose plastic nametag over her left breast named her Iris, nodded her head. 'Family is important,' she pronounced sagely.

She had an ambling gait that made Gabe want to stride ahead of her. It wasn't that he was impatient; it had more to do with being keyed up.

Although he certainly had been informed of Magda's state, Gabe had no idea of what to expect. In the photograph salvaged from its hiding place behind the cupboard, she appeared to be in her forties (although Percy had assured Gabe and Eve that Cribben's sister was in her early thirties: she just *looked* ten years older), a stiff, austere figure with a granite-like face, her eyes black and intimidating. She'd be in her nineties, and her once dark hair would be white or at least grey. He wondered if her hard features would be softened by wrinkles, if her rigid bearing would be mellowed by time. Would her heartless glare now be subdued?'

Gabe and the nurse passed by doors on either side of the corridor, some of them open to reveal sparsely furnished rooms, taken up mostly by narrow beds. They seemed empty of residents at the moment, but as they walked by one closed door near the end of the passage, it crept open a few inches. A small woman, whose unkempt grey hair hung over her creased face in thin straggles, peered out at him with watery eyes and he felt uncomfortable under her scrutiny. He heard a small, crusty snigger come from her, and then he was past the door.

The nurse turned to face him outside the open doorway of the next room, the last room along the corridor.

'Here we are, Mr . . .?' she said, eyebrows raised, questioningly.

'Caleigh,' he supplied for her.

'Yes, of course, you said before. Mr Caleigh. Magda's

inside. We always have her door open so we can keep an eye on her. Not that she's ever any trouble. Magda's as quiet as a mouse – quieter, actually – and rarely moves from her chair once she sits there after breakfast. We have to come and fetch her at mealtimes, but apart from that she stays in her room all day long. Never socializes with the other residents. She has her own little toilet and washroom, so she comes out of her room only to eat and when it's her bath day.'

Iris spoke in a normal voice, not bothering to lower its tone in deference to the woman on the other side of the doorway and Gabe wondered if Magda was deaf also. Couldn't be. The nurse or receptionist would have mentioned it otherwise. He guessed that if any resident, or patient, was always passive and silent, they would probably end up being treated as an imbecile or vegetable.

Stepping up to the doorway and looking over the nurse's shoulder, the engineer immediately set eyes on Magda Cribben.

Although there was an easychair in the room, the aged woman was seated on a hardbacked chair by the tidy bed.

'Now, I'll leave you to it,' said Iris, moving aside to let Gabe through. 'It's all right, she will hear you, but don't expect a response. If she does speak, believe me, we'll all come running. They tell me she hasn't spoken a word since the last world war, even though there's nothing physically wrong with her. Not a peep, not a whisper.'

She called into the room, this time using a louder voice. 'A gentleman has come to see you, Magda, isn't that nice? He's a relative from America and he's come all this way to visit you, so be nice to him.' The nurse winked conspiratorially at Gabe, but he did not react. 'Go right in, Mr Caleigh. You can pull the armchair round or sit on the bed, whichever you prefer.'

With an unconvincing smile, she ambled away, back in the direction they had come.

Gabe entered the room.

*Who is this man? He was a stranger, she'd never seen him before, and he was certainly no relative because she had none. Only Augustus, her dear brother, gone now, gone a long time ago. Perhaps that was for the best – they would have persecuted him if he hadn't drowned. But she did not want this strange man in her room; he wasn't even smartly dressed. Nobody ever came to see her, no, nobody ever came. Except for that one time, but it was long ago and in a different place to this, somewhere where they kept her locked up and where they were always asking questions – questions, questions, questions! But she never let them know, she never answered their silly questions – that would have been too dangerous – and eventually they had given up. Yes, he had visited her there – not this man, but the one who knew everything. He had come to her out of curiosity, not for love. Years ago that was, but she remembered it clearly as if it were yesterday. The doctors didn't know it but her mind was still razor sharp – how else could she have kept up this pretence? – her memory unimpaired. Oh yes, she remembered the other man quite clearly.*

'Ms Cribben, my name is Gabe Caleigh.'

*Who? She didn't know anyone called Caleigh. Did she? No, she would have remembered. She wasn't stupid as everyone thought she was. Just because she wouldn't speak, it did not mean she'd forgotten how to. Oh no, that would have been too risky. Did they still hang people these days? She couldn't be sure. And she certainly couldn't ask.*

*The stranger had made himself comfortable now, he's sitting on the edge of the bed* – her *bed. Who had given him permission? Improper, that's what it was. Most inappropriate behaviour, a strange man alone with a poor defenceless woman who could not even protest! The very idea! It was a good thing the door was open or he might have tried anything. On her bed, indeed! Such insolence, such bad manners.*

*She wouldn't let him know she was cross, though. She would not reveal her outrage. She wouldn't even look at him any more.*

'Currently I'm living at Crickley Hall with my family.'

*Crickley Hall! There it was. He would try to trick her, he'd ask about the house, what happened there . . .*

'Do you remember Crickley Hall, Magda?'

*Oh such atrocious manners. He was addressing her by her Christian name as if he were a friend or an acquaintance. Trying to be familiar because he wanted to ask her questions. But no, she wouldn't be tricked, she wouldn't speak to him, no, she'd not say a single word. He wasn't even English, he was what was commonly called a Yank. The Yanks were coming to help Britain fight the Germans. No, no. The war had ended, hadn't it? It was over a few years ago. Ten? Fifty? A hundred? It was a long time since, if she remembered correctly. And she did remember correctly, didn't she? Yes, she did, more than anyone else would ever know.*

'When you were in your thirties you lived in the house called Crickley Hall with your brother, Augustus Theophilus Cribben.'

*He knows something! He knows something about Augustus and he's trying to trick me into telling him about what happened that time in Crickley Hall. That horrible night when the river broke its banks and the river beneath the house rose up through the well. She had escaped just moments before the flood had come, when Augustus was – no! She must not even think of it! Her heart was pounding and he might hear it. It would give her away. She must calm herself, reveal nothing in her expression. 'That the time may have all shadow and silence in it.' Shakespeare wrote that. See how acute her memory was? After she had been found the next morning, they had explained what had befallen Augustus and the children – what they* thought *had befallen them – but she had not betrayed herself, she had not shown any emotion, even though inside she had been devastated, her heart and soul left raw and damaged. She had been cunning, though: she had pretended to be in deep shock. No, that wasn't quite true – she* had *been in deep shock – but she had fooled them all, the doctors who had examined her, the police and the various officials. Even the pious prig, the Reverend Rossbridger (yes, see how sharp her memory was?), had been duped when he had come to the hospital, pleading with her to save her brother's righteous name (and, of course, his own by association). He had wanted her to refute the outrageous but necessarily covert report and the rumours that followed it, stories of how Augustus had shut the orphans in Crickley Hall's cellar on the night of the flood. Surely Augustus would not have acted so wickedly, Rossbridger had pleaded. The guardian has cherished those unfortunate children. Certainly he was firm with them, but he was loving also, and taught them the way of the Lord. Speak out, dear Magda, the old fool had begged her, defend your brother's honour. But she would not speak out, the truth would only defile Augustus's good name even more.*

*And then, many years later when she was in the bad place where they had locked her away and she thought she'd finally been forgotten, another man came to speak with her. But this one she knew well, even though he had changed, for he had been her willing ally once.*

*He had been aware of everything – all that had taken place that last night and all that had gone on before:* everything *– but he, too, had plied her with questions, questions, questions, and* *she had played dumb, she had not broken her silence even for him, she'd not said a single word. She wasn't going to be gulled into admitting anything! She was just a dumb old lady with no memories and who played no part in the present world.*

*Curiously he had looked satisfied when he left her all alone again (which was how she liked it – no temptations to speak then). He had never returned, though, and that was fine too. Her own company was good enough for her! Perhaps he didn't know they'd moved her to this place, where she had the door open all day (she had closed it several times when she'd first arrived, but they had scolded her, so she didn't do it any more. That was perfectly all right, though – they could spy on her as much as they liked, but they wouldn't catch her out, she was too clever for them).*

'Back in 1943,' Gabe said doggedly, aware that Magda was paying no heed, as if she were in a world of her own, 'you and your brother were custodians of a bunch of evacuees sent down from London because of the war. Do you remember that? Just nod your head if you do, you don't have to speak.'

*Now this man was interrogating her! Had he no respect for a frail old woman whose only pleasure was solitude? Why was he asking about the best-forgotten past? Hadn't she suffered enough, didn't she still have the nightmares? Surely she had paid the price for what had happened at Crickley Hall. None of it was her fault anyway – she'd left the house when she realized her brother had lost his mind. She couldn't have helped those children – Augustus was too strong and he might have turned on her! She had run out into the storm, and then walked miles to get away from Crickley Hall and her brother's madness. She couldn't, she wouldn't be blamed! At least, not for that night. Her grievous sin came before then, but she'd only committed it out of love for her Augustus, knowing he would have been in serious trouble with the authorities should they learn just how rigorous was his rule. The young teacher – what was her name? She knew it, she was sure, because her memory was razor sharp. Miss Linnet, that was it! Miss Nancy Linnet – the young teacher had to be stopped. Magda would not allow the betrayal! The girl had been soft with the children, pandering to them, treating them as if they were special. Well, they weren't special, they were unruly and needed strict discipline, a hardy regime to mould them into proper young persons! Augustus had the right idea, he knew the value of chastisement, and Magda always carried out what was expected of her. She revered her older brother.*

*The children learned respect, just as they learned their lessons, yet still they rebelled and still Augustus had to punish them. But finally, it all became too much for him: Augustus's mind snapped. His rage was awful and his actions frightened even her. First the Jewish infant (how she and her brother hated the Jews! They were the real reason, with their worldwide conspiracies and profiteering, for the war in Europe) had been dealt with, then the children who had attempted to run away. But in the end, it was she and the boy who had fled, frightened by Augustus's madness, not sure how far the insanity would drive him, afraid for their own lives.*

'Magda, how about I get a pen and some paper? Couldn't you write down your answers? You used to be a teacher, so obviously you're an educated woman.'

*Hah! Flattery now. As if she would betray her brother. They had told her a long time ago that Augustus had drowned within the walls of Crickley Hall, so if his soul were weighed down by sin – a sin caused by his own derangement – he had paid the price. Now his soul should be left in peace.*

*They had also told her that the children had perished with him in the flood. How little these people knew! Perhaps they thought another shock would move her to speak, might unlock her mind and release her from the amnesia (the false amnesia!), but she had been too clever for them. She had not reacted at all; not one tear of grief had fallen from her eyes. She could tell her interrogators were suspicious about the deaths of the children, but they had no proof of what really happened that night. None at all. They didn't even know the fate of the young teacher with the ugly withered arm. And they never would. Not even on her own deathbed would she tell them. 'In dumb silence will I bury mine.' The great bard again, put so aptly. No, the secret would die with her.*

'Y'see, Magda, weird things have been going on in Crickley Hall lately. My wife thinks the place is haunted. She figures there must be a reason for it. Now personally, I don't go along with all this ghost, uh, stuff, but I have to admit I've been pretty shaken by some of the things myself.'

*What did he expect her to say if she chose to speak?*

'We can't understand why the kids weren't at the top of the house, you know, above flood level? What were they doing in the basement? The mystery is why were they down there in the first place? Common sense should've taken them to high ground, wouldn't you agree?'

*No, she wouldn't agree at all. The man wasn't going to trick her even if he could read her mind.*

'My wife's theory is that the kids were put down there as some kind of punishment. Maybe just to scare 'em. But your brother took it too far, he kept them there when the flood came. My wife, she figures that those children have somehow come back, as ghosts, I mean, and they won't leave until the mystery's solved. She wants to help them move on, but there's no way of knowing how they were trapped. Although you were found miles away next morning, she thought you might've been there when those kids were shut away. But maybe you weren't, maybe you'd already left before the flood hit. Seems likely, otherwise you'd have drowned with your brother. But either way, we'd like to know. At least it might stop my wife wondering, kinda let me off the hook.'

*Let him off the hook? What language was this young man speaking? Oh yes, the nurse had said he was from America. Magda decided she didn't like Americans. Why had it taken them so long to join the war effort against the Germans? Which was a stupid and needless war anyway. She and Augustus liked the Germans. They were a fine race of people, strong and adamantine in their beliefs and pursuits. Not like the insidious Jews, the murderers of Christ. And not like the Americans with their impudence and slovenly speech. Not like this impertinent individual before her now.*

'Look, we know how badly those kids were treated. We found the Punishment Book, y'see, and it's all written down, every detail of the punishments given for so-called misbehaviour – the canings, the whippings with a leather belt, making 'em go without food, the cold baths, standing still for hours in their underwear. Pretty harsh on a bunch of orphans, the eldest of 'em no more than twelve years. Sure, I know things were different in those days, but even so, you and your brother were a tad excessive, don't you think? The authorities would've thought so too if they'd ever found out. What puzzles me is why you didn't destroy the book – oh, and the split-ended cane we found with it – instead of just hiding it. Why was that, Magda?'

*Because Augustus would not allow her to! He said every transgression and its consequence had to be recorded as evidence of their exemplary guardianship. But, always the pragmatic one, she knew the powers that be would never approve of their methods for controlling disobedient boys and girls, so, with his grudging acquiescence, she had hidden the book and the thrashing cane away. Inspectors might arrive on any day of any week, so it was best that they find no handwritten testimony to the punishments. Both book and stick could easily be retrieved whenever they were required.*

'And for some reason there was a picture stashed away too. Of the kids and you and your brother.'

*And the trainee teacher, the silly girl who protested and threatened to betray them with exaggerated stories of how the children were treated! Well she had been dealt with and the photograph put away with the other items because the young girl's image served as a constant reminder and Magda did not like to dwell on just how she had silenced Miss High-and-Mighty Linnet. But Magda was too proud of the photograph to get rid of it. It displayed Augustus and her in all their authority, a permanent tribute to their fine achievement and dedication. Before, they had been mere teachers with limited powers, but then the opportunity had come along to become tutors and custodians of eleven evacuee orphans for the duration at Crickley Hall, far from the war-torn city. She and Augustus had been chosen for the post from above all other applicants. No, she could never have destroyed that photograph. She swelled with pride just thinking of it. If only Augustus had not suffered the headaches, the excruciating pain that had him crushing his head between his own hands to suppress it. It was the headaches that slowly deranged his brilliant mind, leaving him with fits of uncontrollable anger. It was the agony of them that caused the insanity.*

'Okay, I'm done here. It was my wife's idea to drop by anyway. I didn't expect much, and that's what I got. 'Cept for a slight reaction in your eyes. I caught it twice, just a flicker, even though you wouldn't look at me. Once when I said my wife thought Crickley Hall was haunted, and then again when I mentioned the photograph. Both times it was just a stab of fear. Well, it looked like fear to me. It came and went fast, but it was there.

'Maybe you're trapped inside a world of unresolved guilt,

living in a hell all your own. Who can say? If I've got it wrong, I apologize. Didn't mean to bother you. So long, Magda, I hope you really don't remember.'

*He was going! At last he was leaving the room. Curiously, she was tempted to break all her years of silence to speak to him. She wanted to defend her righteous brother. And herself, of course. But silence had protected her for a long time now – a century, it seemed – and she was not about to break it for this brazen young man. In truth, she had remained quiet for so long that she wondered if her voice had atrophied along with her tired old body. Damn this stranger, and damn all those others, all those officials and medical people who had tried to make her communicate! There, this man had caused her to curse. But God would forgive her. He had forgiven her for everything else, even the killing of the teacher, because He understood the necessity. God was with her always.*

*Besides, she hadn't cursed aloud, had she? So it didn't count.*

Gabe was more disgusted with himself than impatient with Magda Cribben. She may have been one hell of a bitch when she was young, but now she was just a shrivelled-up old lady who looked so frail a sharp sneeze might cause her whole body to disintegrate. In the photograph he'd found she appeared so formidable, with her colourless face and black, shadowed eyes and stiff posture. Now she was a relic of her former self, a pathetic hunched figure whose bone structure seemed to have shrunk beneath her flesh. Yet, oddly, she did not have an elderly person's vulnerability; there was still something scary in her unblinking gaze. Had he really seen a flicker of fear in her eyes, though, or were both times only in his own imagination?

At the door he glanced round for one last look at her: she remained staring at the blank wall.

Well, at least he'd kept his promise to Eve, he thought to himself as he strode out into the corridor.

He had only taken a few paces when the partially open door he and the nurse had passed by earlier swung wider. A thin, brown-spotted arm reached out to him.

'Mister,' a low, raspy voice whispered.

Gabe stopped and saw the same wrinkled face that had peered out at him before; now there was more of it to see. The woman with grey straggly hair clutched a worn pink dressing gown closed tight against her flat chest and he could see the hem of a nightdress hanging low round her skinny ankles and slippered feet.

He drew close and she narrowed the gap in the door again as if fearing he might attack her.

'D'you need something?' Gabe asked. 'Can I get a nurse for you?'

'No, no, I jus' wants to speak to yer.' She had an accent almost as broad as Percy's. 'Yer've been to see her ladyship, haven't yer?' The elderly resident didn't wait for a reply. 'No one ever comes to see her. Got no relatives, no friends either. Give yer the silent treatment, did she?' She gave a sharp cackle.

'Yeah,' said Gabe. 'She never spoke a word.'

'Likes to pretend she can't speak, that one does, likes to play dumb. But I've heard in the middle of the night when everyone's s'posed to be sleeping. Walls're thin d'you see, an' I don't sleep much nowadays. I listen an' I hear Magda Cribben speakin' plain as day. She has nightmares and she moans somethin' awful an' talks to herself. Not loud though, not so the night nurse might come down to her. I can hear all right though. Puts my ear against the wall. Thinks they're comin' to get her, see?'

'Who? The police?' It was a fair assumption if Magda had played some part in the children's deaths. Guilt might still be hounding her.

The woman became tetchy, almost cross. 'No, no, not the police!' Her voice dropped to a conspiratorial whisper again. 'It's the kiddies she's scared of. She thinks they're comin' back to get her for what she done to 'em. She cries out she's sorry, she shouldn't have lef' 'em alone. She don't do it fer long, jus' fer a coupla minutes most nights. She can speak all right, despite what they thinks here. I know, I can hear her.'

She closed the door a little more, as if even more cautious.

'An' sometimes, sometimes I gets frightened too 'cause I can hear somethin' else. Soft little feet runnin' past my door an' goin' into her room. Goin' in to haunt her 'cause of what she done.'

It was ridiculous but Gabe felt the hairs on the back of his neck stiffen.

## 47: GORDON PYKE

Loren skipped off the people-carrier, gave a wave to her new best friend Tessa (ignoring the scowl she received from Seraphina, who sat silently but grumpily in the back seat of the vehicle) and hurried across the road to the bridge. She hardly registered the dark red Mondeo parked behind her father's Range Rover and whose driver's door was beginning to open. She was too eager to get out of the rain and tell her mother about Seraphina, who had turned up for school that morning nursing a sore-looking nose and without a word to say to Loren. Loren had expected more trouble from the hefty girl when she eventually returned to class, but Seraphina had ignored her all day (although Loren had caught some dirty looks from her). Loren knew it was wrong, but she felt pleased that punching her seemed to have worked, for Seraphina's intimidation had stopped. Mum would be relieved there was no further problem, though she would hide it, and Dad would be delighted, but he wouldn't show it in front of Mum.

She reached the wooden bridge, rain seeming to *thud* against her woollen beanie, and quickened her pace. Unfortunately, she didn't realize how slippery the bridge's planks were.

One foot slid sharply forward and she went down, her

other leg collapsing beneath her, bending so that her bare knee whacked against the wood. She cried out in pain and surprise, her school bag falling from her shoulder, spilling some of its contents onto the bridge.

Momentarily numbed by the shock, Loren was unable to move. She sprawled on the wet boards, her weight on one elbow, eyes smarting with welling tears. Mustn't be a baby, she told herself. Her leg wasn't broken, it just hurt a lot. Looking down at her injured knee, she saw blood beads appearing on its scraped skin. She wondered if she would be able to walk properly. Not far to the house, but she was soaked already. She tried to rise on wobbly legs but found it difficult.

That was when a large, strong hand reached under her shoulder and began to pull her up.

Gabe had just come down from the room in Crickley Hall that he used as an office. Earlier that day at the Seapower office in Ilfracombe he had surprised his new colleagues with the news that he had almost solved the maintenance problems of the marine turbine. However, he preferred to work out the details alone, without distractions, and that was probably best achieved from home. He had offered no excuse for his late arrival that morning (after visiting the old folks' home) and none was sought – in any case, as a subcontractor to the company and technically a free agent, he was allowed some latitude, provided he came up with solutions. So Gabe had returned to Crickley Hall mid-afternoon.

In truth, he had wanted to leave early so that he could discuss with Eve his eerie meeting with Magda Cribben. He'd had to phone Eve from the office because his cell phone still wouldn't reach Hollow Bay, although it worked fine outside the area, but it proved difficult to talk freely with co-workers in close proximity. He had told Eve that Magda hadn't said a word to him, that she'd remained silent throughout the visit; he hadn't mentioned the crazy next-door neighbour who maintained that Magda had not lost the power of speech but sometimes spoke in her sleep. As for ghosts running down corridors in the dead of night, well, he thought he'd omit this from his report for now.

Face to face, he told her everything and Eve had become very quiet – if not pale – when he mentioned the crazy woman's assertions that Magda Cribben still had the power of speech, even if it was only when she was dreaming, and that ghosts were also haunting the nursing home. It had all only served to deepen his wife's belief in spirit children.

The engineer had then worked solidly on his design for raising the marine turbine's gearbox and generator above the water level so that maintenance could be carried out using a surface structure and ancillary vessel, and it was late afternoon before he came down again, hungry and thirsty because he had worked through lunch.

He crossed the hall, but before he could enter the kitchen, the loud discordant sound of the doorbell brought him to a startled halt. Through the kitchen doorway he caught Eve's surprised look in his direction. He shrugged and went to the front door to unlock it.

The man standing outside with Loren was tall, at least six foot one or two, Gabe reckoned. The stranger wore a funny little Tyrolean hat with a small stiff feather stuck in its band.

'Delivery of one young lady with a badly scraped knee,' the stranger announced in a deep but friendly voice. Then, smiling, he introduced himself: 'My name is Gordon Pyke. I think I might be of some help to you.'

Gordon Pyke had the kindest eyes Gabe had ever seen. They were of the lightest blue and creases – laughter lines – spread from their corners almost to the man's temples. He looked to be in his sixties – late, or early seventies, Gabe couldn't tell – but his long figure looked strong and straight, only a slight paunch bulging against the lower buttons of his waistcoat, which was worn under a brown tweed jacket. An open fawn raincoat hung over both. He leaned on a stout walking stick that favoured his left leg.

When Loren had explained that she had fallen on the bridge and Mr Pyke had helped her to the front door, Gabe had immediately invited him in out of the rain.

Once inside, the stranger had removed his hat to reveal thin grey-black hair swept back over the dome of his head. He sported a small goatee beard, which was also black flecked with grey, as were the thick sideburns that partially disguised the largeness of his ears. His smile was warm, with teeth so perfect Gabe guessed they had to be manufactured.

Eve came out of the kitchen, Cally following, and went straight to Loren. She bent to examine her daughter's injured knee.

'Oh, you poor thing,' she said sympathetically. 'How did you manage that?'

'I slipped and fell on the bridge,' Loren told her, putting on a brave face even though the scrape was really sore by now. 'Mr Pyke picked me up.'

'I'm sure you'll find it's not a mortal wound,' Pyke said teasingly.

'Thank you for helping Loren,' said Eve, satisfied that the injury really wasn't serious.

'You are Mr and Mrs Caleigh, I take it.' The tall stranger looked first at Gabe, and then at Eve. 'Yes, you're certainly Eve Caleigh. The photograph of you in the *North Devon Dispatch* was an excellent likeness. Not all newspaper pictures are.'

'You saw that?' Gabe was both resigned and suspicious.

'I'm afraid so. Not the sort of publicity one normally seeks, is it? But newspapers enjoy publishing such hokum because they increase circulation figures.'

'Is that why you're here?' Gabe suspected they had one of those sightseers they had dreaded on their hands.

'As a matter of fact, it is, Mr Caleigh.'

Gabe felt his heart sink. He would thank the man, and then get rid of him.

'But not out of mere curiosity,' Pyke continued, 'I can assure you of that.' He smiled at Gabe, and then at Eve.

Eve spoke to Loren. 'Go into the kitchen and wait. I'll be there in a minute to clean your knee and put some ointment on it to stop any infection. It might need a plaster. Oh, and take Cally with you.'

Loren limped off, leading Cally back into the kitchen, while Eve returned her attention to the tall man with the nice smile and pleasant manner.

'So you believe all this nonsense about ghosts,' Gabe said when Loren and Cally were out of earshot.

'No. It's precisely because I don't that I'm here,' came the reply.

Gabe and Eve exchanged glances and Pyke gave a short, deep-throated chuckle.

'I came here, Mr and Mrs Caleigh, because I seek out so-called "ghosts" for a living.' He smiled at Gabe's pained expression. 'You might be relieved to hear,' Pyke went on, 'that rarely, if ever, do I find them.'

Gabe shook his head. 'I don't get it.'

'No. Well, as it happens I don't believe in hauntings either and eight times out of ten I find my disbelief is vindicated. There are no such things as ghosts and, if you'll allow me, I'm confident I'll prove to you that this house isn't haunted.'

'So you're one of those guys who investigate spooky places.'

'I'm a psychic investigator, or a parapsychologist, if you like, and I do investigate houses and buildings where it's claimed – usually mistakenly – that they're haunted by supernatural forces – apparitions, phantom voices or poltergeists.'

'Poltergeists?'

'Mischievous demon spirits.'

'Yeah, I know what they are. I just don't give 'em much credence.'

'Good, then we agree.' But again, Pyke took in Gabe's doubtful expression.

'Let's take poltergeists as an example then,' the self-pronounced psychic investigator resumed. 'Such activity involves objects flying across rooms, doors opening and closing, furniture movement, knocking sounds, even smells – there are a whole range of incidents that can startle or terrify the poor victim. But the fact is, they are often instigated by the kinetic mind energy of pubescent girls, whose emotional and hormonal state is undergoing profound changes. Or they can be caused by individuals who are in high-stress situations.'

'Are you telling us that what has happened here is all in our minds?' Eve's voice was cautious, yet challenging.

'No, I'm only giving you an example of what might be the cause of paranormal activities.'

'You're thinking of Loren,' Gabe guessed.

'Not necessarily, although her age could suggest it's her. But you or your wife might equally be the epicentre of such activity. That is, if either one of you is deeply anxious or distressed at this time. Perhaps you both are.'

Once more, Gabe and Eve glanced at each other.

'Yes,' said Eve, regarding Pyke again. 'Yes, there's much more going on here that isn't mentioned in the newspaper.'

'Then why don't we make ourselves comfortable and discuss precisely what *has* been happening?' Pyke turned first to Gabe and then to Eve, and the warmth of his smile was persuasive.


'Sometimes,' Pyke was explaining, 'energies, especially if they're traumatic or violent, can be absorbed into the very fabric of a building itself, as if the stone and timbers act like a tape recorder, to be released as images or sounds, or both, at some later date.'

The three of them were in Crickley Hall's sitting room, Gabe and Eve together on the couch, the psychic investigator in the high-backed armchair, his cane resting between his legs. Gabe had not yet laid a fire, so the room was chilly and dank.

'It's these type of events that seem to register mostly, because the energy released at the time is extremely potent. It's when those occurrences are subsequently *replayed* as images and sounds that they're taken for supernatural encounters.'

Eve had related some of the unusual incidents that had happened in Crickley Hall that past week and Pyke had listened attentively, making sympathetic noises here and there, a nod of his head occasionally. Sometimes he gave a benign smile, other times a deep frown.

'Now, this house,' he continued, 'is old and full of draughts – although I'd rather call them air currents. They're certainly evident in this room. The building itself is situated in a deep-sided gorge through which winds and breezes are channelled. A sudden fierce gust could easily have caught the swing outside, frightening your youngest daughter and consequently knocking you to the ground. Now, you tell me there's a well to an underground river in the basement area, from which I imagine all manner of air currents rise, and on occasion they probably bring vapour mists with them. Mists that you have misguidedly thought to be apparitions.'

Eve looked doubtful, but it was Gabe who protested, even though in truth he was prepared to believe in the investigator's theories. 'They were scooting all over the place, following each other.'

'Vapours driven by rampant but localized winds. In your own mind you might view them as having purpose or direction, but the reality is that they were merely carried along on the air currents.'

'The banging from inside the closet?'

'All manner of causes. Wind, hot waterpipes, bats, rodents, vibrations . . .'

'But the cupboard door moved; it rattled in its frame,' asserted Eve, 'as if something inside was pushing against it. And when we opened the door, the cupboard was empty, there was no living thing in there.'

'If it were a rodent it would have disappeared through whatever opening it had used for entry. Or it may well have been vibrations from internal piping.'

'Well, there are hot and cold waterpipes running through the closet...' Gabe said uncertainly but willing to be convinced.

'When a person is in shock or frightened, it's all too easy for their own imagination to exaggerate what is really happening.' Pyke leaned forward, his large hands resting over the curved top of his cane. 'Take the cellar door as an example. You claim you always lock it, yet it constantly appears to unlock itself. The lock is obviously faulty, or the frame is slightly warped, probably both, so the locking bolt works itself loose with the continual pressures of the draughts coming from the well below being funnelled up the stairway.'

Plausible, thought Gabe. Just.

'Puddles on the floor? I think perhaps water either seeps up from minute cracks in the cement between the flagstones, or there are slow, tiny leaks in the roof and ceiling.'

'But the puddles disappear,' said Eve, sceptically.

'Obviously not through evaporation, but perhaps the water sinks back into the same cracks that caused them. Those cracks are so fine that they can't be seen unless examined closely. The same applies to those created by leaks in the ceiling – they merely drain away. Puddles on the staircase could be formed by cracks in the ceiling directly above or by rainwater driven in through small gaps in the large window. They would disappear through splits in the stairboards.'

'But I saw children in outdated clothes dancing in the hall,' Eve insisted, her hands clasped tightly over her knees.

'Yes, that's interesting.' Pyke settled back in the armchair again, his voice and his manner somehow calming. 'Tell me, what had you been occupied with just before you had this vision? Sleeping, perhaps?'

'No, it was mid-morning and I was wide awake.' She

thought back. 'Yes, I'd been in the kitchen looking at the spinning top.'

'Spinning top?'

Eve hesitated. 'We found an old-fashioned spinning top in the attic among the other toys. It looked like it had never been used. I oiled it and got it spinning.'

'You spun it?'

'Yes. It was stiff at first, but I soon had it turning.'

'These toys spin very fast, don't they?'

'Very fast. The colours merge into a kind of whiteness as it makes a high-pitched humming noise.'

'What's the pattern or design? They're usually very colourful.'

'It's a picture that goes all the way around. Of – of children holding hands and dancing in a circle.' She knew what Pyke was about to suggest.

'And the figures blended, became a white blur . . .?' Pyke prompted.

'Yes.'

'You watched it spin. I suppose it might have some kind of hypnotic effect if you stare at it too long and too hard. Revolving patterns at certain speeds can induce trance-like states. Is that what happened to you, Mrs Caleigh?'

'I – I don't think so. I'm not sure.'

'I suggest that's precisely what happened; and when you went out into the hall, the vision of dancing children became a reality to you. You were still in a semi-trance, you were in a waking dream.'

'But Cally saw the children too. It was because of her call that I went out there.'

'Auto-suggestion.'

She stared at him.

'I assume you are very close to your daughters. The mother–child relationship is one of the strongest bonds possible, one that's full of intuition and shared feelings. A mother can often know why her baby is crying without there being any physical evidence of something wrong. In the same way, a baby or small child can often sense the mood of their mother without a word being spoken.'

Eve thought of her intuitive connection with Cam, but it was Gabe who spoke.

'What are you saying, Mr Pyke? Cally saw the children because the thought of them was already inside my wife's head?'

'That's exactly what I'm saying.' Pyke thumped the top of his cane enthusiastically. 'The almost hallucinogenic vision of children dancing in a circle was created by the spinning top and was fixed in your wife's mind. It transferred itself to your daughter, who thought she was seeing the real thing and so called out to the mother.'

'Wait a minute.' Gabe scratched the side of his chin, perplexed. 'The night before last, Loren woke up screaming. She said someone had beaten her with a stick. Was that some kinda thought transference too?' He was thinking of the punishment stick they had found earlier that afternoon and how disgusted and horrified both he and Eve had felt at the sight of it.

'No, I don't think so. But there is an underlying emotional tension in this house; I sensed it as soon as I entered. Have you suffered a bereavement recently, or had bad news?'

Eve looked down into her lap, leaving it for Gabe to answer.

'Our five-year-old son went missing a year ago,' he said dispassionately. 'We're still grieving.' Glancing at Eve, he added, 'And we're still hoping.'

'Ah.' Pyke brought his steepled fingers up to his mouth and stared into the mid-distance. 'That could explain much. You must all be in a fragile emotional condition. Perhaps Loren, when she felt herself being beaten, was punishing herself because she is here, safe with her parents, when her young brother is gone. Perhaps she feels guilty. You've heard of the stigmata, people suffering the wounds of Christ on the Cross? It's a rare but accepted phenomenon. An inborn guilt causes those who devoutly believe Christ suffered for the sins of mankind to take on the agony of repentance themselves. I merely suggest Loren might feel some unreasonable blame for your loss and so had to be punished.'

He let out a compassionate sigh. 'I take it there were no visible signs of her pain?'

It was Eve who shook her head; Gabe was too busy trying to understand what Pyke had just suggested to them. The investigator had to be wrong: Loren was a normal well-balanced kid; there was nothing for her to feel guilty about. And besides, she'd never had that kind of dream before.

'If anyone was to blame,' said Eve, 'it was me. I let Cam out of my sight that day.'

'Eve . . .' Gabe reached for her hand to comfort her, even though he had become a little weary of the guilt she imposed upon herself. He wished he could take that burden from her, but even after all this time he just didn't know how.

Gordon Pyke was about to expound further when Loren entered the room bearing a tray on which there were two teacups in their saucers, a jumbo coffee mug that was for Gabe, and a bowl of sugar, a teaspoon dipped into it. Gabe noticed she had even laid out a small plate of biscuits. Cally trailed after her.

Treading slowly so that nothing was split, Loren made her way directly to the investigator.

'I thought you might like a cup of tea, Mr Pyke,' she said respectfully. 'I didn't know if you took sugar.'

Gabe was impressed. Loren was not usually so congenial towards adults, especially when they were strangers. Polite, always. But most times she was too shy to come forward like this. She must have taken an instant liking to the man who had helped her on the bridge.

Eve saw that Loren's injured knee had stopped bleeding, although the scrape looked red and sore. She had meant to clean it for Loren and dab on antiseptic, but Gordon Pyke had kept them talking in the sitting room.

His cane now leaning on the arm of the chair, Pyke stretched forward to take a cup and saucer from the tray. He gave Loren a broad smile.

'No sugar, my dear, but I'll help myself to a biscuit if I may?'

Almost coyly, she returned his smile. She really did like Pyke, thought Gabe again, and he wasn't surprised – there was something reassuring about the big man. Cally, as ever, was indifferent, as she was with all grown-ups.

So far, Pyke had impressed Gabe with his grounded logic for things considered paranormal or supernatural, although he could tell Eve was far from convinced. It broke down to two attitudes, he supposed: the willingness to believe in ghosts or believe in what Pyke was saying. Eve was definitely in the former category and Gabe blamed Lili Peel for that.

After Loren had given Eve her tea and Gabe his coffee, she leaned the tray against the side of the couch and squeezed herself in beside her father. Cally pressed herself against Eve's knees. Both girls eyed the stranger as he bit off half his biscuit. He munched away, a small smile showing through his short beard as though he were content in their company.

But Eve had other ideas: she didn't want her daughters included in this conversation.

'Loren, haven't you got homework to do? And Cally, why don't you do some painting in the kitchen? Loren will help you set it up.'

'Oh let them stay,' said Pyke, the remainder of the biscuit poised only inches away from his mouth. 'They should be part of this. Besides, our conversation might allay some of Loren's concerns. And the little one, well, much of what we say will go over her head.'

You might be surprised at what Cally understands, Gabe thought, but he said nothing. Loren was smiling at Pyke gratefully, pleased to be respected for the sensible girl she was.

Gabe was curious, but not only about hauntings and their rationale.

'Mr Pyke . . .' he began.

'Ask me anything you like,' said Pyke and popped the rest of the biscuit into his mouth.

'I was just wondering how you got into this business.' Gabe was not ready to trust the investigator completely. He was cautious because Gordon Pyke had arrived unannounced and unexpected, and they had allowed him in because of his kindness to Loren. But they knew zilch about him and there was a chance he could be another nut like the psychic, Lili Peel, even though outwardly he seemed sane enough.

'A perfectly reasonable question,' said Pyke cheerfully as he flicked crumbs from his fingers. 'To you ghost-hunting must seem a singularly odd occupation, but for me it's a splendidly unique calling and one, I discovered, that I'm particularly adept at, although investigating psychic phenomena is a passion that came to me late in life. Oh, I had a cursory interest in the paranormal, but my profession took up most of my time. I was a librarian in London, you see. That was a while ago and eventually I left the grime and the clamour of the city to follow a more sedate life as a librarian in Barnstaple.'

Gabe had heard of the town, which was quite a distance from Hollow Bay. So the man wasn't a local.

Pyke paused to sip some tea. Cally was thoroughly bored by now.

'Mummy,' she said plaintively, 'can I play in my room?'

'Yes, of course, dear,' Eve replied. 'Just in your room though – you're not to go up to the attic.'

'No, Mummy.' Cally trotted to the door and they heard her small steps clattering across the flagstones of the hall.

'You have exemplary children,' remarked Pyke.

'Thank you.' Eve was growing impatient. She had already guessed Pyke's purpose in coming to Crickley Hall, but she wasn't sure if she was willing to agree to it. No matter how the investigator sought to explain the bizarre events of the past week, she knew he was fundamentally wrong: Crickley Hall *was* haunted by ghosts. The problem was that Gabe, ever the pragmatist, seemed to be going along with Pyke's rationalizations.

Pyke placed the cup and saucer on the occasional table next to the armchair. 'As a librarian, I found I had lots of time to indulge myself in outside interests. Study of the preternatural became more than just a hobby with me and I soon realized that to become a psychic investigator was not difficult if one had the, uh, aptitude for such work. I found that I had.

'I began to devote my weekends to visiting alleged haunted sites and more often than not I was able to prove that most disturbances were caused by physical aberrations and not by spirits of the dead. I could do this using only the minimum tools of the ghost-hunting trade, if I may call it a trade. Early successes led to more consultation requests, which kept me very busy, so I was pleased to reach retirement age and devote all my time to researches and practical experiences.'

Pyke was retired, thought Gabe, at least sixty-five, obviously older if he left his job some time ago. He looked in fine shape.

'Is this how you find your work?' There was no hostility in Eve's question, but Gabe detected some cynicism. 'You read a wild newspaper story and then just turn up on the subject's doorstep?'

'Well, sometimes, yes,' Pyke admitted. 'I even use a cuttings agency to send me any snippets about hauntings or such. Usually I would find a phone number and ring the prospective client first. If they're not interested, fine; but more often than not, they're only too anxious to get to the bottom of the problem. I also place small ads in the local papers. You'd be surprised how many people believe their houses are haunted.'

'Eight times out of ten,' said Eve. 'Earlier you said two out of ten hauntings are unaccountable.'

'Yes, yes, I take your point, Mrs Caleigh, and you're absolutely right to make it. But in certain cases all the factors cannot be known and sometimes the psychological state of the person or persons involved is not immediately evident. So yes, of course, not all the mysteries can be solved. But that doesn't necessarily mean unnatural elements are at play.'

'But you can't be sure.'

'No, I can't be sure every time. Some mysteries will always remain so, despite our best efforts to understand them. Sometimes, perhaps, a glimmer is all we're allowed.'

There was a silence between them for a moment or two, then abruptly Eve said: 'Mr Pyke, thank you for your kindness to Loren, but I'm afraid we aren't in need of your services.'

'Wait a minute, hon,' blurted Gabe. 'Having Mr Pyke look into things can't do any harm.' Truthfully, Gabe hoped Pyke would bring a little sanity into the house.

'I can assure you, my investigation will not be disruptive. My equipment would be minimal to begin with – a couple of cameras, one with infrared capability, a tape recorder, thermometers, talcum powder and synthetic thread. We can move on to other appliances – sound scanners, magnetometers, thermal heat scanners, and other pieces – only if necessary for a more sophisticated type of investigation. From what you've already told me, I'm fairly sure that won't be the case.'

Eve was shaking her head, but Gabe pressed on.

'And you're certain you can come up with answers?'

'I'll do my best for you, that's all I can promise. I could make a start tomorrow evening.'

'Gabe—' Eve started to say, but Gabe cut her off.

'How much is your fee, Mr Pyke?'

'Oh, I don't charge anything. Any expenses, obviously, but they won't amount to much. You see, I don't do this for financial gain. With my pension and what's left from a modest property inheritance when I was much younger, I'm moderately comfortable financially and have never had the need to charge for my services. The only thing I'd require from you is permission to write a paper on my findings, which I might submit to the London Society for Psychical Research at some later date. They're always interested in the fieldwork of independent investigators like myself. And I would ask you to stay in one part of the house once I've set up my equipment. As that will be at night-time, you'll probably be in your bedrooms anyway.'

'You want to do this at night?'

'Fewer natural disturbances then. People walking about, children playing, visitors – all the usual daytime matters. Besides, that's when most of the incidents have occurred, haven't they?'

'Gabe, I don't want this,' Eve said earnestly.

But Gabe was undaunted. 'Eve, either we let Mr Pyke do his stuff, or we move out of this place at the weekend. Maybe if we find the causes of these things happening here we can fix 'em.'

Eve was about to object again, but she saw the resolution on her husband's face. Once Gabe was set on something, there was no changing his mind. Besides, the investigator might find that Crickley Hall *was* haunted.

And in her heart, that was what she hoped.

The bath was long enough for Eve to stretch full length, her legs straight, only her head and neck above the waterline. It was almost relaxing lying there cocooned and snug in the warm water, her face wet with light perspiration; only her troubled thoughts kept her from dozing.

Tomorrow evening Gordon Pyke would come to the house and set up his equipment, then would keep a lonely vigil through the night while she and her family slept. She wondered if anything more would happen when the place was under observation, something mystical that would prove his investigation pointless. Would the hours pass by peacefully, the spirits choosing not to reveal themselves, not by sound, nor by apparition? Would Pyke's apparatus show that the disturbances had perfectly natural causes? Perhaps the man was right – she *had* imagined the dancing children because her mind was susceptible to images prompted by a simple kiddies' toy, the colourful spinning top. She was aware of how emotionally vulnerable she'd become, worn down by grief and fading hope, but surely she had truly seen them, and surely she had not imagined that dark, evil presence last Sunday, and again yesterday when Lili Peel had also sensed it?

She closed her eyes against the starkness of the bathroom with its black and white tiles and plain bowled light overhead.

Rain pittered on the frosted window and curls of steam rose from the water in which she tried to relax. The warmth felt good against her skin and her thoughts wandered.

Eve was tired – she always felt tired nowadays, but this week had been particularly stressful. Good idea, Gabe, getting us all away from London so that we wouldn't be at home with its memories on the anniversary of Cam's disappearance. She gave a bitter smile. As if it would make any difference, as if it would hurt any less. But Gabe meant well.

She wiped the flannel across her face, water mixing with the perspiration. It was good not to be cold for a change, the house was always so chilly. Full of draughts, Pyke had said – or air currents, as he would have it. He was a tall, big-boned man, but he seemed trustworthy. A gentle not-quite-giant, with a good-natured countenance and a comforting smile. Eve hoped she hadn't been too rude to him, but she knew Lili Peel would be of more help to her. Eve was sure the psychic would reach Cam eventually; it would just take a little time and the right conditions. Hadn't she herself felt him close by?

Keeping her eyes closed, she sank lower into the bath, water covering her chin, almost reaching her bottom lip. So warm, so comfortable. Eve began to drift . . .

Mustn't fall asleep. So tired, though, so wearied by events. And by sorrow. Briefly, she wondered if they would ever find Chester again. Lost dog, lost son. The girls were still upset. Over Cam. Over Chester. One loss too many. Sleepy. Very sleepy . . .

Because her eyes were closed and she was half asleep, Eve didn't at first notice the light above flicker, then dim, then burn out.

But she felt the change in temperature that followed almost instantly. It roused her with a start.

The water she bathed in was suddenly chilled – no, it was

cold and fast becoming freezing. It was as if it were congealing into ice.

Then, there in the absolute darkness, she heard its sound – ice crackling as it merged on the water's surface.

She lifted her leaden arms and her numbed hands came in contact with the thin icy layer. She pushed against it, but already it was firm and wouldn't break.

Her face, just above the waterline, felt the frigidity of the room itself. Her hair stiffened and crackled with ice particles and the cold beneath seemed to press on her lungs, making it difficult to breathe. She tried to call out, but drew in frosted air that constricted her throat. This could not be happening, it was beyond all reason! How could a bath full of heated water freeze over within seconds? It was insane!

The coldness about her body seemed heavy, hardened, and it clamped her limbs, making it almost impossible to move them. And each time she tried to suck in air so that she could scream for help, it was as though a rod of ice had rushed into her throat to stifle any sound. Instead of raising her hands, she pushed them against the bottom of the bath, using her heels too, hoping to break through the glacial surface with her shoulders, but she kept slipping on the porcelain, kept slithering on its slickness.

Desperately, she sharply brought up one knee, the foot of the other leg pressed hard against the end of the bath. She heard the ice crack, sensed it give a little, felt the impact on her knee. But the effort caused her head to sink further down into the water, which rushed up her nose and surged into her open mouth. She panicked even more and threw her body around, writhing in the icy thickness, kicking up with both knees now, one after the other, cracking, then breaking the frozen sheet. Her head and shoulders were completely underwater and her back pressed against the bath's solid bottom.

She was frantic, she was terrified. She did not want to drown.

With a massive effort, she lifted her torso, her forehead breaking through the thin layer of ice that was already forming over the opening where her head had been only moments before. She gulped in a huge breath, not caring that it froze her mouth and throat and invaded her lungs like an arctic breeze, just desperate to take in air so that she wouldn't die.

She opened her eyes to the darkness and that was when vice-like fingers clamped the top of her head and pushed her down again. She went under, not understanding, just fighting for her life, tossing herself around, squirming and wriggling, refusing to be still despite the cold, tight embrace of the water, twisting so that the iron hand that held her could not get a firm grip. Eve burst through the surface ice, this time further down in the bath, one leg over the side, the other one bent, her foot pushing against the slippery porcelain.

Blinking to clear her eyes, Eve perceived rather than saw the dark figure looming over her and this time she did scream, for it was an instinctive, animal cry that was not forced but came from sheer terror.

The piercing sound echoed round the tiled bathroom. Now two stunningly gelid hands grasped her, one in her hair, the other on her shoulder. They forced her down once more, but she struggled so much, the ice breaking up completely around her, that they could not keep her under. She heaved herself upwards, screamed again, and the bathroom door crashed open, dismal light from the landing pushing back the reluctant darkness.

Gabe rushed in and grabbed Eve, hauling her out of the bath, hugging her naked shuddering body close. He tried to calm her, squeezing her tight, hushing her sobs with quietly spoken words.

'It's all right, Eve, you're safe, I'm here.'

He quickly scanned the room and although it was shadowed, he could tell there was no one else in there.

But he smelt the thick cloying stink of strong soap mixed with decay and excrement.

## 49: COMFORT

'But I felt the water, Eve, and it wasn't cold. Tepid maybe, but for sure not icy like you say.'

'You have to believe me.'

'Maybe the light burning out like that scared you and you thought—'

'I didn't imagine what happened, Gabe. The light went off—'

'It was just the bulb. I checked. None of the other lights failed.'

'When the light went off the bathwater froze. Just suddenly froze! I was caught in it. Then someone – *something* – started to push me under. It was trying to drown me! A hand was on my head, it pushed me down. I didn't imagine it!'

'Okay, hon. I'm just trying to make sense of it all.' He didn't say anything about the noxious smell. At a stretch it might only have been the bathroom's ancient drains. He had to face it, though: he was looking for plausible reasons for the weird things going on in this house. 'I suppose really I don't want to believe in ghosts,' he admitted.

'How can you ignore everything that's gone on since the day we moved in?'

He was silent. Eve was right. He himself had witnessed

the strange little glowing lights hovering round Cally while she played in her room; he, too, had heard the scuttling of small feet coming from the attic, and he had been there when the closet door had almost burst its hinges with the banging coming from inside.

Finally, he said: 'You're right, there's something wrong with this place, something bad here. Chester knew straight-away. S'why he hit the road.'

They were in their bedroom, both sitting on the edge of the bed, Eve with her bathrobe wrapped around her. Merci-fully, and perhaps oddly, her screams had not awoken their daughters; they had slept on, the sleep of the innocents. The house was taking their energy.

Gabe slumped, bent over his knees, his hands clasped together. 'I'm beat,' he said. 'We've had enough. We gotta pull out, quit.'

'But there's something good here, too.'

'How can you know that?'

'I've sensed it. So has Lili.'

'We can't go through all that again. Look, if you're right, if Cam did make some kind of contact with you, he can do it wherever you are.' He thought she was deluding herself, but now wasn't the time to voice that opinion. Eve was in a fragile state, she was too strung out.

She leaned into him, one arm crossing to his shoulder. Gabe slipped his own arm round her waist.

'All right, Gabe, we'll leave.'

He let out a sigh of relief.

'But only after Lili Peel comes here again.'

'Eve . . .'

'Just one more time. We can also let Mr Pyke carry out his investigation, if that's what you want.'

'Doesn't seem much point if we're leaving.'

'As you said earlier, his investigation can do no harm. Besides, I'm interested in what he might find.'

'You just wanna see me proved wrong, is all.' He said it lightly.

'No, I want you to be satisfied.'

'You gonna be okay tonight?'

'I'll take a sleeping pill. I feel exhausted, but I doubt I'd sleep otherwise.' The house was sapping her strength too.

She softly kissed his cheek, aware of his confusion, confident of his love. Her lips lingered.

'I was so frightened, Gabe.'

'I know. That's why we have to go.'

Yes, she thought, they should leave Crickley Hall.

But not tomorrow.

## 50: FRIDAY

Eve took the breakfast bowls and mugs out of the hot soapy water and left them on the draining board to dry. She looked out the window at the habitually dismal day. Would this rain never stop? Sighing, she stripped off the rubber gloves and dropped them on the other side of the sink, then emptied the suds into the drain. Loren, disgruntled with tiredness, had finally gone off to school, while Cally, unusually for her, was still upstairs asleep. It would have been a shame to wake her, so worn was she last night; best to let her sleep it out.

Eve realized she would have to do a small shop this morning, just some fresh food for the weekend, but Gabe was in his makeshift office, so he could listen out for Cally. He had told Eve that he thought he'd cracked Seapower's maintenance problem – something about using a telescopic hydraulic pole, its jack on the seabed, instead of a crane fixed to a surface vessel – a boat, he meant – to bring up the marine turbine's below-the-waterline machinery for maintenance work. In a way, she hoped he hadn't found the solution, because if he had, then it wouldn't matter so much if the family returned to London. Gabe could make solo trips to Devon when required.

Contrarily, Eve wasn't ready to abandon Crickley Hall too soon, despite having been scared witless last night. Cam knew she was here, that was all that mattered. He had reached out – consciously or subconsciously, it wasn't important which – from wherever he was being held and had finally found her here. Although Gabe said if there really was some kind of telepathy involved it didn't matter where she might be physically, Eve wasn't sure and was not about to take a chance, not at this stage, not when the contact felt so close. Even now she could *feel* Cam's presence. She knew beyond all doubt that her son was trying to communicate with her. Hadn't he soothed her brow on Sunday with his little soft hand, hadn't his goodness, his purity, forced the dark horrid thing to go away?

Lili Peel could be the intermediary. Eve had to get the psychic to help her again. Cam's message could be channelled through her. Eve took Lili's card from the parka hanging up beside the kitchen door and went out into the hall.

She tapped out the number on the old phone. It took six rings before Lili picked up.

'Hello?'

'Lili, it's Eve Caleigh.'

'Oh. Are you all right?'

'Not good.' Eve quickly told the psychic how the same black spirit whose presence had frightened them so the day before yesterday had tried to drown her in the bath last night. 'I'm scared, Lili,' she admitted. 'But that's not why I'm ringing. I want you to come back to Crickley Hall. I want you to try and contact my son again.'

'After what happened on Wednesday?' Lili sounded astonished – and afraid. 'It came back for you last night, don't you understand? It's too dangerous, Eve, I won't do it. I – I had a similar experience some time ago: an entity, a malevolent entity, came through unbidden. I can't take the chance again.'

'Lili, I *need* you. I know you could help me save my son if you tried. You almost reached him before.'

'Yes, and look what manifested itself instead.'

'But you'd be prepared this time. You could send it away, close it off from your mind.'

'It doesn't work that way. Once I'm in a trance I'm vulnerable, I can't control what comes through.'

'Then don't go into a trance, just use your conscious mind.'

'Don't you see? I can't help it sometimes, it takes me over. I just go under.'

'I won't let it happen, I'll keep you awake even if I have to slap your face. But you could reach Cam without being in a half-conscious state, couldn't you? I'm not even asking you to communicate with the dead. My son is alive, I know it! I only want you to establish a telepathic link, that's all I'm asking. Only you can control it properly, Lili, I'm convinced of that.'

'Your husband doesn't want me there.' Lili was struggling to excuse herself.

'Gabe won't object if it's just one more time. I'll talk to him and it'll be okay. Just try once more, Lili.'

'I'm sorry, Eve.'

'Please. Please, Lili.'

'You don't know what you're asking. Crickley Hall is filled with unrest. There's so much wickedness, so much fear.'

'Is it the children?'

'Yes, their lost spirits. Something is keeping them there. They're frightened.'

'Have you considered it might be the dark man, the thing that terrified us both when you came here, the entity that never quite materialized that day? It was stronger last night. It froze the water and wanted to drown me.'

'Its force is building and I don't have the power to stop it.

Something really bad is going to happen in Crickley Hall – I felt it as soon as I walked into the hall – and I don't want to be there when it does. My advice to you is get out as soon as you can. Please take your family away from that house.'

'We are leaving. Soon. That's why I want one more chance.'

'No, Eve. Not with me. I'm so sorry.'

Eve heard the connection break.

Lili stared at the small cordless phone on her desk. The shop was empty of customers so far, but business would pick up towards lunchtime. Midday Friday was always busy.

She felt awful. She had hated turning Eve down – the woman was in deep mental anguish and desperate – but Lili could not get involved: it was too dangerous. Eve didn't understand, even though she knew there was evil in Crickley Hall. She seemed to have a blind trust in Lili's psychic ability and an unreasonable belief that her son was still alive. It was foolish on both counts.

The truth was Lili was too afraid to return to Crickley Hall after her visit on Wednesday when she had been almost overwhelmed by fear and despair as soon as she'd entered the place. And afraid again later, when that dark thing – *literally* dark – had terrorized her and Eve. What might have been the consequences had not Gabe Caleigh and his daughter walked in at that point? Lili gave a little shudder at the thought.

No, she could not – she *would* not – go back to that house, not for Eve, not even for the children ... She broke off her deliberations and stiffened in her chair. No, she told herself, don't think of the children who had perished there. There was nothing she could do for their earthbound spirits! How could she stand up to the other, the malign, force that haunted the house? Eighteen months ago she had nearly been driven to a nervous breakdown by a spirit that had spontaneously manifested itself, the spectre of someone from her past, someone she had hurt badly, someone who even in discarnate form could not forget.

Lili unconsciously twisted one of her coloured wristbands. She blocked her own thoughts, wishing it were possible to discard certain memories.

The shop door opened and two people, shoulders still hunched against the rain, stumbled through. It was a welcome distraction.


It was just after eleven when Gabe heard the phone downstairs ring.

Bent over his drawing board, he muttered something nasty and snapped down the Rapidograph. He was tempted to ignore the *brilling* tone, but Eve was out at the harbour village store and Cally was sleeping a few doors away. He didn't want his youngest daughter disturbed, because while she was asleep she was no bother to him and he had a lot of work to wrap up before they left Crickley Hall. Gabe almost regretted not having gone into the office that morning; but then, he supposed, there would have been even more interruptions there. He wanted to finish up his sketches this morning and deliver them that afternoon, hopefully the engineering problem solved.

With a resigned groan, he stepped down from the high stool and went to the open door. Maybe it was someone from

Seapower ringing; or maybe it was his own London office, checking on his progress – he hadn't spoken to anyone there for a whole working week.

On his way along the landing, he popped his head into Cally's bedroom to see how she was doing. She was still sleeping soundly, her mouth slightly open, quietly snoring through her nose. Poor mite, she had become as tired as her older sister. Getting Loren out of the door to catch the school bus this morning had been hard work for Eve.

He hurried to the stairs, now having decided to answer the phone, anxious not to miss the call. Might be important.

Crossing the hall's stone floor in sneakers, jeans and half-sleeve sweatshirt, he grabbed the receiver from its cradle.

'Yeah?'

'Gabe Caleigh?'

'Yeah.'

'It's DI Kim Michael.'

Gabe drew in a sharp breath. His heart didn't know whether to sink or be elated. Instead, it became neutral. Michael was the police detective in London who had eventually, when it was assumed that Cam had been abducted, taken charge of the investigation and search.

'Hey, Kim.' Gabe's voice was low and steady. He and Detective Inspector Michael had become almost friends during the long quest to find Gabe's missing son for, although two FLOs (Family Liaison Officers) had been assigned to the family, the detective had taken a personal interest in the case, going out of his way to inform Eve and Gabe of every lead the police were following, of every reported sighting, and every disappointment when they followed them up. He would call in on Eve and Gabe regularly after duty hours, just to see how they were bearing up, encouraging them at the beginning, letting them down as gently as possible as the months went by, his sympathy genuine, unaffected by the official role he played.

'I tried your mobile number first – I wanted to speak to you, not your wife. Couldn't even get a tone though.'

'Yeah,' Gabe responded, 'cell phones don't seem to work in this neck of the woods.' Then, bluntly: 'What is it, Kim?'

The detective was equally blunt. 'We've found a child's body.'

# 51: THE DRIVE HOME

Gabe tried to concentrate on the road ahead as he joined the motorway that led straight into the heart of the capital. Rain lashed the windscreen, keeping the wipers busy, but when he glanced out of the side window he saw there was worse to come: huge grey-black clouds had assembled in the north-east, great over-burdened bulks that were steadily progressing across the country, portents of punishment yet to come. His mind kept wandering back to the conversation with the police detective, the same questions and the same replies repeating themselves like a script that had to be learnt.

A little over three hours ago he had been standing in the great hall, the phone shaking in his hand, while the world shrank around him. He had endeavoured to remain calm as he spoke to DI Michael.

'Have you seen the body itself?' he had asked the detective.

'Yes, I have.'

'What . . . uh, what kind of condition is it in?'

'Gabe, come on. You don't want to know. It's been in the canal for a long time. The pathologist reckons it's been in the water a good few months, possibly a year.'

'For as long as Cam's been missing.'

Silence at the other end.

Then, Gabe: 'Tell me, Kim.'

'It's badly decomposed. As you'd expect.'

Gabe had thought for a few moments, the news taking time to sink in even though he had been expecting – *fearing* – something like this since Cam had been gone.

'Thing is,' the policeman said slowly, 'we need you to ID.' More quickly: 'You don't have to see the body, Gabe, you could just identify the clothes. They're worn and ragged, and the colours are faded, but you should be able to recognize them. The shoes are gone. Eve gave a fair description of what Cameron was wearing the day he disappeared, so no doubt you'll know yourself.'

Of course he'd fucking know: he was there when Eve described the clothes to the police for about the hundredth time. He remembered getting the phone call at the office, Eve too distraught to make it herself, a WPC doing it for her. The fast drive home to be with Eve, hoping, *praying* – he had more faith in God back then – that they would have found his little boy by the time he reached the house. The panic in Eve's eyes, her body-rattling weeping, throwing herself into his arms the moment he walked through the door. Yes, he remembered – that day was seared into his brain.

'Look, Gabe,' DI Michael had said this morning almost exactly a year later, 'I don't think you should bring your wife with you. Come on your own, will you?'

'She's gonna want to be there.'

'My firm advice is that you don't let her. Your son or not, either way, it would be too distressing for her. I don't think she needs to be put through an ordeal like this.'

'Okay. You're right. Someone has to look after Cally anyway – we can't drag her all the way back to London. And Loren's at school, she doesn't get home 'til around four. I'll make Eve see sense.' His shoulders were hunched and he consciously forced them to relax. 'Eve's out, but she'll be back any minute. When I've told her, I'll be on my way. Look, just to be certain, you're talking about the canal that runs past the park, right?'

'Afraid so. The body was trapped a mile or so further on, which was why the divers found nothing when they searched before.'

'You say trapped?'

'Yes, it was inside an old pram – one of those big perambulators – someone had dumped in the water probably years ago. Apparently it was lying on its side among a lot of other junk on the canal bed. There's a council estate along that stretch and residents have been dumping stuff for years. Yesterday, the Underwater Search Unit was searching the area because a local known villain was seen tossing a gun over the canal wall as he was being chased by uniformed cops.'

So, the body had been discovered by chance. Gabe suppressed any cynicism he felt.

'Kim,' he said quietly. 'What do you think?'

'I can't lie to you, Gabe, but it looks bad for you. The clothes—'

'Okay. Where do I meet you?'

'At the mortuary.' The detective gave Gabe the address as well as the mortuary's phone number in case he got lost. 'You've got my mobile number, so ring me when you're approaching London. It'll give me time to get there before you.'

Gabe had hung up. Cally was at the top of the stairs, rubbing sleep from her eyes with her knuckles as she looked down at him.

*

401

Surprisingly, when Eve had returned from the harbour village she had taken the news calmly; perhaps it was because she was almost totally drained, had little more emotion left. Also surprisingly, she had agreed to stay at Crickley Hall while Gabe made the trip to London. She seemed to see the logic of remaining behind with their daughters.

Now, Gabe pushed his foot down hard on the accelerator, keeping to the outside lane, flashing his headlights at other drivers who blocked his way, forcing some to pull over into the middle lane by tailgating them.

Anxious already, Eve's reaction made him even more so. He had feared the finding of a child's body so close to the park where Cam had been lost would leave her broken, hysterical at least, but she had been composed, albeit a brittle type of composure. Her one condition for staying, though, was that he phone her immediately he knew whether it was the body of their son or not. She had kissed Gabe and leaned into him so that he could enfold her in his arms. That was the moment he thought she might break, but she had only trembled against him, and when he lifted her chin with the crook of his finger, she had gazed back with dulled eyes. He realized she was in shock, a numbing kind of shock. He was loath to leave her like that, but he'd had no other choice, he had to find out the truth about their son. And if it was Cam? Right now that was too painful to contemplate.

He kicked down hard on the accelerator once more to get past a lorry that was throwing up spray from the middle lane. The wet greyness of the day closed round him.

## 52: SECOND VISITOR

Iris ushered the visitor into Magda's room at the nursing home.

'There now, Magda, aren't you the popular one? You've another person come to see you. That's two more than you've ever had since you've been here.'

Magda ignored the nurse's prattling and took in the man who had entered.

*Oh, she knew him. He had visited her once before, but in the other place, where they kept a person locked up all the time. But that was a long while ago and he was much younger then, a young man and not the awkward boy she used to know.*

'You can sit in the armchair, if you like.' The blue-uniformed nurse indicated the lumpy soft chair in the corner. 'Magda won't move from her one unless it's to be put to bed. Sometimes I think she's stuck to it.'

The visitor gave Iris a genial smile before making himself comfortable in the armchair, altering its position so that it faced the elderly resident. The nurse left the room and he waited for her footsteps to recede down the corridor before speaking.

'Hello, Magda,' he said. 'Do you know who I am? Do you recognize me after all this time?'

*Of course she did, you fool. Maurice Stafford. Who could forget such a devoted boy?*

She remained silent.

'I came to see you a long time ago when you were in the other place. They don't call them mental asylums any more, did you know that? But then so much has changed since we sat on that cold and wet station platform.'

*When he'd left her alone and frightened, too frozen with fear to get on the train with him when it came the next morning. He never even pleaded with her. He was just gone. Gone for ever, she'd thought. But now he was back for the second time and she wondered why.*

'Won't you speak to me? Won't you say hello to your old friend?'

*Speak? She'd not spoken a word since that day, not even when they found her alone at the station. Why should she drop her guard now?*

'Still refusing, eh, Magda? Is it a game you're playing so you don't have to confess? Either way it's good, it's very good. You can't tell tales on your brother, can you? People would never understand why Augustus did the things he did, especially nowadays. Discipline is an old-fashioned concept.'

He leaned forward and peered at her intently, his cruel eyes searching for any sign of recognition, of recollection. She remained impassive.

*She remembered many things though, dear Maurice. How he had spied on the other children, reporting their misbehaviours to either herself or Augustus. And she also remembered what she and Maurice had done to the young teacher whose prettiness was marred by the ugliness of her withered arm. Oh, they had taken good care of her, the prying, interfering little wretch, but it was Maurice who had killed her, creeping up behind the silly girl and bashing in her head with one of the stouter logs piled on the boiler-room floor for winter fires.*

'You remember what we did to the teacher, Magda? How

we killed her next door to the cellar? I was, shall we say, agitated afterwards, but then I was a mere child of twelve years. You took charge, you knew what had to be done to conceal the crime. We carried Nancy Linnet's body back into the cellar and dropped it into the well. You were brisk and efficient, utterly cold – if there was any trepidation, you hid it from me.'

*Yes, she had hidden her panic: she'd had to be strong for Augustus, she could not allow him to be betrayed. It was only at the very end, on the night of the fierce storm, that she'd had to desert her brother in his madness. She had fled with the boy, Maurice Stafford, braving the storm because they were too afraid of Augustus to stay, terrified that in his insanity he would turn on them.*

'The game was up that last night, we both knew it. Augustus could no longer be protected from the outsiders, the snoopers, the government people – he had gone too far. In the end, he wreaked havoc, didn't he?'

*Those street urchins only had themselves to blame! They were bad boys and girls, incorrigibly wayward! They had planned to run away from Crickley Hall that night and they had to be stopped!*

Magda sat perfectly still on her hard chair.

*But in the end it was she and Maurice who had run away.*

'We defied the storm and reached the train station. We sat on the platform bench, bowed and shivering, until the next morning when the storm had ceased and all was calm once more. But when the train came along, quite early, you refused to get on it with me. You had sunk into yourself, Magda. You refused to speak and you wouldn't be moved. At the last moment I caught the train myself. Your face was as expressionless as it is now. Like stone. I could tell you how I survived in the city on my own for almost a year before I found someone to take me in, but I'm afraid it wouldn't mean a thing to you.'

He rose to his feet.

'You really are mad, aren't you?' he said.

*Certainly not. She was just . . . just cautious, that was all. She could talk if she wanted to, couldn't she? Of course she could. It was safer this way, though. They left her alone now, didn't even try to coax her to speak. To confess. Oh, she could talk all right, but this way was best. This way they thought she knew nothing and could tell nothing. Hah! Fools, all of them.*

'You're harmless, I can see. I came today because I was curious after all these years. I saw you once – what was it, thirty years ago? – when they kept you in a locked cell, and you were as silent as you are now. You've grown old, Magda. You must be at least ninety-three, ninety-five? I don't suppose you even remember me and I doubt you remember anything about those days in Crickley Hall.'

He walked to the door, paused and turned back to regard her.

'Let me assure you,' he said with a faint smile, 'I've never forgotten Augustus Theophilus Cribben and all the things he – and you, Magda – taught me. I hear his call even now. He won't be denied, do you know that?'

Magda refused to look at him. She went on staring at the blank wall.

'At least, Magda, you seem to be at peace in your lunacy.'

The visitor left the room.

*A lunatic? Yes, perhaps she was. Perhaps all the years of silence had finally made her that way.*

*But she wasn't as mad as Maurice. His madness shone from his eyes.*

Magda listened to his footsteps fade away. Inwardly she smiled, but her face did not change expression. Someone might be watching.

## 53: THE MORTUARY

Detective Inspector Kim Michael was waiting for Gabe at the mortuary entrance, which was in the basement of a huge teaching hospital. They shook hands in a perfunctory manner, both men wanting to get through the ordeal of viewing the body as quickly as possible.

DI Michael was just below average height but fit-looking, with dark-brown hair and intelligent greeny-brown eyes that softened his tough features. From experience Gabe knew the policeman was a good listener, whose sound advice and quiet encouragement had helped Eve and Gabe through the bad times after Cam's disappearance. He looked at Gabe sympathetically now.

'How was the journey?' he asked as he led the engineer down a long sloping corridor with pale two-tone green walls.

'I used the motorways, made good time, although the rain didn't help,' Gabe replied.

DI Michael nodded. He stopped before black plastic swingdoors, pushing open one side and ushering Gabe through. The engineer found himself in another but broader corridor with doors left and right, all of them closed except one, the nearest.

'I've got the clothes ready for you,' the detective said,

407

indicating the open doorway. 'Let's see how you do with them before we try anything else.'

Gabe entered and found himself in a viewing room, a long plain table on one side, a few metal chairs set against another wall. To his right was an interior window, the drapes behind the glass closed. It was a viewing window and he wondered if the child's corpse was already lying there beyond the curtains. There was a door beside the window.

On the long table was a semi-clear plastic bag in which items of clothing were bundled. Gabe could just make out a faded reddish jumper lying on a blue anorak.

DI Michael went to the bag and began to pull the rumpled clothing out, laying each item along the table. The woollen jumper was ragged and now closer to pink in colour; when Cam had worn it, the jumper was a vivid red. Gabe almost choked. There were holes where the wool had unravelled or had been nibbled by scavenging fish. He managed to get a grip on himself before moving on to the blue anorak. The colour had paled but it was truer to its original tone than the woollen jumper. Next to this was a tiny vest that had been white but was now a dirty grey, as were the small underpants close by. The material of both was torn and punctured as though river fish had gnawed through to get at the meat beneath. That image caused Gabe to waver and the detective held on to his arm to steady him.

Gabe forced himself to continue looking. The little pair of shrunken jeans came next; they were so drained of colour they were almost white in places.

'As I told you on the phone,' Kim Michael said, 'the shoes are missing, but I forgot to say the socks were gone too. We think the underwater currents took them away. As far as the pathologist can tell, there are no signs of violence on the body before drowning.'

'You're sure?'

'As sure as we can be after all this time . . .'

Gabe could not tear his eyes away from the shrunken, damaged garments displayed on the table. He wanted to sink to his knees before them and wail his son's name, wanted to scream denial. But there was no doubt – the clothing had been Cameron's. Now, as if to confirm the gut-wrenching truth of it, he noticed the tiny crocodile logo stitched to the jumper's chest, some of the stitching broken, the crocodile no longer green but a colourless smudge with only the outline defined. Cam had loved that little cartoon emblem.

'Gabe?' DI Michael had dropped his hand away from the engineer's arm, but he angled his head, trying to look into Gabe's downcast eyes. Gabe knew what was expected of him.

'The clothes belong to Cam,' he said without apparent emotion.

'You're sure?'

He nodded. 'Pretty much.'

'If you are certain, there's no need to see the body.'

'I got to.'

'It's been in the river for a year. Sorry, Gabe, but it's been eaten away, as well as spoiled by the polluted water. It isn't necessary to put yourself through any more. We've got the clothes – you've identified them.'

Gabe nodded towards the interior window. 'He's in there, isn't he, Kim?'

'Yes, he's there. But I'm telling you, there's no need to see the body itself.'

'I don't want to see the body,' Gabe replied grimly. 'I just want to see the hands.'

\*

Gabe slowly sank down onto Cam's small bed, leaned his elbows on his knees and cupped his face in his hands. He was still numb from the shock of finally accepting his son really was dead, that there was no more hope, that their little boy was gone for ever.

With its Shrek posters, brightly patterned wallpaper and robust transporters and the like spilling from an open pine chest, the cheerfulness of the room belied the desolate mood of its occupant. A Lion King mobile hanging from the overhead light-fitting stirred only slightly in the draught he had caused by entering the room. Early evening shadows gradually deepened and cohered as he sat there, his heart a dead weight, his thoughts dulled by the trauma of unbearable truth.

At the mortuary, Gabe and DI Michael had gone through to the room where Cam's poor decomposed body was laid out beneath the green sheet. Horribly, a few strands of hair – blond hair that had been bleached white by the dirty shifting waters – protruded from one end of the sheet and Gabe had forced himself to look away, to concentrate on the only parts of the body he needed to see. The mortician who had accompanied them had been considerate; he had pulled up the cover so that the exposed hair was concealed. Then carefully, after instructions from the detective, the man had folded back both sides of the green cloth, revealing the corpse's hands and arms.

Gabe had felt nauseous and horrified when he saw the skeletal fingers, scraps of corrupted flesh still clinging to the digits and the wrist. He had sucked in a sharp breath when he compared the little fingers of both hands and found the one on the right was shorter than the one on the left.

He had wanted to see no more than that, but the temptation to draw back the sheet and reveal the whole of the body was almost irresistible. It was Kim Michael, as if reading

# THE SECRET OF CRICKLEY HALL

Gabe's mind, who deterred him. He tugged gently at the engineer's elbow and led him back to the viewing room next door. Gabe knew he would always be grateful to Kim for that: full sight of Cam's despoiled little body would have haunted him for ever. He officially identified the corpse as Cameron Caleigh, then left the mortuary and drove to his Canonbury home.

Ringing Eve was the hardest thing he had ever done in his life, but unexpectedly she had not broken down or become hysterical; rather she had taken the news calmly, as if he were telling her something she already knew so it was no shock. He realized her denial this past year had been a sham, something she would never admit even to herself – *especially* to herself. Part of her had rejected the idea that Cam was dead, but another, deeper, part of her, had already accepted his fate.

He sat on Cam's small bed, with its gaily patterned duvet, its pale blue pillow, and his emotions began to surge, to rise to the surface, overwhelming that numbness he felt, finally bursting through so that his chest spasmed, his shoulders shuddered, and the tears he had held back for so long flooded his eyes and wet his cupped hands. It was as if at last he had been given permission to grieve properly.

He remained weeping for his dead son until the room's darkness was almost complete.

Sam Pennelly, landlord of the Barnaby Inn, wiped the bar counter with a teacloth, surveying the room as he did so. It was all very well keeping the pub open all day, but where was the trade? Two customers, that's what he'd had since three o'clock. Old Reggie (as he was known) with his halves of bitter, each one lasting at least an hour before he ordered another, was sitting there in his regular place by the fire, cloth cap and muffler still in place but his storm coat laid over a chair opposite. Because he was long retired, Old Reggie spent most afternoons and evenings in the Barnaby, ready to engage anyone who gave him a greeting in conversation, but most of the time content to sit alone and no doubt reminisce about the old days. Earlier, when he'd ordered his first half-bitter, he had complained about the inclement weather, likening it to 1943 when Old Reggie was just a nipper and the constant rainfall had caused the Great Flood. Sam didn't like such talk – it made his other customers edgy, afeared it might happen again.

'Can't resist the force of nature,' the old boy had remarked glumly as he'd handed over the exact amount for the beer. Mebbe he was right, but there was no cause to go alarming people. Some villagers were even talking about moving out, going to stay with relatives or friends on safer ground until the downpours had passed, but Sam saw no sense in that, not when it meant he might lose his regular customers. In any case, the widened estuary and fortified embankments would see the village all right if a flood ever occurred again.

He wiped his hands on the teacloth and his eyes wandered to the bar's other solitary customer, who sat at a small corner table. The man seemed thoughtful too, mebbe reminiscing like Old Reggie.

Sam was glad of his custom. Large brandies, the man drank, and he'd had two since he'd arrived. The landlord frowned. He hadn't said much to his customer, just the usual pleasantries when the first Hennessy had been ordered, no more than a polite welcome and a short exchange about the foul weather, but Sam had thought he recognized the man. Couldn't place him, though.

It came to him then. The man was an infrequent visitor to the inn, dropping by once or, at the most, twice a year. Sam only remembered him because he always had the same tipple: a double brandy, always a Hennessy, and never with ice or soda. Yes, the man had been coming in for a few years now, always as a stranger because of the length of time between visits. Not one for conversation, Sam recollected, just a 'good day' and a 'thank you' when he took his drink.

Without a newspaper or book to read, Sam's occasional customer seemed to be concentrating on the glass of brandy before him on the small round table. He was certainly lost in thought. He had a half-smile on his face.

Maurice Stafford was hardly aware of the coppery-gold liquid in the tumbler. His fingers encircled the bowled glass and he leaned his elbows on the tabletop, but although he gazed into the brandy, his thoughts were on other things. Like the old man who sat by the pub's warm fire, he was sifting through his memories, remembering a different era . . .

Most of the evacuees had been collected by the LCC (London County Council) from meeting points at schools, orphanages and town halls all over south London and brought by coach (or charabanc, as they used to be called, Maurice reflected with a faint smile) or bus to Paddington railway station, while a few had been taken there directly by fretful and remorseful mothers. Hundreds of children were gathered on the station's great concourse, all with identity labels attached to collars or coat buttons, gas-mask boxes hung around their necks, a few possessions in cardboard suitcases or brown paper parcels tied with string. Ministry of Health and Board of Education officials were in charge of the mass exodus of children, and they were fraught with disorganization and noise.

Maurice stood and waited with nine others from the same orphanage. None of them were crying like many of the evacuees, because they had no family from which to be parted. In truth, the ten of them regarded the evacuation as an exciting adventure. At the last moment, another boy joined them, hurriedly brought there by two members of the RCM (Refugee Children's Movement). Documents were checked by officials before the five-year-old boy, Stefan Rosenbaum from Poland, was formally handed over. After the first evacuee-laden trains had departed the station, the eleven orphans were herded towards an already crowded carriage and put on board. One of the older orphans, a girl called Susan Trainer, had immediately taken charge of the overwhelmed Polish boy, holding his hand tightly and calming him with soft words he did not understand.

After a long journey, the eleven orphans were taken off

the train by their adult guardians at a town none of them had ever heard of in North Devon, and from the small rustic station a yellow bus carried them to a house in Hollow Bay called Crickley Hall, where they were cheerlessly greeted by their new custodians, Augustus Theophilus Cribben and his sister Magda.

Cribben was openly furious at the addition of the Polish refugee, while Magda was plainly hostile towards him. They had not been expecting the boy. The guardian, who had accompanied the children from London, explained that it had been a last-minute arrangement. Stefan's parents had been shot when they tried to flee Poland with their son, and he had been brought over to England by other escapees and turned over to the authorities. The boy was shy and spoke very little English.

Cribben had gone through the relevant papers concerning Stefan's status with a fine-toothed comb before reluctantly accepting the boy into his care. He had stated his disapproval of the situation forcefully and the temporary guardian looked relieved to get away at last.

On that first day, and despite the long journey the children had made, the harsh regime began. They were immediately ordered to wash themselves, two at a time in the house's one bathroom. A waterline was marked in the bathtub of three inches rather than the government's water-saving limit of five inches. The tepid water was only changed twice during the bathing and Magda supervised it from a chair on the landing outside the bathroom, issuing orders through the open doorway. Even Maurice, who was considerably bigger and older than the other boys, had to share the bath, as did Susan Trainer, who at eleven was the eldest girl.

After the communal bathing, it was nit-seeking time. Magda carried out the searching with a metal comb. Then everybody's hair was cut short, the boys having a pudding basin placed on their heads to set a line for the barber's clippers that Magda used, the hair up to that line so short that the lower scalp and back of the neck was exposed to the air. The boys looked ridiculous and the girls fared not much better – they had to have short bob-cuts that just covered their ears. As well as a toothbrush each and a spare set of underwear, the LCC had provided the orphans with black plimsolls, which they were ordered not to wear inside the house (which would be for most of the time, their only outings being the Sunday-morning visit to the local church) so that they would not leave scuff marks on the floors and stairs, nor make undue noise.

After a meagre meal of mincemeat and boiled potatoes (this was to be their staple diet from that day on) they were sent up to the dormitory, which was a capacious converted attic where iron cotbeds were set out. There was no excited chatter between the children as they undressed for bed. At the orphanage, Susan had been allowed to tell bedtime stories, but not here in Crickley Hall: the children were instructed to go to sleep immediately after Magda had switched off the lights.

They were an austere twosome, Cribben and his sister Magda, and they made it clear from the start that they would tolerate no dissension or misbehaviour from the children in their charge. Ominously, Cribben had used his split-ended cane the very next morning when Eugene Smith, nine years old, was late down for the assembly in the hall (the orphans had to present themselves washed and dressed in two lines at precisely six thirty every morning). Breakfast would follow after prayers in the big drawing room, which also doubled as a classroom. Eugene hadn't appeared 'til the rest were all seated at the two long trestle tables that were used as desks during school time, and Cribben had flown into a fearsome rage. The nine-year-old was made to bend over in front of the others and Cribben administered six hard strokes of the cane.

*Swish-thwack!* Maurice had never forgotten that sound. Neither had he forgotten Eugene's screech of pain. *Swish-thwack!* Six times. By the end of the caning, Eugene had been reduced to a blubbering wreck.

Cribben and Magda's very presence was intimidating – no, it was downright *scary* – and Maurice knew he had to ingratiate himself with them as quickly as possible. He was not only big for his age, long and gangly, but he was also smarter than the other children and certainly more cunning. He did not relish that cane leaving red stripes across his own backside and he determined to do anything to avoid it.

As luck would have it, his chance to gain favour with the Cribbens came the very next day.

The parents and baby brother of two of the evacuees, Brenda and Gerald Prosser, had been killed one night in the Blitz when a German bomb had fallen on their home (the father had been on leave from the army at the time, prior to being shipped overseas). Their parents' bedroom, in which the one-year-old baby also slept, had been totally demolished, while Brenda and Gerald's bedroom had hardly been touched. With no relatives to take them in, the sister and brother had been sent to the orphanage. That had been almost three years ago, and ever since the deaths of their parents and sibling, they had feared the nights, afraid that a bomb might drop and this time kill them too. So they had taken to sleeping, sometimes together, beneath their beds. The punishment of their friend Eugene had traumatized them so much that on the second night at Crickley Hall, Brenda had taken the blankets (there were no sheets) from her own and Gerald's bed and laid them on the floor under her bed. They had slept the night there, cuddling together. Maurice, who was a natural sneak, had informed on them the next day. As punishment the Prossers had been caned across the palms of their hands, six strokes each, with Gerald collapsing in wails and tears after the third stroke. Magda had to support him and force his arm straight so that Cribben could finish the chastisement. Both children were left with livid red weals on the hands and their punishment noted in a big black book that Cribben kept.

And so it continued, Maurice telling tales on the other orphans and soon earning small rewards for the betrayals. Discipline at Crickley Hall was rigid, unbending, the rules of the house too many for Maurice to remember now, but severe punishment was the penalty for breaking them. Sometimes it would be Cribben's cane or Magda's strap (she always wore a thick leather belt round her waist which she would snap at any rule-breaker's hands and legs). Other times it might be fasting for a day, or being made to stand silently in a corner for six hours or more. Toys and board games were not allowed, even though Maurice knew there were some in the house because he had helped Magda carry them – they were sent by orphan-concerned charities – up to the storeroom next to the dormitory, where they were locked away. On Saturday mornings, however, the evacuees were allowed to play on the swing the young gardener had rigged up for them on the front lawn. Only two at a time though, just for the benefit of passers-by who would think it was part of the children's recreational fun. In particular, it was meant to impress the vicar of St Mark's, the church further down the hill; the Reverend Rossbridger liked to pop in for tea and biscuits with the Cribbens from time to time. It was not long before even those innocent sessions on the swing became another form of punishment.

Maurice quickly became Magda's preferred child and loyal servant to Augustus Cribben himself. The other children hated him for this (as they had hated him in the London orphanage before) because they knew he spied on them, that he reported the slightest misdemeanour on their part to the Cribbens, and that he stirred up problems for them with their guardians. Susan Trainer got into the most trouble, because Maurice disliked her in particular – she was too lippy and always defending the smaller kids, especially the Polish boy. Stefan Rosenbaum was constantly picked on by Cribben and Magda; that Stefan understood very little English didn't help matters.

But Maurice enjoyed it all. He liked the strictness and it was fun to see the other boys and girls get punished. He loved the brutality of the canings. And quite soon Cribben saw Maurice's potential.

## 55: LIGHTNING

Gabe was heading west in the Range Rover and making reasonably good time despite the Friday-night exodus from the city. Now on the motorway, he was able to pick up speed, illegally keeping to the fast lane, once again flashing his headlights at any vehicle that impeded his progress, tailgating them if they didn't pull into the middle lane. It was a foolish thing to do, reckless and heedless of others, but he wanted to reach Hollow Bay as quickly as possible. He was in no mood to dally.

Eve had not wanted him to return to Crickley Hall that night because she felt he would be too exhausted both physically and emotionally. She would comfort Loren and Cally when she broke the terrible news to them. They, in turn, would console each other. For him to drive back that night was too big a risk, especially as it was raining still.

But Gabe hadn't liked the sound of his wife's voice. It was too dispassionate. Eve was too calm, too collected. She had to be in shock. Maybe she had nothing left, her emotions wrung out. Whatever the answer, Gabe had to be there with his wife and daughters; they would need his love and support, as he needed theirs.

Rain suddenly hit the windscreen so fiercely he was momentarily driving blind. He eased up on the accelerator and turned the wipers on to a swifter speed. Other vehicles were also slowing down and he groaned aloud. He didn't need this.

The change from light drizzle to absolute downpour was dramatic and unexpected, like driving into a waterfall. Gabe saw that the sky ahead was black and, just to make things worse, there was a lightning flash that bleached road and countryside, followed by the distant rumble of thunder.

Gabe swore and flicked his headlights at another driver who was blocking his way. He pressed down harder on the accelerator pedal and once more gathered speed.

## 56: MEMORIES

He drained the last of the Hennessy and pondered whether or not to have another. Glancing at his watch, he decided it was still too early to leave.

Rising from the table, Maurice went to the bar. An attractive but rather sluttish girl, who had arrived a short while ago, was serving. The man Maurice assumed was the landlord or pub manager was standing at the far end of the counter, talking to a couple of customers. The place was just beginning to get busy.

Maurice ordered another large brandy, his third, and smiled at the girl he'd heard the landlord call Frannie. Keep the change, he told her, and took his drink back to the small table.

The old man with the cloth cap was still gazing into the fire. Frannie had livened it up with a few fresh logs when she had come on duty. The fire-gazer had an inch or so of the half-bitter left in his glass and Maurice wondered if it would take him another half-hour to drain it.

Maurice sipped his own drink, enjoying its bite, taking his time because he had plenty of that, plenty of time yet.

He settled comfortably in the chair and went back to his memories.

*

Augustus Theophilus Cribben was a deviant: a masochist and a sadist. But Maurice did not understand such terms in those days. In fact, to Maurice, Cribben was a kind of god. And in three short weeks, the boy was to become an acolyte of the god. He always remained afraid of Cribben, but still he idolized him. Cribben was lord and master of Crickley Hall and Maurice was only too pleased to be his servant, for it gave him power too: domination over the other children, influence with Magda, and the approval of his master – especially that.

He found ways to please Cribben and Magda, watching over the other orphans, controlling them whenever Cribben or his sister was not present, making them stand in two straight lines at assembly in the hall, reporting them if they talked or played after lights out, and generally conspiring with the guardians to make life miserable for the evacuees. When they all marched down the hill to church on Sunday mornings, Maurice always walked at the back with Magda, ready to point out any chatter or mischief from the boys and girls in front. He also kept alert during the Mass, on the lookout for misbehaviour or whisperings among them.

Soon, he had inveigled his way so much into his guardians' good books that he was allowed to stay up long after the others had gone to bed, although he had the habit of sitting on the narrow staircase just below the open hatchway so that he could listen to anything they might whisper about the Cribbens or himself. Augustus Cribben never seemed to sleep: he would walk the landing, pace the flagstoned hall, climb the broad stairway – and sometimes stop at the bottom of the narrow staircase leading to the dormitory, waiting there as if listening for the slightest noise, the quietest of murmurs, hoping to catch the children out, ready to stomp up those wooden steps and deal out immediate punishment – he always carried the cane with him. Then, in the evenings, he began to take Maurice to his bedroom.

There he would instruct the boy to kneel at the bedside with him and pray. Such prayers could go on for two hours or more and such was Cribben's fervour, so intense were his supplications, that Maurice's boredom was never noticed.

It was on one of those nights that something took place that was totally bizarre to the boy – bizarre then, but soon, with repetition, becoming an acceptable part of the evening ritual.

Cribben had been suffering a severe headache all day. Migraine, Magda had informed Maurice when they were alone one day, a condition Augustus had endured all his adult life and which was made worse when they were caught up in an air raid, the house they occupied demolished by a German bomb. Augustus had been trapped in the parlour, beneath half the ceiling that had fallen in, sustaining a serious injury to his head. His life was spared, but from that day the migraine attacks were even worse than before. So bad had they become that sometimes the pain carried him to the very brink of insanity. The attacks were punishment for his past sins, her brother had declared, and this he truly believed even though his life had been pure, his adoration of the Lord absolute.

But one day, Augustus suddenly knew what must be done to relieve this sickly pounding in his head, for it came to him as an epiphany: only further pain, further punishment, could release him from his affliction; only this further penance could absolve him of his sins and thus take away his suffering. Pain defeated by more pain. Magda would have to punish him to the limit of his endurance so that his sins would be washed away by the physical contrition.

One night, as Maurice prayed with Cribben, intoning

prayer after prayer, most of them of repentance, the guardian had leaned his head on the bed, his hands clawing at the single sheet. Cribben's face had been ashen all day, his treatment of the evacuees even more stern than usual. At times he had clutched his head in his hands and moaned and even Magda had been wary around him, as if he might explode into violence at any moment. Instinctively, the children had become more subdued than usual (if that were possible) and had avoided even meeting his pain-raddled eyes. They crept quietly around him, never once raising their voices beyond a murmur.

Maurice, kneeling beside Cribben at the bed, watched with a kind of awed anticipation as his master's shoulders jerked with smothered sobs.

After several moments, Cribben seemed to pull himself together. He turned towards Maurice, who saw his guardian's gaunt face was even whiter than usual and drawn with the agony of his headache; tear trails glistened on Cribben's hollowed cheeks.

'You have a duty, boy,' he said to Maurice tightly. He pointed to the commodious wardrobe that dominated one side of the room. 'You're tall, Maurice: you can reach it.'

The boy was confused as he gawked first at the wardrobe, then back at the kneeling figure.

Cribben's order seemed squeezed through his lips, as if pain and impatience were constricting his throat. 'Fetch it, boy!' he hissed.

Bewildered, Maurice nevertheless scuttled over to the big wardrobe. He regarded it blankly.

'You'll find it hidden away on top,' Cribben told him fretfully. 'If you stretch you can reach it. Hurry, fetch it to me!'

Anxiously, Maurice stood on tiptoe and raised his arms above his head, his taut belly pressed against the wardrobe's closed door. He ran his fingertips along the edge and felt nothing at first. But when he stretched himself even higher, his whole body straining with the effort, he touched something lying there out of sight. It was light, for it moved easily when he nudged it. Working his fingers to draw the object closer, he soon realized what Cribben wanted brought to him. He pulled the long thin stick off the wardrobe and faced the guardian with it.

Like the punishment cane Cribben flogged the children with, this was split into several strands at one end; however, there were tiny iron studs impressed into the separate slithers of wood, there to inflict even greater pain when used as a scourge.

'Yes,' was all that Cribben said as he rose from the bed, his eyes glazed with either tears or fervour, and proceeded to remove his jacket. The rest of his clothes followed until he was completely naked. Maurice's eyes widened when he saw the stripes and barely healed weals on Cribben's body, across his chest but mainly across his thighs and lower legs. The studs had also left their marks as small red puncture wounds and short sore-looking scratches. The boy understood that the cane had been used on Cribben before – many times before, for some of the marks were old and faded while others were fresh, almost livid.

'This is my personal instrument of chastisement – it hasn't been sullied by those sinful wretches. You know what to do, Maurice. You must do it fiercely,' Cribben urged – no, *he implored* – the boy, who was still afraid and uncertain.

He jumped when Cribben screamed at him.

*'Punish me! Let the pain absolve me of my sins!'*

What those sins could have been, Maurice had no idea, for his God-fearing master was surely without the stain of sin upon his soul. But then, who could tell what dark and covert thoughts tortured the man? Maurice only knew that his own mind possessed many thoughts and images that might be deemed sinful.

Cribben knelt at the bedside again and he threw his upper body across it so that his back and buttocks were exposed. Maurice felt a strange thrill of excitement.

*'Make it hurt, boy, let me feel its sting!'*

In shock, and without further thought, the boy obliged, though his first couple of strokes were tentative.

*'Harder, boy, harder!'* Cribben shouted.

Maurice brought the cane down harder, the strokes clearly defined on the guardian's pale flesh, together with small pricks of blood made by the metal studs.

*Swish-thwack!*

*'Lord, let the pain wash away the corruption of my spirit, help me atone for the evil that is mine!'*

*Swish-thwack!*

Maurice struck with more passion, enjoying the sound the cane made on skin and bones, encouraged by the whimpers and cries it brought from his master – *excited* by the hurt he was causing. Oh, it was glorious. It aroused feelings inside him that he'd never before experienced. It made his groin tingle and caused a new and exquisite sensation, a wonderful feeling that he wanted to go on for ever.

Cribben, his face laid sideways on the bed so that the boy could see his expression, seemed to be in some kind of delirium, his open lips formed into an agonized grin, his eyelids fluttering as if he were about to faint. His hips were inches away from the bedside and Maurice saw something he didn't quite understand, something he'd never seen on any other man or boy before.

Cribben's erection was enormous, its engorged globular tip pressed into the bed's thin mattress.

# JAMES HERBERT

'Yes,' the guardian moaned in a low, parched voice. 'Yes, more. *Harder now!*'

Eventually Cribben had had enough. 'Good boy, good boy,' he gasped as he rested his head and shoulders on the bed. 'Go to your room now, boy, and pray for your soul. Mine too. Go.' He sounded exhausted.

Maurice had walked to the door and opened it to find Magda waiting outside on the landing. She had been silent but a wisp of a smile had told Maurice she was pleased with his labours.

The flogging of his master was not the last. It was just the beginning.

## 57: FRIDAY EVENING

Lili had closed the shop and gone upstairs to her flat. It had been a slow day, unusual for a Friday, but the lack of trade hadn't bothered her too much. Business was always good around Christmas-time and, of course, in the summer months when tourists were like locusts in this part of town. She could have used some distraction that day, however.

She took a bottle of wine from the fridge, uncorked it, then filled a glass almost to the top. She went into her small but neat sitting room, taking both glass and bottle with her. Still standing, she tasted the wine before setting the bottle down on a glass coffee table.

Put the TV on, or not? She weighed up the option in her mind. Not, she decided. Even if it meant having some kind of company in the room, there was hardly anything worth watching nowadays and she hated reality shows (whose reality was it supposed to be anyway? The lives they showed were nothing like her own or anybody's she knew).

Lili walked to the window and looked out at the storm. So hard was it raining, she could barely make out the lights from the shops and houses across the road. She shivered. The rain was unrelenting, sudden gusts of wind throwing it at the glass in wintry flurries. Lili pulled the curtains closed and turned away, going to the comfortable beige armchair that faced the television screen. The window behind her rattled in its frame.

She sat, sipped her wine and brooded. Too many evenings like this. Alone in her little flat above the shop, drinking wine, sometimes 'til a whole bottle was empty. Lili never got drunk, though. No matter how many glasses of wine she had, she always ended up sober. The second or third glass might give her a lift, but it invariably led downhill to depression after that. She wished it had a different effect, wished it would wipe out certain memories. Never did, though. If anything, consumption of wine revived them. So why did she drink? A shrink might know.

Placing the glass next to the wine bottle on the low coffee table, she relaxed back into the chair. Something else that rekindled times past. She was looking down at one of her wristbands. With a deliberate shrug of her shoulders as if to say, 'Who cares?' she pulled off the coloured band and stared at the thin, fading scar across her wrist. There was another one hidden on her other arm.

*Stupid cow!* she thought, not because she had tried to bleed to death, but because she'd done it all wrong and had been saved by a young Asian doctor in the Surrey hospital's A and E department. Seven years ago. Since then, she had learnt that the most successful way to slit your wrists was *down* the veins, not across them.

So she had been saved and made to feel foolish in the process. Why kill yourself just because an affair that had been doomed from the start had ended predictably badly? Don hadn't been worth it; his wife deserved him. For three years they had been lovers and in the end he'd refused to leave his wife as he had promised. It was not even that there were children involved: his wife (Don had complained) was barren.

Lili had fallen in love with him at the minor pharmaceutical publicity agency where she'd found her first job after leaving art college. She had been a junior art director, Don was the marketing manager. Love very nearly at first sight. Ha-ha, witty, because she was psychic and had the power of second sight. She should have known the outcome from the beginning then.

In the end, he had chosen Marion, his wife, but even so, Marion was not satisfied. The bitch had made Lili's life hell after she discovered where she lived. Phone calls, hate mail, threats and even physical confrontation – Marion would not leave Lili alone. Marion the mad woman. Who wanted revenge. Soon to die of cancer.

After her swift but ghastly death, Lili and Don had not tried to rekindle their love for each other: she because he had let her down irrevocably, had turned his pledges into lies; he because he was weighed down by too much guilt. So Lili had changed her life. Certainly they could not work together in the same company, which was too small to get lost in, and he was not going to turn his back on a good job, especially after such a profound tragedy. No, Lili had been the one to leave. It seemed inevitable to her, the only thing to do.

So her father had helped her financially, as had the bank, which thought her idea was sound (it was at a time when banks were practically throwing money at borrowers in order to hook them for life with an almost scandalous pay-back interest rate). She had enough money to lay down a deposit on the charming little high-street shop in Pulvington, North Devon, that had been advertised in the property section of *The Times*. The mortgage she took out was from a building society that had an office in the same town. The shop had previously sold ladies' high fashion, which apparently had low appeal to the local women, but Lili had fallen in love with it the moment she stepped through the door.

# JAMES HERBERT

The town was crammed with tourists in the summer and
Lili had the idea of selling craftworks, light hats, paintings
and exquisite but not too expensive hand-tooled ornaments
and jewellery. All executed by herself and local artists (who
were easy to find by placing ads in the local press). Tourists
always wanted something to take home from places they
visited, either as gifts or keepsakes; also the indigenous
population would be interested if the work was quality and
the price right.

And her idea appeared to have merit – the shop attracted
a lot of customers in the first few summer months. Unfortunately, she hadn't given much thought to the winter season,
when most of the tourists had disappeared and dark days
did not encourage locals to buy what might be regarded as
frivolities. So as a sideline, and to help make up for loss of
trade, Lili returned to giving psychic readings, again putting
ads in the local newspapers and her card in shop windows.

Both occupations balanced out well – readings could be
given in the evenings or on half-day-closing afternoons, so
they never interfered with the day-to-day running of the shop
– her reputation as a psychic soon established itself locally.

Unfortunately, the past had not been left behind.

It was on a Tuesday evening that the dead wife of her ex-
lover had returned for more revenge. Lili was at an elderly
woman's small bungalow on the outskirts of the town, her
client a widow of several years who had come to wonder if
her late husband was in a happy state of being (apparently
he'd been generally disgruntled for most of their married life)
wherever he was now, or if gloom had followed him into the
next world. Older women usually wanted to know about
relatives or loved ones who'd passed over, while younger and
middle-aged females (nearly all her clients were female)
generally wished to discover their own futures, good or bad

(Lili only relayed the good, unless the bad was a warning of some kind that could be acted upon).

This was the second visit Lili had made to this particular woman, a Mrs Ada Clavelly by name, the first time being only a partial success – her husband had come through and given indications that he truly was Ada's late partner in life by referring to things only he and his wife would know about, but his voice had been distant, as if from a long way off (which, of course, in a metaphysical sense it was), and Lili had hoped for a clearer 'sighting' this time.

On that particular late-spring night, however, something occurred that had almost destroyed her confidence as a 'seer'. In fact, something happened that terrified both her and her sitter.

Instead of the spirit or voice of Ada's long-departed husband coming through, Marion, Lili's ex-lover's wife, had made her presence known. Through Ada, herself.

Sometimes Lili could talk to a spirit as if it were in the same room, but on rare occasions it might speak to the client through Lili's own mouth – it had happened to Lili only twice since she'd known she was psychic and clairvoyant, and she had never encouraged the phenomenon, it just happened that way. But this time, the spirit had used Lili's client, Ada, to speak through.

Lili could only stare as Ada's very features seemed to alter. Even though she was sure that this was an illusion conjured by a voice that was instantly recognizable for its husky venom – Lili still clearly remembered the phone calls and the face-to-face confrontations between herself and Marion five years before, the low threatening voice that had risen through the octaves to evolve into a shrill shrieking – it seemed so real. With Marion's words came her visual image, transmuting another living person's features into her own likeness. It was incredible and something Lili had never before experienced. She was stunned by it.

The possessed woman lunged across the table between them and spat and hissed into Lili's face. Ada's grey hair had stiffened as if charged with static (Lili actually heard the faint crackle of electricity coming from Ada's hair) and the room itself sank to a wintry coldness that frosted breaths.

Clawed hands tried to scratch the psychic's face, but Lili pulled back in time and the widow's brittle fingernails scrabbled in the air before falling and raking Lili's blouse. Lili screamed but the malevolent entity that had appropriated the widow's body did not have the power to make it rise from the tabletop. Instead it lay collapsed on the table, where it twitched and writhed as though in seizure.

When she had screamed, Lili had jumped to her feet, knocking her chair over. Hands to her mouth, she could only stare down at the jerking body on the table as Marion's shrieks died, her borrowed power spent, her curses becoming murmurs and finally dying away altogether.

The poor widow woman was left in a state of shock, although she wasn't aware of what had taken place, only that she was very, very frightened. As was Lili.

She had helped Ada sit back in her chair and quickly brought a glass of water from the kitchen for her to sip. But Ada remained trembling for a long while after and Lili was afraid to leave her alone like that, even though she herself was desperate to get out of the room and away from the bungalow lest the transfiguration recur. She had stayed with the suddenly frail, weeping woman for as long as it took to settle her, to reassure her that nothing like it was going to happen again (a reassurance that lacked conviction).

Lili had told Ada that she had been momentarily possessed by a rogue spirit, an evil one that sometimes came through unbidden. The psychic hadn't explained about her ex-lover's dead wife whose soul, tormented by jealousy and reprisal, had somehow reached out from the dimension in which she now existed to hurt the person she still believed had wronged her.

Unsurprisingly, Ada Clavelly had not wanted to see Lili again; as for Lili, she vowed never again to make herself vulnerable to unearthly forces. Since that evening she had endeavoured to block her psychic sensing and refused to contact the dead any more. Nevertheless, she was still susceptible to psychic vibrations, even though she did her best to ignore them.

That had been eighteen months ago and her resolve remained firm. She had tried to help Eve Caleigh because the poor woman was desperate and had pleaded with her. It had not turned out that way: something evil had manifested itself through Lili and she couldn't let it happen again.

But now, on this Friday night, alone in her flat, she was aware of metaphysical disturbances around her, as if there was a riving beginning in the thin dividing fabric between life and death. Somehow she knew Crickley Hall was at its centre.

She gave a little start and almost spilt her wine as the wind outside threw rain at the windowpanes. Lili shivered, but it was because of an inner coldness and had nothing to do with the temperature of the room.

Her hand shaking, she lifted the glass and sipped more wine.

## 58: MORE MEMORIES

Maurice Stafford, now a man – an *old* man of more than seventy years who looked and *felt* much younger – glanced around the room. The inn was filling up despite the storm raging outside. People looked forward to their end-of-week tipple. For some it might be the only social evening of the weekend. Dreary little lives, sad little people. If only they knew the pleasure that comes from fulfilling a duty. He had been looking forward to it for a long, long time, but circumstances had never been right. This night they could not be better.

He drank more brandy and wondered whether to finish it in one big swallow. No, make it last. He had plenty of time, but didn't want to refresh his glass. He wanted to keep a clear head. Too soon to go to the house, though, so take your time with the Hennessy.

Despite the hubbub around him – the telling of stale jokes, the laughter, the complaints and warnings about the inclement weather – Maurice ignored it all.

He easily slipped back into his reverie.


Now Maurice had learned that inflicting pain was so agreeable it thickened the penis (Magda had told him the proper word for his willy or wee-wee thing all those years ago when he shared her bed, although she had emphasized it was a *bad* word, a *dirty* word), he was willing and eager to enjoy the experience again. And he soon discovered that the beating was not the only aberration (this particular word one that he learned later – many years later) of Augustus Theophilus Cribben's, in his quest for absolution, for not only did he need his soul to be cleansed by pain but he also wanted the vessel in which his soul resided to be cleansed.

On several occasions, Maurice was charged with the task of scouring Cribben's body from tip to toe, using a strong carbolic soap and a stiff-haired brush of the type used for scrubbing floors. Cribben would stand in three inches of water (the same amount he allowed the children) in the bath and Maurice would start with his face and wiry hair.

*'Harder!'* the guardian would demand of the boy in a voice that was almost guttural. *'Purge my wicked flesh, boy, drive out the impurities.'*

And as with the flogging, Cribben's penis would engorge until it stood fully erect. Maurice scrubbed hard as he was bidden, grimacing with the effort, and Cribben's skin turned blotchy red and raw. How his guardian stood the rough scrubbing of brush and harsh soap, the boy could only wonder. Eventually Cribben's neck and back would arch, his arms rise to shoulder height, and he would stare at the bright light in the ceiling, his eyes wide and glazed as if hypnotized, his mouth stretched open, yellowed teeth laid bare, and Maurice would scrub even harder, aware of the pain he was causing, Cribben's chest, his legs, his groin, livid with the scraping, scored by the hard bristles of the brush.

Finally, the purged man would all but collapse, his hands grabbing the edge of the bath as he bent down, legs almost giving way beneath him, hissing at Maurice to cease, to give him respite, his body chastened, his sins absolved.

In later years, Maurice was also to wonder that Augustus Cribben had never once molested him during a session either of scourging or scouring, even though Cribben was clearly aroused (did he never notice that Maurice was aroused too?). Magda, on the other hand, was a different matter.

He had found her waiting for him outside the bathroom door as usual after the scrubbing of her brother and this time there was a peculiar lustre to her usually cold eyes. After he'd closed the bathroom door behind him, leaving the naked man alone to continue his now-gibbering prayers, she had beckoned Maurice to follow. Cribben's sister led the boy along the dingy landing to her bedroom, where she had drawn him in by tugging at his shirtsleeve. She brought him to her bed and, still wordlessly, she lay him down on it. She turned off the bedside lamp and he heard her undressing in the darkness.

If Magda was disappointed with her young lover – he may have been big and mature for his age, but he *was* only twelve years old! – she didn't reveal it. Instead, she told him to pray with her and beg the Lord's forgiveness for the mortal sin they committed, only they must do it quietly so that they wouldn't be heard by her brother should he pass by her door during his nocturnal prowling. An hour later, after many repeated acts of contrition, Maurice was allowed to leave and sneak up to the dormitory.

Next day, Magda was her usual cold, stone-faced self, although she treated him with less severity than the other boys and girls. Augustus Cribben also regarded Maurice with less asperity, never once using the cane on him nor punishing him in any other way – not that Maurice ever did anything to occasion the guardian's displeasure. In a way, he had become part of Crickley Hall's ruling triumvirate, although his own power was limited to informing on the other orphans and keeping them in order whenever Cribben or Magda were busy in other parts of the house.

And so it went on: the flogging, then scrubbing of Augustus Cribben, the loveless trysts with Magda. All this went on while the other children lived in misery, with daily punishments, sparse rations and lack of love (which was the most needed).

The little Jewish boy was singled out for particular punishment. Maurice was delighted to tell Magda that Stefan had climbed into Susan Trainer's bed one night and slept with her until morning call. Magda was disgusted (and perversely pleased) to hear of such naughtiness and Stefan was at once taken down to the bitterly cold, damp cellar and left there all day and all night, on his own in the dark, the only sound he would hear being the rushing water at the bottom of the well. It was a dreadful punishment, for the total darkness could conjure all manner of monsters and demons in the mind of a five-year-old child, especially one who was already traumatized by personal tragedy. Susan Trainer had protested, shouting at both Cribben and Magda, and had received six strokes of the cane for her trouble. Maurice had smirked when she continued to plead for the little boy and had taken six more strokes, this time across the knuckles of her hand. That had shut her up all right, although she had howled with pain. When Stefan had been brought up from the cellar next day, he was pale and quieter than ever before. He was cowed.

Maurice enjoyed himself at Crickley Hall. He revered Augustus Cribben, who remained the dominant one; even during the canings and scrubbings, the boy was merely his acolyte, his chattel, which suited Maurice fine. And Maurice also enjoyed his secret liaisons and alliance with Magda, even

JAMES HERBERT

if her body was skin and bones and her breasts were tiny and flat (such imperfections did not bother the boy; his sexual awakening was too glorious for criticism). Life, if a little austere, was good at Crickley Hall and he revelled in it.

But then that interfering busybody Nancy Linnet had come along and tried to spoil things.

# 59: THUNDER

Loren and Cally were in their room, both of them subdued. Eve had waited 'til Loren returned from school, and then had explained to them both that their brother would not be coming back to them, that he had drowned a year ago when she had lost him in the park. The two sisters had sobbed in their mother's arms for a long time afterwards, but Eve had not wept with them. She did not understand why this was so, only that her thoughts – and heart – were numbed; there were no reserves of emotion left. She knew the certainty of Cam's death should have broken her, but she realized that perhaps she had been broken that first day he'd gone missing. And every single day that followed.

So instead of grieving she had kept herself busy, tidying the house, washing the kitchen floor (so much mud trodden in because of the mucky weather), making the beds, laying new fires in the sitting room and the great hall, anything to keep herself occupied. It wasn't that she didn't think of Cam – his lovely face was a constant image on the screen of her mind, but only partially formed; it was when she closed her eyes that all the colours and features of his face were filled in. She was coping, that was all she could say of herself, but she did not know how long it would last. Until her emotions filled to spilling point once more, she supposed.

Right now, she was preparing her daughters' evening meal while they rested (their crying seemed to have left both girls utterly worn out). As she checked the softness of the boiling potatoes with a sharp knife, she heard the rumbling of distant thunder. Crossing over to the kitchen sink, she leaned forward and peered out of the window.

It was too dark to see much outside but when, after a few seconds, sheet lightning stuttered along the gorge, she saw the swing beneath the big oak rocking from side to side, pitched by strong winds. The bridge was lit up too, and the boiling river that passed under it. Disconcertingly, the water level was high, almost brimming over the top of the riverbank. The sight made her drop the knife into the sink.

The thunder that followed the lightning was much louder now, as if it were rolling round the gorge itself, and its noise made Eve cringe. Gabe. She needed Gabe to be with her. But she had urged him not to drive all the way back from London. He would be weary with all the travelling, plus he must still be shocked, having had to identify Cam's little body (he hadn't told her how their son looked, but she realized that after a year in the water – No! she mustn't think of that, she mustn't try to picture the condition his body would be in!). She insisted that her mind should stay on Gabe. All she knew was that she needed him here, with her and the children. But he shouldn't drive, not all that way, not in this weather. Would he see sense and stay in London?

A fierce gust of wind shook the window and kitchen door, causing Eve to take an involuntary step backwards.

She heard other parts of the house creak, contracting timbers, storm-battered windows, the oaken front door shifting on its hinges. Eve hated this place. Even though it was she who tried to persuade Gabe to stay, she loathed Crickley Hall for what it was: a morgue in which eleven children had perished along with their cruel guardian. You could almost feel the house's pitiful history . . .

She gave a little shudder. So cold, always so cold here.

The lights suddenly dipped, brightened, dipped again, then became bright once more.

*Oh, please no*, Eve thought almost drily, *please don't let the power blow. That's all we need on a night like this.*

She jumped when a loud crash came from the hall. Walking quickly to the kitchen's inner door, she went out into the hall to see what had made the racket. It happened again, but this time she saw the cause.

The cellar door had swung open, its edge hitting the wood-panelled wall behind. The door began to swing back in rebound, but it stopped halfway and was thrown wide again.

Eve hurried forward, shoes briskly clattering on the stone floor. She caught the door just as it was about to repeat the process and smash into the wall behind it. Holding it still, she looked into the dark cavernous cellar below, the draught that came up the steps from the well strong enough to ruffle her hair. It was silly, but to her the dense blackness there seemed to be pressing upwards as though riding the current of chilled air.

Eve closed the door and locked it, even though she knew it wouldn't stay shut. The key was icy to her touch.

# 60: THE KILLING

Maurice Stafford had decided another Hennessy was in order – but no more after this one, didn't want his breath to stink of alcohol when he went up to the house – and he had brought it back to his cosy little nook in the inn. He hooked his walking stick over the curved back of his chair.

The pub was getting even busier and he detected a collective nervousness in the drinkers' banter, their occasional laughter just a decibel or two louder than it ought to have been. Oh, they felt comfortable enough inside the bar, but he doubted any one of them was unaware of the storm outside for one single moment. The *crack* of thunder was directly overhead now; it had moved across country and found a nice little harbour bay to torment. It was quite funny to watch the inn's patrons glance towards the thick leaded windows whenever lightning flashed or thunder boomed. Bumpkins, the lot of them. Not his type of folk at all. But then, there were very few that were. Maurice wasn't very fond of people.

He picked up his previous train of thought. One day, Nancy Linnet had arrived at Crickley Hall, sent there by the education department to help out with the teaching of the evacuees. Probably they didn't know what to do with her.

Prissy Missy Nancy Linnet couldn't do enough for Augus-

444

tus and Magda at first. Pretty little face with tumbling locks of copper-coloured hair and Maurice had been quite smitten with her until he realized the shawl she wore round her back and over her lower arms concealed a hideous deformity. Oh, that spoilt the effect all right, that marred her looks. Her hand was a withered twisted claw, the arm above it up to the elbow just as unsightly. But she couldn't hide it all the time. When her shawl slipped and Maurice saw the disfigurement it had almost made him sick. God's punishment for her past and future sins, Magda had quietly told him. The Lord was wont to punish in this life as well as the next.

The young handyman/gardener had taken a shine to her, though, as if he didn't notice the horrible affliction. It had turned out to be propitious when Percy Judd was drafted into the army and taken away from Crickley Hall.

She loved the kids. Spoilt them. Always smiling at them and patting their heads as if they were angels from God. Didn't have a clue how to discipline them, although they always behaved when she was around; they weren't afraid to open their mouths to her. The kids adored Miss Linnet.

Well, she never patted Maurice's head. He couldn't even remember her smiling at him. Maybe the first couple of days. Then she turned against him, even though he tried to please her. So he turned against her, reported her soft ways with the orphans to Magda, knowing Magda would tell Augustus.

But as the weeks went by, the teacher became more and more rebellious, protesting whenever Augustus had cause to chastise the older children with the cane, and actually blocked his way when he tried to punish the younger ones by the same means. She was against all other punishments too, the denial of food, the hall vigil, Magda's leather-belt strapping – she decried all these punishments.

Then one day it happened: Miss Linnet threatened to go

to the school authorities and denounce the Cribbens for the cruel (her word) way they treated the evacuees. Susan Trainer had been the catalyst.

It was evening and the children were taking their turns in the bath. Susan had been washing the smaller ones until it was time for her to dip into the three inches of water with Brenda Prosser. Maurice had been at the landing door that led up to the dormitory, making sure the children went straight to bed after their baths, when a panicky scream had pierced the air.

Magda Cribben, at her usual place on a chair outside the bathroom, shot to her feet. Over the balcony, Maurice saw Augustus quickly striding across the hall, alerted by the noise. His footsteps were heavy on the stairs and he passed by Maurice with a look of thunder on his face. Maurice followed him to the bathroom's open door, where Augustus stopped abruptly, the boy almost bumping into him. Maurice peered over his guardian's shoulder.

Brenda was out of the bath, dripping water onto the tiled floor. She was naked and shivering, her frightened eyes on the cowering figure still in the bath. Magda slapped her face to stop her gibberings.

The naked figure in the bath was Susan and her legs were bent, her shoulders hunched, and blood was visible on her fingers as she clutched herself between her legs. The blood had streaked her legs and turned the bathwater red. Maurice remembered the scene as if it were yesterday.

'Susan's hurt,' Brenda wailed, pointing at her older friend.

Maurice was fascinated, not by the sight of two nude girls, Susan with her budding breasts, but by the blood on Susan's legs. Augustus seemed to be transfixed.

'Stop it, child!' Magda told Brenda briskly, and pushed her

to one side. The teacher's eyes narrowed and her voice was full of disdain. 'You horrid, dirty girl,' she rasped at Susan. Grabbing a damp towel from the metal rack, she shoved it at the distressed eleven-year-old. 'Use this! Soak up the bleeding!'

'What is it, miss?' Susan asked timorously. 'Am I dying?'

'Of course you're not.' There was no compassion in Magda's reassurance, only anger and disgust. 'There's nothing the matter with you.'

'Why am I bleeding?'

'Because you're impure. This is a woman's illness, a curse from the Lord to punish them for Original Sin.'

'But I haven't sinned, miss. I promise, I haven't done anything.'

'Well, you must have. You're far too young for *menstruation*.' She spat the word out, as if it's mere expression was iniquitous. 'You're a wicked girl!'

Augustus finally spoke, and his voice was brutal. 'She must be kept away from the others or her uncleanliness will taint them all.'

In the corner of the bathroom, Brenda was now crouched and sobbing. Susan had shrunk away from Magda and was cringing against the tiled wall.

'Please help me,' she pleaded, first looking at the woman, and then at the man.

Magda snatched her wrist. 'Come with me. We've a place for dirty girls.' She pulled Susan to the edge of the bath and, to stop herself falling, the girl stepped out still clutching the reddened towel to her body.

Augustus grabbed her by the other arm and Maurice quickly stepped aside as brother and sister brought the bowed girl out of the bathroom between them.

'My clothes!' Susan shrieked, dragging her feet.

Augustus and his sister merely tightened their grip and pulled her along the landing.

'You will not need clothes where you're going, child,' Magda sneered.

The other children had gathered at the bottom of the stairs to the dormitory, none of them daring to venture out onto the landing. Two of the youngest, Stefan and Patience, were clinging to Eugene Smith, both of them crying.

Maurice would never forget the shame on Susan's face as she was led naked past her friends, and he would never forget the smugness he felt as he trailed behind, even though he was mystified by the girl's condition. Had she cut herself somehow, would she bleed and bleed until she was dead?

Susan screeched as the brother and sister dragged her down the stairs and across the grand hall, spots of blood dropping behind her as if to mark her path. They ignored her desperate entreaties, for she knew where they were taking her. Maurice watched from the landing balcony and was afraid for himself. There was grim spite on Magda's hard face, while Augustus stared resolutely ahead, his deepset black eyes burning wickedly, a glistening of spittle on his thin lower lip. It was then that Maurice, only twelve years old but big for his age and both cunning and smart, truly understood that there was madness in his guardian, which ran just beneath the surface, ready to erupt at any given moment. The boy had witnessed the man's wrath many times, but this evening there was a light behind Augustus's dark eyes that hinted at barely suppressed violence and insanity. Maurice sensed it as much as he saw it and he was in a terrified kind of awe. Somehow, perception told him he would always be in terror and awe of Augustus Cribben, even after the man was dead.

Magda waited at the cellar door as her brother took the recalcitrant girl below. The sound of Susan's shrill remonstrations came back out into the hall, amplified by the cellar's brick walls and the narrow staircase. Suddenly, her cries were cut off.

Maurice heard heavy footsteps on the creaky narrow stairs, and then Augustus stood in the doorway next to Magda. The children, who had at last crept out onto the landing to look through the balustrade, all scooted back upstairs to the dormitory. Brenda Prosser, having dressed and left the bathroom, followed after them. But Maurice continued to watch, scared but fascinated. At that point, he seriously wondered if Susan Trainer had been murdered in the cellar. Augustus's words to his sister swiftly put an end to this notion.

'She'll remain there until the impurity has been purged from her body. I've counselled her to pray for her damaged soul and she is not to eat until her discharge is complete.'

'That will be days, brother,' Maurice heard Magda say.

Augustus's features were like granite, tough and uncompromising. 'That will be her penance. You'll give her water only.'

Without another word being said, Magda locked the cellar door and followed her brother into the sitting room that was used as an office. Another entry for the black book, thought Maurice, glad that his own name had never featured on its pages.

He sat on the stairs for a while afterwards, waiting to be called by his master or mistress. An hour went by and still they hadn't left the office, so reluctantly Maurice made his way up to his bed in the dormitory.

It was the next morning that things began to go wrong at Crickley Hall.

Maurice Stafford settled more comfortably in his corner seat at the Barnaby Inn. As he sipped his last brandy, he listened to the storm that raged outside. It was ironic that as a boy he had looked much older than his age, for now he looked much younger than his seventy-five years. The crowd in the bar had thinned out considerably, some customers having openly admitted they were worried about the ceaseless downpour and the effect it might have on the high moors. All were aware of the harbour village's history, even though the last great flood was more than sixty years ago, and they wondered if all the precautions taken since were enough to avert another disaster.

Maurice placed the bowled glass on the table and smiled to himself. He was unconcerned. He'd survived one flood, he could survive another. At ease with himself, he resumed the contemplation of his former life.

Miss Linnet. Miss Nancy Linnet. That fucking seditious little bitch. Maurice rarely swore, even in his thoughts. Augustus Cribben wouldn't like him to swear. But it was difficult not to be furious with the teacher who had upset everything.

He remembered she had arrived at Crickley Hall that morning at her usual starting time of 7.45. As soon as she'd gone into class she noticed that one of her pupils was missing. Where is Susan Trainer? she asked the children. No one answered at first, they were too frightened to, but when Miss

Linnet asked again, Brenda Prosser, the ten-year-old girl who had been with Susan in the bathroom the previous night, hesitantly spoke up. She told the teacher that Susan was locked in the cellar. Miss Linnet had been aghast, especially when she learned the girl had been down there all night, and then she had been angry when she found out the reason for the punishment.

She marched straight out of the classroom.

Maurice gave Brenda a threatening look. 'You're in trouble,' he told her.

Timid though they had become at Crickley Hall, the older children crowded round the classroom's open door and listened. Only Maurice was bold enough to take a step outside the door.

They could hear Miss Linnet remonstrating with Magda Cribben in the office, and although they could not catch every single word, they caught the drift of what was being said.

The young teacher was telling the older woman how outrageous it was for Susan Trainer to have been incarcerated in the cellar all night. Magda's replies were spoken in a low, even voice, but the children could tell she was cross. She warned Miss Linnet not to interfere, that school discipline had nothing to do with her. Only when Miss Linnet insisted that Susan had done nothing wrong, that what had happened was perfectly natural for a growing girl, did Magda raise her voice.

*'The girl is dirty! She's too young to bear the curse! She must have done something very wicked to have such punishment brought down on her so soon!'*

'There is too much punishment for all the children in this school. They are afraid even to speak. It's all I can do to coax a smile from them, so browbeaten are they.'

'Mr Cribben will hear of this impertinence,' Magda responded stiffly.

Maurice remembered that Augustus Cribben had left the house earlier that morning to catch the bus to Merrybridge where he had business in the local council offices.

'Very well.' Miss Linnet sounded defiant. 'I want to take the matter up with him. The situation cannot continue like this. I've a mind to report you to the school inspectors and the local authorities.'

With that, the teacher strode back through the office doorway and went straight to the cellar door. As always, the key was in the lock and she turned it with a swift twist of her good wrist. Reaching inside, she switched on the stair light, and they heard her clumping down to the well room below.

She must have had a conversation with Susan Trainer, or at least spent time comforting her, for it was several minutes before she reappeared again, now with the naked girl, who cowered against her, ashamed and exhausted. Susan held the blood-sodden towel to her lap, but blood still managed to drip and leave tiny spots across the hall's stone floor. The older children were frozen in the classroom doorway, watching the teacher help their friend up the broad stairway, taking her to the bathroom or dormitory. But when Magda appeared in the office doorway, her face incandescent with rage, they scattered back to their desk tables.

It was evident when Miss Linnet returned to the hall that she and Susan Trainer had had a long conversation. Her small pretty lips were set in a grim line and anger blazed fiercely in her hazel eyes. As usual, her long knitted shawl covered her withered arm and hand, but her other hand was clenched into a tight fist. She marched across the hall and went straight through to the office to confront Magda once again, who had already returned to her desk.

Maurice still lingered by the classroom door, and half turned to hush the other children who were whispering excitedly to one another. Wary of him, they fell silent immediately.

He listened again to the sound of Miss Linnet and Magda's voices.

'... down to the village pharmacist ...' the young teacher was saying. 'I shall purchase the appropriate items for poor Susan and show her how to use them.'

'You will not leave the classroom this morning,' said Magda and Maurice thought there was a trace of uncertainty in her otherwise stern tone. 'The girl may use old towels 'til the flow ceases.'

Flow? Flow of blood? Maurice was too confused to understand any of it. Was Susan bleeding from somewhere inside her body? If so, how had it happened? Perhaps Magda would explain it to him later. All he knew at that moment was that Susan had committed some grave sin for which she was being disciplined.

'Don't be absurd.' Miss Linnet's voice was raised. He had never heard her speak like this before; she was usually so quiet and well mannered. 'She needs proper sanitary towels and she must have them as soon as possible. Her first period has frightened her and made her unwell. I don't think spending the night without clothes in a cold damp cellar has helped matters.'

'How dare you speak to me in this manner?' Uncertainty had now been ousted by Magda's indignation. 'Mr Cribben will hear of your impudence the moment he returns. You, a chit of a girl, barely an adult yourself, daring to speak to me in this fashion.'

'I shall look forward to that moment. I've a few things to say to him about the running of this establishment. You and your brother are unnecessarily cruel to these orphans ...'

Maurice was amazed at the defiance in the teacher's

attitude. He would never have guessed she had the gumption to act so boldly. Until now, she had appeared to be a timid little creature.

'. . . and it has to stop. They deserve to be treated kindly and without these dreadful corrections you impose on them. I've spoken with Susan and she has told me of your despicable punishments when I am not here. I've suspected it was so since I first came to Crickley Hall. The children are too meek and fearful – no, terrified – of you and Mr Cribben, and I didn't quite understand the reason. Now I know all of it, and I will not allow it to carry on. I intend to contact the authorities by letter and insist they send inspectors to investigate my complaints. I shall make sure the children speak up.'

'You will do no such thing.'

Maurice almost shuddered at Magda's menace.

'Nothing will prevent me. I trust you will take charge of the class while I go to the village for poor Susan?'

She came to the door again and Maurice heard hurried footsteps behind her as Magda followed. Miss Linnet had got as far as the open cellar door when Magda called her. She turned to face the woman who stormed towards her.

Magda shouted into the teacher's face. 'You will not leave this house!'

Maurice had never seen Magda so angry. Cross, yes, severe, it went with her nature, but never before had he watched her lose control like this, not even when she had cause to strike the children with her leather belt (but then, that was always carried out coldly). Her hard features were contorted, her face more white than usual, and her words had been spat out – literally, for he had seen the spittle fly from her mouth.

At first, whether in shock or to create space between herself and the raging woman, Miss Linnet retreated a step so that her back was to the open doorway behind her. But then she stood her ground, her face red as Magda's was white. She seemed consciously to control herself.

'Susan needs help, not punishment,' she said firmly. 'All the children need care and attention, not constant hardship, which is all they get from you and your brother.'

'You will not leave this house!' Magda repeated, taking another step closer to the teacher. 'Go back to the classroom immediately!'

Maurice felt his heart pound and he forgot to take a breath.

'You wretched child with your shrivelled arm. What have you done to cause the Lord's castigation?'

'I was born this way,' Miss Linnet replied evenly, Magda's jibe somehow calming rather than upsetting her. Perhaps experience of similar cruel remarks had taught her how to deal with it. 'Now please move out of my way. I'm going to the village.'

Magda's fury finally erupted. 'You evil girl!' she screeched and took another step towards the teacher, her arms stretched forward as she came. With great force she pushed at Miss Linnet's shoulders.

Astonished, the teacher teetered on the threshold of the cellar stairway. But Magda did not stop at one push. Incensed – and afraid of betrayal – she pushed the teacher again, even harder this time, and Miss Linnet toppled backwards.

Maurice watched in fascinated awe as the teacher fell into the darkness behind her. He heard her body tumbling down, striking the side walls as well as the steps as she went. Curiosity overcame trepidation and he ran forward to see what had happened to the young woman; the sound of her body hitting the concrete floor below with a resounding crunch came back up to him.

Magda seemed frozen to the spot when he reached her. She was staring into the cellar's blackness, but her eyes were unfocused, seeing nothing at all.

'Have you killed her, miss?' (Even when they were in bed together he called her 'miss'.) He turned away from her to squint into the gloom.

She did not answer and when he looked round at her, he saw something that might have been panic in those cold black eyes of hers. Then she appeared to gather herself – her shoulders twitched and stiffened, her chin lifted a fraction.

She spoke slowly and firmly, brooking no dispute. 'You saw what happened, Maurice. It was an awful accident. Miss Linnet missed her footing on the stairs.' Her voice hardly wavered at all when she said, 'Go down and see if she's badly hurt.'

His eyes returned to the pit. All he heard was the urgent susurration of rushing water from the well. He didn't want to go down there. Not alone.

'Maurice, did you hear what I said? I want you to go down to the cellar and see how Miss Linnet is.' She reached forward and gripped his shoulder. Her hand felt like an iron claw through his flannel shirt.

'But . . . but what if she's dead, miss?'

'Don't be silly, boy. It was only a fall due to her own carelessness.'

'Miss . . .?'

'Did any of the children see the accident?' There was a noticeable quiver in her voice and a restlessness about her eyes.

'No, miss, they were all at the tables.'

'So only you witnessed her accidentally fall.'

He took in a long breath. 'Yes, miss.'

'Good boy. Well, now you must go and see how Miss

Linnet is. Here, I'll turn on the light for you.' She reached past him and stabbed at the light switch.

It was still dingy, but he could just make out a curled bundle lying at the foot of the stairs, a bundle he knew was a human body. He was startled when he thought he saw the shape twitch. He turned back to Magda. He was almost as tall as her and their eyes were level.

'Will you come with me?' he asked her nervously.

'Is that necessary, Maurice? Can't you go alone? The other children are unsupervised.'

'I'd prefer it if you come with me.' It was almost a whine.

She gave it a moment's thought and he could see the panic was still there at the back of her eyes. 'Very well,' she said stiffly, 'we'll go together. You can lead the way.'

As he hesitated on the top step, he was sure he saw movement below again.

'I don't think she's dead, Miss Cribben,' he whispered and Magda froze. It was then that he realized that Magda Cribben did not want the teacher to be alive.

Maurice momentarily closed his eyes as he remembered the frightening descent to the well cellar. Had it really been all those years ago? It was still vivid in his mind.

The brandy glass before him on the small table was nearly empty. Mustn't have another, though, had to keep a clear head. Yet he couldn't go up to the house too early. Make this one last then, drink the remains very slowly, appreciate its flavour.

*

Nancy Linnet was moving. She was pushing and pulling her battered body further into the dark cellar. She was desperate to get out of the light from the stairway, dim though it was, for she could hear footsteps approaching, heavy on the creaky wooden steps, and something – call it primal instinct – told her Magda Cribben was not coming down to help her. So Nancy dragged herself across the hard dusty floor, biting into her lower lip with the pain the effort caused her.

She knew that one of her legs was broken, because it was useless to her and hurt terribly, especially so each time she drew it along after her. Something was wrong with her back too, for her spine was numbed and her shoulders barely working. Tears of pain dropped from her eyes into the dirt beneath her and, although it was difficult to see, she continued to shuffle herself forward. She had to hide before Magda could hurt her again and at least the dingy light from behind helped her make out a deeper shadow ahead. When she blinked the tears away, she was able to see the black haven more clearly for a moment or two.

It was the entrance to the boiler room and if she could reach it, she would be able to hide there. She would have to be very quiet and very still, though, once she got inside. If only she could use both arms the effort would be so much easier, but her right arm had always been ineffective, just a withered limb that marred her life with its ugliness. So she managed with her left arm and her left leg to haul herself across the floor. She suddenly realized it was not only tears that were blurring her vision, but it was the blood streaming down her forehead also.

The boy, the sneak, the bully, watched from the bottom of the stairs. Magda had switched on the chamber's inadequate ceiling light and he could make out the figure on the floor as it crawled through the entrance to the boiler room. One of the teacher's legs dragged uselessly behind her and it seemed to be bent the wrong way. As if mesmerized, they both watched the teacher's progress. Gradually, her body slithering awkwardly, she disappeared inside the boiler room and the darkness devoured her.

Without further hesitation, Magda made her way to the boiler room and Maurice went with her. A churning mix of emotions caused his heart to beat even faster. There was anger at the teacher for threatening to betray his guardians and there was dread of the outcome now. Reigning over both was a feeling of excitement that made his limbs tremble and his brain tingle.

Although in shadow, they saw the shape of Nancy Linnet's prostrate body lying near the centre of the rough-bricked room. The light switch was just inside the entrance and Magda quickly pressed it on. As in the well cellar, the overhead light was dull and covered in dust, so that a dirty greyness prevailed with dark shadows at its edges.

Miss Linnet was still trying to drag herself on her belly but, too weakened, she was making no more progress. The fingers of her good hand scrabbled uselessly against the litter-strewn floor and one foot scuffed away at the dirt behind her without catching. Her once glorious hair was matted with silky blood, and because she lay with her cheek against the ground they could see that her lips were moving, although no sounds, no moans, no murmurs, came from them.

Magda raised a hand to her throat and her mouth dropped open. Maurice saw there was alarm rather than compassion in those black eyes of hers.

'What shall we do?' she said tonelessly, the question inwards, not meant for Maurice who stood by her side. 'She'll tell. She'll destroy us.'

It was the first time Maurice had seen weakness in the woman who had bizarrely become his mentor and mistress, and it distressed him.

'It was an accident, miss, like you said.' Anger began to override any fear that he felt. But it was excitement that continued to make him tremble.

'She'll say otherwise.'

'No, she can't! I'll tell everyone it was her own fault. I saw it happen.'

'She'll say I deliberately pushed her because I didn't want her going to the authorities. She'll tell lies and half-truths about Augustus and me. She'll make terrible trouble for us. They won't understand our methods, she'll tell them we're unkind to the children, and if they believe her they'll close the home. Our reputations . . .' Magda's mouth clamped shut: what would happen to their reputations seemed too horrible to contemplate.

'No!' shouted Maurice. He didn't want to leave Crickley Hall. He liked the things he did with Augustus and Magda. He liked lording it over the other orphans. 'I won't let her!' His words came out as a screech. He rushed forward and kicked the broken bundle on the floor. 'I won't let her!'

Taken aback by the suddenness of his anger, Magda could only watch as he ran to the pile of logs heaped against the back wall next to a hill of coke. Maurice picked up a short but stout log with both hands and a faint smile touched her thin mouth as she realized his intention. A cruel gleam of satisfaction shone from her narrowed eyes.

Lifting the heavy log high over his head, Maurice tottered back to the recumbent body, which was now twitching rather than moving. Magda made no attempt to stop him – she didn't want to stop him – as he stretched his arms, then brought the bludgeon down with all his might on Nancy Linnet's blood-soaked skull.

The sound of wood smashing against thin bone was hideous, a kind of popping-crunching that made Magda flinch despite herself. The teacher's injured leg jerked, the fingers of her outstretched left hand quivered.

Maurice raised and brought down the thick log again, perhaps even harder this time, and the teacher's exposed temple caved inwards. Maurice fell to his knees, but still he raised the log again and smashed it against the head that had already become a mess of pulpy gore. Nancy Linnet lay perfectly still beneath him, yet still he struggled to lift the deadly weapon. Only when Magda stepped forward and gripped his wrist did he stop.

'Enough,' she said quietly but firmly. 'She's dead, Maurice, the girl is quite dead.'

He froze and looked down at the blood that had spattered his knees and the front of his sleeveless jumper. He threw the log to the side as if afraid to be caught with it. His lower lip trembled and his eyes were wide in shock. But although fearful, he was glad, glad that the teacher was gone, glad that she couldn't interfere any more. His excitement had not abated. He even felt mildly proud of what he'd done – until he began to think of the consequences.

Would the police come and take him away? Would they lock him up in jail for the rest of his life? He looked pleadingly at Magda and saw she wore the faintest of smiles.

'She deserved it, Maurice,' she soothed him. 'She would have betrayed us, she would have undone all the good work Augustus and I have achieved. Now quickly, we must dispose of the body.'

'Miss . . .?'

'Have trust in me, Maurice.'

To him, it was the kindest she'd ever sounded.

'Come now, help me lift her.' Magda reached down for the teacher's legs. 'You're a strong boy – take her beneath the shoulders.'

First, they rolled the body over so that Nancy Linnet's half-open glazed eyes looked up at the ceiling.

'What are we going to do with her?' He felt no remorse and his fear was rapidly diminishing. Even the prospect of going to prison did not worry him. Magda had said to trust her, and he did, implicitly. He had no doubts at all that she would make things all right.

'We're taking her next door,' replied Magda, grunting softly with the effort of lifting the corpse's lower body.

Maurice's hands slid under the teacher's shoulders and he heaved her up. When alive, Nancy Linnet had looked as light as a feather but, although he certainly was a strong boy, he discovered a dead body was a dead weight. He and Magda struggled to carry it through the opening into the well room.

'Where will we hide her, miss?' Maurice managed to ask between gasps for breath.

'Where she'll never be seen again,' came the calm response.

'But what if the police find out?'

'They won't.'

Magda had not only thought of a place to put the corpse, but had already worked out a reason for Nancy Linnet's absence. Without prior notice, the young teacher had announced she was returning to London that very day. Magda would go down to the village in the afternoon and tell Miss Linnet's landlady that the teacher wanted her clothes and few small possessions sent on to her. A sudden crisis in the family,

Magda would explain to the landlady and anybody else who might be interested (it was just as well that Nancy's sweetheart, young Percy Judd, had recently been called up for military service and had left to help fight the nonsensical war or he might have caused a fuss).

She brought Maurice and the body to a stop by the well's low wall, but did not lay down her burden. The rushing of the river below seemed to satisfy her.

Maurice realized the intention immediately. His eyes widened, both excitement and trepidation still burning in them.

'You know what we're going to do?' Magda regarded him levelly.

The boy nodded twice.

'The currents are strong in the Channel,' she continued, Miss Linnet's ankles tucked beneath Magda's arms, her hands holding the teacher under the knees. 'Her body will be swept out to the ocean and, with luck, it will never be found. Now, over the wall with her.'

They rested the body on top of the stone wall for a moment, then tipped it over the side. It was a deep drop, but the turbulent sound of water below almost covered the resulting splash.

Magda leaned over the circular wall and peered into the black pit as if to check that the corpse had been flushed away. Maurice copied her, but could see nothing, not even the bottom of the well. Finally, she straightened and regarded him with a cold – colder than usual – countenance.

'If you ever tell anyone of this,' she warned Maurice grimly, 'then you will follow suit. Remember, it was you who bludgeoned her with the log. It was you who killed her.'

He replied earnestly, 'I won't tell anyone, miss, honest.'

'Good boy.' She gave him a wintry smile. 'Come to my room tonight. You deserve a reward.'

The reward would be as much hers as his, he was already cynical enough to know. Suddenly, Magda no longer looked old to him – she looked ancient.

# 61: STORM

After skidding for the second time, Gabe decided to slow down. Fortunately, the Range Rover's stability control and four-wheel drive had helped him avert anything serious, but he knew he had to take greater care: he had no desire to make Eve a widow and his children fatherless.

Forcing himself to ease up on the accelerator, he wondered how his daughters had taken the news of Cam's death. Loren would have been distraught, while Cally ... Well, maybe Cally would cry without fully comprehending the whole implication of losing a brother, what loss of life truly meant. He felt his own eyes moistening again and he shook his head as though that would stem the tears. He had to get a grip, couldn't afford to cry, needed clear vision to see the road ahead. Driving was dangerous enough on a night like this.

By now he had left the second motorway behind and was on a smaller, country road. The windscreen wipers were on double speed, but still the glass kept filling up. The rain was not just falling on the car but was pounding it, and the wind buffeted it whenever there were gaps in the hedgerows. He passed through lonely villages that looked battened down for the night, and other vehicles that were travelling more cautiously than he. Several times he had to wait for a clear stretch of road to overtake cars and lorries in front; the headlights of oncoming traffic were intensified by the rain on the windscreen, blinding him so that he was forced to bring the Range Rover down to a crawl until they had gone by.

It was a nightmare drive and, he figured, a fitting end to a nightmarish day. At that time, Gabe had no way of knowing that the nightmare would continue long into the night.

Lightning flared, followed by a deep roll of thunder in the distance.

The row of small terraced cottages had been almshouses in days gone by, built for the needy of the parish but now individually owned. They were remote, set back from the main road and reached only by a rough track. In today's market, estate agents would refer to them as *bijou* residences, and they were the type of properties sought after by city dwellers who dreamed of holiday homes or boltholes in the country. Percy Judd had been lucky enough to have lived in one of them all his life, so price was never a factor as far as he was concerned, although he had been assured of a small (but not that small) fortune by frustrated local agents and developers should he ever decide to sell.

Inside the cottage, which was at the end of the row, Percy sat in his tiny living room in front of a roaring fire, his outstretched slippered feet almost in the hearth, while the storm outside raged, shaking windows and rattling the room's front door like some weather-beaten traveller seeking refuge for the night. He was warm and comfortable, settled there in his old, favourite (and only) armchair, a mug of cocoa in one hand, a self-rolled cigarette in the other.

With no faith in the electricity supply in such extreme

weather (power cuts in the district were not infrequent when conditions were bad), Percy had lit two oil lamps, one of which stood on the inside sill of a window, the second on the room's centre table. They and the fire in the grate gave the room a cosy glow; yet despite appearances, the old man felt uneasy.

He was wary of this kind of weather for, although he had been away on National Service with the army when the flood of '43 had occurred, he had heard so many first-hand accounts of that night he felt almost as if he had been through it himself. And last time, he remembered being told, the rainfall had been heavy but not as consistent as these past weeks. Not that he had cause to be afraid: this row of low-roofed cottages was high up on the hill that ran down to Hollow Bay and well away from the river itself. No, it was the properties that stood on either side of the riverbanks and the village itself that were in danger should the worst happen.

A mewling caught his attention. The dog was curled up on the rug in front of the fire, inches away from Percy's feet, and it suddenly looked towards the door. It whimpered and turned its head towards Percy, then back at the door again.

'Not tonight, fellah,' he said to the dog in a low gentle voice. 'It's a wild 'un out there, too stormy fer me to be takin' yer out. Jus' settle down now.'

But the animal was fidgety, restless. It uncurled itself and aligned its body so that it directly faced the door that rattled and shook in its frame. It gave a sharp yelp.

'Hush now. Nothin' to be gettin' excited about. Yer been out once tonight, no need to go out again, not 'til it's time fer bed.'

Percy flicked the last of his cigarette into the fire and reached down to pat the dog's back reassuringly.

The dog whined.

'What's troublin' yer, lad? Hear a fox out there?'

A shuttering flash of lightning filled the room's two small windows and thunder cracked so loudly overhead that both man and dog flinched. The dog jumped up and ran to the door as if desperate to escape the close confines of the living room. It whimpered frenziedly as it scratched at the wood.

When it stood back and gave a long howling moan, a deep sense of foreboding came over Percy. There was something *bad* in the air tonight and it wasn't just because of the storm.

## 62: FRIENDLY EYES

Maurice drained the brandy, unable to make it last any longer. He smiled to himself as he remembered the day he and Magda had dumped the young teacher's corpse into the well. At that stage he'd felt little fear, only a frisson of excitement and an anxiousness to please Magda and Augustus Cribben. The troublesome Miss Linnet was out of their lives and nobody was any the wiser. Magda had covered up the murder perfectly: even the children believed the teacher had abruptly left for London without saying goodbye because of urgent family matters. They had missed her, sure enough, moping for days afterwards, and Susan Trainer was the worst. She was profoundly disappointed in Miss Linnet and spoke to no one for a week, but even she thought that the teacher had abandoned them and returned to the city. The school authorities had merely been miffed at the teacher's unprofessionalism and, what with the war going on and all, they had made no effort to contact her or, if they had, they hadn't tried very hard, nor for very long.

Magda had not told her brother the full story, had just kept up the pretence that Miss Linnet had absented herself. Augustus was not concerned: he was relieved that she was gone.

Scrubbing the cellar and boiler-room floor had been a bothersome chore, but Magda and Maurice had worked at it together. After they had cleaned the relevant areas, they had swept dust back over them so that the lighter patches would not stand out. No one would ever know what had happened down there, least of all Augustus.

Maurice smiled to himself again. Magda had kept her promise to reward him that night, though her reactions as ever were mechanical and her orgasms without abandonment. She never once lost her breath. At least he had learned from her. As he had learned from Augustus. Yes, Augustus had taught him the exquisite pleasure and the power of inflicting pain. It was just a pity that the psychiatrist who had had Maurice sectioned when he was a young adult did not appreciate or understand such joys.

Maurice's smile turned sour at that point. Some things are best forgotten.

Pulling back his shirtcuff, he checked his wristwatch. Time to go. Time he made his way up to Crickley Hall.

He stood and shrugged on his raincoat. Allowing the walking stick to take some of the weight off his left leg, Maurice leaned to pick up his hat from the table. He put it on, then lifted the empty brandy glass.

As he went by, he placed it on the bar.

Sam Pennelly, landlord of the Barnaby Inn, broke off his conversation with two local lads at the other end of the bar and sauntered down to where the customer had just left the glass.

'Thank you, sir,' he called after the tall man who was limping towards the pub door. 'Now you take care if yer drivin'. Some roads might be flooded already.' *And yer've had four stiff brandies*, he thought, *so you're over the limit*.

# THE SECRET OF CRICKLEY HALL

The tall man turned his head and in acknowledgement touched the brim of the funny little hat he wore. The landlord smiled back, thinking what friendly eyes his customer had.

A gust of wind drove heavy rain through the door when the customer opened it and the landlord watched as Maurice Stafford pulled the hat with the small feather sticking out of the headband more firmly down on his head before stepping out into the storm.

## 63: INNOCENTS

It was no good. She couldn't put them out of her mind. Not Eve and her family (although their predicament did weigh on her conscience), but the children who had perished in Crickley Hall. Lili could not stop thinking about them.

Their spirits were troubled and Lili sensed only she, or someone else with her gift, could help them. But she did not know how.

Why were they bound to that miserable intimidating house? Why hadn't their spirits passed over peacefully? Was it because they were still traumatized by their own deaths? Was something holding them there in a lonely neverworld of fear, were they somehow dominated by another force, one that was malign? She had felt it herself, had been terrified when it almost materialized in front of her and Eve. She dreaded the thought of facing it again.

But the children. They needed her help. She was convinced of it. But she had vowed never again to put herself in that position. And what if she did and next time it was the ghost of Marion that manifested itself? Would that be as terrifying? She couldn't help cringing in her chair as lightning flashed and thunder roared overhead.

Lili poured another glass of wine and her hand shook as she brought it to her lips. Oh God, help me, tell me what I should do. Those poor innocents should not have to suffer any more. They had been tied to Crickley Hall for more than half a century, they should be allowed to continue their journey. They shouldn't be afraid ever again. But how could she help them, what could she do?

A sob escaped her. Why was she so drawn to Crickley Hall? What was calling her from there? The children themselves? She could almost hear their small voices pleading with her, but surely that had to be in her own imagination. Was guilt causing her mind to play tricks, inventing these voices because somewhere in her deepest subconscious she felt responsible for them? Why else would she have been gifted – or cursed – with extrasensory powers if not to help lost souls find their way?

With the back of her hand, Lili wiped away a tear that had trickled down her cheek.

She couldn't ignore them. The child spirits were desperate, she could feel their mood. They needed her so badly and she could not refuse them. Suddenly, her determination grew stronger. For the sake of her own peace of mind, she had to do something for them, even if it meant putting herself in danger. And even if Eve's husband didn't want Lili there, she knew she had to go back to Crickley Hall, she had to do what she could for the children.

She sensed that things were stirring in the old house, that secrets were waiting to be exposed. Perhaps when they were, the spirits would find peace. Perhaps she would, too.

Lightning flared and thunder seemed to heave itself at the room's two windows as if to challenge her resolve. Lili trembled, but she would not give in to her fears. She put the wine glass down on the coffee table, then picked up the keys that were in an unused ashtray on the sideboard.

She headed for the door.

# 64: FLIGHT

Maurice Stafford stared out at the rain through the windscreen of his Ford Mondeo. The storm buffeted the car and bent the trees, the high walls of the gorge creating a natural channel for the wind that came off the moors and tore down to the sea. His car was parked in the short bay close to the bridge that spanned the river leading to Crickley Hall. Debris – branches, foliage, even rocks – was already piling up beneath it and Maurice wondered how long the wooden structure would last before it was smashed and carried away.

Curiously, his Mondeo was the only vehicle in the parking area beside the road; the Caleighs' Range Rover, which had been evident yesterday, was missing. Did that mean the husband was away from home? Maurice had slowed down before turning into the parking area so that he could get a good look at the house across the river and was able to make out a figure in the kitchen. Even at that distance he could see that it was a woman, so it had to be the wife, Eve Caleigh. Well, that was just fine and dandy, because if the man was away, then it would make his own task – his *duty* – all the more easy.

Something thumped against the Mondeo's windscreen causing Maurice to start. A loose tree branch rattled against the glass for a few moments before it was dislodged by a fresh gust of wind.

A truly dreadful night, he thought, so much like the night he and Magda had fled Crickley Hall in fear for their lives. In the shadows of the car's interior, Maurice grimaced as he remembered.

They had run from the house, terrified of the madness they were leaving behind. Augustus Cribben's final descent into total insanity had been swift, the terrible pains in his head driving him there it seemed. Of course, Maurice had come to realize, Augustus was always on the verge of insanity – his ways had never been entirely normal – but circumstances and excruciating pain had combined to throw his brain into a maniacal disorder that had become uncontrollable. Fortunately for them, they had left before the floodwaters had come, before the bridge had been swept away by the river that had risen above its banks, and they staggered into the storm, coatless bodies (there hadn't been time to grab their coats) flailed by rain and tree branches, battered by great billows of wind that almost blew them off their feet. It was a torturous journey that had them clinging to each other, every footstep forced, their bodies bent almost double into the gale.

Magda would not allow them to take shelter, nor even rest a while, for she had a destination in mind and it was far away from Hollow Bay, so far away that she could never be linked with the dreadful things taking place in Crickley Hall that night. Maurice could only be led by her, for he had no one else and did not want to die. Occasionally, he looked up to see Magda's face in profile and it was a mask of misery and horror. Once, she returned his look, as if she had felt his scrutiny, and as lightning strobed, he saw the same madness in her eyes that had been in her brother's: her eyes were wide open, even against the bolts of rain that pelted them, the pupils black and large, and they seemed to have no focus, seemed to stare right through him. The lightning flashes ceased and she was just a dark silhouette. But he could not erase the sight of her derangement from his mind. And as they stumbled, trudged, staggered through the wind and rain, both of them so soaked that they imagined their bones were wet, Maurice came to realize that he had been wrong to think that he had held some power over the Cribbens, that he had some control because he beat and scrubbed Augustus and gave Magda pleasure when they were naked in her bed. He now understood that he had no domination over them at all, he was there to do their bidding, a slave to be rewarded with treats and favours. This was why he would not have been safe back in Crickley Hall with the other children, why he followed Magda so blindly now. Augustus was his master, Magda was his mistress. Without them he was just another parentless child.

They used smaller lanes mainly, where high hedges gave them some protection against the wind, and passed no other person, motorcar or cart as they struggled on. They had travelled several miles when Magda dropped to her knees, then threw herself to the ground.

'*Augustus . . . what have you done?*' she wailed, the words torn away by the howling wind.

Maurice knelt on both knees beside her and tugged at her shuddering shoulders.

'*Please,*' he shouted over the noise of the storm, '*we can't stop! There's nowhere to hide!*' He meant nowhere to take cover, but it came out as hide.

She beat at the rough roadway with the heels of her fists,

her back juddering as she sobbed. Then, without another sound, she rose to her feet, swaying with the wind. She stared at the boy, but again it was with wide vacant eyes.

'Where are we going?' Maurice pleaded.

But Magda just turned away and walked on as if there had been no interruption to their journey. He quickly caught up and clung to her elbow.

They stopped only twice after that, once when a stout tree branch fell into the lane before them, and again when Maurice tripped over some soft and sodden creature – a rabbit or small fox – lying dead in a puddle on the ground.

Although their weather-hindered journey must have taken several hours, Maurice had lost all sense of time and was surprised when they reached the outskirts of a town. There were no streetlights or gaslights in this part of the country and only a few upstairs windows were lit as they made their way along the road. Magda's bent body was stiff and she seemed to be walking mechanically, like a wind-up toy. She spoke not a word to him, but when they came upon the deserted railway station, he at last understood that this had been their destination all along. The station master's quarters and the ticket office were closed, for these were now the very early hours of the morning, but Magda led Maurice through a side gate and along to the very end of the platform where there was a backless bench. Despite the exposure, she sat them both down and Maurice huddled against her for protection. She remained stiff, upright now, her back ramrod straight, ignoring the boy, lost in her own breakdown.

Leaning close to her ear, Maurice asked, 'Are we catching the train? Are we going to London?'

There was no response, but he assumed that was the idea, to get back to the city where no one would find them and no one could blame them for what had happened in Crickley

Hall – and he was, after all, *only* a child. Maurice saw no future beyond that.

As the hours moved on to dawn, the storm abated and the winds died. They weren't to know that the gorge and Hollow Bay had been flooded and that there was no one left at Crickley Hall to bear witness to what had taken place there. No, Maurice and Magda were in their own world, Maurice drenched and shivering, hunched up as close to Magda as he could get, she still staring straight ahead, also drenched but her body rigid, her face expressionless, features hard as if made of stone.

As often was the case in the aftermath of a heavy storm, the morning was bright and clear, the smell of raw damp earth heavy in the air. Somewhere in the distance there came the *clang-clang* of a fire-engine bell.

Still they waited and the sun began to dry out their clothes a little. Eventually, someone strolled out of the ticket office onto the platform, but it was too far away for the man to see them properly. As the hours went by, more people arrived on the platform, but none wandered down to the far end. Only Maurice was looking – Magda was still in a place of her own – and he saw a uniformed station master or guard step out of his office and check his pocket-watch, then glance towards them.

Maurice, sitting on Magda's right-hand side, sat back so that he was shielded by her body. He felt guilty, because they hadn't bought tickets.

All the uniformed man saw was a lone woman dressed entirely in black waiting for the morning train at the far end of the station. She was too far away to make out her features, although he could tell her face was very pale. He checked his watch again, a piece that had served him well for twenty years with its large sharp numbers and fine black hands, then peered in the opposite direction to the single woman, towards the west. He sensed the rumble on the railtracks before he actually heard it, a trick he'd picked up over the years – it was as if the rails were trembling ahead of the sound – and his eyes squinted as he waited for the London train to appear round the bend half a mile away.

For the benefit of the waiting passengers on the platform, he barked out the train's ultimate destination and the major towns it stopped at along the way.

Maurice heard the station man call out London and he ducked his head forward to see the train's approach. It soon chugged in and with a hiss of steam and a squeal of brakes the engine and first carriage came to a halt just past him. Doors began to open and slam shut again. No passengers alighted, for this was the train's first stop after leaving its departure point of Ilfracombe.

He looked at Magda, but she was not paying attention, she was just staring at the cream and dark-red carriage that was opposite them. He tugged urgently at her elbow and she took no notice.

'Magda,' he said in a quick hushed voice as if others might hear, 'we must get on. It'll take us to London. Please, Magda, before it starts up again.'

No response though. She was like an alabaster statue sitting there, so white was her colour, so still was her body.

'Please, Magda!' He was desperate now.

And then, when she wouldn't move, wouldn't acknowledge him, a coldness flushed through Maurice. He was completely alone again. The alliance between himself, Augustus and Magda was over. Augustus would be sent to jail for what he'd done – even hanged – and Magda would lose her job. No, worse than that. For murdering the teacher, Nancy Linnet, she would be put in prison for the rest of her life. Unless she told the police and the judge that he, Maurice, had struck the fatal blow that killed Miss Linnet, and she had only helped him get rid of the body. She wouldn't tell them it was she who had pushed the teacher down the stairs, she would blame it all on him!

He slid a few inches away from Magda on the bench and searched her profile. Would she tell on him? She didn't seem right in the head, it was as if something had closed down inside her. Why wouldn't she speak to him, why did she just sit there?

The slamming of the doors had finished now and he peeked past his silent companion to see the station man looking in the opposite direction, checking all the carriage doors were shut and there were no more passengers trying to board at that end.

Maurice knew he had to make a decision right then. If the police caught him they'd send him to Borstal, where all the bad boys went; or maybe, even worse, they'd put him in a grown-up prison because that's what they did with anyone who had murdered another person. Perhaps they'd even hang him, like Augustus. How old did you have to be before you got the rope?

Maurice ran for the carriage as a whistle blew and, once aboard and the train was slowly moving out of the station, he looked through a window at the solitary figure sitting there on the platform bench. Magda did not seem to see him as he passed.


Maurice Stafford – the older Maurice Stafford, no longer a boy but a man of seventy-five years who now lived under a different name – tried to flex his left knee in the limited space beneath the Mondeo's steering wheel. His leg always felt worse when the weather was cold or wet, a flaw in his otherwise healthy body, and he thought back to when the injury had occurred.

The accident had happened when he was still a boy scavenging in the ruins of the bomb-blasted city, stealing from grocery shops whose owners displayed their wares – fruit (limited) and vegetables (basic) – outside in boxes on the pavement, or from barrows in the markets. At night he slept in partially demolished houses, and on particularly cold nights he went to the underground shelters that some families still used even though the bombing appeared to have stopped (this was before the flying bombs, the V-1s and V-2s, Hitler's newest weapons, began their reign of terror). Most of the families shared their rations with him after he had explained that his father had died overseas and that his mother was an ambulance driver on call that night – he would tell anxious women that his mother always dropped him at a shelter before she went on to do her duty. It was never difficult to attach himself to families or women.

In fact, he had used a large family group – three boys, one about his own age, two girls and their mother – to get past the ticket collector on the day he'd arrived in the heart of the capital on the West Country train, the day he had left Magda Cribben sitting alone on the distant platform. From their chatter, he had gleaned that the boys and girls were evacuees like himself and that their mother had decided to bring them home to London now that the bombings had stopped; it was simple to merge with them among all the other arrivals, then pass unnoticed through the barrier, the collector having no time to count the tickets.

The hauntings had begun just before he broke his leg – indeed the first one was the prime cause of the injury. It had been a chilly April night and he was in a house whose upper floors had been gutted. Maurice snuck into a corner over creaky floorboards, pulling the collar of the over-sized overcoat that a kindly market porter had given him tight around his neck and jaw. Moonlight shone through two glassless windows, spreading across the floor of what once must have been a front parlour. All furniture and ornaments had been salvaged (or looted), for the room was quite empty save for rubble and shattered glass. Weary from a morning's work and roaming the bustling streets – war or no war, the city carried on as normal, the difference being that most of the women wore cheap, dull or homemade clothes, while the majority of men were middle-aged or elderly, those that were younger usually wearing military uniforms, and there were walls of sandbags protecting doorways and tape criss-crossing windows – Maurice soon drifted off to a fractured sleep, too uncomfortable and cold to lie peacefully.

He wasn't sure what woke him – a policeman outside on his rounds, an ARP warden on his way somewhere – something had interrupted his uneasy slumber anyway. He peeked out from his corner, the lapel tips of his coat touching over his chin. If there had been a noise – maybe a rat scuttling through the debris – it was gone now. Maurice snuggled down again, a shoulder fitting into the corner, but no sooner had he closed his eyes than he opened them again. Squinting, he peered into the shadowy corners opposite. There was someone standing in one of them, he was sure. Someone moving in the blackness. Moving out as if to cross the room in his direction.

He gave a little whimper and drew his knees up to his chest, trying to make himself smaller, less easily seen. The shape stopped in the clearly defined light from one of the windows and he saw that it was a man. And there was something familiar about him, the skinny body, the white hair lit by the moon, the rigid stance. Maurice recognized who it was from that alone.

How had Augustus Cribben found him here in London? How could he know where Maurice sheltered? Why was he naked? How could he walk through the rubble without disturbing it or making a noise? Then the boy realized the moonlight was shining *through* the figure! Maurice caught his breath.

At the orphanage before Crickley Hall, one of the female carers, a hefty woman with a ruddy face and wiry hair, had delighted in telling the children bedtime stories about hauntings, and she had claimed that all ghosts were transparent, you could see right through them. And now Maurice could see the shape of the smashed windows through Augustus Cribben.

The boy's eyes bulged as if ready to pop from their sockets, and the hairs at the back of his neck seemed to divide and stand straight. Was Cribben dead? Was this his ghost?

Maurice screeched, a high-pitched terrified sound that shot through the murky London air. He scrambled to his feet, his shoulder brushing against the wall, wiping off dirt and dust, while the ghost, now unmoving, looked on. The boy screeched again, pushing his back into the corner as if to sink through it. The room had become bitterly cold and

Maurice saw his own breath materialize in front of him. The limpid image of Augustus Cribben remained still, but Maurice could feel the eyes, even though they were hidden in shadows, boring into his.

Never before had Maurice been so frightened, not even when he and Magda had run out of Crickley Hall all those months ago. It was as if something bad, something frigid had seized his mind, his body. What did the ghost want from him?

With a panicky wail, he made a dash for the doorless opening on the other side of the room, skirting round the flimsy vision that merely turned to follow his progress. He was halfway there when the bomb-weakened floorboards collapsed inwards, sending Maurice plummeting down into the basement below.

Timber and bricks fell with him, three bricks joined together glancing off his head, debris of cracked floorboards landing on his left leg, pinning it to the stone floor. The blow to the head, although stunning him and causing blood to pour, failed to distract him from the pain of his broken leg.

Maurice screamed and screamed before passing out and the last thing he saw as he slipped into unconsciousness was a face looking down at him from the opening above. It wasn't Cribben's face.

An indistinct bulk sitting in the darkness of the car, he bit into his lip. The rain, the wind, was unremitting and Maurice flinched at the bitter torment of memories.

His mood had changed. The calmness had left him for the moment.

It had been the first of the hauntings that were eventually

to undermine his sanity. Followed by the dreams that had lost him his freedom for a while when he was young.

The man who had rescued him from the cellar (and perhaps who had chased away the ghost) was an ARP warden called Henry Pyke, and he and his wife, Dorothy, would play an important part in the boy's life from then on.

The national dailies carried the story of the 'mystery boy' found in the ruins of a building and who had lost his memory due to a blow to his head (it was thought). It made the front pages for more than a week, his photograph, which had been taken while he was in hospital recovering from his injuries, printed large for the first three days, the caption beneath appealing for anyone who knew the boy's identity to come forward. No one ever did. The picture released to the press was too bleached out, worse when it was reproduced, and a bandage covered his forehead, so that even the market traders for whom he had done odd jobs failed to recognize him.

The boy had been unable to tell the authorities anything about himself – what his name was, who his parents were, how he came to be in the bomb-gutted house where he was found. His photograph was even circulated among the troops in England and abroad, but still no one claimed him for their own. Eventually it was suggested that perhaps both his parents had perished in the earlier Blitz, and the boy, lost and confused, had roamed the streets ever since. There appeared to be no other explanation.

Public interest waned and the story was relegated to a couple of column inches on the inside pages, while the front-page headlines returned to more urgent world events.

JAMES HERBERT

The anonymous boy spent the next six months in hospital recovering from his injuries – his left leg had been badly broken – and the doctors hoped his memory would return of its own accord. But it never did.

Because of his size and his evident maturity, the patient's age was approximated at fourteen years, and Maurice, whose memory was fine, did not disagree with them (he was by now thirteen years of age anyway). Henry Pyke, the Air Raid Precautions warden who had discovered Maurice and carried him up from the cellar, had taken a special interest in the boy and had visited him several times a week at the hospital. As time went by and the 'lost' boy remained unclaimed, the warden began to bring his wife to see him. Theirs was a childless marriage and for years they had longed for a son or daughter. They grew so fond of Maurice, who was shy and well-mannered and had a wonderful shine to his eyes, that they decided that if the boy's parents or relatives were not found soon, then they themselves would apply to adopt him for their own. And that was precisely what happened. The authorities had not known quite what to do with the amnesic boy, and the Pykes had provided the ideal solution. They would allow the couple, who were in their early forties and now unlikely to have a child themselves, to foster the boy for a year or so with a view to full adoption.

Maurice Stafford, who had not forgotten his name or how he had returned to London, nor the horror he had left behind in Crickley Hall, was renamed Gordon Pyke.

The Pykes were gloriously happy with their new-found son, who hobbled around on crutches while his injured leg strengthened, and the boy did his best to conceal the unpleasant side of his nature, a task that was not difficult for him over the first few months. But then the nightmares had begun, prompted, he had always felt, by the fresh attacks on

486

the city, this time pilotless rockets sent over from the coasts of Europe by the desperate Germans. The doodlebugs, as the first V-1 rockets were nicknamed, brought hell back to the capital. The drone of their engines was feared, but the silence when the engines cut out and the flying bombs dropped through the sky were feared even more.

Henry Pyke was killed while on duty in a school hall acquisitioned by the ARP when a doodlebug fell on it and completely destroyed the building. Seven other people lost their lives with him.

The nightmares that came to plague young Gordon Pyke were intense and damaging. They made his nerves bad; they made him neurotic and paranoid.

These terrible dreams varied in content but were constant over the years. In one (the first one he had), he is on a train and he can see Magda Cribben's white face outside the window. Her mouth is open but he can't hear her shouts. Her pale fingers claw at the glass as the train begins to move, slowly at first, then picking up speed, leaving Magda behind, her face ugly in its contortions. He is always struck by an acute loneliness as the train leaves the woman far behind. In another, he is standing at the foot of the stairs in Crickley Hall and all the other orphans who had been evacuated with him are higher up, each to a step, and he feels deep shame as they stare down at him, for he knows they are all dead. When they beckon him, silently inviting him to join them on the stairs, he doesn't move. He can't, he's paralysed. So the dead start to come down to him and he can see the emptiness in their eyes, the lifelessness of their corpses; he can smell their decay. In yet another, he is flagellating Augustus Cribben's nude body with a bamboo cane, and as he does so, the skin parts, wounds open, Cribben's abused body becomes raw red meat and no longer recognizable as human. But he can't stop the flogging, he wields the cane until the meat begins to pulp, then disintegrate, and the gore puddles at the feet of the thing that is no longer a man but now a mashed carcass that starts to corrupt and rot and fall away until finally it is nothing more than boneless lumps of flesh in the spreading pool of blood. Even then he cannot stop; he continues to thrash the bloody mounds, and the cane itself becomes red and slippery until it slides from his hand and he falls to his knees in the muck he has created. He always woke up at that point, shivering yet sweaty, clammy, peering round frantically, searching for anything lurking in the darkness of his bedroom. The final nightmare in the cycle of four has him up to his neck in cold water that is as black as the space around him. A circle of dull grey light comes from high above, and when he feels the slimy walls they are circular. Naturally he is frightened in this predicament, but the real fear comes when he realizes there is something in the inky water with him. He can't see it, but he can sense it. As something brittle, like the decayed fingers of a claw, wraps itself round his wrist he starts to scream and it becomes a real, waking scream that seems to rebound off the walls of his room.

Yes, the dreams were bad, for their consistency as much as their nature, but it was the second appearance of the ghost that had him gibbering on the floor of his bedroom, his curled body pushed tightly into a corner, his hand scratching frantically at the wallpaper and his teeth chattering, his eyes bulging.

It was late at night and he was lying in bed, just beginning to doze, hoping that his sleep would be dreamless, when he heard the familiar sound.

*Swish-thwack.*

He was afraid to open his eyes, but also afraid not to. He

could feel the room had become icy and the air was foul, as if a large rat lay dead and mouldering beneath the floorboards.

*Swish-thwack.*

He forced his eyes open.

Because of his nightmares, he always slept with the ceiling light on, so anything in the room was plainly visible. Only too visible. The figure of Augustus Cribben was coming slowly towards the bed, and this time it was not transparent, it was as firm and solid as when Cribben was alive. Only twin gleams of light could be seen of the shadowed eyes, but the lips plainly moved as if the vision was speaking.

It had to be a ghost, but it looked so real!

The cane came down hard on the bedspread and, impossibly, he saw dust rise from the material. The cane came down again and this time it hit his leg, the one that had been broken by his fall into the cellar, and although the pain was mostly absorbed by the cover, it was still strong enough to release the scream that had struggled to escape him the moment he saw the ghost.

He leapt out of bed and cowered in the corner of the room where he stayed, blubbering, until his adoptive mother burst through the door and ran to kneel beside him. It took Dorothy more than an hour to convince her adoptive son there was nobody else in the room.

His behaviour from then on was alarming. He twitched every time she touched him and shrank away when she tried to take him in her arms and comfort him (now widowed, Dorothy needed comforting herself, especially from the son she had always longed for). Gordon wouldn't speak to her either and he refused to meet her gaze: he hunched his shoulders, leaning over the walking stick he now used (the break in his leg had never healed properly), and his eyes darted craftily as if he had some secret to keep. He became agitated whenever it was time for bed and for three nights running she had to rush into his room, brought there by his dreadful screams. On each occasion she found him huddled in the corner of the well-lit room, his body shaking, his eyes wide.

Only then did Dorothy seek medical help for him and her GP immediately sent the boy for psychiatric treatment.

'They'll soon sort him out,' was the doctor's opinion.

But once in the mental home, Gordon, like Magda Cribben before him, withdrew into himself even more, blocking out the world so that nothing could reach him, especially the lunatics he was forced to share the ward with. He could not escape the ghost, though, nor the nightmare dreams of Crickley Hall, but in time he learnt to control his reaction to them.

When Cribben's ghost now appeared, Gordon would stifle his own screams with a fist to his mouth and a hand over his eyes. The horror was still there, but self-preservation had always been his strength. He wanted to leave this place of mad people and to do so he knew he had to appear inwardly and outwardly normal. He did not care for their drugs and physical restraints.

When the nightmares came, he learned to be still when he awoke from them, not to cry out or complain, to weep silently beneath the bedclothes until repetition hardened him even against tears.

He could not tell his personal psychiatrist of what he had done and what he had witnessed at Crickley Hall – if he did he probably would not have been released for years, if ever. So when he came out of what had become his own self-imposed shell, he made up stories of explosions and houses toppling down onto him and big holes opening up to swallow him and the sound of sirens, air-raid warnings constantly ringing in his head.

The medical profession had become used to dealing with shell-shocked victims during and after the war, and the psychiatrist easily recognized the condition in Gordon Pyke. He also knew of the boy's history, how he had suffered from amnesia, forgetting how he had become parentless and alone: who knew what trauma he had endured before? Gordon had finally started to talk freely and seemed to be making a sudden, rapid recovery. After five months of confinement, Gordon was released.

However, the relationship with his adoptive mother was never the same again: after all, it was she who had agreed to his internment in a mental hospital. He rarely spoke to her now and, as he grew older and taller, his attitude towards her became menacing. She started to be afraid of him.

Although the war was long over, conscription was still mandatory for eighteen-year-old males and when he reached that age, he received his call-up papers for National Service. Fortunately, as he saw it, he was rejected by the military because of his invalid status – he still used a walking stick. His psychiatric history would probably have excluded him anyway. So now, Gordon Pyke, who had decent school reports (ironically, he was placed in a lower year – which was more suited to his real age – because of his absence from school due to injury and time in the psychiatric hospital), found a job as a junior librarian in a library not far from where he lived.

The hauntings and nightmares continued through the years and they were always terrifying, even though he had become used to them. Perhaps inevitably, the hauntings aroused in him an interest in the supernatural. Were ghosts possible, did he *really* see the ghost of Cribben, or did he imagine it? He read the books on the subject stocked in his own library and they gave him an appetite for more. He visited bookshops that specialized in the supernatural and paranormal. If others had witnessed such apparitions, the phenomenon not just in his own mind, then maybe the haunting *was* genuine. In several books he discovered that ethereal bodies were created when the consciousness of a dying person leaves the body and exists somewhere between the spiritual and the physical, often because of the trauma of death itself, or because there is something left unfinished for them in the real world.

It caused him to wonder if that was why Augustus Cribben was plaguing him now. If that were the case, then why did the ghost appear to him? How could he help Cribben resolve something left unfinished? It was a question to which Pyke had no answer.

Gordon Pyke, once known as Maurice Stafford, shifted rest-lessly in the driver's seat of the Mondeo. His leg was giving him particular gyp tonight. Always did in cold or wet weather, but this was worse than ever. He rubbed his knee with his big hand. He had to curb his impatience. Let the family settle in for the night.

He wiped mist from the side window with the sleeve of his coat and peered through. Rainwater was running fast down the lane, creating its own shallow river. Lightning flared and the crack of thunder soon followed, so loud it made him want to duck his head.

This is so right, he thought, so much like the night he

and Magda had fled Crickley Hall. Would there be another flood? he wondered. Well, that would make things perfect.

To restrain his agitation, he went back to his memories.

His adoptive mother, Dorothy Pyke, with whom he still shared a house, had passed away from a fatal dose of flu that led to pneumonia when Gordon was twenty-eight. It was a relief to him – they had despised each other for years. Surprisingly, in view of their strained relationship, she left the house and the small amount of money she had managed to save from her widow's pension to him. But then, who else did she have to leave anything to? He soon sold the house and moved into a small rented flat, placing the modest amount that came from the sale and the money he had inherited into a deposit account in a bank.

Now that he could afford it – his salary as a librarian was pitifully low – Pyke took to visiting prostitutes, particularly searching out the older variety who were more than happy to provide the kind of service he required. In fact, it made the job easier for them because they did not have to pretend enjoyment. The deal was that they had to keep perfectly still and exhibit no passion whatsoever while he used their bodies. (Initially, he had tried the younger whores but was always disgusted by their squirming and sighing, feigned or otherwise.)

For a while – less than a year – he was married. Pyke, with his apparent courtly manners and his gentle eyes, was attractive to certain women. He was tall, and well built too, which added to the attraction. His new wife, Madeleine, was almost pretty despite the thick horn-rimmed glasses she wore and the size of her teeth that kept her lips permanently parted. An avid reader, she was a member of his library and her borrowing of books increased after he had mildly flirted with her one day as he stamped her choices for that week. At first enthralled with her husband, she did her best to please him, but as the weeks went by she began to resent his lengthy silences and his constant brooding. In sleep he was often unsettled, sometimes waking up with a start, his pyjamas damp with perspiration. But never did he explain his dreams to her.

His method of making love was decidedly odd and a great disappointment to her. He demanded that she remain passive when they had sex (Madeleine was a virgin and hadn't known quite what to expect, though she was sure it wasn't this), that she should not respond in any way to his attentions. If she expressed the slightest passion, if she breathed too sharply or too deeply, he would abruptly bring the engagement to an end. Although he did not rage at her, he would become even more distant.

It did not take long for her to realize that all his good manners and apparent kindliness were a sham, meant for others to think well of him, whereas in reality he was a cold, remote man who was indifferent to everybody else. But what finally repelled her was when he told her she was to submit to beatings. With a stick. A stick that had lain hidden on top of the bedroom wardrobe, a thin yellowish stick that must have been purchased from a school supplies outlet, for one end was crooked so it looked like a headmaster's cane.

She refused. He beat her anyway.

Madeleine, her back, arms and legs stiff with throbbing red stripes beneath her blouse and skirt, packed her bags and left him the following day. Pyke didn't care much: he had expected this plain and timid little thing to be pliant to his will. Because of her dowdiness, her lack of glamour, she would be grateful to be moulded to his liking. Her wails of protest and her pitiful tears when he flogged her that night had spoilt his pleasure, for he had begun to crave the stimulation of inflicting longed-for pain again. Madeleine was a grave disappointment to him.

The divorce took ages to go through (as it did in those days) but by then Pyke had found someone else to help satisfy his needs, an ageing homosexual he had met in a Soho dive. It was almost perfect, because the man was only a little older than Augustus Cribben had been, and he gloried in pain, begged for chastisement. Although Pyke was always aroused, there was never any sex between the two men: Pyke didn't consider himself 'queer'.

It was only when he went too far in one of their sessions, beating his partner in sado-masochism so brutally that he turned the man into a bloodied, howling mess, that the arrangement was swiftly brought to an end. The unfortunate victim, who had suffered far greater pain than he had ever imagined or desired, threatened to go to the police and have Pyke arrested for attempted murder. Pyke ran and never went back to the seedy drinking club where they had met. Fortunately, he had used an alias (ironically, the name Maurice Stafford) during their association and the beatings had only ever taken place in the other man's humble little flat above Berwick Street market.

The hauntings and the nightmares persisted, although the ghost gradually became less dense, as if it were losing power, and the dreams became less vivid, but nevertheless still harrowing. Over time he learned to accommodate both. But eventually a strange compulsion to see Crickley Hall once again nagged at him and he could not understand why. It wasn't sentimentality: he still feared the place and was unable to erase the memory of that last terrible night from his mind. He felt that his own guilt lay there, waiting for him to return and acknowledge it.

One year, when he was in his mid-thirties and on a summer break from the library, he took the early-morning train and went back to Hollow Bay. He caught the bus from the station to the harbour village and stared hard at Crickley Hall when he went past. It was as grey and grim as ever, but he felt no sensation whatsoever: good or bad, it was just a sombre unprepossessing pile standing on the other side of the river with the gorge rising sheer behind it. He alighted from the bus at the bottom of the hill, then walked back up. Crossing the short wooden bridge, he took the path to Crickley Hall's front door and, without hesitation, knocked the gothic door knocker loudly.

There was no answer, nobody came. When he knocked once more and still no one came to the door, he looked through all the ground-floor windows, even those at the back of the house where the gorge wall, with its thick vegetation, rose dramatically just feet away from the building itself. The house appeared unoccupied, for dustsheets covered the furniture and the kitchen's counters and tabletop were bare. Pyke was disappointed that no emotion was aroused in him; yet somehow he felt drawn to the place, even though there seemed to be no answer for him there. The hauntings remained a mystery.

Back at the village, he visited its only public house, the Barnaby Inn, and ordered himself some sandwiches and a gin and tonic. While there, and on his second drink, he got chatting to an elderly, roughly dressed man who looked like a local, the kind of regular customer who had nothing better to do than spend his lunchtime and evenings in a pub, a solitary drinker who welcomed conversation with anyone who would give him the time. When Pyke enquired about the village, the old boy inevitably mentioned the great flood that had engulfed it during the war, the biggest and most awful event in Hollow Bay's history. Sixty-eight folk were killed that night, eleven of 'em orphans, who'd been evacuated from London to Crickley Hall, the big house up the hill. Their guardian drowned with 'em as well. Only person to survive were a teacher, guardian's sister apparently, an' she must've got away before the floodwaters came down the gorge. They say she's never spoke a word since the day she were found. Shock, they reckoned. Shock, because all them kiddies in her charge was dead, as well as her own brother. Couldn't remember her and her brother's name after all this time though.

Keenly interested, Pyke had asked what had become of the woman. Although he hadn't known Magda's true age at Crickley Hall, Pyke guessed she was probably into her sixties by now. That is, if she were still alive.

Last I were told, came the reply, she were put away in the loony bin. Ilfracombe had the only one in them days. Can't say what become of her after that.

Pyke found Collingwood House by journeying to Ilfracombe and making enquiries at the seaside town's main library. He was given directions to the mental home and he walked nearly two miles to get there, his bad leg protesting most of the way. It was an old redbrick building sparse in embellishment and quite unlike the psychiatric hospital he had been confined to as a youth. This was a mental *home*, a place for lost causes. In the olden days it would have been called a lunatic asylum.

Inside, he could have sworn there was the tragic smell of mental decay, although it was surely a combination of boiled cabbage, detergent and piss. Again he was reminded of his own incarceration all those years ago and he had an urge to flee the building; but he was too curious to leave.

At the reception desk, he enquired if a Magda Cribben was still a patient, and the receptionist checked a list and informed him that yes, Cribben – only surnames in those days – was a long-term resident (she emphasized resident as though patient was an ugly word). He used to be one of her pupils, Pyke told the uninterested girl, and he had only recently learned of the ex-teacher's circumstances. He had been very fond of Miss Cribben, so would it be possible for him to visit her?

He waited while the receptionist conferred on the internal line with someone of authority and when she finished her conversation she said yes, although it was not strictly visiting hours, he would be allowed to see Cribben, and that was only because Cribben rarely received visitors – in fact never, as far as the receptionist knew, and she had been employed at Collingwood House for the past five years. A male nurse dressed in white jacket and trousers duly arrived and led Pyke down a long corridor on the ground floor. The walls were painted a lifeless grey and there were scuff marks and scratches along its length as if the inmates had struggled all the way when being taken to their rooms or padded cells. As he followed the nurse, whose thick biceps were evident beneath his tight, starched sleeves, Pyke was warned that, frankly, it was pointless to visit Cribben because she was a zombie – the nurse's own appraisal of his patient's condition – and hadn't said a word to anybody since she'd arrived at Collingwood House back in 1943. He knew this because colleagues had passed it on when he himself joined the staff. Pyke wondered if she would recognize him after all this time.

He was startled by her gaunt figure and her ashen face and hands. Magda never had much weight, but now she was skeletal, and although her complexion had been pallid before, now it was almost bloodless. She seemed to have shrunk – but then he had grown taller. The hardness had not retreated from her features with age and the lines on her tight skin were many and deeply etched. Her cheeks were sunken, but her jaw was still strong. She was dressed in black, which was no different from before, and the hem of her skirt ended just above her bony ankles. Her eyes, though, were as black and sharp as ever. Yet they showed no reaction when he entered the tiny cell.

Even when the nurse had left and they were alone there was no acknowledgement. She was sitting bolt-upright on a hard wooden chair beside her narrow bed and there was nowhere else for him to rest except the bed itself. He stood, putting all his weight on his good right leg.

Pyke started by reminding her of Crickley Hall and all the things they had done together, a sly conspiratorial smile on his face, nothing on hers. He talked of her brother and the harsh regime that had governed the orphans' home that was also a school and there was no recognition. But he was glad at last to speak to someone about his hidden past, even though he might just as well have been yakking to himself for all the response he got. Her eyelids did not flicker when he mentioned the murder of the young teacher and how, together, they had disposed of the body. He felt satisfied when there was no response, for this was good, their secret was safe. He had always worried about someone else knowing of his crime, but Magda was not only mute, she seemed to have forgotten the deed. Her mind was blank, she had lost all memory of it. She had even forgotten that last horrendous night that haunted him still because of his own guilt. After all, it was he who had informed on the other children. It was he who had betrayed them.

He left Magda Cribben with mixed feelings: disappointed that he had no one with whom to share the past – and they were exciting times for him – but also relieved that there was no one left to expose his former life as Maurice Stafford.

Although his exterior inspection of Crickley Hall had been fruitless, he remained drawn to it, for his few months there as a boy had marked him for life, an experience that had shaped his nature – and, though he could not know it, his destiny.

When Pyke returned to London and his job as librarian, he asked for a transfer. Somewhere in North Devon, he indicated. Meanwhile his interest in things otherworldly continued and he soon found himself fascinated by all aspects of the occult. But the dreams came back with full force and Cribben's ghost had regathered its strength, although now it appeared as a murky blackness, barely resembling the figure of a man, more of a noxious ragged mist, a strong unpleasant odour always preceding the manifestation. Despite its lack of clear definition, Pyke always knew it was Cribben's shade, for its overwhelming malevolence was the same and with it there always came the familiar *swish-thwack* sound, only as a kind of distant echo it was true, but nevertheless there to remind him of the punishment cane, the harbinger of pain that had terrified the orphans of Crickley Hall so. The dreams also revived their intensity – and their clarity – so that sleep became an ordeal once more. Pyke suffered his second psychological breakdown.

Considered to be a danger to himself as well as others when his rages got out of control, he was involuntarily committed to the psychiatric ward of a large London hospital.

Fortunately for Pyke, treatment for mental illness had improved significantly since he was a boy and within three months his condition had improved enough for him to be discharged (the doctors weren't to know that his apparent return to normality was because the hauntings and the power of the nightmares had waned again, making it easier for him to cope).

His position at the library had been generously held open for him, although the chief librarian regarded Gordon Pyke's request for a transfer to the West Country a priority: the slower pace of life would be of benefit to his neurotic employee. As luck would have it, a vacancy for an assistant librarian shortly came up in the large Devon town of Barnstaple and Pyke duly went down to the beautiful county and took the job.

Growing older did not dim his interest in psychic phenomena and spontaneous psychic activity. If anything, his fascination with the subject increased as the years went by, for he longed to know what lay beyond death and he needed to be assured that Cribben's ghost was not hallucinatory, a figment of his own imagination (which would mean he truly was mad). He read the works of respected psychical researchers from which he learned that certain people could attract and concentrate psychic forces. He also learned that nobody yet knows the boundaries of what is considered normal, nor the extremities of that which is considered supernormal. He learned practical methods of detecting the possible presence of a ghost by the simple use of a thermometer or thermograph: when a ghost is present it seems to create a partial vacuum which results in a drop in pressure and temperature (the atmosphere certainly became cold whenever Cribben's spirit appeared to him). And it was also reaffirmed to him that a ghost is generally an earthbound spirit trapped in the physical world because of trauma at death or unfinished business (what could Augustus Cribben have left unfinished? he asked himself yet again). He also learned that a violent act can sometimes leave a psychic imprint on a place that later will attract supernatural activity (even *he*, so very much alive, was strangely drawn to Crickley Hall, so why not spirits too?).

Pyke was absorbed with the works of psychic investigators and began to wonder if he himself could become one. Divorced, a routine, undemanding career, plenty of spare evenings and weekends – why not become a part-time ghost-hunter? He certainly had good knowledge of what was involved by now. Over the following months he acquired some of the basic equipment recommended for such investigations, simple things like notebooks, thermometers (including the greenhouse type), coloured pencils and crayons, synthetic black thread as well as white cotton thread, tape measures (one of them an architect's thirty-three-foot leather-cased winding tape), talcum powder, drawing pins, graph paper, torches, and also more expensive items like cameras for colour, black-and-white, and infra-red film, a Polaroid camera, tripod, digital camcorder, spring balance (for weight of objects if moved), strain gauge (for measuring force to open or close doors), voltmeter, portable sound-recorder, frequency-change detector, instruments for measuring atmospheric pressure, vibration, wind force and humidity, and a magnetometer. There were other more expensive and sophisticated items that would be useful, such as closed-circuit television, a capacity-change recorder, or an Acorn computer that had the ability to monitor changes in temperature, light and vibration, and having sound-recording equipment attached, but Pyke decided he'd collected enough for his amateur status. The good thing was that no licence or degrees in psychic phenomena were required.

He joined various associations connected with parapsychological studies and psychic research and attended spiritual meetings (which he was surprised to discover thrived in both towns of Barnstaple and Ilfracombe) where he made useful contacts. Through these, and by placing small discreet ads in local newspapers and freesheets, he began to gain clients who wanted his 'expertise' in investigating hauntings in their homes, pubs and once even a theatre. His efforts generally met with success, often finding quite natural reasons for supposed supernatural or paranormal activity, while at other times confirming that yes, there was a ghost or ghosts on the premises.

When Pyke reached the age of sixty-five, he retired from the library and devoted more of his time to ghost-hunting. There were never very many cases to investigate or explore, but just enough to occupy him in his retirement. He had even written papers on some of his investigations and submitted them to the London Society for Psychical Research, which had never published any but had kept them on file, commending him for his work. In order to drum up more business, he made use of a cuttings agency which sent him any news items or features from the south-west journals concerning suspected or alleged hauntings. These he would follow up by getting in touch with the 'victims' involved (always quickly, to get in before any fellow investigators who used the same methods of finding cases) and offer his services. The fact that he was financially comfortable (he had never squandered his small inheritance and the money he received from the sale of his old London home, and there was still a reasonable residue left) meant he did not have to charge would-be clients – he only asked remuneration for his expenses – and this made him instantly attractive to them.

He invariably presented himself as a knowledgeable and

sympathetic sceptic and his apparent normality, plus his engaging manner, swiftly won people over. Yet despite his usual successes and resolved cases, he had never discovered the cause of his own hauntings.

Over a period of time, he had approached four reputable mediums in the hope that they would come up with an answer to the mystery, but the first two had regarded him with something like fear in their expressions and had asked him to leave immediately, while the third had cried out, then collapsed in a heap on the floor only moments after going into a trance. Her husband, who had been present, demanded that Pyke leave the house and never come back. The fourth and last, without even going into a trance, had warned him that he would be tormented by hauntings until something was resolved and only he could know what it was. Bewildered, he had asked the medium how she knew this, but she had avoided looking at him directly in the eyes and refused to reply. But as he had reluctantly turned and was walking away, she called after him, her voice quiet yet her words distinct.

'It will only get worse for you,' she had told him. 'Unless you fulfil his wish – no, his *command* – if you don't, you'll never be free of him. It'll become unbearable, you'll suffer . . .'

But he refused to listen any more as he hobbled away, moving as fast as his bad leg would allow. The medium had not provided any answer, she had just given him a dire warning, filling him with fear for the future.

That was a year ago and the medium had been right: the hauntings had become worse, worse than when he had been a boy even. Pyke had begun to be afraid for his sanity again, for the ghost of Augustus Cribben now came so close to him that he could smell the putridity of its inner core over the noxious fumes that accompanied its presence. The atmosphere would become so cold that his body, which was in paralysis, felt like ice, a frozen vessel in which his mind was trapped. He was afraid to sleep, night or day, because the dreams had found fresh vigour and were as clear as reality, and they came to him at any time. He was exhausted and nervous, and he knew he could not go on like this, that the hauntings and nightmares would break him as they had before, only this time he would not recover, this time he would be broken for good.

Then, just five months ago, depleted and desperate, he did something he should have done long, long ago, for it gave him the answer for which he had been searching, the way of resolution.

He used the microfiche reader facility in the same library where he had once been employed and he sourced the front pages of national and local daily newspapers for October 1943.

With these he had travelled back to the past.

Now it was October again. Late October. But it was the present. Not quite the same day as when the Devil's Cleave had become a huge conduit for the wind as well as a giant gutter for the swollen river and rainwater from the moors, but close enough.

Gordon Pyke sheltered from the storm in the metal cocoon of his car, reliving his life and anticipating the final closure from the years of torment.

Enough of memories, he mentally snapped at himself. Time to deal with the present. It was as if all the years since leaving Crickley Hall as a twelve-year-old boy had been leading up to this point, as if he had been directed – *driven* – back to this ugly old house. Tonight was perfect. It wasn't quite the same date, the day and the week were different, but that was okay, it didn't matter because everything else was right. Tonight he would free himself.

Fierce rain assaulted his face and shoulders when he pushed open the Mondeo's door. He climbed out awkwardly, gritting his teeth as he cricked his knee. The wind nearly tore the hat from his head, but he clamped a big hand down on it in time to save it. With both hands he gripped the narrow brim and secured the hat firmly. Reaching back into the car he drew out his sturdy hardwood walking stick, then pulled open the rear door and dragged out a huge worn leather suitcase. It was heavy, but he was a large man and still strong.

He straightened, paused for a moment to look across the foaming river at Crickley Hall, then made his way to the bridge.

## 65: THE DRIVE BACK

Wind-driven rain lashed at the Range Rover's windows and bodywork, and Gabe took the bend in the road cautiously. The roadway was so narrow that another skid might take him into a ditch on one side, or into the trees on the other, despite the vehicle's stability control. Nothing was foreseeable on such a vile night.

It was just as well he had slowed down because the road dipped just beyond the curve and rainwater had created a mini-lake across its surface. Even the ditch on the left was not enough to carry the water away. Normally, he would have changed down to a low gear and driven steadily through the flood, confident that the 4x4 had the height and power to pass through it, but his headlights lit up another vehicle ahead which had become immobilized in the middle of the road.

Two heads turned round to look at him through the other car's rear window, their anxious faces lit up by the Range Rover's strong lights, and he saw it was a young man and girl trapped in their Ford Fiesta. They looked too young to be married, nothing more than teenagers. Maybe this was their first date, Gabe thought, and the guy had made a jerk of himself trying to take the flood too fast or too slow, the Fiesta in the wrong gear.

Gabe thumped the steering wheel with the heel of his hand. All he wanted to do was to get back to Eve and the girls, to be there with them in their mutual grief. He didn't need this.

The driver's door of the Fiesta opened and the young man stepped out into the water, which came almost up to his knees. He splashed towards Gabe, desperation on his face. Gabe pressed a button and his side window slid down. Ignoring the rain that battered his face, he stuck his head out, an elbow resting on the sill. Despite the weather, the kid approaching him wore only a Kaiser Chiefs T-shirt over baggy trousers. Tree branches were waving with the force of the wind and ripples coursed across the newly made lake that concealed the roadway; the Range Rover shuddered with each fresh gust.

'*We got stuck!*' the other driver, who was, as he had thought, no more than a teenager, shouted out pointlessly when he got as far as the Range Rover's bonnet.

'*Yeah, looks like you did,*' Gabe called back. He was impatient to get on his way.

The drenched kid came up to the side window and Gabe couldn't help but feel sorry for him. The teenager's long hair was now plastered to his scalp and the soggy T-shirt stuck to his skinny chest.

'*The car just stopped halfway through,*' he bellowed mournfully into Gabe's ear. '*We didn't realize the puddle was so deep.*'

Puddle? The way ahead was concealed by a mini-lake.

'*Can you help us?*' the kid pleaded hopefully.

'*I can get you out of it,*' Gabe shouted back, '*but I don't know how well your engine's taken it. You may not get it started till it's dried out again. You've probably sucked up water through the exhaust.*'

The drenched kid looked forlorn, rainwater dripping off

his nose. *'We need to get to the next village. My girlfriend lives there.'*

*'How far?'*

''Bout five miles.'

*Good*, Gabe thought. He wouldn't have to go out of his way if he gave the couple a lift. *'Look, I haven't got a tow rope, but if you put your car in neutral, I can push it out from behind. When we're out of the flood, steer towards the side of the road. You can leave it there and I'll take you to your friend's place, then you can get a garage to collect your car. Doubt you'll get anyone out tonight, though, not in this weather.'*

They both jumped when they heard a sharp *crack* from across the road. A stout branch of a nearby tree snapped off and dangled by sinews over the road.

*'Let's get to it,'* shouted Gabe.

*'Thanks, man. I owe you.'*

The young guy splashed back to his own car and through its rear window Gabe could see him explaining the situation to his girlfriend. Still lit up by the Range Rover's headlights, the girl turned and waved back a thank-you.

Gabe engaged first gear. 'Okay, let's see what we can do,' he murmured to himself and set the 4x4 in motion.

## 66: GHOST-HUNTER

The wind blew the front door wide open and rain flew in with it when Eve answered the croaky doorbell.

The tall figure of a man stood on the doorstep, a walking stick in one hand, a very big suitcase set on the ground by his right leg. Lightning flared behind him so that his face and body were momentarily in silhouette. The boom of thunder quickly followed and Eve almost recoiled from the sound.

She was still in an emotional daze from news of her son's death, although outwardly, and for the sake of her daughters, she appeared calm and collected. She waited for the other person to speak.

'Mrs Caleigh?' the big man queried even though he knew full well who she was. 'Gordon Pyke. We met yesterday.' He was puzzled by the lack of expression on her face, but nevertheless he smiled warmly.

'Mr Pyke,' she said at last.

A cold draught wrapped itself round her body and rain spat at her through the doorway.

'Yes,' he confirmed again. 'You and your husband agreed that I should come back tonight to make tests.'

'Tests? I'm sorry . . .'

'May I come in? I'm afraid the storm is rather fierce.'

Eve stepped aside as he hoisted the suitcase and came

into the house. She was too confused – and her senses were too blunted – to object.

'You do remember, Mrs Caleigh?' Pyke took off his little hat and smacked rain from it against his thigh. He rested the brown leather suitcase on the stone-flagged floor.

Eve shut the front door, exerting pressure as the wind fought to keep it open. Although they could hear the gale outside and the rain lashing the high window, it became comparatively quiet inside the grand hall.

'Yes, of course,' she said distractedly in answer to his question. 'But I didn't expect you . . .' Her words trailed off.

'Oh yes, that was the arrangement. Your husband was rather keen that I help you with your problem.'

'Problem?'

'The suspected haunting. I'm here to look into the matter. There are no ghosts here, I can assure you of that.' Pyke was sticking to the line he'd used on Gabe Caleigh, that of a pragmatic sceptic. 'Even better,' he added, 'I'll prove it to you.'

His natural smile was disarming. He indicated the dripping suitcase. 'If I could just set up my equipment? I promise I won't get in anybody's way.' He beamed his kind eyes on her and the smile beneath his small, grey-streaked beard was warm, charming. Somehow, understanding. She caught the whiff of alcohol on his breath. 'We need to agree on what rooms can be off-limits to you and your family once I've prepared them. I'll have cameras and sound-recorders in them, you see. And instruments for measuring movement and pressure change. Also, don't be surprised if you find talcum powder sprinkled on the floor or furniture. It's for possible footprints and handprints. Quite easy to vacuum up after-wards.'

'I'm sorry, it's not . . .' Eve was going to say, it's not

# JAMES HERBERT

*convenient*, but the word was hardly apt for the circumstances. 'We've – we've had very bad news today,' she finished lamely.

'Oh, my dear Mrs Caleigh, I'm so sorry.' His sympathy sounded perfectly genuine. 'Is there anything I can do?'

She shook her head dispiritedly. 'No. Thank you. It's my little boy. I told you yesterday that he'd been missing for a long time and today we learned that – that he's gone for ever. He's dead.'

'Dear God. That's dreadful.' One of Pyke's big hands reached out and rested on Eve's shoulder for a moment, its pressure light. 'Would you like to talk to me about your son?'

He wondered why her eyes were not puffy from crying. She seemed to be taking her loss surprisingly well. But then her tone of voice suggested that her mind was in another place. It was not that unusual for the shock of sudden tragedy or bereavement to numb a person's feelings, dull their senses, so that they appear detached and withdrawn rather than mortified.

'That's very kind of you,' she replied solemnly, 'but no, I've spent most of the evening talking to my daughters about Cam – that's my son's name – and now they, we, need time to grieve.'

'How are your daughters taking it?' Pyke oozed concern.

'Loren's terribly upset – that's the older one you helped yesterday.'

He nodded.

'And Cally,' Eve continued. 'Well, she cried a bit, but she's too young to understand . . .' Her voice trailed away again.

'How old is Loren? She's twelve, I think you told me.'

'Yes, just twelve. She's with Cally in their bedroom now, trying to deal with it. She's putting on a brave face for me, I think.'

512

'Is your husband not at home?' Pyke already knew Mr Caleigh wasn't, but there was no harm in checking.

'Gabe's still in London. He had to identify the body. I hope he's all right.'

*Excellent*, thought Pyke. 'You know, yesterday he was very keen for me to carry out an investigation into the unaccountable disturbances in this house. Despite your mutual grief, I'm sure he would have wanted me to carry on. If I'm successful – which I know I shall be – in providing proof to you that Crickley Hall is not haunted by ghosts, it will be one less thing for you to concern yourself with.'

Eve thought of telling Pyke about last night, how she had nearly drowned in the bath, strong hands seeming to push her down, submerge her in the water whose surface had turned to ice, but did not have the energy to explain the inexplicable. Pyke was on a fool's errand – she, herself, had witnessed too many weird things in this house for there to be rational explanations – but she was too weary, too played out, to try and convince him.

He was still babbling on, but she barely took in a word he was saying. She didn't even consider him insensitive, so sincere did he appear to be.

'I promise you'll hardly know I'm here. I'd start at the top of the house, the attic room from where you said you heard running feet, then I'd be interested in examining the cellar, which may be the root cause of some extraneous noises you've been hearing. The well, the underground river, damaged or worn foundations and all that. Do you have decent architect's plans of Crickley Hall, by the way? No? They might have helped me, but never mind.'

Eve's will had been wearied by grief. She cast her eyes downwards as if deliberating, while in truth all she was thinking about was her dead son. Her thoughts were interrupted by a small voice from the stairway.

'What does the man want, Mummy?'

Cally had a frown on her podgy face as she stood hand in hand with Loren on the square landing at the turn of the stairs. She was in her pink pyjamas, while her big sister was wearing a light-blue nightie that hung down to her bare ankles.

'This is Mr Pyke,' Eve told her patiently; she had hoped Cally would be fast asleep by now. 'He's come to see about all those strange noises we've been hearing. He wants to make it all right.'

'Good,' proclaimed Cally. 'I hate the noises because there's no one there. I like the lights though.'

Pyke didn't know what lights the little girl was referring to. But his attention was on Loren. His smile contained both delight and sympathy, his kindly eyes the secret of the trick.

'Hello, Mr Pyke.' Loren managed to raise a smile. Her face was blotchy from dried tears and her eyelids were red-rimmed. Her shoulders were slightly hunched forward, another outward sign of her anguish. She looked very vulnerable.

Eve quietly called across the hall to her youngest daughter. 'Cally, you need to be in bed sleeping.'

'I'm too sad to sleep, Mummy. Is the man going to make the noises go away?' She rubbed an eye with a knuckle.

Eve turned back to Pyke. 'I'm not sure—' Again she was interrupted.

'Mrs Caleigh. Eve. Your husband was quite definite.'

'But not right now, not tonight.'

'I'm afraid I'm going away in a few days,' he lied. 'Tonight is the only time I'll be available. I promise I'll have answers for you by tomorrow morning. I won't even have to stay here overnight if you don't want me to, although that would be preferable. I only have to arrange my paraphernalia, a camera here, a sound-recorder there, a length of cotton across a doorway somewhere else. All I require is a couple of hours or so. You can go up to your bed without worrying about me – I can let myself out and come back early in the morning if you'd rather I didn't stay.' Yes, it would make everything easier if they were sleeping; that was the original plan anyway.

'Normally,' he went on without giving Eve a chance to speak, 'I would sit in a chair somewhere in the house, the hall itself or perhaps the attic room, so I could keep an eye on things, check my equipment every now and again. I just wouldn't feel right if I didn't do something to help you and your family at such a sad time.'

His compassionate smile broadened, but not quite into a grin.

'Besides, I've driven a long way this evening and through the worst weather I've ever known.' (Which wasn't exactly true because he and Magda had braved a similar storm all those years ago.) 'It would be a shame if it were a wasted effort.'

Eve felt her will sink, and it was already at a low ebb. Pyke was persuasive, he had a sincere manner; but it wasn't his entreaties that were wearing her down, it was because nothing else mattered to her right now. She could tell that Loren was taken with Gordon Pyke despite her obvious emotional pain over Cam. Perhaps she saw him as the grand-dad she had never had? Perhaps if Loren accompanied the ghost-hunter as he set out his tools of the trade and explained each one's purpose she might be diverted from her sorrow for a short while. For the first time ever, Eve abdicated from parental responsibility to pass it on to her eldest daughter.

'What do you think, Loren? Should we let Mr Pyke go

ahead and flush out bats in the roof or mice in the cupboards?' She chose not to mention ghosts. 'You were there yesterday when we spoke about it.'

Loren had led Cally down to the bottom of the stairs. The nice, tall Mr Pyke was smiling encouragingly and she could almost feel him willing her to say yes.

'Dad wants Mr Pyke to do it, doesn't he?' she said to her mother.

'Circumstances have changed,' Eve replied, struggling to keep bitterness from her voice.

Loren's face clouded over for a moment and her thoughts skitted elsewhere; she was still shocked by her brother's death even though she had been expecting the worst for months.

'You told Cally and me we have to try and carry on as before – before Cam got lost.' There was something like anger in her tone, but it wasn't directed at her mother.

Eve gave in. She looked up into the investigator's gentle eyes and spoke resignedly. 'Very well, Mr Pyke. Put your equipment wherever you think it might be useful. Loren will show you the cupboard on the landing where most of the noises have come from, while I get Cally back to bed. Then she'll take you up to the dormitory – sorry, it's now just an attic as you called it.'

'I'm anxious to examine the cellar where the well is.'

'Yes, of course. I'll take you down there myself when you've finished upstairs. You might want to put some kind of contraption on the cellar door – as I told you, it just won't stay shut.'

'Certainly. I'll use a spring balance and measure the amount of force it takes to open it. It's probably due to strong draughts. And you won't enter the rooms I've sealed?'

'As long as we know which ones they are.'

'I'll site my movement-triggered cameras and tape record-ers, but won't set them 'til you're all out of the way in your beds.'

'I'd rather you didn't stay the night.'

'That's fine. I'll leave late and return first thing tomorrow morning. As long as you keep clear of my little, er, traps, there'll be no problem.'

'I hate to turn you out on a night like this . . .'

'Perhaps the storm will have broken by the time I'm done here.' Besides, now he didn't have to wait until the husband was asleep. 'I'm sure I'll be all right.'

He lifted his suitcase and looked towards Loren again. 'So lead on, young lady; I'm entirely in your hands.' *How true*, he thought, *oh so very true*.

Loren produced a wan but polite smile. Cally only scowled at the man when her big sister dropped her hand.

Lili drove cautiously, slowly, her nose only inches away from the windscreen. The Citroën's wiper blades did their best, but the rain seemed to be *hurling* itself at the glass, making visibility extremely poor. Several times she had almost resolved to turn back and go home, for some of the minor roads were flooded with pond-like puddles and each time she went through one she worried that the car might stall and leave her stranded. Yet she kept going, driving steadily, determined to reach Crickley Hall that night. That *crucial* night. She could still hear echoes of the children's calls in the deeper caverns of her mind, too distant to catch their words, but knowing – sensing – her help was needed.

She ducked her head instinctively every time there was a lightning flash followed by a thunderclap. Lili had never realized that thunder and lightning could continue for such a long time; the thunderclouds had remained localized and that puzzled her, for surely the high winds should have moved them on?

Another car was ahead of her and its brakelights were constantly winking on and off as if the driver were being even more cautious than Lili. Maybe it was a good thing. She needed to keep her speed down and, anyway, following another vehicle made things easier for her. Let them make the mistakes.

The car in front, however, soon turned off onto a side road, leaving Lili to fend for herself. Suddenly blinded by blazing headlights coming at her from the opposite direction, she pulled up sharply, thankful there was nothing behind. Three cars went by, all of them on full beam, the second one dazzling the first's rearview mirror, the third dazzling the second's, a dangerous way to be driving, especially on such a treacherous night.

More lightning, more thunder. A good night for hauntings, she half joked to herself. If anything, she discovered, it was more hazardous travelling along main roads than down country lanes, for the high hedges of the latter offered some protection from the battering wind, even though the branches of some trees bowed perilously close to the Citroën's windscreen and roof.

Coming to a crossroads, she could just make out the signpost, one of its four arms pointing directly ahead to Hollow Bay. She checked left to right, and left to right again, squinting into the storm for headlights approaching in either direction. The road was eerily empty of traffic now; but then, what kind of fool would be out on a night like this? She gunned the engine and shot towards the relative safety of the opposite lane, a mighty burst of wind rocking the small car halfway across. Her hands gripped the steering wheel firmly, keeping the car on course, and then she was in the narrow lane, this section of it at least protected by tall, grassy banks. Hollow Bay was now no more than a couple of miles away, she reassured herself. Not far. Just difficult with all this wind and rain. No going back now, Lili told herself. Despite the heavy dread she felt. Besides, it was that dread that was drawing her to Crickley Hall. She was needed. By the children. She was sure.

After another nightmarish mile, Lili reached the turn-off for the harbour village and was mercifully aware that it wasn't too far to the house from this point. Wind whistled round the vehicle and rain pummelled it ceaselessly. Thinner trees waved and bushes shook wildly. Lili anxiously rubbed the steam of her breath from the glass in front of her with the sleeve of her coat; she had to keep leaning over the steering wheel to get even closer to the windscreen just to see the roadway ahead as shooting rain pounded the road's surface like exploding bullets. The psychic bit into her lower lip and her knuckles were white on the wheel.

Then it happened.

Lightning forked its jagged way down from the turbulent skies to strike an elm tree on Lili's left. Sparks flew out from it and a small fire flared. With a sharp grinding sound the trunk began to split. Her scream was muted by the thunder that quickly followed as the tree started to fall towards her, and it might have been fright or reflex that made her stamp on the accelerator. Branches that were still in leaf scraped against the car's rear window as the tree toppled with a mighty, juddering crash and Lily only stopped the Citroën when she knew it was well clear.

The psychic twisted round to look back and all she could see through the rain was a thick mass of branches and leaves completely covering the road. She let out a shuddering breath as she turned and rested her forehead on the top of the steering wheel.

*Oh God, that was close*, she thought. *Oh dear God, that was very close.* Her whole body was trembling, especially her neck and shoulders which, paradoxically, also felt taut.

She took a few moments to calm herself before starting the car again. Trembling still, she drove onwards to Crickley Hall.

*

There was a vehicle parked in the short bay area, but it wasn't Gabe Caleigh's. Lili knew he drove a Range Rover and this was another make entirely, a Ford of some kind. The rain was beating down so hard and the night was so dark – except when lightning strobed; then everything became a dramatic silvery-grey – she couldn't even tell its colour. The Range Rover was not to be seen and she briefly wondered if the Caleigh family had left the house. But then she saw the dull glow of a lighted window across the river. She parked close behind the Ford and her headlights revealed it to be a Mondeo, dark red in colour. A shallow spray haloed its roof as rain bounced off the metal.

As soon as Lili got out of her car she was drenched, her blonde hair darkened and flattened to her scalp. She wished she had brought an umbrella along – her mind had been too preoccupied when she had dashed from the flat – but then dismissed the idea: it would easily have blown away in this gale. Leaning forward, shoulders hunched almost to her ears and holding her coat closed with one hand, she made her way to the bridge.

Pausing before stepping on to it, Lili looked over at Crickley Hall. There were lights on in most of the windows, she now saw, upstairs and down; she thought she even saw a glow coming from the small attic windows. Holding onto the handrail, the psychic put one tentative ankle-booted foot onto the bridge and stopped. She could feel the wooden structure shaking beneath her.

Dark though the night was, she could see the white spume of the hurtling, swollen river. The wild waters were only inches below the foot planks of the bridge, and spray misted over the boards so that they were dangerously slippery. She gripped the handrail more tightly.

Lightning zigzagged from the sky and in its argent

illumination the river looked terrifying, as if about to burst its banks. Broken tree branches, twigs and loose shrubbery cluttered against the rail on the other side, and the rail she held onto quivered in her grip.

With great trepidation, she placed her other foot on the bridge. It seemed even more shaky now that she had both feet on the walkway, even more unstable. Sliding her hand along the soaked rail, Lili warily moved further on, the wind whipping rain against her exposed face, her boots slipping on the bridge's slick surface. Halfway across she felt the whole structure shift, as if the raging water underneath might carry it away. The bridge only moved an inch or so, but nevertheless it was enough to make her panic.

The psychic ran the rest of the way, her feet skidding on the boards, only her hand on the rail saving her from falling. Just before she reached the end, the bridge lurched again as if to break free of its supports, and the movement, slight though it was, sent Lili staggering forwards so that she crashed to her knees onto the pathway.

She hurt her hands taking her weight, and her knees would have been grazed had she not been wearing a coat and skirt that covered them. Picking herself up and grimacing at the sharp sting in both hands, Lili hurried towards the house, crouching against the rain. Something caught her shoulder, a hard knock as if someone had punched her, and she wheeled round, expecting to be attacked. She saw movement in the darkness of the night, something small and rectangular falling away from her. The swing was lit up by another flash of lightning and it was coming back towards her at speed. But this time she was able to step backwards off the path so that it missed her. She sensed its heaviness as the wooden seat reached its highest point a foot or so above her head.

Although the psychic knew its motion was caused by the

gale-force wind, she could not help but feel that the swing had hit her deliberately, conspiring somehow with the lightning-felled tree and the unstable bridge to keep her away from Crickley Hall.

Chiding herself for being melodramatic and almost letting her imagination run away with her, Lili continued her difficult journey to the house.

She got to the big front door and pressed hard on the bell button by its side. The storm was too loud for her to hear anything from inside and she pushed the bell once again, then banged on the wood with the heel of her fist.

'*Eve!*' she called out. '*It's Lili Peel. Please come to the door!*'

Certain it wouldn't work but trying it anyway, she turned the old painted-black doorknob and was surprised when the wind blew the door inwards.


Her matted hair flat against her head, its ends dripping raindrops onto the floor, Lili entered Crickley Hall. The wind blustered in behind her, bringing rain with it. She quickly pushed the front door shut, fighting the wind to do so.

With the door closed and the noise of the storm muffled, the psychic turned to face the grand hall again. She had half expected to be overwhelmed by invisible presences like the first time she had arrived here, but there was nothing – she sensed no overwrought spirits, nor anything bad oppressing the atmosphere. The vast, stone-flagged room that felt like some self-aggrandizing billionaire's mausoleum was devoid of unearthly energies. But there were puddles of water, some as big as pools, scattered around the floor. Lili regarded them curiously, then movement caught her eye.

'Lili?' she heard a surprised voice say.

Looking up, the psychic saw Eve Caleigh peering down at her from the hall's balcony. She had obviously emerged from a room along the landing. Lili heard Eve draw in a sharp breath when she saw the puddles that lay around the ground floor. Eve quickly went to the stairs and hurried down them, her face showing concern. She avoided the water as she came towards Lili.

'It *must* be the rain,' Eve said quietly, as if to herself rather than to the psychic.

Lili saw the usual aura of sadness round Eve, but now its greyness was deeper and more lifeless.

'Sorry, Lili,' Eve apologized as she drew near. 'I heard the doorbell, but I was settling Cally into her bed. I'm hoping she'll drift off to sleep soon.'

Lili looked at the other woman with pity. 'Eve ... your son. I'm so sorry.'

Eve stammered. 'You – you know? You sensed that?'

'He's at rest now. Nothing more can ever harm him.'

She thought that Eve might crumble, might break down in tears, but the bereaved mother was strong and regained her composure. Lili was relieved.

'What brought you here tonight?' Eve asked detachedly. 'The weather ...'

'I couldn't let the storm prevent me from coming. It's important that I'm here. I think you'll need me.'

'I don't understand.' Eve gave a small shake of her head.

'I can feel it now. The house felt empty a few moments ago, but now I sense something coming through, as if they've been waiting for me.'

'The children?' Eve stared intently into Lili's green eyes. 'I felt something impending all morning, but I thought it was because of Cam.'

'No. I told you, your little boy is at peace. What's going to happen tonight is nothing to do with him.'

'That's why you came here? The children brought you here?'

'They called me. I had to come.'

A week ago, she might have thought the psychic's words were self-delusional, but everything had changed for Eve now. Eve *believed* Crickley Hall was being haunted by the ghosts of children who had once lived in the house. But they were not alone; there was a darker entity here also. Eve herself sensed this.

Her question was in earnest. 'Why do you think they've called you, Lili? There has to be a reason, doesn't there? The hauntings must have a purpose.'

But in answer, the psychic merely closed her eyes and mentally reached out to the orphans who had died in Crickley Hall. Nothing happened. She could not visualize them. Yet the first time she had entered the house she had almost been overwhelmed by a great pressure, an emotional barrage that had made her feel faint. She knew there was contact between herself and the spirits here – she sensed their unhappiness, their pleadings – but they had not come through clearly. Something or someone was holding them back. Something or someone they feared. And now she could sense it herself.

Lili's eyes snapped open as if she had been physically stunned. Whatever it was, it was feeding off the psychic energy of the house's occupants, including her own. She could feel strength draining from her.

'It's more powerful than them,' she murmured, more to herself than Eve.

Eve touched her arm. 'Lili, are you all right?'

But the psychic looked puzzled rather than weakened.

'There's something very wrong.' Lili looked around, her eyes wide. She looked at the cellar door, which was ajar; she looked up at the L-shaped landing, which was empty. She looked at the broad, imposing staircase and she shuddered.

'Sometimes stairways act like a vortex for spirits,' she told Eve. 'It's because there's so much energy there with people using it all the time, and the spirits are drawn to that energy. There's something there but I can't tell what it is.'

Lightning flashed outside the tall window over the stairs, blanching each separate pane of glass. Thunder seemed to roll along the roof itself.

'Eve!' Lili suddenly said, making the other woman start. 'D'you have anything that belonged to the children? The children who died here, I mean. Anything that might have been left behind years ago.'

Eve shook her head and was about to say no, when she remembered the items Gabe had found hidden behind the landing cupboard. The Punishment Book, the thin, supple cane – the photograph of the Cribbens with the children!

'Wait here,' she told the psychic and dashed into the kitchen, leaving Lili alone in the cavernous hall.

Lili took a moment to study the pools that spread across the floor. There were no drips from the high ceiling that she could see, and how could the water seep through the floor if there was a cellar below? Maybe there was a layer of earth or a cavity between floor and cellar ceiling that rainwater could have soaked into from underneath the property's solid walls.

Eve hurried back from the kitchen clutching a photograph in one hand and a child's colourful toy, an old-fashioned spinning top, in the other. She showed Lili the spinning top first.

'It's a toy Gabe and I found in a locked storeroom next to

the children's dormitory. There was a lot of stuff in there – more toys and school things. All the toys were old but looked new. We think they'd never been used.' Eve eyed the spinning top nervously. 'Once we'd wiped off the dust, it came up like this. When I was alone last Monday, I spun it and saw the ghosts of the children.'

'You mean you saw their images in the top?' Lili pointed to the graphics printed on the spinning top's metal shell.

'No. I saw real children here, in the hall. Except they weren't real, they were ghosts. They were dancing in a circle. But Mr Pyke suggested that watching the top spinning – listening to the humming noise it made as it spun fast, seeing the colours turn to white – might have caused me to hallucinate.'

'Who's Mr Pyke?' Lili asked, curious.

'He came yesterday. He calls himself a ghost-hunter, a psychic investigator, and he convinced Gabe he could prove the house wasn't haunted. He's here now, upstairs in the old dormitory arranging his equipment. Loren is with him.'

Eve realized that Pyke and her daughter had been gone a long time. Mr Pyke may have been charming, but what did they know about him? She began to grow anxious.

The psychic took the toy from Eve and inspected it.

'Maybe the children did play with it before it was taken away and put in the storeroom.' Lili lightly ran her fingers over the top's brightly coloured surface. 'I can feel a connection with them.'

'And here's a photograph Gabe found. It was hidden behind a false wall in a cupboard upstairs.' Eve proffered the old black-and-white picture.

Lili placed the spinning top on the floor at her feet and accepted the photograph. She felt her heart leap when she held it in her hands, for at last she could see the children who had come to Crickley Hall as evacuees, she could know what they looked like.

She examined each face in turn, beginning with the back row, frowning once, then moving on. She came to a pretty young woman whom Lili assumed was one of the teachers; there was something infinitely sad in her countenance.

In the middle of the front row of smaller children and seated on chairs were a man and woman of similar features to each other. They both looked hard, mean, and they seemed to regard the camera with hostile suspicion. A disturbing flutter ran through Lili and she quickly looked away.

But her eyes returned to the one child – although he looked more than a child and was certainly older than the others – that she had frowned at before. The boy was grinning, the only person in the photograph to do so, but his eyes did not match the grin. They were sly, mad eyes. Lili sensed it.

She swayed unsteadily and Eve thought the psychic was about to faint again. But Lili caught herself.

Pointing at the grinning boy in the photograph, she said: 'D'you know anything about him?'

'As a matter of fact, I do,' Eve replied. 'The gardener here has worked for different owners of Crickley Hall for ever, it seems. Percy was even here when the evacuees came down from London to stay. He told us about that particular boy and it was nothing good. The other children didn't like him, but apparently he was a favourite of the Cribbens. I think his name was Maurice. Maurice something-or-other. Stannard? No, it was Stafford. Maurice Stafford.'

'I sense bad things about him.' Lili frowned again and this time it was more deeply, more concentrated. 'There's something wrong with him. I think he was very wicked.'

'He was just a boy,' Eve said. 'He was too young to be wicked.'

'This one was born that way. It wasn't something he learned. There's some kind of connection between him and the two adults at the front. You called them the Cribbens – husband and wife?'

'Brother and sister.'

'Yes, the likeness is obvious. This boy, Maurice Stafford, he learned evil from those two. I can feel it so strongly. Oh God – ' the photograph shook in the psychic's hands – 'it's becoming clearer. He did the children great harm.'

She closed her eyes.

'They're trying to tell me, the children are trying to speak to me. They're here. Eve, the children are still in this house. They've never left it.'

Her eyes opened.

'Can't you sense them?' she asked Eve.

And Eve could sense something. No, she could hear something. A susurration of whispers. Growing in volume, filling the corners of the hall. She gasped when the colourful top on the floor began to turn slowly.

The sounds were of young voices, all whispering words she could not understand because one overlaid the other, all mixed together so that they were incoherent. But she knew they were frightened voices. The clamour rose, but still only in whispers, and the top spun faster. Eve looked at Lili, confused and mystified.

'They're trying so hard,' said Lili as she gazed in wonder around the vast room. 'But there's something preventing them.' She gave a shiver. 'There's another entity here, but it won't come forward. Not yet.'

The psychic stared down at the spinning top whose colours were beginning to blend, to become murky, and then to become a white blur. A humming sound came from it that was neither musical nor harsh, but which ascended to a steady *thrum*. And the whisperings now sounded like the soft flurry of distant birds on the wing.

But then a voice, a real voice, a man's voice, interrupted everything, even though it was just a murmuring coming from the landing above.

The spinning top began to wobble as it slowed down and its humming grew deeper in tone. Colours appeared on its tin surface once again and the dancing figures started to become clearer. Suddenly, the toy lurched, faltered, then fell onto its side to roll away in an arc, coming to a stop behind Eve. The whisperings ceased.

Lili inclined her head, searching for the source of the new voices. Loren came into view from a doorway along the landing, followed by a tall man, and it was his voice they could hear. The girl kept looking round at the man, as if taking in every word he said.

The couple paused and through the balcony's railings, Lili saw Loren pull open a cupboard door. The man's voice was strong and clear enough to be understood from below.

'We'll come back to it after I've had a word with your mother about the attic. I shouldn't like anything to be disturbed up there now I've set up.'

'That's Gordon Pyke,' Eve told Lili. 'He's the investigator.' Then, as if she had only just noticed: 'Lili, what happened to those sounds? The whisperings.'

The psychic continued to look up at the two people on the landing, who were now making their way to the stairs.

'Lili?'

The psychic dropped her eyes to find Eve staring at her. 'They've gone. Something disturbed them. I think they were frightened away.'

'It was the children, wasn't it? The orphans who drowned in this place all those years ago.'

'Yes. Yes, I believe – I'm *sure* – it was.'

Pyke and Loren were descending the stairs and Lili saw that the man, who had a small goatee beard, was very tall. Something – an intuition – seemed to click in her mind as she watched him, but the thought hadn't yet made itself apparent. Pyke had left something at the top of the stairs; it was a large suitcase.

Leaving the stairs, the so-called 'ghost-hunter' walked round the puddles with Loren. 'You appear to have been flooded,' he remarked needlessly as he looked around the hall. He craned his neck to peer up at the ceiling. 'Don't worry, I'll find its root cause and then we'll be able to stop it happening again.'

Something about the man was bothering Lili as he and Loren came towards them. As Pyke approached, she gazed intently into his eyes.

The sensing hit her like a physical blow, almost taking her breath away.

*Oh my God!* she thought. Then, urgently and aloud: 'It's him, Eve! He was the boy in the photograph. The one you called Maurice Stafford.'

## 68: OBSTRUCTION

Gabe brought the Range Rover to a sliding halt, the bonnet nodding at the leafy fallen tree one foot away.

Hell! This can't be happening!

Travelling too fast, he had almost smashed into the obstacle that sprawled across the country lane, seeing it only just in time to slam on the brakes. He thanked the Lord for quick reactions and EBA – Emergency Brake Assist. Electronic traction control had helped also, preventing the vehicle from going into a skid.

The Range Rover's full-beam headlights lit up the blockage and Gabe quickly surveyed it. Lightning stammered and illuminated the scene even more and from where he was sitting he could see that the toppled tree filled the full width of the lane, its branches having crushed the tall hedges on the right, its split trunk creating a solid barrier on his left. Gabe slumped back in his seat in momentary despair and uttered a sound that fully formed would have been a curse. Thunder roared.

Without further hesitation, he pushed open the driver's door and stepped out into the storm. His eyes narrowed against the driving rain as he pulled up the collar of his reefer jacket and tucked one lapel beneath the other to protect his neck. Closing the door with a thud, he moved towards the high barrier of branches, the vehicle's headlights helping him assess the damage ahead. He walked to both sides of the lane and found no way round the obstruction. At least, not in the Range Rover.

He was about to climb the grass verge where the shattered tree stump still smouldered, the fire caused by the lightning strike extinguished by the wind-blown rain, when he was distracted by a single light approaching down the lane behind him. As the light drew closer it shone directly into his eyes, dazzling them so he was forced to raise a hand in front of his face.

The voice fought to be heard over the storm. *'Mr Caleigh? Is that you?'*

Gabe blinked and was able to make out a dark figure behind the torchbeam as it was lowered a little.

He raised his own voice. *'Who's there?'*

The torch was dropped even further so that its beam pointed at the ground. By the reflected glare of the Range Rover's headlights he recognized the approaching figure. The man with the torch wore a storm coat with the hood up over a flat cap.

*'Percy? That you?'*

*'Yers, Mr Caleigh,'* came the shouted response. *'It's Percy Judd. Had an accident, has yer?'*

Gabe could barely comprehend the old gardener's words over the noise of the gale and pounding rain, but he caught the name all right. He waited for Percy Judd to get closer before speaking again.

'What the hell you doing out on a night like this, Percy?'

The gardener leaned close to Gabe's ear.

'Goin' to the same place as you, Mr Caleigh. Makin' my way to Crickley Hall.'

Gabe jerked his head away in surprise. 'Right now? Why?'

Percy seemed reluctant to explain. He could hardly tell

his employer that it was the incessant whining and then howling of a dog had brought him out of his home this stormy night. That and his own very real sense of unease. 'Worried about the weather, sir,' he only half lied, again talking directly into Gabe's ear. 'It's flood weather, Mr Caleigh, jus' like las' time, them who remembers tell me.'

'I thought it couldn't happen again.'

'Nothin' can stop the waters pourin' off the moors, not when it's been rainin' fer weeks an' the storm's this fierce. It's the build-up, y'see. All the precautions can only limit the damage, can't stop the floodin' itself.'

*Great*, Gabe thought to himself. *Something else to worry about.*

'I tried phonin' the house,' Percy went on, 'but the lines must be down. Couldn't get nothin', jus' a dead line.'

As lightning flashed again, Gabe pointed at the fallen elm. He waited for the thunder to roll away before attempting to speak to the old man again. Percy stood there unbowed by the wind and rain, his back straight, rainwater dribbling from the peak of his flat cap which protruded from the hood.

'Road's blocked all the way across,' Gabe told him. 'Can't get round it in the car.'

Percy quickly appraised the situation. 'Then we'll have to walk round it, sir. Not too far to Crickley Hall from here; we'll make it all right.'

'You still wanna' go there? You don't have to, you know – I can take care of things myself.' He was only thinking of the old man's stamina. It was still a long way to Crickley Hall no matter what Percy said.

'No, I wants to go with yer. Set my mind at rest, like.' He seemed resolute.

Gabe clamped Percy's upper arm. 'Okay. I appreciate it. Let's find a way past the goddamn tree.'

He leaned into the Range Rover and switched off the engine and lights, but turned on the hazard lights to warn any approaching vehicles on that side of the lane. Together, bending into the gale, Gabe and Percy headed towards the charred tree stump on the grass verge. Without the car, it was going to be one hell of a journey, thought Gabe.

# 69: ESCAPE

Never had Eve seen a personality change so fast. One moment Pyke was striding towards her and Lili, bringing Loren with him, his limp hardly evident as he avoided the puddles, only friendly curiosity in his eyes (he had been regarding the psychic), the next his face was screwed up into a snarl, nothing but fury now blazing from those same but frighteningly different eyes.

His slight limp was no impediment as he marched towards Lili, raising his thick stick over his head as he came.

Lili took a step backwards and lifted her arms to defend herself from the blow that surely would follow. Loren froze, her complexion paling, her mouth open in consternation.

'Don't—' Eve began to say, but Lili screamed, drowning the next words, the sound shrilling through the great hall.

Pyke – Maurice Stafford? Lili had said he was Maurice Stafford! – barely paused, the walking stick quivering at the end of its backward arc, about to come crashing down. His face was a mask of sheer hatred and wrath, as if the exposure had revealed his true nature.

Lili kept her arms high to protect herself, her terrified scream reaching its peak.

All the lights flickered.
They went out.

Shocked, and with Lili's scream ringing in her ears, Eve reached out for Loren in the darkness. Just before the lights went off she had seen Pyke's walking stick begin its descent, then heard it strike something – she knew it was Lili, for the scream turned into a howl of pain. Footsteps clacked on the stone floor, but Eve could see nothing until the lightning flashed outside and the grand hall was illuminated by a stark silver-white coruscation that came through the tall window over the stairs.

In the sequence of still-lifes caused by the lightning's strobing, Eve saw that Lili was retreating to the front door, was pulling it open, was rushing out, was a black silhouette against the flashing light that spilled through the portal.

Lili had already begun to duck and hold up her arms to protect her head when all the lights flickered then died, only the absorbing thickness of her coat sleeves preventing serious damage to her right forearm when the stout cane struck. Her scream turned into a painful cry.

Horror had gripped her the moment the man once known as Maurice Stafford had come striding purposefully towards her, the walking stick held aloft as a weapon, his face rendered ugly by its expression. She managed to recover enough to turn and run.

Lightning lit up the hall as her panic drove her to the front door, her boots clacking on the flagstones, her right arm numbed by the blow and hanging down by her side, her left hand stretched before her. When her hand touched wood, her fingers scrabbled for the doorknob; she found it, twisted it, pulled the nail-studded door open and escaped into the storm-filled night.

Almost blinded by the fierce stuttering light, she ran across the rain-sodden lawn, mortal dread of what she had left inside the house (and it was not only the limping man that caused this dread, for she had sensed other terrors lurking within those solid walls) driving her on. The wind seemed to contest her progress and she had to lean into it, her left hand raised palm outwards to keep the rain out of her eyes. Thunder boomed as the soft wet earth sucked at her boots with each stumbling stride and she cringed under its power.

She failed to see the heavy, black seat of the swing as it hurtled towards her from the darkness. It struck her right temple, stunning her so badly that she fell.

Lili lay there in the close-cropped grass with rain hammering at her outstretched body, the fingers of one hand curling into the muddy soil. She tried to lift her head, but it took too much effort.

Lili passed out.

# 70: EPICENTRE

Eve reached into the darkness for Loren, but could barely see her own hand in front of her.

'*Loren!*' she hissed, but there was no response.

The lights of the black iron chandelier high overhead suddenly came on, dimly at first, then seeming to catch, growing brighter. They dimmed again, as did all the other lights around Crickley Hall that were switched on. Brighter once more, then waning to a lacklustre but steady glow that threw shadows and created gloomy recesses around the hall and landing.

Eve realized what had happened. Somewhere in the Hollow Bay area power lines had been struck by lightning or blown down by the gale – either way, electricity to homes in the locale, and probably the whole of the harbour village too, was out. Crickley Hall's generator, the generator that Gabe had fixed and serviced only last Sunday, had kicked in and was now the power source for the house. The light was weak, barely adequate in fact, but it was better than total blackout.

She saw the tall man – Pyke, Stafford, whatever his real name was! – standing by the front door which he had just slammed shut.

He looked at Loren, who was standing frightened and disorientated a few feet away from her mother, then at Eve.

'Your friend won't get far,' Pyke said in an unexcited, almost friendly, way. 'Not on a night like this. And even if she does manage to find help – which I doubt very much; those people who've chosen to stay in the area will be locked inside their homes with barricades round their doors and windows – well, by then it will be too late.'

*Too late for what?* Eve asked herself. She had stepped towards Loren and held out her hand again for her daughter to take. Loren's hand was cold and shaking in her own.

'Do you feel it, Eve?' Pyke asked, his glittering eyes seeking out every corner of the vast room and even searching the high beamed ceiling. 'The hall is the epicentre of the psychic activity. The spirits are gathering here, their vigour is almost palpable.'

Pyke was blocking the front door. His coat and hat, which he had discarded earlier, were hanging on the rack by the door, but it was obvious he was not going to put them on and leave. Eve began to back away and Loren kept in step with her, regardless of the puddles they trod through. If they made a break for the kitchen to escape by its outer door, Pyke would cut them off in a few strides. He held his walking stick like a weapon.

Eve had never been so afraid. Oh, she had suffered more than just fear since Cam had gone missing, but this was different. She knew that this was a dangerous situation and her fear was for herself and Loren – and Cally upstairs, of course – for the man at the door exuded menace. She had thought him so kindly, so mannerly, and now his eyes seemed to gleam with malice.

Loren was squeezing her hand so tightly that it hurt. Eve fought to keep the nervousness from her voice.

'What do you want from us, Mr Pyke?' She had put the

question mildly, her tone even, as if she might be enquiring of a grocer the price of tomatoes. Somehow she had to humour this man, get him to respond in a non-hostile way.

'Dear woman, it's what the house wants from me that's the problem.'

He moved away from the door, taking two steps towards them. Eve and Loren backed off even more, matching him step for step, their direction taking them towards the stairway.

'I don't understand, Mr Pyke.' Humour him, *humour* him, Eve told herself. Why had he hurt Lili Peel? Just because she'd recognized who he was? But now they, she and Loren, knew his true identity, so what would he do to them? And why did their knowing he was Maurice Stafford matter? What had Stafford done and, my God, why wasn't he dead, drowned like the other evacuees?

Her heel kicked the first step and she and Loren came to a halt.

She prompted Pyke, who had not stopped advancing. 'How can a house want something from you?'

'By now, you're fully aware that Crickley Hall is possessed, Eve.'

Oh so friendly; his voice was so matter-of-fact and soothing. It was his eyes, those once so engaging eyes, that were deranged.

'You told us there were no such things as ghosts,' Eve said as she took the step with Loren, both of them moving backwards, their eyes never leaving Pyke's.

'No, I said in many cases there are perfectly natural explanations for what might be considered supernatural episodes or so-called manifestations. But – and I freely admit, they are in the minority – there sometimes are genuine hauntings that cannot be rationalized.'

'The children – their *spirits* – they really are here?' Moving as steadily as possible, Eve took the second step. Loren rose with her.

'*Of course they are!*'

Eve flinched at Pyke's anger.

'Can't you feel their presence, woman? Can't you see they're all around us? My God, they're almost visible.'

And as Pyke said the words, Eve thought she saw something flit among the shadows of the room. Small, insubstantial shapes. Lighter shades of darkness.

'But they aren't alone.' Pyke sounded perfectly reasonable once more as he limped towards Eve and Loren, now leaning heavily on his cane. 'Their guardian is with them. Augustus Cribben. You might say he was Maurice Stafford's lord and master.'

Mother and daughter had discreetly risen another step.

'Wasn't Augustus Cribben in charge here during the last world war?' Eve ventured warily. She wanted to keep Pyke distracted for the moment, afraid of the harm she was sure he meant to do them. She could see the insanity dancing in his eyes. 'He was the children's custodian and teacher, wasn't he?'

Her mouth was dry and she fought the urge to turn and run with Loren, to get to the bedroom where Cally slept and lock the door. Was there a key in the lock? Eve couldn't remember.

Pyke limped to a halt, his brown brogues in a puddle. His cane took some of his weight. 'Augustus Cribben was more than that: he was a god to his sister and me; we revered him. But the other evacuees? Well, they were just afraid of him.'

They were on the third step now; a few more and they would be on the little square landing at the turn of the stairs. That was when they'd make a break for it, Eve decided. She kept her voice steady, even though she wanted to scream and flee.

'The children were afraid because he was cruel to them. Wasn't that it?'

'Who told you that?' Anger shared the insanity of his gaze and it made him even more frightening. 'I suppose it was that old busybody, Percy Judd. Oh yes, I know he still keeps his job here as gardener and maintenance man. But he was always an outsider who liked to poke his nose into other people's affairs. He was a rather stupid individual then and I'm sure the passing years have added nothing to his intellectual powers. Hah! He probably still wonders whatever became of his sweetheart Miss High-and-mighty Nancy Linnet. Well, Magda and I attended to her.'

Eve dared to ask. 'You – you got rid of her?'

'No need to be coy, Eve.' The comity was back in his manner. 'She was a busybody too. We had to kill her, had no other choice really. We disposed of her body down the well.'

They could no longer wait until they reached the turn in the stairs: Eve jerked her daughter's hand and they both spun round as one and climbed as fast as they could.

But Gordon Pyke was surprisingly swift for a man of his size and age – the thought occurred to Eve as she ran that he must be in his seventies! – and he sprang forward and adroitly caught Eve's ankle with the hook of his walking stick. He yanked hard and she fell heavily against the next set of stairs, bringing Loren down with her. Eve grabbed at a rail as they slithered back down.

'*Mummy!*' Loren screeched, and Eve quickly put an arm round her as they sprawled there.

'It's all right, baby, it's all right.' Eve looked at Pyke, who had calmly sat down on the small landing, his right foot resting at an angle on the first step down, his left on the one below that. He laid his walking stick down behind him, its hooked end pointing at Eve. Lightning from outside lit up one side of his face as he looked their way and Eve thought his grin was the most evil grimace she had ever seen.

He waited as thunder split the air and rolled away into the distance. When it was quiet again he spoke. 'Please don't worry yourself, Eve. It isn't you I want.'

In the poor, generator-powered light she saw his grin slip to a smile and his eyes had lost that manic gleam she was so afraid of. He seemed his old charming self again. But Eve drew up her left leg so that her foot was out of reach.

Stretched out on the rain-sodden lawn, Lili murmured something that was not quite a word. The fingers of one of her hands had clenched, digging shallow grooves in the soil.

It wasn't exactly a dream she was having, it was more of an extrasensory perception that conveyed itself as *if* it were a dream.

Thoughts, sights, came to her. She began to see what had happened to the evacuees at Crickley Hall in the month of October sixty-three years ago.

'The little Jewish boy was the first of the children to go. You might say he was the cause of all their deaths. And the young teacher; she was partially to blame.'

Gordon Pyke had leant back against the rail so that he faced Eve and Loren on the stairs. His walking stick was close to hand should mother and daughter attempt to escape up the stairs again.

'Augustus and Magda Cribben hated the Jews, blamed them for the whole of World War Two, in fact,' Pyke sniggered. 'They thought Hitler had got it about right – exterminate all Jews, with their global intrigues and secret cabals. I honestly believe the Cribbens hoped the Germans would win the war.'

He gave a wry shake of his head and his thoughts lingered for a few moments.

Then: 'Now what was the boy's name? He was the youngest of the children. Oh yes, Stefan. Stefan Rosenberg. No, Stefan Rosenbaum, that was it. See how well I remember? It's as if it was yesterday. God, how angry Augustus was when he found out the authorities had foisted a Jew on him. And how the boy suffered because of it.'

Eve shivered and pulled Loren closer. Her daughter was trembling and seemed afraid to make a sound.

Pyke continued in his mild-mannered way. 'Our guardian made a discovery about the boy one day. I should mention that Augustus was very ill at the time. He'd always suffered severe headaches, according to his sister, Magda, but a head injury during the Blitz had caused more and, apparently, irrevocable damage to his brain. At least, that was Magda's opinion.

'Augustus was going through one of his bad spells when the headaches were almost paralysing, and Stefan Rosenbaum had done something wrong – I forget precisely what it was; I think he'd wet his bed, something like that – and Augustus was about to punish him. In a rage, Augustus made the boy drop his trousers – this time the misdemeanour was serious enough to warrant a caning on bare flesh. When Stefan did so, Augustus saw that he hadn't been circumcised. All Jewish males had to be circumcised, Augustus screamed. Magda pleaded with her brother, but this was the beginning of the madness . . .'

Lili's murmur became a groan. There were scenes being played out inside her head, like a dream but not a dream: it was a psychic vision. The event was in the past and it was shocking.

*A little boy. A little boy with dark hair and large frightened eyes. He is in the grip of a man who seems familiar to Lili. The man is wicked. And insane.*

*He's shaking the little boy, screaming at him, and the boy is wailing in terror, which only makes the man more angry and the shaking more violent. There are other children around, but they are frightened too and so they run away to hide, to hide from the man whom Lili now recognizes from the old black-and-white photograph, the children's guardian, the man Eve had called Augustus Cribben. He is picking up the howling boy whose trousers are bunched around his ankles. The man is taking the boy into a room where there are tables and benches set out like a schoolroom. He lays the boy on the main desk, the teacher's desk, and tells the woman – the woman must be Magda Cribben, Lili realizes – to hold the boy there and wait.*

*Augustus Cribben soon returns and Lili cries out in her semi-conscious trance, for in his hand he holds a gleaming cutthroat razor, no doubt the very one he uses himself for shaving.*

*Magda Cribben brings up a hand to her throat and she pleads with her brother not to do this, that the authorities will find out if anything happens to the boy. But her brother is undeterred: he reaches for the boy's tiny penis.*

*To one side stands a tall boy, one of the orphans yet not one of them. There is an excited glint in his eyes.*

*Cribben calls for him to help pin the dark-haired boy down and Maurice Stafford eagerly comes forward. He leans his strong upper body on the younger boy's legs so that they are trapped, and his hand presses down on the little boy's chest, holding him flat on his back against the table.*

*Augustus slashes with the razor.*

*But the cut is too hasty, too imprecise, too deep, and the blood spurts from the little boy's penis . . .*


'Stefan bled and bled,' Pyke went on and Eve felt nauseous. How could a man do that to a child? 'But Augustus didn't care. He tossed the severed flesh into the wastepaper bin and left the room as though anything else that happened was nothing to do with him.'

Pyke stretched his left leg and forcefully rubbed his thigh as if to encourage circulation.

'Magda did her best to save the boy, but the bleeding just wouldn't stop. In his pain, Augustus had cut away too much of the penis itself, not just the foreskin.'

He sighed as though there were some regret over what had occurred, but Eve was soon to realize it wasn't because of the harm done to poor young Stefan.

'All that followed was because of the Jewish boy.' Pyke scowled with resentment, as if events might have turned out otherwise but for the bodged 'operation'. 'Magda ordered me to bring towels, and then more towels, but nothing could staunch that bleeding. The boy was draining of colour before our eyes because of blood loss. Naturally, taking him to a hospital or calling a doctor wasn't an option; how could we have explained the injury? No doubt Augustus would have been imprisoned for what he had done and Magda too, probably, for being an accomplice. I didn't care for my own chances either: they had special places for naughty boys in those days. All the other children would have ganged up on me, they would have told the police what a bad person I'd been. They never liked me.'

Eve could hardly believe what she was hearing. Pyke was now wallowing in self-pity. But while he was preoccupied she took a sly glance up the stairway behind her. If she and Loren could only reach Cally's bedroom there might be a chance to barricade themselves in . . .

Light in the vast room dipped and she wondered if the generator in the basement could take the strain of running all the electrics in Crickley Hall. Perhaps Gabe hadn't done such a good job on it after all, and if the lights went out once more, it might give them another opportunity to get away from Pyke. But then the lights came up again, although their glow was weaker than before.

In the darker regions of the hall there seemed to be a slight movement, lighter shadows shifting inside the darker shadows again. The air was heavy, oppressive, the kind of heaviness that usually came *before* an electrical storm. The fine hairs on Eve's arms bristled and there was an uncomfortable creeping sensation along her spine, the arctic breath of ungovernable fear. Oddly, although the source of light came from high above – the iron chandelier and the landing light – it was much *darker* round the ceiling, as if a blackness were hanging there, a kind of murky fog that was pressing down on the room below.

Pyke appeared not to have noticed, or if he did, he was ignoring it. Rain rattled the tall window.

He began to speak again, revisiting a past that was obviously important to him. 'Magda knew we couldn't save the boy, although by God, she did try. Stefan was fading away fast and she realized what we had to do. We had used the well to get rid of the teacher's body before; we could use it again.'

Despite her terror, Eve was aghast. Magda Cribben and Pyke – or Maurice Stafford as he was then – had murdered Nancy Linnet and thrown her corpse into the well, knowing that it would probably be swept out to sea by the subterranean river. Then they had decided to do the same with Stefan.

'Magda said that we would tell the authorities that Stefan Rosenbaum had wandered down the cellar alone – which was strictly out of bounds for the children, of course – and had accidentally fallen into the well. The wall round the well is very low so it could easily happen. In all likelihood, his body would never be recovered and none of the other children had witnessed what Augustus had done to the boy, although they must have heard the screams. Magda was sure they'd be too scared to speak out.'

My God, thought Eve, was Pyke insane even then, as a boy? All three of them – the brother and sister and Maurice Stafford – must have been crazy to imagine they would get away with such a crime.

Pyke flexed his knee to loosen the joint. 'So that's what we did. We dropped Stefan's body down the well. To be perfectly frank with you, I wasn't sure he'd bled to death by then. I don't think Magda was sure either.'

The revelation seemed to numb both Eve's body and her mind. She had to stop this madman getting his hands on her daughters.

Pyke gave a laboured shake of his head as if chiding himself for something. 'We had underestimated the interest that had been aroused in the disappearance of the teacher, though. She had been gone several weeks and could not be traced, despite the efforts of the education authorities to find her. We had assumed she wouldn't be missed, not with the kind of disruption a war brought to the country.'

He studied Eve, then Loren, with half-hooded eyes. 'The very day after we rid ourselves of Stefan Rosenbaum, we received notice that government inspectors were to visit Crickley Hall. Oh, it might well have been a routine call, something the inspectors were apt to do from time to time, but Magda thought not. She thought suspicions had been kindled by Nancy Linnet's abrupt departure.'

His gaze was momentarily on Loren, although his mind seemed elsewhere.

'Magda was in a state of panic,' Pyke continued, 'while Augustus was merely outraged that the authorities should even presume to inspect his province. The stress only made his pain worse and the usual method of relieving some of it had no effect whatsoever. In fact, it hadn't worked for some days, which was why Augustus finally lost all reason.'

The lightning and thunder came again and it was as though those elements were chained to the house itself; the storm just did not seem to be moving on.

Pyke changed position on the landing, sitting on its lip, thick wrists resting on his knees, head turned to take in Eve and Loren. His back was to the cane, which lay across the landing.

'Are you growing tired of my reminiscences, Eve? It gets more interesting, I assure you.'

Tentatively, she said: 'My husband will be home soon.' It was a feeble warning.

Pyke responded almost cheerfully. 'No, you told me he'd gone off to London. Even if he were on his way back, he'd have stopped somewhere to avoid the worst of the storm. Nobody sane travels in this sort of weather.'

'What would you know of sanity?' She spat the words in spite of herself.

'Ah, aggression. That's quite understandable. You don't know why I'm here yet?'

'You were supposed to be proving there are no ghosts in this house.'

'I lied. Unfortunately – especially for me – there are such things as ghosts. To my regret, I've been haunted for most of my life. I'll explain it all to you, I promise.'

There was that affable and concerned person again. Pyke was like an emotional chameleon, changing so fast it was difficult to keep up with him.

Eve fought to control herself when she said: 'I want to know the real reason you came here tonight and why you attacked Lili Peel.'

'Lili Peel. So that's her name, is it? Well, I'm afraid your friend was interfering where she shouldn't. How did she know my original name?'

'She's psychic.'

'She must be very good to pick up on it like that.'

'I showed her an old photograph of the Cribbens and the children – the evacuees – who were here in 1943. You were among them.' Eve was still waiting for the right moment to dash up the stairs with Loren.

'I see. But does that mean you knew my name then?'

'Our gardener pointed you out the other day when Gabe found the picture.'

'I remember the time it was taken; all the other children were so glum.'

'They had good reason to be.'

'Yes. Where is the photograph now?'

Eve indicated the hall. 'Down there, near the spinning top.'

'Dear Lord, I even remember that toy. It was one of the few items we were allowed to play with and that was only when the local vicar called in for afternoon tea. The Reverend Rossbridger, if I remember correctly. He thought well of Augustus Cribben – another disciplinarian, you see. He and Augustus were two of a kind in some ways. And of course, both strong believers in the Almighty.'

Eve thought that Pyke might go back down to the hall to retrieve the photograph, but either he was too canny or he'd already lost interest in it. He seemed to be growing restless, one foot tapping on a lower step. Loren's breaths were coming in quick shallow gasps.

'How did the children come to drown in Crickley Hall?' Eve was still playing for time, a distraction, something that would give them a chance to make a break for it. Unaware that the phone lines were down, Eve prayed for the phone across the hall to ring, *anything* that would draw his attention for a second or two. He had a bad leg, he'd have difficulty chasing them (although he had moved remarkably quickly when he had attacked Lili). She was taken aback by his answer to her question.

'None of the children drowned,' he said. 'They were all dead before the floodwaters broke.'

Eve stared. Her fear of him reached new heights. 'But everybody said that's how they died,' she managed to say.

'Oh, everybody *said* it, but that doesn't necessarily make it so. I'm sure there were those in the community who had their suspicions. And those who found the bodies – the police and a few members of the rescue services – must have realized the truth. Possibly Reverend Rossbridger was informed that the children had been murdered and the blame had to lie with Augustus Cribben, who also died that night.

'I only discovered he died of a broken neck and multiple piercings to his body when I searched back through old newspaper stories of that time. I've visited his grave in the church cemetery down the hill and, disappointingly, his marker is quite humble. It's also situated in a very neglected part of the graveyard. Yes, I'm certain the authorities were aware that Augustus killed the children in his care with his bare hands. The marks on the children's necks could hardly have gone unnoticed.'

Appalled, and further shocked, Eve could only react by saying, 'But you – he didn't kill you. How . . .?'

'I told you I would explain.' Pyke was finding it a relief finally to share his secrets with someone who was neither dumb nor mad like Magda. 'There was a terrible storm that night of the flood, much like this one tonight, which makes it all the more apposite. No thunder and lightning that night, though, just heavy rainfall. None of the children were sleeping . . .'

Lili groaned and tried to lift her head again, but it was no use: it sank back to the drenched earth.

It was almost cosy lying there. She hardly felt the rain that battered her, even where it drummed on her head and neck; she could not feel the cold at all. No, she was snug, dozing in and out of consciousness, half dreaming, but aware those half-dreams were more like revelations.

Lightning exposed the brown, churning river nearby, its level reaching the top of the banks. Woodland detritus, that which hadn't entangled behind the short wooden bridge – the *unstable* wooden bridge – was swept along by the current and carried down to the harbour estuary where the twin rivers, the Bay River and the underground Low River, met.

Lili felt rather than saw the hugeness of the room she was in, a room whose only lighting was from strategically placed oil lamps so that shadows hung like dark drapes around its walls.

*There is movement, a sound followed by a warning whisper as small figures appear from a doorway on the landing above the hall.*

*Nine children make their quiet way towards the broad staircase at the end of the L-shaped landing, shoes in their hands, stockinged feet almost silent on the wooden boards. They stop and hold their breaths whenever a floorboard creaks and move on only when there is no reaction to the noise. The older children hold the hands of the younger ones. No one must speak, Susan Trainer has told them all, and no one must cough, sneeze or make a noise of any kind, especially when they passed by certain closed doors behind which their guardians would be sleeping.*

*Down the stairs they come, in twos, with the eldest, Susan, leading the way, unable to prevent a cracked stairboard creaking here and there even if the children's soft feet tread as lightly as possible. They are all dressed apart from their outdoor coats, which hang in a row on the rack beside the big front door. They will put them on, along with their shoes, before leaving the house.*

*They steal into the great hall, all of them shivering with trepidation and cold, following their leader, who is as scared as any of them but does her best not to show it. She dreads to think of the consequences if they are caught.*

*Despite the terrible storm outside, tonight she will take the children away from Crickley Hall. They can no longer stay in the house: it's too dangerous. Mr Cribben has done something bad to little Stefan, something horrible, and the children haven't seen their friend since. Susan is afraid Mr Cribben might do bad things to the rest of them, for he seems to have lost his mind; there is no telling what he might do now. They will make their way down to the village and knock on the door of the first house that has a light in its window. They will beg to be taken in and Susan will tell everything – their cruel treatment at Crickley Hall, the punishments, their meagre rations, the missing boy.*

Lili Peel, lying prone on the ground more than six decades later, witnessed this as if she were a ghost herself, hovering close to the terrified orphans, hearing their thoughts, sensing their emotions. But unable to help. Unable to intervene in any way. Her heart reached out to them, for she already knew their bid for freedom would fail.

*They are almost halfway across the hall, heading for the coat rack and the locked and bolted front door, when it happens . . .*

Pyke smiled as he related the story, but there was no humour in his eyes. The expression in them, Eve observed, ranged from lunacy to kindness, then to an emotionless vacuity, which was how they were at present. Dead eyes. *Deadly* eyes.

'You see, I had overheard Susan Trainer's plan to escape the night before,' he said. 'I'd just left Magda's room – she was so worried about her brother, who had taken to his bed all that day because of his illness. The pain in his head was so bad he could barely think, and daylight – any bright light – made his agony even worse, so much so that he could hardly see.'

Pyke changed position, resting his back against the railings once more so that he could face Eve and Loren.

'I sat on the stairway just beneath the hatchway into the dormitory and I listened to the whisperings, heard Susan scheme to escape Crickley Hall. She was aware that Augustus was demented with pain by now and that she and the other children were in danger. She intended to sneak out of the house with them the very next night. Susan knew the front-door key was kept on a hook in the kitchen and she would fetch it while the others were putting on their coats and shoes.'

Pyke gave a short snigger as he remembered his own cleverness.

'Oh, it was a fine escape plan. They would leave the house, closing the door behind them. Every child in turn had to promise to be silent when they left the dormitory; the smaller ones were made to promise twice.

'Once outside they would go down to the village, avoiding the vicarage because they were aware of Reverend Rossbridger's friendship with the Cribbens. They didn't trust him and Susan was sure they'd get no sympathy from him. In Hollow Bay they would find someone to take them in and as soon as their story was known, the police would be called and the Cribbens taken off to prison.'

The snigger was followed by a throaty chuckle, but the mood quickly passed.

'The children had forgotten I liked to spy on them. Yes, I gained valuable bits of information when I listened to them out of sight on the stairs, titbits that earned me rewards from the Cribbens. That particular night I crept back down to Magda's room and told her what I'd overheard. Augustus was too ill to be informed right then, but she revealed the children's plan to him the very next day. Unfortunately, she failed to realize just how ill he was. His mind had snapped, although it wasn't evident at that time.

'Augustus kept to his room that fateful day. But when night-time came . . .'

Lili, a silent witness, watched the orphans lift their coats from the rack, the bigger children reaching for those belonging to the younger ones and handing them down. She allowed her mind to follow Susan . . .

. . . *who is tiptoeing towards the kitchen. The kitchen door is closed and the girl gently turns its handle, pausing for a moment as the door creaks. A bunch of keys is hanging from a hook just inside and the long front-door key is among them.*

*Afraid to open the door any wider, Susan reaches in and her trembling hand runs up the wall searching for the large keyring. The keys jingle as her fingers brush against them and she quickly stops the sound by pressing them against the wall. She feels the long one with the palm of her hand and, although frightened, she allows herself a small smile. Slowly she lifts it.*

*And that is when cold, hard fingers reach round her wrist to paralyse her for a moment.*

*Susan cannot help but shriek. She pulls her arm back and so powerful is her fright that it is wrenched free from the grip round her wrist. The kitchen door is pulled wide open and there in the darkness stands the naked figure of Augustus Cribben. He is without clothes because he has been flagellating his own body for most of the evening. The fresh marks on his pale flesh are still livid.*

*All the children scream in terror. Dropping their shoes and their feet slapping against the stone floor, they disperse in all directions. Three of them scurry into the classroom and conceal themselves beneath the tables. One more shuts himself in the cupboard beneath the stairs, while another chooses a storage closet set in a wall to conceal herself in. Three others, one of whom is barely six years old, flee up the stairs and hide in the landing cupboard where brooms, brushes and an iron bucket are kept. They pull the door closed after them and crouch on the floor as far back as they can go, pressing into the black-painted wall behind them. They clutch each other tightly and shiver in the darkness. They wait.*

Lili felt their horror and she stirred on the wet bed of grass and mud. She moaned in protest, but the vision continued. Like the children, she cannot escape.

*The naked man holds a long thin stick whose end is split into wicked slivers that spread the pain when struck against flesh. This is his own personal cane, the one he keeps in his room for himself alone, the other cane, defiled by the sinners he had used it on, temporarily hidden by his sister because the school inspectors are soon to visit. His gnarled left hand grabs the girl's wrist again, for shock has frozen her to the spot, unable to run away. She now squirms and tries to pull away from him, kicking out at her captor, her stockinged feet having little effect. The keys fall from her grasp and skid across the floor.*

*Cribben handles Susan roughly and she is crying with terror and desperation. He lays into her with the cane, her thin cotton dress offering no protection at all, and she screams.*

*Two figures appear looking over the balcony down into the great hall. Magda Cribben and Maurice Stafford have left the bedroom where they have patiently waited for much of the night, ready to leap into action and help Augustus deal with the would-be absconders. Their eyes widen in alarm as they see the naked guardian drop the cane and grab Susan Trainer by the throat.*

*Her cries cease immediately as her throat is squeezed and her windpipe crushed. Her feet pummel the floor for a few seconds and her once-pretty eyes bulge as if pushed from behind. Her tongue protrudes from her yawning mouth, her face begins to turn a purplish red, her young body stiffens as she is lifted by her neck. Urine spatters the flagstones beneath her, while her hands feebly pull at the naked man's wrists. Finally, her hands fall away and she goes limp. Susan is dead.*

*'Augustus! No!' The anguished wail is from Magda, who leans over the balcony to beseech her brother. Maurice is too dismayed to move.*

*Cribben bends to pick up his punishment cane and he strikes it hard against his own body as he advances across the hall towards the cupboard beneath the stairs. There are long welts and red stripes all over his body, and old scars where self-inflicted wounds had run deep.*

*Cribben reaches the cupboard and yanks the door open. There is a screech from inside and he leans in to drag out six-year-old Wilfred Wilton, who tries to resist but is no match for his guardian's manic strength. Once again, the cane is dropped to the floor and Cribben's powerful hands reach round the boy's throat. Wilfred is murdered in silence.*

*Hand to her breast, Magda wails,* 'Oh dear Lord, what can we do, what can we do?'

*Her brother picks up the stick and strides towards the closet located in the hall's oak panelling. As he walks he continues to beat his own body.*

Swish-thwack! *is the sound it makes.* Swish-thwack! *almost a single emanation.*

*The wind outside blows rain against the tall window in a sudden fierce burst, but nothing distracts the man with the cane. He stops in front of the cupboard, opens its door, stretches inside to pull out seven-year-old Marigold Welch by the hair. Her screams are cut off as he strangles her, Cribben's rage making it no effort at all. He lets her lifeless body fall to the floor and slowly looks towards the classroom.*

'No, Augustus!' *Magda implores him and she runs towards the top of the stairs.* 'You mustn't do this! They'll lock you away! Or they'll hang you. Augustus, they will hang you!'

*But of course, it is already too late.*

*Maurice follows her, his long gangly legs making it easy for him to catch up, even though she is running. They descend the stairs together, dread in their hearts . . .*

'But by the time we got down there,' Pyke told Eve as coolly as if he were commenting on a slow game of cricket, 'Augustus was at the classroom doorway.'

Loren was now perfectly still in her mother's arms and Eve worried that she might be in shock. As for Eve herself, she was completely unnerved as Pyke recounted his horrific tale. She could have wept for the poor innocents who had been forced from their hiding places to be brutally killed, but she knew she mustn't break down, she had to be ready when the chance to flee came.

'Magda stood in front of her brother, blocking his way, begging him to stop. When I tried to help her, pulling on his arm, trying to divert him from the classroom, he turned and looked at me as if he were seeing me for the first time. Then he started lashing out at me with his stick. I fell to the floor and curled up there so he couldn't hurt me too much. I'll admit, I became hysterical, in fear for my own life, and it was only when Magda fell across me that he held back. It was as if he suddenly remembered the other children, because he stared through the classroom doorway. Perhaps one of them screamed or scraped a chair, distracting him from me.

'He left us lying there, both of us weeping with pain and despair. But before he went in, I saw his face, and I've never forgotten it. It was full of hatred and anger – no, wrath would be the better word. He was possessed by it. Nothing would stop him murdering every one of those children. I knew it, Magda knew it. But what we feared most was that he would turn on us once all the others had been dealt with. It was in his eyes, a madness, when he stared at us both.'

Pyke fingered the end of his walking stick, but did not pick it up.

'Magda knew there was no going back now. We might have been able to account for the teacher's absence and we could cover up Stefan's death by saying he'd broken the strict rules and gone down to the cellar on his own the only time the cellar door had been left unlocked, but how could we explain the deaths of all the other orphans? No, we were in an impossible situation.

'Magda's face became grim, more stony than I'd ever known it to be. We had to leave the house, she told me. Leave the charnel house before we ourselves became victims. We had to get far away from Crickley Hall. I think by that time she had cracked like her brother. Oh, you wouldn't know it to look at her, but there was a distance in her manner, as if mentally she had already left Crickley Hall.

'We didn't even stop to put on coats; we fled the house as we were. The keys were lying on the floor just outside the kitchen and Magda picked them up and unlocked the front door. We didn't care about the storm, we just wanted to get away from the carnage. I had no idea where we were going, or what we were to do: I went with her and once outside she never spoke another word. Of course, I didn't realize it at the time, but she was in shock, terrified of her own brother, knowing that they would *both* be in terrible trouble. Something inside her closed down that night and apparently she has remained in that state 'til this day. We stumbled through the storm for most of the night, fortunately missing the flood that created even more havoc.'

He shook his head at the thought.

'And while we fled, Augustus Cribben's rampage continued...'

The grooves that Lili's tense fingers had dug in the soft earth had grown deeper so that only the second knuckles of her hand were visible. She remained physically snug in her semi-conscious condition, as if cocooned from the rain, but her mind was in panic as Cribben went on with the killings . . .

*Three of the orphans are concealed beneath the tables that are used as desks in the makeshift classroom. Gloomy light from the hall spills through the open doorway and they silently pray they will not be discovered in the shadows under the tables. They listen to the familiar sound – swish-thwack! it goes, swish-thwack! – and it is growing louder as the guardian draws close.*

*Cribben pauses on the threshold and he knows where the children are hiding.*

Swish-thwack!

*The swift sharp pain on his bare thigh is exquisite, but it fails to subdue the burning agony inside his head. He feels his brain must explode into molten fragments.*

*Oh Lord, he silently beseeches, relieve me of this cruel burden! Take away this penance and I will serve you all my days!*

*He sways, almost staggers, and his eyes are shut tight against the suffering. One hand presses his brow in the vain hope of absorbing the worst of it. Augustus Cribben forces his eyes open again and even the feeble light from the oil lamps hurts them. Almost overwhelmed but driven by pain, he squints into the shadows and finds the small crouching figures hiding under the tables.*

*It's these worthless children who should and would be punished. They had tried to sneak away from Crickley Hall, no doubt to spin their lies and accusations of maltreatment to anyone who would listen. How he despises these wretched ingrates and sinners. He will not allow them to spread their falsehoods. No, tonight they must pay for their treachery. Tonight their iniquitous souls will be offered up to the Lord before they can be corrupted irredeemably. Only then could a benevolent God grant them His forgiveness.*

*Like a lightning bolt from a troubled sky, a fresh excruciating pain sears his brain and he howls his confusion and distress. The children! They were why he was being punished! He must find them all and give them up to the Lord before their corruption was complete.*

Swish-thwack!

*He moves into the classroom and the orphans cower, try to make themselves even smaller. But the tables are swept aside and they are exposed. Cribben grabs the nearest child, seven-year-old Mavis Borrington, and it is easier to twist and snap her neck than choke her. While he throttles nine-year-old Eugene Smith, the third child scuttles into a corner and buries his face in his hands, his body curled up into a tight ball. Seven-year-old Arnold Brown becomes perfectly still as if by not moving he will not be noticed. But he is mistaken.*

*First, Cribben flogs the screaming boy's back with the cane, and when his victim tries to crawl away, Cribben stands over him. The guardian leans over Arnold and cups his strong hands beneath the evacuee's chin. Cribben jerks the boy's head backwards and relishes the sound of small bones breaking.*

*There are still three more to account for. He looks about him, but there is no one else – no one living – in the room. He is breathing heavily with the exertion, but there is a gleam in his black eyes that indicates a spiteful lunacy.*

*He leaves the room and continues the search.*

Swish-thwack!

*He makes his way upstairs . . .*

## 72: FEAR

Pyke was now standing on the small square landing beneath the tall window, the torchère behind him; sitting had proved too uncomfortable, his knee was aching. He contemplated Eve and Loren, who still lay sprawled on the stairs, the frightened girl comforted in her mother's arms.

'I returned to London on my own, you know.' He appeared to be boasting, as though he had achieved something heroic and grand. 'A mere lad of twelve years. And I survived, even though there was a war on; or perhaps it was because of the war that I went unnoticed for some time. Eventually I found a home and was adopted by a well-meaning but simple couple who had no—'

Eve had had enough. Scared and disturbed as she was by Pyke's gruesome story, and without knowing how much more she – and Loren – could take, she interrupted him. But she kept her voice falsely mild because she did not want to antagonize him.

'Mr Pyke, I asked you before: what do you want from us?'

'Ah, I can tell I'm boring you. But decent exposition takes time. Besides, it's almost a relief to unburden myself of the knowledge I've carried around with me for decades. The only other person to hear it is completely batty. Magda Cribben neither speaks nor responds to anything put to her; she doesn't even indicate that she understands what's being said. So you see, it's good to share the secret of what happened in Crickley Hall all those years ago with you.'

Fear and uncertainty were beginning to turn into a rising anger and Eve knew she had to control it. After learning that Cam really was dead she had felt almost doped, somehow remote from everything around her. She hadn't become hysterical as might have been expected; she hadn't even wept. She had spent the rest of the day in a listless and detached state, her exhaustion almost overwhelming. That was why she had allowed this man into her home tonight, her will softened by tiredness.

But now she was alert, adrenaline rushing through her system like a whirlwind. She had to stay calm though, for Loren's sake and her own. Eve had to watch her tone so that it revealed no hostility, nothing to arouse this lunatic's ire.

'We can't help you,' she said. 'Whatever it is you want from us, we can't help.' She was emboldened by his reaction – or lack of reaction. 'Please, can't you just collect your equipment and leave? We trusted you.'

'Yes, you did. You did trust me.' He smiled. 'That was your mistake, though.'

'Mistake? I don't understand . . .'

'You invited me into your home. That was a huge mistake. But meeting your daughter, Loren, outside confirmed what was meant to be. I knew her destiny immediately.'

Eve stiffened, any calmness she might have had swiftly vanishing. She tensed her body, ready to pull Loren to her feet.

He seemed to read her thoughts. 'Let me finish, Eve. Let me explain why this has to happen.'

Pyke rested both hands on the back of his walking stick.

'My life after Crickley Hall would have been fine except

for two intrusions. If I told you that both literally drove me mad for a time, I'm sure you'd believe me. You would, wouldn't you?'

Eve was careful. Yes, she could see the madness in his eyes. He was as crazy as his guardian, Augustus Cribben. He was as demented as Magda Cribben. Perhaps Pyke had caught it from the brother and sister like some virulent kind of disease. Or perhaps it had been their mutual insanity that had once united all three of them.

'Sometimes a culmination of events can induce a break-down,' she ventured tentatively, nervously. Instinct, and the incident with Lili, told her he was a very dangerous man.

He seemed to be looking into the distance but in fact his gaze was inwards. When he spoke it was almost to himself.

'I think I could tolerate the dreams, although they wearied me. But the hauntings . . . the hauntings are more than I can bear.'

'You told us yesterday you didn't believe in ghosts,' Eve said, genuinely surprised.

'Yes, yes,' Pyke replied impatiently, his attention having returned. 'You said that before and I told you I lied.'

Eve was ready to kick out with her feet if he came close. But Pyke hadn't done with talking.

'I suppose I could live with the dreams even though they came night after night, relentless in their consistency, always the children accusing me of betraying them.'

He banged his walking stick against the floor.

'But I could bear that! I could live with the dreams if only Augustus would stop torturing me, if only he would leave me alone.'

Eve gasped. He was *truly* insane. And yet . . . and yet hadn't *she* felt a presence in this house, something foul, something vile? The ghost of Augustus Cribben? Perhaps she was becoming a little unhinged herself. But a question nagged at her: why should meeting Loren mean so much to him? It confirmed what was meant to be, he had said. *What* was meant to be? *What* was Loren's destiny? Already scared, a terrible dread began to rise from deep inside her.

'The hauntings began soon after I returned to London. At least I heard the sound of his cane thrashing against flesh – I knew that sound. Oh yes, I had come to know it well – then his spirit would manifest itself. Even in spirit he would raise that cane against me and I felt its pain as if it were real, even though I'd never physically been struck by it.'

Eve remembered the other night when Loren had screamed in bed, claiming someone had beaten her.

Pyke visibly shuddered. 'Sometimes his image was weak, as if he were slowly losing power. The smell was always there, though, the whiff of strong carbolic soap which he always used to cleanse himself, but mixed with an aroma of what might be described as rotting corpses. At other times the apparitions are strong, as clear to me as you are now, and that's when he seems to sap my energy, leaving me weak and afraid. Sometimes he's completely black and that's when I fear him most.'

Pyke cast his eyes downwards as though studying the end of his walking stick; but his thoughts were elsewhere again, perhaps reliving the hauntings.

'It took me many years to realize the reason for his visits.' Pyke's voice was low. 'Augustus wanted something from me, but still I didn't know what it was.'

Lili wanted to escape the slaughter, was desperate to wake from the brutal scenes of remorseless, pitiless violence. But her mind was held captive to the horror and she was compelled to watch . . .

*. . . There are only three children left alive in the house and they huddle in the sable darkness of the cupboard on the landing. Brenda Prosser, aged ten years, and her younger brother Gerald, aged eight years, and Patience Frost, who is only six years old, clutch each other tightly, the youngest girl in the middle. Patience has wet her knickers.*

*They have heard the screams echo round the great hall, all of them abruptly cut short. A long silence follows as their guardian searches other rooms downstairs for them. Then the dreaded sound comes to the three survivors, faint at first, but growing louder by the moment.*

Swish-thwack!

*It's coming closer. Up the stairs.*

Swish-thwack!

*The children cling together, shivering as one. Gerald's teeth are chattering and his sister claps a hand over his mouth. They mustn't make any noise at all. Gerald and Patience are crying and Brenda's eyes are wide and startled, for she cannot comprehend what is happening to them.*

Swish-thwack!

*Growing louder.*

Swish-thwack!

*Almost one sound.*

Swish-thwack!

*Pausing a few moments as though the wielder of the stick is looking into doors along the landing.*

Lili now sees and hears everything through the eyes and ears of one of the children hidden in the darkness . . .

*. . . Footsteps approach, softly because the predator wears no shoes, coming closer, the children afraid to breathe, every few*

*seconds the cane making the sharp thwacking sound they know so well. The light footsteps stop.*

*He is outside the cupboard door.*

*All three shriek as the door suddenly swings open. They dig their heels into the floorboards as they try to push themselves as far back into the cupboard as possible. Gerald is now wailing and Brenda is shouting, 'Get away! Get away!' They hunch their shoulders and press their foreheads against their bent knees, and they refuse to see the naked man who is leaning through the open door, the long, thin stick with the splayed end in his hand.*

*One by one Cribben draws them out and one by one he murders them. He strangles the boy and snaps the neck of the little girl. Brenda is last, and he grabs her ankle and yanks hard so that she slides out onto the landing. This girl's struggling body is held off the floor by her neck, as was Susan Trainer's only minutes before, and her feet kick out at him uselessly. But he doesn't feel the blows; nothing could detract from the pain inside his head. He squeezes, tighter and tighter, and Brenda's frightened, despairing eyes almost pop out of their sockets with the pressure, and her tongue, its tip trapped by her lower teeth, curls over to bulge from her mouth.*

*Like her young friend Susan, Brenda involuntarily urinates, and its stream spatters Cribben's legs and feet. He takes no notice. His only purpose is to extinguish the lives of these disloyal and ill-behaved miscreants who had been given into his care. Nothing else matters.*

. . . And in her psychic vision, the unconscious Lili Peel was held aloft and was slowly being strangled. Her own legs jerked in the mud and grass on which she lay, and her eyeballs pushed against their lids, her tongue began to emerge from her mouth, as if she herself suffered the young girl's imminent death. She started to panic, needing air, the hands that squeezed her neck so strong and relentless. But as life passed from the last child, so Lili escaped her corpse. Still senseless yet still 'sensing', Lili's vision continued . . .

*Cribben allows the child's lifeless body to fall on the floor. He retrieves the punishment cane that is lying on the landing. He stands still. Something is not quite right, but the torturous pounding inside his head will not allow clear thought. Has he dealt with all the children? He isn't sure, he cannot think.*

*It suddenly comes to him, though. Eleven evacuees had been sent to Crickley Hall, but despite his blinding pain he knows he has despatched only nine. Then he remembers Stefan Rosenbaum – the Jew! – has already been accounted for. That meant one was missing.*

*Where was the eleventh child?*

*Cribben resumes his search . . .*

And Lili lost the psychic nightmare, although not for long.

## 73: INSANITY

Eve drew up her legs, resting the flat of her foot on the small square landing at the turn of the staircase, ready to use the leverage to push herself up. She still didn't know Pyke's intentions, but there was no doubt that they were bad as far as she and Loren were concerned. And every instinct as a mother told her they would be particularly bad for Loren. As he talked, Pyke kept looking at her daughter, showing more interest in her than Eve. If she could keep him talking, they might get a chance to escape. Or Lili might possibly get back with help.

He looked up at the window as stuttering lightning bleached all its glass white again. He waited for the thunder to die away before he spoke.

'So what did Augustus Cribben want from me?' The question was put mildly enough and Eve was aware that it was rhetorical. 'What caused him to reach out from his grave to me? If I were psychic I might have known long ago. If Augustus's spectre were stronger, he might have been able to communicate his needs to me.'

Pyke's smile was bitter.

'It was only comparatively recently that I found the answer,' he said. 'God only knows why I hadn't done it long ago – at least I would have the reason for the hauntings that have affected my state of mind all these years.'

Let him talk, Eve advised herself. Pretend interest and let him ramble. She exerted pressure on Loren's shoulder to warn her she was going to make a move soon, and was reassured when her daughter pressed a hand against Eve's back as if to say she would be ready. Pyke's lengthy narrative had allowed Loren to get over her initial panic, although she was still rigid with fear.

Eve continued to force herself to be polite and rational. 'Why does there have to be an explanation for Augustus Cribben to haunt you? Doesn't that sort of thing just happen?'

'No, dear woman, it does not just "happen",' he chided her. 'There are always reasons for hauntings. Some people may bear a grudge when they pass over and their spirit returns for revenge. Or the deaths might have been so traumatic that the spirit does not even realize he or she is dead. Sometimes there is some unfinished business or other left behind that has to be resolved. The last of these applies to Augustus Cribben.'

Pyke frowned as though the thought disturbed him more than he could say.

'You see, Eve, Augustus had eleven evacuees in his charge here at Crickley Hall.' He emphasized the number again. '*Eleven* children. That last night he'd punished only nine, all slain by his own hands. He knew the Jewish boy, Stefan, had died earlier, his body despatched by myself and Magda, but it still meant only ten children – *his* children – were dead. So where was the final one, the eleventh child?'

He had posed the question as though expecting an answer from Eve. When she didn't respond he seemed disappointed. Pyke continued.

'Of course, I was the eleventh evacuee in his care. Maurice Stafford, my name then, was the missing child. Augustus wasn't aware I'd run away with Magda, with me in fear for my life and Magda in fear for her future. Who knows? He was so uncontrolled he might even have killed his own sister.'

Pyke breathed out a long sigh of resignation. 'Augustus wanted to claim *all* the children. That was his right, they had been given to him.'

Eve discreetly rose on an elbow, very slowly so that Pyke would not notice. An awful suspicion was beginning to dawn on her.

'I only understood this,' he went on, 'when I went through the journals of that period in a public library. October 1943. The Hollow Bay flood made all the front pages, even though there was a war going on. After all, sixty-eight people were drowned or crushed to death in the disaster and the village was almost destroyed. Even more poignantly, so the newspapers pointed out, eleven of those who died that night were orphans who had been evacuated from London for their own safety. Eleven children who were in the care of Augustus Cribben.'

Pyke nodded to himself. 'There was the answer for me, laid out in stark black and white print on the front page of the national dailies. Such tragic irony. Children sent to the safety of the country because London in wartime was too dangerous.

'Two of the evacuees' bodies were never recovered and it was assumed they had been swept out to sea by the river that runs beneath the house. After all, the rest of the orphans' bodies had been discovered in the cellar where there was a well to the underground river, so the assumption was natural enough. No one knew that Stefan's body had been dumped in the well on another day, and I, of course, had absconded to London.'

Eve and Loren were almost sitting erect on the stairway by now and Eve's dread was deepening. She forced herself to speak normally. 'I still don't understand what this has to do with us.' She said this despite her suspicion.

He took a sudden step towards them and stamped his walking stick on the bare boards of the small landing. Both of them flinched.

'Don't you see?' he said excitedly. 'Isn't it clear to you after all I've said? The eleventh child doesn't have to be me: it can be another child!'

The shock, her suspicion now voiced, caused Eve to collapse back on the stairs. Loren squeezed her mother's arm in a tight vice.

Pyke leaned towards them, sinister, threatening, yet his voice still pleasant. 'When I read the local rag's story of a haunting at Crickley Hall, two trespassing children claiming they had seen the ghost of a naked man in the house, I knew the ghost of Augustus Cribben had returned to Crickley Hall – perhaps it had never gone away! The newspaper story said a family was renting the house, a husband and wife with two daughters, one of them twelve years old, exactly my own age when I stayed here in 1943. It couldn't have been more perfect!'

The insanity in Pyke's eyes was dangerously bright.

'His plaguing of me had become more intense of late, more powerful, and now I understood why. The conditions had become so appropriate!'

'Mummy—' Loren began to say, but Pyke's zealous babble cut her off.

'Loren can substitute for me, don't you see? I was his favourite, but I know he'll accept another child in my place. I'm sure he will approve my sacrifice to him. Augustus will have his eleventh child and I'll finally be free.'

Eve could not help herself. 'You're completely mad. This

whole thing is crazy. The police will find you. Lili will tell them you were here and attacked her. They'll lock you away for life.'

He actually chuckled. 'Would that really matter, if I was free of the hauntings? Perhaps even the dreams will stop when everything's resolved.' His face became artful. 'I'm prepared to take the consequences – after all, what's wrong with being pampered in an asylum for the next few years, because they will say I'm mad, won't they? I'll play the same game I think Magda Cribben has played all these years.'

He straightened and smiled as if pleased with himself. He took a step back and leaned against the landing railing behind him.

'You know I expected your husband to be here tonight,' he said. 'I had intended to get his permission to stay overnight to monitor the equipment I was going to set up around the house. When I was sure everyone was asleep I was going to steal Loren away from her bed and take her down to the cellar. When it was done, I was going to leave quietly.'

'They wouldn't put you in a psychiatric institute,' Eve said coldly. 'No, you'll rot in prison.'

'I don't think so.'

'*I won't let you take my child!*' Eve shouted at him defiantly but more scared than she had ever been in her life, more scared even than the day Cam went missing, if that were possible (perhaps because then she had hope).

His reply was so twisted in logic and so affably put that a violent shudder ran through her.

He said: 'But, Eve, I only want *one* of your daughters.'

That was when she had no doubt at all that this man was *seriously* crazy, and all the more dangerous: he couldn't be reasoned with.

Lightning blazed against the window and thunder cracked

almost immediately afterwards, momentarily diverting his attention.

'*Run, Loren, run!*' Eve shouted and they both jumped to their feet, Eve pushing at her daughter's back to hurry her up the stairs.

But although surprised by their sudden break, Pyke's reaction was swift. Even before the thunder had rumbled away he had turned his sturdy walking stick upside down so that its curved handle was pointing away from him as he leaned forward. He hooked Eve's ankle with it and her own impetus brought her crashing down, jarring her chest and one elbow against the edges of the stairs.

'*Do you want pain, Eve? Because I can give you pain,*' Pyke bellowed.

Loren's scream bounced off the walls, ceiling and flagstoned floor. The girl stopped climbing and reached back for her mother, tugging at her arm to help her rise again.

'*Leave me!*' Eve cried at her. '*Just run, get away!*'

But Loren refused to leave her mother behind. She slipped a hand under Eve's shoulder and desperately tried to lift her.

The walking stick descended fast and struck Eve's back so that she sprawled on the stairs once more.

She half turned and kicked out, her foot hitting Pyke full in the stomach. He nearly toppled backwards, but somehow managed to regain his balance. Only slightly winded, he raised the heavy stick again.

Eve pulled herself free of Loren's clutching hands, turning all the way to defend herself. It was too late, though: the walking stick came down and hit her on the side of her head. She fell back and in a daze she heard Loren's frightened cry and then another, smaller voice, Cally's voice, yelling from the top of the stairs.

'*Leave my mummy alone!*'

Eve turned onto her stomach and tried to raise herself on hands and knees, but she was struck across the back of her shoulders next and everything went black.

The 'vision' swam back into Lili's head. She had lost it for a while as her other senses, the normal ones, began to resurface, leading her slowly towards consciousness. There was no choice but to accept the returning images . . .

*The guardian who is called Augustus Cribben, still naked, his pale flesh scored with striped wounds and old scars, is collecting the small corpses that are scattered around the house.*

*He carries the children's bodies to the head of the cellar stairs, then bundles them down, their still warm bodies rolling over and over until there is a lifeless pile of them at the bottom. The roar of coursing water rises from the well and fills the chamber with its sound, for the river below is in tumult.*

*Susan Trainer is the last child to be gathered up and this one he drags across the flagstone floor because he has grown tired with all the killing and carrying, and the fiery demons inside his head refuse to give him peace. His mad eyes are bloodshot with the pain.*

*Cribben shuffles the corpse onto the top step, then pushes it over with his foot so that it tumbles down to join its companions in death.*

*He presses both hands against his temples as if to squeeze out the agony, but there is no relief.*

*Shambling to the centre of the hall, he picks up the stick he had left lying there while he completed his body-disposal tasks. He shouts out as he flails his own flesh with it, not as a penance but as a distraction from the fiercer pain inside his skull.*

*After a short while, Cribben lumbers to the hall's broad*

*stairway and climbs to the small landing. Rain gusts against the glass of the tall window with awesome force and the howling wind rattles the wood. He turns round to face the hall, the brutal studded cane held aloft as he stretches out his arms in adoration of Christ. He has discharged his duty.*

*He has offered up the souls of the children to his God. And found absolution for his own tortured soul.*

Lili's 'vision' finally faded completely and she stirred on the drenched earth.

# 74: THE BRIDGE

Lightning lit up the house across the river and Gabe, who had been unable to make out the dark building through the heavy sheets of rain, took a moment to absorb the sight of it. *Yeah*, he thought drily, *it even* looks *like a haunted house, especially on a night like this.*

The lightning stuttered and died, and as thunder shook the skies almost directly overhead, Crickley Hall all but disappeared into the murk once more. There didn't seem to be any lights on – no, if he looked hard, Gabe could just detect faint glows in some windows. But they were very dim and that wasn't because of the rain. He wondered if power from the main grid had failed and the house's generator had kicked in; if the machine wasn't running at full capacity it might account for the weak lighting.

Gabe leaned in close to his companion. *'You okay, Perce?'* He had to shout to be heard over the storm.

*'I'm all right, Mr Caleigh,'* Percy yelled back. *'But I don't like the look of that river.'*

He was right. They were standing in the roadway, the bridge and river only a few yards away. By the bright but rain-limited beam of Percy's torch Gabe could see the ferocious white spume that reared and tossed on the roiling water, whose level was almost up to the top of the riverbanks.

It didn't look like the swollen river would be contained for much longer.

The engineer had noticed the two cars in the short parking bay and he thought he had seen the small two-door Citroën before. The other vehicle, a dark-red Mondeo, he didn't recognize. Who the hell would be visiting on a night like this?

Gabe and Percy hadn't said much to one another as they had battled the storm, but the old gardener's concern over Crickley Hall had the American worried. The house had survived the previous flood, hadn't it? So Eve only had to get herself and the girls upstairs and trust in the building's solid, thick walls to withstand any floodwaters. Although power lines were vulnerable in this kind of weather, Gabe was also concerned that Percy hadn't been able to reach Eve by phone. He didn't like the idea of Crickley Hall being totally cut off.

The gardener directed the torchbeam towards the bridge ahead of them.

'*I don't like the looks of that, either,*' he declared, and Gabe nodded. Nor did he.

Natural debris – branches, a small tree, shrubbery and no doubt dead animals – was piling up on one side of the bridge, and the structure itself was visibly unsteady, shaking as if about to break free of the concrete bases on both riverbanks. Crossing it was going to be a risk.

'*Percy, we gotta get over the bridge right now, before it goes,*' Gabe shouted into the gardener's hood-covered ear. '*But, look, maybe you don't. No point in both of us chancing it.*'

'*I'll come along with yer, Mr Caleigh. We'll hafta' be quick though.*'

Gabe didn't argue: there was no time. Soon the bridge was going to break away under the strain. He clamped his hand around the old man's upper arm. '*Let's go, then!*'

Percy led the way, shining the torch down at the ground before them as they went. Gabe had never felt so wet in all his life: his reefer coat felt twice as heavy as normal and his hair was plastered to his scalp. Although his coat collar was up, rainwater still managed to soak his neck; his jeans were now a darker shade of blue and even the socks beneath his boots felt damp. They plodded over the muddy patch in front of the bridge and paused to make a closer assessment of the wooden structure's condition.

Percy stood to one side so that he could examine the thick stanchions supporting the bridge.

'*One of 'em uprights has come away,*' he informed the engineer. '*The whole blamed thing's gonna tear free afore long, but that were why it were built this way, so's it don't act like a dam.*'

'*That's helpful, Perce. Shall we get across now?*'

Gabe placed a tentative foot on the sodden slippery boards. The bridge shook under him.

'*Got an idea, Perce. Let's just run for it.*'

Percy clapped him on the back and without another word they raced towards the other side of the bridge.

They almost made it together, but the surface was too slick with spray and slime. Percy's feet skidded from under him and he went down with a bone-rattling thud.

Gabe, who had made it all the way before his companion had fallen, turned back for him and as he reached down to haul Percy to his feet, the whole bridge lurched. The deck tilted and the engineer went down on one knee. Percy began to slide towards the left-hand rail and might have slipped through the struts had not Gabe grabbed him. Unbalanced himself, Gabe managed to clutch the limb of a tree that was poking through the struts on the right-hand rail. It jerked forward a little, then held firm, and Gabe was able to draw Percy towards him using the branch for leverage.

The bridge continued to lurch and tilt, and it was obvious to both men that the weakened structure was going to break away at any second.

'*On your feet, Percy!*' Gabe yelled, one hand under the gardener's shoulder. Letting go of the branch with his left, he now grasped the top of the rail.

The other man rose shakily, using Gabe for support. A sharp judder, then another lurch. Something – a hefty tree branch probably – smashed against the engineer's curled fingers, but he ignored the pain, well aware that if he should let go, he and Percy would slide off the bridge into the water below, for the rail on the other side had broken, leaving a gaping hole just inches above the turbulent river.

He yanked Percy up all the way and shouted: '*Keep hold of my arm and work your way along it to the other bank!*'

Percy didn't bother to reply: he followed Gabe's instructions. First he clung to the engineer's taut upper arm, moving along the elbow and then the wrist, his boots threatening to skid from under him with every step he took. When he reached Gabe's upraised fist holding the rail, he lunged for the right-hand rail and clung to it. He had stuffed the torch into one of his storm coat's huge pockets, so he had both hands free.

The bridge was now leaning perilously at one end, the nearest to the lane, and it began to sway with water splashing over its planks.

Percy quickly stumbled and slid his way towards the path, and finally he reached it. Even though he was out of breath and his arms and legs were shaking with the effort, he brought out the torch again and pointed it at Gabe, who was

JAMES HERBERT

still struggling to pull himself along the rail, his feet constantly slipping on the wet boards. The incline was becoming more and more acute so that it was almost impossible for the engineer's boots to gain purchase, but he battled on, slowly drawing closer and closer to the bridge's end. Then, just as he was about to grab Percy's outstretched hand, the structure lurched once more, violently this time, and Gabe thought he would be swept away with it. He hadn't counted on the old gardener's tenacity, though.

Percy dropped the torch onto the ground and leaned forward as far as he could from the very edge of the path. He clasped Gabe's coat with both hands and, with surprising strength for a man of his age, pulled the engineer off the bridge.

There was a loud ear-splitting cracking as the bridge behind Gabe collapsed. The broken structure was instantly carried away by the rising river and all the detritus that had been banked up behind it followed.

Gabe bent over, hands on his knees, and fought to suck in lost breath. By the time he straightened, Percy had the torch back in his hand and was shining its light at him.

'Th-thanks, Percy,' he stammered, then realized his gardener wouldn't have heard him over the storm. '*Much obliged*,' he said, louder this time.

'*Yer did right by me, Mr Caleigh,*' Percy growled loudly. '*A favour for a favour.*'

Gabe saw evidence of a faint smile on the old man's face.

As one, they turned to look at the house, both of them breathing heavily. Lightning flared and its thunder boomed.

'*Did yer see the same as me?*' Percy was looking at Gabe for affirmation. '*The lightnin' lit it up, over there near the tree.*' He aimed the beam at something – no, someone, Gabe realized – stretched flat out on the lawn close to the big oak tree.

They hurried towards the prone figure and for one heart-freezing moment Gabe thought it might be Eve lying there in the rain. It was certainly a woman – he could see slim fashion-booted legs beneath the hem of her coat. But Eve didn't have a coat of that light colour: she favoured darker tones for overcoats. As they drew near, he noticed the coat sleeves were pulled up slightly and the woman wore bracelets on both wrists – no, not bracelets: wristbands, coloured wrist-bands. He was beginning to understand who she was before they reached her. He had thought the small car in the lane's parking area was familiar, because it was the same one that had been parked there when he returned from work on Wednesday; it belonged to the psychic, Lili Peel. But by the torchlight he saw this person's hair was dark, whereas the psychic's had been light blonde, so maybe he was mis-taken, this was someone else.

He had almost reached her when Percy, who was slightly behind him, shouted something and pulled him back by the elbow. A dark object swished past Gabe's head, missing him by inches. It rose higher, then paused in the air as if held by the wind. As it swung back, Percy's torchlight caught it and Gabe saw it was the swing that was suspended from a lower branch of the oak.

As they watched, one of its rusty chains snapped, spoiling the swing's momentum. The edge of the loose seat was now low enough to be snagged by the ground, the broken part of the chain acting as an anchor. The swing dangled there, stirred by the wind but unable to rise any more.

'Thanks again, Perce.' Gabe realized that the swing might well have brained him had it connected with his head. He wondered if that was what had happened to the unconscious woman lying at their feet.

She was moving slightly, lifting her head and shoulders off the ground. Gabe dropped down on both knees beside her while Percy kept the light on her face. She groaned and her head bowed as if she were going to rest it on the grass again.

Gently, he touched her shoulder.

'What happened to you?' he asked, his voice just loud enough to be heard over the gale.

She turned her face towards him and was blinded by the light. She raised a shaking hand to shield her eyes.

'Who – who are you?' she asked so quietly Gabe hardly caught the words.

He saw that it was Lili Peel. Her hair was dark because it was rain-soaked and flattened against her scalp and face. He inched closer.

'It's Gabe Caleigh, Lili. Eve's husband, remember?'

As if relieved, she closed her eyes for a second or two. When she opened them again they were wide with shock.

'I ran away,' she managed to say, and Gabe had to move even closer to understand. Their faces were only inches apart. 'I left them there in the house. I'm sorry, I'm so sorry, but I was afraid. I thought he was going to kill me.'

She attempted to sit up, but it was too soon. She rocked forward and looked as if she were about to pass out again. Gabe quickly helped her to turn round, his arm lifting her at the back. Lili wiped her damp face with the flat of her hand and mud was smeared over her cheeks and nose.

Gabe kept his arm around her, supporting her, and Percy played the light on them both.

'Who was going to kill you, Lili?' Gabe urged. 'Has anything happened to my wife and daughters? Quickly, you gotta tell me.'

He was about to leave her there and get into the house fast, but she gripped his wrist.

'Oh God, I know what happened to the children,' she said breathlessly, ignoring his question. 'He murdered them all. The evacuees who came here during the war.'

Percy, only just able to hear her even though he bent near on one knee, said: 'Who murdered them, miss?'

Lili looked from one man to the other, the torch held low so its glare would not blind her again.

'The – the guardian – he killed them,' she stammered. 'The man called Augustus Cribben. I recognized him from the photograph Eve showed me. He killed them all except for the one who ran away.'

Percy was confounded, wondering how this woman – this girl, really – could know the children's fate when it was so long ago.

'He – he strangled them,' Lili went on, her eyes staring into the rain. 'He broke the necks of the smaller ones. I sensed it. I saw him do it.'

Gabe glanced at Percy. 'Lili's supposed to be psychic,' he hurriedly explained. He suddenly remembered the other car, the Mondeo parked in front of her Citroën. 'Is someone else in the house?' he asked urgently. 'Is someone threatening my family?'

'Yes!' she exclaimed, looking directly into Gabe's eyes. 'The boy named Maurice Stafford. I mean the man – the man who now calls himself Pyke. Oh God, you've got to help them before it's too late. He's going to harm them, I'm sure—'

But Gabe was already sprinting towards Crickley Hall.

## 75: THE SACRIFICE

The front door was shut but unlocked.

Gabe burst through, sending the heavy nail-studded door crashing back against the wall. Rain gusted in with the wind behind him as he came to a startled, skidding halt.

A great darkness, like a black fog, spread across the ceiling, wispy grey tendrils of it drifting down from the mass. It almost covered the iron chandelier, dimming its already weak lights so that the whole room was gloomy with shadows. With it, or from it, there came a foul fetid smell, an odour like raw sewage, that clogged the nose and throat. He nearly retched with the stench. A different kind of coldness settled over his body like a tight silk shroud.

A shrill cry from Cally brought him back to his senses. She was standing next to her mother halfway up the hall's broad staircase. Eve was sitting on a stair, a hand up to her lowered head, Cally's arm round her shoulders. Dark liquid oozed through Eve's fingers, blood from a cut in her head.

'*Daddy, the nasty man hit Mummy!*' Cally's face was screwed up as if she were about to break into tears.

He ran across the hall, splashing through large puddles without questioning how or why they were there, his only thoughts for his wife and daughter. Loren's absence had not hit him yet. He bounded up the stairs.

Eve heard him coming and looked down at him. The panic on her face shook him.

She extended her bloodied hand as if to ward him off. *'No!'* she screeched. *'Loren, help Loren!'*

Gabe dropped to his knees on a lower step so that his face was level with hers. 'Eve, what is it? Where is Loren?'

*'He's taken her to the cellar! The well!'*

He took her by the shoulders. 'Who has? What're you talking about, Eve?'

'Pyke! He came back. He's mad, Gabe! He's going to kill her!'

Gabe was confused, astonished. But he did not waste another moment. He hurtled back down the stairs, taking two at a time and leaping the last few into the hall. All kinds of dreads ran with him. Loren! Pyke! Why the hell would Pyke – no time to think, he was at the open cellar door.

He went through, hardly slowing, descending the creaky cellar steps in a rush, his hands brushing the rough walls on either side for balance, almost stumbling near the bottom but catching himself before he could fall.

Emerging into the cavernous basement room, he took it all in in an instant: the roaring of the underground river whose sound was amplified by the circular wall of the shaft and then further enhanced by the cellar's stone walls, the dank earthy smell of the poorly lit chamber – the two figures, Pyke and Loren, standing by the lip of the old well.

Loren was struggling, her back to Pyke, his big hand round her neck, pushing her head and shoulders forward so that she was forced to look into the deep well. She was crying hysterically.

With no interest in conversation – reasons why, warnings, pleadings, humouring the bastard – and barely breaking stride, Gabe launched himself at the man threatening his daughter.

Although Pyke had heard the footsteps coming down the stairs, he had not expected such a swift reaction, and he involuntarily pulled away in surprise, bringing the girl back from the edge with him. He attempted to raise the walking stick he held in his other hand to meet the attack, but the engineer was hurtling in to him before he had a chance to use it.

All three of them went to the floor, Pyke uttering a cry at the impact, but Gabe rolled over in the dirt and dust, coming up on one knee to face his adversary again. Loren was lying on one side, a hand grasping the edge of the low wall; her hysteria had abruptly stopped.

As Pyke started to rise, Gabe threw a punch at him and the tall man staggered away, sprawling backwards onto the floor again. Gabe quickly moved towards Loren, who still lay on her side next to the well. He bent over her and pulled her to a sitting position.

'*Are you okay, baby?*' he asked over the noise of the underground river.

She looked back at him with bright scared eyes, her cheeks smeared with tear-streaked grime. She must have fought Pyke all the way, he thought. Loren flung herself against him and sobbed on his shoulder.

'It's all right,' he reassured her, not sure if she heard him, 'nobody's gonna hurt you.'

Suddenly, he felt her stiffen, her hands gripping him.

'*Dad!*' she screamed.

Over her father's shoulder, she had seen Pyke getting to his feet.

Gabe whirled, but he was at a disadvantage, on his knees, one arm still round Loren.

The thick walking stick came down heavily and he just managed to get his left arm up to block the blow. The stunningly sharp pain paralysed his arm right up to the shoulder and he gasped at the shock of it. Ignoring his numbed arm he forced himself to his feet.

Pyke faced him, the walking stick wielded before him like a sword, keeping Gabe at bay. There was sheer malice in his narrowed eyes and the engineer wondered how he had ever thought those same eyes were kindly. Gabe's injured arm hung uselessly by his side and Pyke realized his own advantage.

Gordon Pyke was a big man and, despite his years, he still had a big man's strength. He was also swift, and when he drove at Gabe's lower belly with the walking stick the engineer was not quick enough to avoid the unexpected move.

Gabe doubled over, the wind taken out of him. He felt as though he had been kicked in the gut by a horse. He stayed on his feet, hands clutched to his stomach, but he was vulnerable.

Raising the stick high over his head, Pyke brought it down with all his might and it splintered and broke in half against Gabe's half-turned back and left shoulder.

Gabe staggered with the blow, but he refused to go down. He tried to straighten up to be ready for another assault and only just managed to dodge the next strike. But he was dazed and he reeled backwards, unbalanced, then fell to the floor to sprawl helplessly in the dust.

Loren screamed again and tried to go to her father, but Pyke, the remainder of the broken walking stick still in his hand, stood in her way. He held it like a knife, its jagged, splintered end pointed towards the ceiling. She gazed up at the tall, bearded man and he was smiling queerly, his sharp eyes blazing into hers. She tried to duck away so that she could get round him to her father who lay on his back on the other side of the well. But Pyke, who certainly was both quick and strong for a man in his seventies, easily caught her, grabbing her arm and dragging her back to the edge of the deep, dark pit.

Below, the loud turgid river surged upwards and around the well's stone wall, creating a spinning, black-centred vortex that rose and fell with changing pressures.

'Please let me go!' Loren pleaded, but Pyke merely took pleasure in her panic and pushed her closer to the low circular wall.

'*Pyke!*'

The big man took time to look across the dingy chamber at Gabe, who had risen on one elbow, pain evident on his creased features.

Although the lighting was feeble, Gabe could see the gleam in Pyke's eyes skittering between insanity and excitement.

'If you harm her I'll kill you,' Gabe said in a low growl. A fine warning to give, but the engineer knew he was helpless to stop Pyke. The pain across his back and shoulder was now excruciating and his left arm was useless for the moment.

'Don't think of this as a sacrifice,' Pyke returned. 'Think of it more as a demand accommodated.'

Gabe didn't know what the hell the man was talking about, or if he'd heard him right, and he didn't care. He had to do something and he had to do it fast. But what? Even if he got to his feet and rushed Pyke there would be no time to save Loren. The lunatic only had to give her a small shove and she would be gone.

He shifted his position slightly, getting ready to charge Pyke anyway, and his elbow nudged something that scraped metallically against the stone floor. In desperation, he glanced down and saw that the object by his elbow was the same length of thin but heavy iron, a small round hole at its centre, he had casually tossed aside when Cally had called him from the top of the stairs five days ago. In a flash and quite incongruously, given the circumstances, it came to him that the metal bar was the blade of the old Flymo hover-mower he had seen leaning against a wall in the garden shed. Someone – probably Percy – had brought it down to sharpen its edges, then discarded it.

Pyke was pushing Loren closer and closer to the edge of the well, while she did her best to resist, screaming and digging her bare heels into the floor, the struggle hopeless against the big man's superior strength.

In the blink of an eye, Gabe was on one knee, his body crouched forward, the heavy blade in his right hand, held in his fingers by one end. He skimmed it through the air and it spun like a boomerang. He had aimed high for fear of hitting Loren and his aim was true.

It seemed to take an impossibly long time but it struck Pyke squarely on the forehead, sending him toppling backwards, his grip on Loren released.

Unfortunately, she was leaning too far over the opening and she teetered on the brink, her arms flailing the air to prevent herself from falling.

But it was no use. She began to drop.

## 76: DESPERATION

Those brief but vital moments of trying to save herself were just enough for Gabe to spring forward like a runner off starting blocks and dive towards Loren.

With a heart-piercing scream she fell, her arms outstretched, the whirlpool below eager to receive her. Even as he landed on the low wall encircling the well, Gabe was reaching out to grasp her wrist as she went. Unfortunately, he had to use his left arm, the fingers of the right wrapping themselves over the top of the wall for support, and the agonizing wrench almost forced him to let go of his daughter. But he hung on, taking her weight with his numbed arm and injured shoulder, straddled face down on the wall, half his body hanging over the edge, only his right knee pressing into the outer stonework and his right hand clenched hard against the top of it keeping him there.

Loren dangled perilously, her bare legs kicking air. The small desperate cries she uttered were lost in the cacophony made by the rushing water. The deep centre of the whirlpool rose as if to meet her halfway, but fell back again when river currents below the surface shifted. Panic-stricken though she was, Loren tried to help her father by swinging round and reaching for the wrist of the hand that held her own. Her fingers tightened around it and Gabe grunted with approval: his hold on her was more secure.

Yet her weight was beginning to drag him off the wall. '*Try . . . to get . . . a foothold*,' he urged with gasping breaths.

She must have heard him, for she raised her legs and searched for a jutting stone or a shallow indent with her feet, but her toes kept slipping off the slimy, mossy stonework of the well's interior wall.

Gabe was strong, but the balance was all wrong; he couldn't get enough leverage to pull her up. Even so, at any other time, he would have scooped his daughter out of the well with ease – her weight would have meant nothing to him – but now his arm was numb from shoulder to fingertips and there was little power in it. It was all he could do to maintain the grip.

Time and again, he attempted to draw her up, but whenever he brought her closer to him, his strength failed and she was lowered again. A thousand red-hot needles seemed to prick his shoulder with each effort and the stone he sprawled upon pressed hard against his cheek and chest. Gritting his teeth, his body tensed, he tried to lift Loren once more, his numbed arm trembling with the exertion, more than half his body now drawn into the opening. When she reached up with her free hand and managed to clutch at his shoulder, the added pain there was almost unbearable. Her fingers slipped away and she hung over the void, her teeth biting into her lower lip so that she wouldn't scream. She looked up and saw the desperation in her father's eyes and she was even more afraid, if that were possible.

Her weight was gradually and inexorably dragging Gabe over the brink, no matter how hard he resisted with his other hand and knee pushing against the outside of the circular wall.

'*Don't let me go, Daddy!*' she cried up at him, pleading with wide terrified eyes.

'Never,' he grunted in a strained low murmur, more to himself than his daughter. He would not let her go. Even if it meant falling in with her, he would not let go of Loren.

There was a sudden distraction. He became aware of movement in the cellar and he raised his head an inch or two, quivering with the effort. As he had feared, the dark shape of Pyke was rising over the opposite side of the well.

His back to Gabe, the big man bowed his head into his hands and rocked slightly. Then he straightened and slowly turned around.

There was a gash on his forehead where the blade had hit him – Gabe had been aiming for his throat – and Pyke raised a hand to it and examined the blood on his fingertips. He regarded Gabe with a cold, furious glare.

'You shouldn't have done that,' he said as if chiding a naughty child, his anger completely contained.

Gabe barely heard his words over the commotion of the underground river, so mildly were they spoken.

'Now you will be included,' Pyke added. 'And your wife, and your other brat.'

'You're crazy!' Gabe spat out. His body shifted a fraction of an inch across the wall and he fought desperately against Loren's pull.

'Naturally that will be my plea,' Pyke replied tartly, pleased with himself. 'Put away for a few years, playing the game with psychiatrists and various busybodies, then, when they realize I've miraculously recovered my sanity, they will have to let me go. Care in the community is the worst I can expect.'

'*They'll never let you out. You'll rot inside an asylum for ever, Pyke!*'

'We'll see,' he said brusquely, the matter closed as far as he was concerned.

Gabe laid his cheek back on the wall, relieving the strain to his neck for a moment. *Help me, God*, he prayed silently and guiltily, and without hope because the only time he'd ever asked God for help was when Cam went missing. *Just give me one chance now.*

He looked down at Loren, desperate for an idea, anything to cancel the maniac and get her out of the well. She stared up at him, quietened now, just hanging there. Beneath her, the water swirled and spumed, hungry to take her. Hungry to take them both.

Raising his head once more, he saw that Pyke was bending over, reaching for something. Metal clanked against the concrete floor and Gabe knew that the big man was picking up the blade he had thrown at him. With his walking stick broken, Pyke needed another weapon.

Pyke straightened and he was smiling. A cruel smile. A satisfied smile. He tapped the metal bar against the palm of his hand and his smile corrupted to a sneer. A little unsteady because of the wound to his forehead, he took a step towards the well where the engineer lay defenceless.

But Pyke suddenly halted. He turned his head to one side, as if listening.

Gabe had heard nothing over the sound of the subterranean river.

Now Pyke was turning all the way round as though something had caught his attention.

Gabe turned his head a little more to see what was engaging Pyke's interest.

It was barely visible, but something stood in the black entrance to the boiler room.

It was watching them.

It was strangely compelling, its mere presence in the doorway enough to render Pyke immobile. Yet it was in shadow, an unknowable and unclear adumbration. It might have been a figure.

Gabe shivered, a reaction so strong that it shook his whole body in spite of the weight he bore and the awkwardness of his position.

Pyke dropped the heavy blade and stood transfixed. He gave out a small moan.

They both stared at the dark, undefined shape in the opening of the boiler room.

It seemed like minutes, but it could only have been seconds before the thing moved. With great deliberation, as if each footstep were considered, it came forward unsteadily from the doorway, and although emerging into the dismal light, it seemed to carry the shadows with it so that it was still difficult to determine. But as it drew nearer – nearer to Pyke – it appeared to take on a definite form.

Still determinedly keeping hold of Loren, Gabe realized it was the slight figure of a woman or girl, for it wore a faded skirt that ended just above the ankles. Sodden leather shoes whose metal buckles were brown with rust and corrosion were on her feet. Her gait was awkward and slow, for the right foot dragged behind so that it scuffed and scraped the stone floor. Each dull *thud* of a footstep was followed by the dragging of the damaged leg, the sound muted yet somehow clear over the amalgam of other sounds.

Water dripped from its – her – bedraggled clothes.

Her head and narrow drooped shoulders remained in shadow, outside the dim circle of light cast by the overhead lightbulb, but the ends of tangled and matted hair could be seen hanging stiffly against her chest. Over a soaked tattered blouse, she wore a colour-drained shawl that hung over her shoulders to wrap loosely round her elbows. One hand was grey, almost white, and it was bloated, as if it had been a long time in water. The other hand was different: it was clutched tight against her chest and it was inverted, the fingers turned inwards, like twisted claws, and so thin they looked skeletal; the wrist was also misshapen, the flesh withered and creased, disappearing beneath a ragged sleeve, suggesting the deformity included the rest of the forearm.

The shadowy figure steadily advanced on Pyke, whose stillness continued; he seemed stricken by the sight of her. But as she drew near he took a faltering step backwards. For some reason, he glanced at Gabe, perhaps to reassure himself that the other man was seeing the same as he. Pyke suddenly looked every day of his seventy-five years.

The world around Gabe seemed to recede, and with it the cacophony of noises – the constant churning of the swollen river below, the muffled rumble of the storm above, the heavy pounding of feet descending the cellar steps – all these diminished to a background susurration as he stared at the hideous walking corpse that came towards Pyke.

Who took another uncertain step backwards.

But the thing that had once been a living being moved

closer, closer until there was only a short space between it and the tall man.

And her face and shoulders came into the light.

Pyke screamed – an unnaturally high sound for a man of his size – as he looked into the grey, bloated face before him.

The swollen flesh was corrupted in parts, the lips gone as if eaten away by tiny parasites, so that long, gumless teeth were exposed in a frightening rictus grin. The temple and cheekbone on one side looked as if they had been crushed by something heavy and hard, and the top of her head was grotesquely dented as if the skull beneath her hair had caved in. The eyes were lidless as if the thin layers of shielding skin had also been nibbled away, and they peered hugely from the skull and what was left of the puffy and ruptured flesh of the face. They gaped lifelessly at Pyke, who again stepped backwards in shock.

He was too near the edge of the well and his calves bumped against the circular wall. He stumbled, he tried to save himself, but it was no use. Pyke fell and his scream echoed round the solid walls of the well.

Gabe could not help but watch as the big man plunged into the whirlpool below, Pyke's hopeless cry suddenly cut off as he was swallowed up by the spinning water.

His head and shoulders appeared again as he was spun by the fierce current and Gabe winced at the horror in Pyke's insane eyes. Big hands scrabbled at the stone wall but, as Loren had already found, its surface was too slippery to hold on to and the drowning man screeched one last time as he was drawn inescapably into the vortex.

The last thing seen of Pyke was a hand reaching out from the maelstrom as if grabbing for life itself. Then he was gone.

All sound around Gabe suddenly returned and, over the liquid roar of the river, he heard his daughter calling to him.

*'Daddy! Please! Oh please!'*

He pulled with every ounce of strength he had left. But the effort almost sent him over the edge. Just when he thought he'd lost the battle and was going to fall with his daughter into the well, another arm reached past his shoulder and took hold of Loren's free hand.

Suddenly her weight was as nothing and together the two men lifted Loren out of the well with one strong heave.

Father and daughter rolled off the low wall and dropped exhaustedly onto the cellar floor. But Gabe soon pushed himself up on an elbow and searched behind him. And saw that the creature that had intimidated Pyke to his death was no longer there.

'Did you see her, Mr Caleigh?' Percy asked earnestly as he knelt beside the engineer. There was an elated shine to his faded eyes. 'Did you see her, my beautiful Nancy?'

## 78: THE LIGHTS

The engineer made no comment. If Percy's ghost was different to his, then so be it. Who knew how the supernatural presented itself to different people? The old gardener saw what he wanted to see, memory ruling his vision. None of that mattered though, Pyke was dead, drowned, and Loren was safe. Hell, they were *all* safe from the lunatic.

Gabe had to wonder at himself. He had accepted that he, the sceptic, the unbeliever, had just seen a ghost, a ghost that had sent Pyke to his certain death, an apparition that had vanished when the deed was done. It was incredible to Gabe, but he had undeniably witnessed everything with his own eyes. Now there was no doubt that Crickley Hall really was haunted.

He helped Loren to her feet and hugged her tight. She had run out of sobs, but she was still shaking.

'Percy,' he said, looking round at the gardener, 'thanks. I'd have lost her if it wasn't for you. I owe you again.'

Percy stood there catching his breath, a glow still in his moist eyes. He gazed round the cellar as if he might catch sight of his lost love once more; or at least, sight of her ghost.

Gabe interrupted his search. 'We oughta get back upstairs to Eve. She didn't look so good.'

The old man nodded once, the noise from the well drowning the deep sigh he gave.

The engineer picked up his daughter and bit into his lower lip at the stab of pain in his shoulder. Loren wrapped her thin legs round his waist and he carried her to the stairs; he began to climb them with weary effort, glad to be leaving the dank and dingy basement.

With one last lingering look towards the black portal to the boiler room, Percy followed.

On the hall's wide staircase, Lili tended Eve as best she could, while Cally fussed over her mother, patting her shoulder, anxiety causing her little lower lip to tremble. The psychic dabbed a folded handkerchief on Eve's head wound, staunching the small flow of blood.

'It's not too bad,' she told Eve. 'There's not much blood now, but I think you'll have a sore head for a while.'

There was a dull, throbbing ache in Lili's own head, the consequence of being knocked out by the swing earlier (or maybe the results of the nightmarish visions that followed as she lay unconscious on the ground, she thought). She took the bloodied handkerchief away from Eve's head to examine the injury and was relieved to find the bleeding appeared to have stopped completely.

The hall was growing darker and Lili peered up at the ceiling, frowning at what she saw. She had been aware of it as soon as she entered the house with the old man when they had come after Gabe Caleigh: a slowly swelling darkness hung over the hall, a smoke-like substance from which dusky wisps descended like tendrils, the blackness sinking after them, deepening gradually so that soon the hanging lights of the iron chandelier were consumed. The smell, though, the fetid stink of corruption and bodily waste, seemed to permeate the hall, as did the extreme chill.

Eve tried to rise from the stair she rested on, but Lili pressed down on her shoulders to keep her there.

'I won't lose her, I won't lose her,' Eve repeated as she tried to resist the psychic's efforts.

'Loren will be all right,' Lili assured her quietly but firmly. 'The other man went down to help Gabe. Everything will be okay, you'll see.' But the psychic was more concerned than she let on. The person who now called himself Pyke was very strong. And fast. He had attacked Lili so quickly she'd barely had time to duck away from the blow. She hoped Gabe Caleigh was as capable as he looked.

Cally was the first to see the three figures emerge from the cellar and she shouted excitedly, 'Daddy, it's Daddy! He's got Loren!'

Eve moaned with relief, swaying so that Lili had to hold her steady.

The first thing Gabe noticed as he carried Loren from the cellar was that the great expanse of darkness overhead had deepened and become even denser than before. It had swallowed up the hall's upper reaches, almost smothering the chandelier and landing lights so that it was difficult to see across the vast room. Nevertheless, he could just make out Eve, Cally and Lili Peel on the stairs.

He was assailed by the stench that ruined the air, but he ignored it in his haste to reach Eve. As he splashed through puddles, Loren in his arms but looking round towards her mother, lightning flashed outside and washed the hall with its stark silver-white brilliance. The thunder that followed was like the boom of close cannon fire. He had never known a thunderstorm go on so long.

With Percy behind him, Gabe mounted the stairs and settled Loren in Eve's arms. Mother and daughter clung to one another, and their tears mingled on each other's cheeks. Gabe knelt beside them and squinted through the gloom at the blood smeared across his wife's forehead. She opened her eyes and they shone mistily with an emotional mix of joy, relief, fear and gratitude. He leaned forward and kissed her gently.

Lili interrupted. 'What happened to Pyke?' Her expression was anxious as she twisted the blood-soiled handkerchief in her fingers. Even in the encroaching gloom, Gabe could see her face was deathly pale.

'He's gone,' he replied, looking up from his wife.

Now there was alarm in the psychic's eyes.

'Pyke fell into the well that's down there,' Gabe added. 'It was an accident.' This wasn't the time to give her the full story.

'He's dead?' It was said in disbelief.

'I goddamn hope so,' he replied bitterly. Then: 'Yeah, he's dead. It's over.'

But his sense of smell picked up another odour amidst the concoction of foul stenches that polluted the atmosphere, one that was oddly familiar: a harsh aroma of strong soap. He noticed that Lili was looking past him, staring at something lower down on the staircase.

'Oh no,' she said in a low, quavering voice.

## 79: THE FLOOD

Despite the noise of the storm, the howl of the wind and the beating of rain on the tall windows, and as quietly as the words were spoken, each one of them looked up at Lili, who was on a higher step, then followed the direction of her stare with their own eyes.

It had no definite form to begin with – it was stronger than a mist, yet of no particular substance – but it evolved quickly, forming a definite shape as they watched in total silence. Within moments it had taken on the configuration of a man. A naked man, who held a slender stick in one hand. A man whose pallid body was cross-hatched with livid red stripes and blood spots over old weals and scars. A man with white hair that was shaved above the ears and whose black penetrating eyes glared back at them from dark shadows beneath a high, prominent brow.

He stood on the small, lower landing and Percy, who was a few steps below the others, voiced his name.

'Augustus Cribben,' he said in dismayed awe.

As if to dramatize the announcement, lightning strobed through the window over the stairs and the naked figure on the landing lost substance again, became translucent, nothing more than a vague apparition through which the landing rail and the torchère with its empty vase could be clearly seen.

But when the searing light flickered away and thunder filled the air, it took on bulk once more, became a seemingly solid entity.

Gabe heard Loren give out a little shriek and Eve froze in his arms. Cally gripped his injured shoulder tightly, but the pain did not distract him. Percy took a stumbling step up, moving away from the pale spectre.

'Oh dear God . . .' Gabe heard Lili say from behind.

He half rose from the stair he'd been kneeling on, his body tensed as if he might throw himself at the bleeding and scarred phantom below.

As they watched, the ghost of Cribben raised the cane and whacked it against his own bare leg. *Swish-thwack!* was the sound it made. Those dark eyes focused on Loren.

Then Cribben moved forward as if to climb the stairs, eyes never leaving his prey.

Cally screamed, a frail cry over the storm, and Eve gathered Loren up and began to push her further up the stairs. Eve shivered as she went with her daughter, her head turned as if afraid to let the monster below out of her sight. The wound to her head was forgotten; everything was sharp again, in focus, the dizziness gone. It was all only too real.

In front of Gabe, Percy stopped climbing and stood his ground: Cribben was not going to get past him. Gabe, too, had resolved not to let the threat pass by; he clenched his fists, even though he wondered what the hell he could do to something that had no real body. Yet it looked so solid, so convincing, that he could not help but assume it had the power to physically harm a person. He swore under his breath.

But as the darkness above swelled and sank lower, rendering the lights to dim, useless glows, the hall becoming as night, Lili pointed upwards and cried out, 'Look! Look into it! Can you see them?'

Gabe glanced up and noticed lighter shadows moving within the murky black fog-like mass, shapeless forms that flitted and weaved in the greater darkness. There were many of them and they conspired to dive down into the thinner lower layers as if to burst through, but they swerved and soared again each time they came close. Until one finally broke away, seeming to use a wispy tendril that dropped from the core as a conduit, and it was quickly followed by another and another, emerging as white shadows that swooped towards the ghost on the stairs.

They swirled round Cribben as if to harass him, and soon they were joined by more white shadows, whirling round and round so that he appeared cocooned in them. He tried to beat them off with his punishment cane, but they deftly avoided it, then resumed their torment. Cribben's mouth opened in a defiant roar, his features deranged, but no sound emanated from him. The whirling white shadows began to condense, almost as if they were solidifying, and soon they had shrunk into small, glowing orbs, the lights Gabe had come upon in Cally's room days go. He tried to count them as they continued to beleaguer Cribben, but they were too fast and mingled too much.

They swarmed round Cribben like angry bees round a rambler who had disturbed their hive, darting to and fro, touching his phantom skin as though to sting, while he – it – swiped uselessly at them with the cane, silently screaming his annoyance. And then they were gone.

Gabe gaped. The tiny balls of light had shimmered once, then disappeared, leaving the ghost alone on the small landing. Cribben dropped the cane and brought his gnarled hands up to his temples as if in terrible pain. Did ghosts feel pain? Or was it the memory of pain? Gabe had no idea.

Lifting up his arms and turning his face towards the

ceiling, Cribben stood with his eyes closed and his mouth open wide, the tendons in his neck stretched and visible, as though real, his spine arched in his apparent agony. Fresh blood pulsed from the self-inflicted wounds, weals appearing, opening up and immediately festering, while scars reddened and seemed ready to burst.

Gabe felt a sudden trembling at his feet. He looked down and the staircase beneath him was shaking. They all became conscious of a deep rumbling and Percy put out a hand to the wall to steady himself. The wall was vibrating. For a few moments they forgot about the vision on the landing below.

The rumbling grew into a steady roar and the whole building seemed to be shivering, even though its construction was of thick solid stone. Dust drifted down from the ceiling, falling through the thinning fog that had all but concealed the chandelier's lights. An earthquake, Gabe told himself, and he reached back for Eve's hand. Cally skipped down a couple of steps and threw her arms round his leg, while Loren buried her face into her mother's chest. The noise was becoming unbearable, frightening, rising to a crescendo, and the house was shaking as though an invisible force was running through its structure.

On the square landing Cribben continued to rage.

With a tremendous crash, the floodwaters smashed through the tall window, sending glass shrapnel slicing into the phantom before it. Gabe toppled backwards onto Eve and Loren with the shock, taking Cally with him, but he saw Cribben engulfed by the deluge and swept away, only his bloody hands appearing above the torrent of water. The ghost was slammed against the opposite wall as if it were human and Gabe thought, if the body had been real, then almost every bone would have been shattered such was the impact.

It was only Lili who understood that this was how Augustus

Cribben had originally died, that this was a replay of his very last moments, and that unless his spirit passed over and ceased to haunt Crickley Hall, he would never rest in peace.

Still more water poured through the open front door to join with the main body of floodwater and surge around the grand hall, sweeping away furniture, bursting through into other rooms, lapping at the stairs, channelling down the cellar steps and flowing into the well, where it joined forces with the underground river to rage down to the sea bay. Soon, the whole cellar and boiler room next door were completely flooded.

Gabe groaned when the lights dimmed even more, then failed as the generator below was overwhelmed. Fortunately, Cally was still clinging to his leg and he could feel Eve and Loren's forms beneath him; he roughly hauled them to their feet.

Lightning brightened the hall again and he saw the flood-water was rising fast, its turbulent level already washing over the stairs just below where they all cowered.

'*Come on!*' he yelled over the roll of thunder. 'The house is solid, but we gotta get higher. No way of telling how far the flood's gonna reach, but we should be okay on the top landing. If we have to, we can go all the way up to the dorm.'

Light dazzled them as Percy switched on the powerful torch that had been tucked away again in a pocket of his storm coat. He turned its beam towards the swelling waters and they saw something bright carried through the doorway to the cellar: it was the spinning top and it quickly disappeared from view, riding the current like a rubber raft.

Percy yelled at Gabe, pointing the torch in the engineer's direction: '*The floodwater will funnel into the well! It shouldn't rise much more than this!*'

'*Maybe! But we'll be safer if we move up!*' Gabe called back.

Percy showed the way ahead and they began to climb the trembling stairs. Before stepping onto the gallery landing Gabe, with Cally carried in his right arm, snatched a quick look over the stair rail into the hall. There wasn't a lot to see in the darkness, but he noticed that the tiny lambent orbs were back.

They skimmed above the surface of the rough swirling water like excited fireflies, exuberant with energy.

He counted nine of them.

The river was unbelievably calm that morning, fast flowing still, but no longer swollen or threatening. The air smelt strongly of damp earth, and natural debris lay scattered everywhere: shrubbery, bushes, leaves, twigs and tree branches, even stones and sizeable rocks. Here and there, and particularly on the lower slopes of the gorge, whole trees had been uprooted. Two yellow Sea King rescue helicopters passed low over Crickley Hall, heading towards the bay, the sky above them a near-perfect blue with only a few puffball clouds floating in its expanse. A wide pre-constructed metal bridge spanned the river in place of the wooden bridge that had been swept away. Various vehicles, including an olive-green military lorry and two police cars, one unmarked, cluttered the nearby lane. (Pyke's Mondeo and Lili Peel's Citroën had been carried off down the hill by floodwater some time during the night and were now floating in the bay along with other wrecks and overturned fishing boats.) Parked on Crickley Hall's muddy front lawn were an ambulance with its rear doors open, a police van and a Land Rover 90.

Loren and Cally were glad to be outside in the sunshine and had watched the comings and goings of policemen and various rescue team personnel with interest. The most exciting were the police divers, but the girls had not been allowed to follow them into the house. If their mood was a little subdued it was because Cam's death had been confirmed and only partly due to the dramatic events of last night, which so far seemed to have had no harmful effect on either of them (nevertheless, Loren, in particular, would be closely watched over the next few weeks for any delayed reaction to the ordeal she had been put through). They had managed to catch some sleep, at first in their parents' arms on the landing overlooking the flooded hall, then later in their own beds while Gabe and Eve kept guard outside their room with Lili and Percy.

A group of men, Gabe Caleigh among them, had gathered by the big oak tree where a broken swing hung forlornly from a branch, one end of the seat resting on the damp grass, its rusty severed chain curled on the ground like an iron snake.

Gabe was speaking to the yellow-jacketed man on his left, the deputy chief of the emergency services, Tom Halliway. 'Thanks for all the attention. I'm sure you gotta lot to do in the village.'

'Not as much as we expected,' Halliway replied. 'Hollow Bay got off comparatively lightly because of the flood precautions taken over the years. Plenty of cars swept away and overturned, several properties seriously damaged, but overall there's been no great harm done to the village. The main thing is, there's been no loss of life as far as we can tell. Sorry, didn't mean to disregard your friend.'

'Pyke? No, he wasn't a friend. Barely knew him. He turned up two days ago calling himself a psychic investigator, looking for ghosts.'

The uniformed policeman to his right, Chief Superintendent Derek Pargeter, remarked: 'Because he'd seen the article in the *Dispatch* this week, you told me earlier.'

'Uh-huh. The guy had read the crazy story about Crickley

Hall being haunted, said he wanted to disprove it – or prove it, I'm not sure which now. So we let him go ahead with his investigation.'

'Last night.' It was a statement, not a question.

'Yeah. Last night. He was setting up his equipment when the flood hit. Poor guy never stood a chance. He was swept down into the cellar.'

The thin-faced policeman nodded gravely. 'Poor man. Wouldn't have stood a chance because of the well there.' He jerked his head towards the house. 'The divers should have completed their search by now, but I doubt they've had any luck in finding the body; it would have been carried out to the bay by the underground river – the force would have been incredible. The coastguard and sea rescue helicopters will keep a lookout for Mr Pyke's body, but the currents along this coast can be unpredictable.'

Gabe looked down at the ground and said nothing. He and his family, with Lili Peel and Percy Judd, had spent the night huddled together on the landing, ready to move to the upper floor should the water rise to a threatening level. Once Loren and Cally had fallen asleep and been put into their beds, the group had discussed everything that had happened in the past week as well as the whole story of the evacuees and their horrific deaths. Lili had spoken of the vision or 'insight' she'd had while lying semi-conscious on the lawn after having been hit by the windblown swing – if it *had* been windblown, that is – and Eve had wept at the children's fate. But they all agreed that the true story of all that had gone on should be kept to themselves. Who would believe the truth anyway? As far as anyone else was concerned, Gordon Pyke had been unlucky, in the wrong place at the wrong time.

It was Gabe who had put the question: 'Who could've guessed the authorities had hushed up the real causes of the evacuees' deaths all those years ago?' The question rhetorical, he had gone on: 'As Percy told Eve the other day, the lid was kept on it because if the fact was ever known that the kids' bodies had strangulation bruisings round their throats, a couple of them with broken necks, then no caring parent would ever let their child be evacuated. Then, was it in the public interest to know in time of war? What about the morale of the country? Y'know, all that stuff. Besides, their only suspect was already dead – he'd paid for his crimes, so no point in dragging it all out into the open. The cane strokes and scars on Cribben's *naked* body – ignoring the fresh cuts from flying glass – must've got the authorities and police thinking something was not quite right about the guy. The only possible witness they had – maybe she was a suspect too, at first – was Cribben's sister, Magda, and she wasn't saying anything any more.

'I guess the vicar at the time – Rossbridger? – knew the truth of it, because he had Cribben's body buried in a neglected part of the graveyard and well away from the evacuees' graves. Rossbridger would've kept the secret outa self-interest – it might've damaged his reputation.'

Gabe's surmise had given them all something to think about during the hellish long night.

Halliway interrupted Gabe's thoughts. 'Not much more we can do here, Mr Caleigh. The last of the floodwater has been pumped from the cellar – most of it had already drained into the well anyway.'

'Thanks for what you've done,' Gabe said gratefully, shaking Halliway's hand.

The stocky deputy chief merely nodded and walked to his mud-caked Land Rover, where he was joined by two other members of his team. Before climbing in, he turned and called back to Gabe.

'Your vehicle's more or less where you left it last night. We just moved it to the side of the road when we cleared the fallen tree. Good thing you left the keys in the ignition.'

'Right. I'll go get it later. We're moving out today.'

As the Land Rover backed across the bridge, a policeman in wet Wellington boots came hurrying out of the house. Gabe hadn't noticed him before but he now recognized PC Kenrick, who had called on them earlier in the week after the two local kids had got a fright in Crickley Hall.

The policeman went straight up to the chief superintendent.

'The divers have brought up two bodies, sir,' he said breathlessly.

'What? Two?'

'Sir. And neither one was an adult male.'

Gabe looked at Kenrick in surprise.

'One is a small boy,' the young policeman went on, 'and the other is what's left of a woman – they could tell it was a woman by the hair. The paramedics will be bringing out the bodies in a moment.'

'In bodybags, I hope,' said his superior officer. 'What condition *are* the bodies in? I presume they've been down there for a long time unless you, Mr Caleigh, haven't been entirely frank with me and more than one person lost their life last night.'

He eyed Gabe suspiciously.

'No, just Pyke. Those other bodies have been there a long time,' said Gabe. 'Since 1943, I guess you'll find. I think they're what's left of a young boy and a female teacher who disappeared back then.'

'Good Lord. You're serious?'

The engineer nodded. 'They both went missing around that time.'

'No, that can't be right, sir.' Kenrick was addressing his superior. 'The woman maybe – apparently she was caught up in a niche in the rocks of the riverbed and she'd rotted. She's almost a skeleton.'

So, Gabe thought, Nancy Linnet revealed herself to Pyke – and himself, of course – in what was probably the worst stage of her decomposition. She meant to terrify her murderer.

'And the boy?' Pargeter asked the constable, irritated that he had to prompt. 'What's the condition of the boy's corpse, Kenrick?'

'That's just it, sir. The boy. He's hardly been touched. His body hasn't rotted at all.'

'Don't be foolish, man, there has to be some decomposition or bloating even if the body has only been there a short time.'

'His skin is like pure-white marble. Oh, and so is his hair. Totally white. He's only wearing a jumper and one sock, and they're stiff, like rotted cardboard, colours almost washed out of them by the water, which suggests the body has been down there a long time. But the paramedics don't think he drowned: they're saying he might have bled to death.'

The chief superintendent was astounded. Gabe was thoughtful.

The young policeman continued: 'The boy had been mutilated, sir. Around the genital area. It looks like an injury that was never treated. The divers found him on a small shelf, almost a fissure in the rockface. He was wedged inside it above the water level. Even over the past few days when the river's been swollen and fast flowing, it still wasn't able to dislodge the body.'

He stopped to draw in a breath.

'The divers say it's like an icebox down there and it's

almost as if the body was hermetically sealed, that's the only way they can explain it.'

'Are you sure it's not just in a state of rigor mortis?'

'No, sir, this is different.'

'But that means the body would have had to be insulated.'

'I know, sir. That's what they reckon. Like I said, the boy's corpse resembles white marble, too hard even for rigor mortis. The flesh can't even be squeezed. It's like a statue. It's unnatural, sir.'

'You're telling me,' agreed the chief superintendent. He scratched the morning stubble under his jaw; it had already been a long day and it wasn't noon yet. 'The pathologist might be able to throw some light on it. And there's no sign of this man, this Gordon Pyke?'

'The safety lines the divers were attached to limited their search a bit, but they had a good look around the area close to the well bottom. The body of the boy and what was left of the woman were all they found.'

Gabe was thinking of Stefan Rosenbaum: had the young Jewish boy, still alive when he had been dropped into the well, managed to drag himself from the river into a cavity in the rockface, to die there alone and in utter darkness? It was too gruesome to contemplate.

The two police divers emerged from the house at that point, the tops of their rubber suits peeled down to the waist, diving equipment in their muscled arms. Both men looked pale, their expressions grim, as they made their way to their vehicle. Behind them came the paramedics carrying a bodybag on a stretcher gurney. Because of the plastic bag's size and shape, Gabe knew it contained the remains of Nancy Linnet.

*

Inside Crickley Hall, Eve quietly wept, while Lili Peel avoided looking at the bodybag that contained the small preserved body of Stefan Rosenbaum. They had witnessed the condition of both bodies when the paramedics brought them up from the cellar to be bagged and put on stretchers. Nancy Linnet was no more than a skeleton dressed in faded rags, but the boy was in an almost perfect state, although his skin and hair were bleached pure white.

To Eve, he had looked beautiful, the hair that fell over his forehead still full, although colourless, his features reposed as if in sleep. Instantly, she knew it was Stefan's presence she had felt last Sunday when she had dozed in the sitting room. It hadn't been Cameron who had come to her and soothed her brow, calmed her fears, but this little boy, Stefan. Or, that is, his ghost.

She wept not just because of sadness, but also because she now knew for certain that death wasn't the end. Lili had told her that most spirits passed over as easily as walking through an unlocked door; it was only the troubled spirits who lingered in this world, those spirits who needed some resolve to their past life, whether by revenge, atonement or conclusion. Eve desperately wanted to believe her. So she did.

The paramedics returned to collect the second bodybag and, as they gently placed it on the stretcher, Eve wondered if the boy's soul could now rest in peace or would forever be lost in Crickley Hall. There seemed to be no way of knowing for sure.

Chief Superintendent Pargeter had departed and PC Kenrick was trudging across the metal bridge to his patrol car parked in the lane. He stepped to one side to let the police divers' van pass, then went on his way.

Gabe was about to go back into the house when a sound made him stop and look towards the bridge. The girls had also stopped dead in their tracks and they looked in the same direction as their father. The sound that had caught their attention was a dog's excited bark, one that was so familiar to them all.

Percy Judd had left Crickley Hall earlier that morning after an uncomfortable and cold night on the landing with the others, checking on the water level in the hall every few minutes or so until they were sure it wasn't going to come anywhere near the top of the stairs, none of them, apart from Loren and Cally, catching a minute's sleep. By late morning the next day, the temporary bridge having been put in place, he was looking all of his eighty-one years and Gabe, when the danger had passed, had tried to persuade him to take a nap in his and Eve's empty bed, but Percy had declined, saying he'd 'gotta bit of business to tend to at home'. Now he was back and restraining a dog that was desperate to cross the bridge and get to the girls.

*'Chester!'*

Both Loren and Cally had screeched the name together. Chester finally broke loose from Percy's grip and, trailing the leash behind, raced towards them as they raced towards him. They met at the end of the bridge, Chester throwing himself at them, knocking Cally over (although she didn't seem to mind, she was giggling at the pet's antics so much). His tail wagging furiously, Chester slobbered all over the sisters, barking happily between licks.

Gabe whistled and Chester was off like a shot, tearing across the grass to reach his master, his barks becoming short gasps of joy. So eager and so intoxicated with delight was Chester that he almost bowled Gabe over too. The engineer could not help but chuckle as he tried to calm the dog down and avoid Chester's slavering tongue at the same time. When Gabe finally declared, 'Enough, enough,' and stood, the dog ran back to the girls to be fussed over again. Meanwhile, Percy was crossing the lawn towards him.

'What's the story, Perce?' Gabe called out, frowning his bewilderment but happy to have Chester returned.

'Sorry, Mr Caleigh,' apologized the old gardener when he was still a few steps away. 'I couldn't tell yer afore 'cause yer'da wanted him back.'

The engineer shook his head, still puzzled. 'I don't get it.'

Chester was rolling in the grass now, wheezing in pleasure at the fuss being made by the girls.

Slightly out of breath, Percy stood before the engineer, his face flushed a little more red than usual. 'All the pets run away from Crickley Hall. Any new tenant who brings a dog or cat with 'em to the house soon loses 'em. None of 'em settle here. I found your dog, ol' Chester there, wandering up the road the day he ran away. Looked like a drowned rat, he did, all soaked an' sorry fer hisself, so I took him home with me. Intended to keep him with me until you folks decided to move out. I knew it wouldn't be long; never is. I did it because it were best fer the animal, hope yer'll understand that, Mr Caleigh.'

Gabe grinned. 'Sure I understand, Percy. You did the right thing. Chester was miserable here.'

'No, he were scared, that's the truth of it. Some animals sense things that most people can't. It were the dog's howling and whining that made me come to the Hall las' night. I knew it were because something were wrong here. Oh, I sensed things was not right days ago, but it were Chester that decided me.'

'We'd have been in real trouble if you hadn't shown up.' Gabe stuck out a hand and Percy shook it.

'That's all right then,' the old gardener said, his face creasing into a smile. He took on a look of concern. 'How's the missus now? She all right?'

'You mean her head? The paramedics treated the whack she took – it wasn't too serious, they said. Still wanted her to have it checked out at the hospital, though, but Eve, well, she plain refused to go. Gotta nasty bump though, right where Pyke hit her with his walking stick. Some bruises on her legs too, but yeah, she *is* okay.'

Gabe glanced towards the house, its front door open wide. 'Come with me and see for yourself,' he invited Percy.

Percy looked at Crickley Hall with some trepidation and Gabe thought he was going to decline his offer. But then the mood passed and the old man's face relaxed.

'I'll do that, Mr Caleigh. I'll come inside with yer. The badness is gone, I jus' know it.'

Together, they walked to the front door.

# 81: ENDING

Gabe saw that his wife had been weeping when he and Percy entered the house. She and the psychic were standing a few yards from the front door and Lili had her hand on Eve's shoulder, as if offering comfort. He splashed towards Eve through the thin remaining puddles and took her in his arms; she leaned into him and he held onto her.

'You saw the bodies?' he asked in a gentle voice.

Eve nodded against his shoulder. 'The boy,' she murmured. 'He was so beautiful.'

Lili spoke. 'He was the reason the others were held here. They couldn't – or *wouldn't* – pass over without him. Their power was limited, blocked by Cribben's, but they gave you signs – the sounds from inside the landing cupboard, the cellar door that wouldn't stay shut, the sounds of scattering feet from above in the dormitory – all those things to make you aware of their presence and their history in this place. You saw them almost in reality, Eve, when the spinning top had somehow taken your mind to a different level of consciousness. Your youngest daughter saw them easily, usually as little lights, because her mind is still fresh and open to them. Mostly, though, they drew spiritual energy from Loren, which is why she's felt so tired inside the house. Pyke knew she was the key to the hauntings.'

'Is that why he tried to kill her?' Eve asked numbly.

'No. It was as he said himself: Loren was the sacrifice, the one to take his place.'

Eve drew in a sharp breath, thinking how close it had been. If Gabe hadn't . . .

'You see,' Lili went on, 'the children gave you signs, whereas the spirit of Augustus Cribben gave you warnings. He didn't want you to interfere because he stood between Stefan and the other spirits. He refused to let go, he wanted power over *all* the evacuees. He considered they belonged to him in life and also in death. Ultimately, he was mad, and so was his spirit.'

Eve gave a shiver and raised her head. 'Is that possible?' she asked of Lili. 'Can a person carry insanity into the next life?'

'Some psychics assume many ghosts are either disturbed or distressed – why else would they choose to haunt the living?'

'When we talked last night,' Gabe said, 'you told us that you knew Gordon Pyke was the kid in the photograph, this Maurice Stafford, as soon as you laid eyes on him: I don't understand – Pyke was an old man, nothing like the boy.'

'There was something about Maurice that never changed. The thumbprint was the same.'

Gabe shook his head, not understanding.

'I'm sorry, it's difficult to explain – you have to be psychic yourself to understand. Let's just say that, like a thumbprint, everybody's aura is individual and although it can vary through life, depending on illnesses and emotional states, its essence remains identifiably the same. Psychics can pick up on that singularity.'

Lili solely addressed Eve. 'When you showed me the

photograph of the evacuees I was immediately drawn to Maurice Stafford. A peculiar evil emanated from his image and when I saw that evil personified coming towards me . . . well, I panicked. I'm so sorry I ran away, Eve. It was the shock . . .'

'He tried to kill you, Lili. Of course I don't blame you for running. What else could you have done?'

'Something braver?'

Eve smiled. 'You did the right thing. Just by coming to us yesterday, you did the right thing. I know how reluctant you were to get involved in spiritualism again. You're probably even more reluctant after last night.'

'No. I'm not afraid any more. For almost two years I've dreaded the return of a certain spirit who wished me harm and I vowed never to use my psychic ability again because of it. Now I realize I can't turn it on and off like a tap. But this particular spirit didn't show last night when it would have had the perfect time to hurt me; now I'm sure it's finally gone, it's passed over peacefully. It's something I sense rather than can claim.'

Lili's smile took in all of them and even though there was dirt on her face and her clothes were dishevelled, her green eyes sparkled and her smile was radiant. Bright sunlight shone through the broken window over the stairs and it created a golden-halo effect around her tousled yellow hair.

She had stopped speaking and, without turning her head, her eyes looked to one side as if she were listening to something the others couldn't hear.

Then she said, a quiver in her voice, 'Oh God, they're stronger than ever.'

Gabe, Eve and Percy eyed her in surprise, and Eve with some trepidation. The hall was bright with sunlight, the shadows of the night vanquished along with the group's fear. Yet all was not quite right; there was a tension in the air compounded by a coldness that stiffened them.

'They're back,' said Lili, simply, turning to point towards the broad staircase.

They followed her direction and Eve gasped as she clung to Gabe's arm. Percy stood rigid, his lipless mouth open, his weary eyes squinting.

'Lord mercy . . .' he uttered.

Nine small figures were standing on the stairs, one to a step, all of them looking over the banister at the people below. Five girls, four boys, their apparitions clear, defined, as if they were of real flesh and blood. Four of the girls wore dark brown berets, the last one hatless but her hair was in two pigtails tied by tiny pink ribbons; only two of the boys wore caps. They were all dressed in outdoor clothes – overcoats and jackets – and each one carried a cardboard gas-mask box, the string across their chest. They looked as though they were going on a journey.

The nine visions were perfectly still and perfectly silent. They continued to stare.

Gabe made to take a step forward, but Eve kept her grip on his arm, holding him there. He regarded her quizzically, but her eyes were on the children and her half-smile puzzled him.

'Eve . . .?' he ventured.

'Wait, Gabe,' she responded softly without taking her attention off the children. 'Wait and see.' She knew something was about to happen.

Lili closed her eyes and she was smiling too. 'The children have come for them,' she said breathlessly.

Percy suddenly felt weak, as if his energy were draining

away. He staggered slightly, but steadied himself through sheer force of will.

The oldest girl, the one Eve thought must be Susan Trainer, shifted her gaze from the four people to the open cellar doorway. The battered door hung by one hinge against the wall.

Lili spun round when the rest of the children looked across the hall at the dark open doorway, and she stared at it too. Her hand went to her throat as she waited.

Gabe heard the noise on the cellar steps, footfalls that were distinct over the low background rush of the river that ran beneath the house. He glanced at Eve when the grip on his arm tightened and he saw that her eyes were shining from some inner joy, while he felt nothing but apprehension. Surely nothing more could happen? He felt what was now a familiar cold prickling sensation at the back of his neck.

The footsteps grew louder. Something moved in the shadow of the cellar doorway.

'It's all right,' he heard Lili say softly and he wasn't sure who she was addressing.

They emerged from the cellar together, the young woman leading the boy by the hand.

The group of people watched in awe and stunned silence. Percy gave a little moan, a kind of whimper. Eve pressed even closer to Gabe. Lili held both hands up to her cheeks.

'Nancy . . .' the old gardener said under his breath.

She wasn't very tall, but her form was slim, compact. Her hair hung in shiny copper ringlets round her pale pretty face. Her clothes were no longer bedraggled, her long skirt no longer faded; the buckles on her shoes now shone with reflected light, and dark stockings covered her ankles. She still wore the woollen shawl round her shoulders, but her right hand and arm were no longer withered and twisted but smooth and as pallid as the rest of her skin. She was smiling and the fine shallow mist of her aura was luminous in its radiance.

She held the boy's hand in her own once-deformed hand, and he came shyly into the hall with her, his wide dark eyes looking about him, taking in the room and its puddle flagstone floor, flitting over the watching people so that they knew he was aware of their presence. The colour in his hair had returned and it fell darkly over his smooth forehead. Stefan and the young teacher moved across the hall and, although their hollow footsteps could be heard, the shallow pools of water they walked through went undisturbed.

Gabe felt Percy brush by him as if the old man wanted – *needed* – to confront the ghost of his lost sweetheart, but it was Lili who held him back.

'It's Nancy—' he began to say, but Lili gently stayed his words.

'You can't communicate with her, Percy,' she told him. 'Please don't interfere with what's happening.'

He looked uncertainly at the psychic, then back at the two figures crossing the hall. His shoulders relaxed and his eyes softened moistly. 'She's so ... she looks so ...' he tried to say. 'Nancy looks so lovely, as she always did.'

Lili turned to Eve, who appeared absorbed by the phantom boy. The psychic sensed Eve's thoughts.

'Your little boy has passed on, Eve,' she said quietly but firmly. 'Cam isn't in our world any more, not even in spirit, like these children.'

Eve seemed dismayed. 'How do you know?' It was almost a protest.

'Because they're telling me so.' Lili indicated the spirit children on the stairs.

'But – but they're not saying anything.'

'They don't have to speak to converse with me. Trust me, Eve. Cameron is in a better place where nothing can hurt him, not even your own grief. He hasn't forgotten you, though, nor his father and his sisters. He knows you'll all be together again some day.'

Gabe slipped his arm round Eve's shoulders and she pressed into him, comforted by his presence and Lili's words.

The ghosts of Nancy and Stefan had reached the stairs when the ghosts above them began to weaken, fading so that the wall and smashed window behind them could be plainly seen. They evanesced to swirling vapour, shimmering when they shrank to tiny balls of light, each one bright, each one incredibly lambent, as if with joy.

They glided down the stairs and circled the teacher and the boy, spinning faster and faster, creating flight-trails of white mist that soon enveloped Nancy and Stefan, who laughed silently with the thrill of it. Their images grew paler, then dwindled, the two apparitions condensing like the others to become small dancing orbs of brilliant gold. The little balls of light mingled, spun around each other, flying high, then low, swooping and skimming around the grand hall, touching its ceiling, glancing off the walls, weaving elaborate, effortless patterns of dazzling sunlight.

Gabe was dizzy just watching them. It was wondrous, a spectacle of breathtaking luminance that elevated his emotions so that he began to grin, then to chuckle, then to laugh. And his companions were smiling, then laughing at the light show too.

One ball of light led the way to dive at Gabe, Eve, Lili and Percy, the others following almost in formation, sweeping between them, circling round and round, pulsating with energy, colours changing to the higher spectrum of a rainbow, so that Eve and Lili cried out in delight while Gabe and Percy laughed with the sheer pleasure of it. One round light settled on the old gardener's cheek and when he touched a hand to it, it flew out from beneath his fingers to land on the opposite cheek; but it was soon gone, rejoining the others in their display, and Percy's hand lingered on the side of his face as fingertips might touch a dampness left by a kiss.

Eve sensed the misery of the past year lifting for, although she would still mourn her son, she knew now for certain that life always continued, but in another form, perhaps even in more than one. At last she embraced happiness again, at last she realized Cameron was not truly gone but was waiting for her in another place.

Suddenly, as if on command, the whirling lights flew high into the air and gathered together in one blazing whole. There the dazzling mass hovered for a moment, then swooped through the glassless window into the bright day where it outshone even the sun. Then it was gone, vanishing rather than flying away.

Gabe was the first to recover. He studied his wife's upturned face and took heart at the joy he saw there. Her eyes shone with unshed tears and her smile was almost rapturous. With Lili and Percy, she continued to gaze out into the daylight as if expecting the lights to return.

At last, Lili said: 'It really is over now.' Her smile had become wistful.

Gabe turned Eve so that she faced him in his arms. He looked over her shoulder at the psychic. 'It's resolved?' he asked Lili. 'They've left this place for good?'

Lili nodded. 'They're complete: there's nothing to keep them tied to Crickley Hall. Augustus Cribben has no power over them any more.'

'And Augustus Cribben himself? Has he gone?'

Her smile faltered. 'I don't know, but I don't feel anything here. After all, he got his eleventh victim.'

'Pyke?'

She nodded again. 'Maurice Stafford. I sense the house is empty for now, although Cribben might not have understood it's time to pass over. His bitterness could still keep him here in spirit, the lesson unlearned, his own evil clouding everything.'

'Then let's leave,' said Gabe firmly. 'Haunted or not, the sooner we're out of Crickley Hall, the better I'll like it. You okay, Percy?'

The gardener wiped a tear from his eye with the knuckle of a finger. 'I am, son,' he replied. 'It's like the young lady says, there's nothing here any more. It's just a big old ugly empty house an' I hope it stays that way fer a long time to come.'

A sound of barking outside distracted them all.

'Gabe . . .?' Eve looked up into her husband's face. 'That sounds like – no, it can't be.'

Gabe grinned as Chester appeared at the open door, Loren and Cally giggling behind him. The dog waited on the threshold for a second or two, as if uncertain. But as soon as he spotted Eve, he bounded and scooted through puddles towards her. As Chester slavered all over Eve, who had made the mistake of kneeling down to his level, Gabe caught Percy's eye.

Percy gave a reassuring nod of his head. There was nothing here to frighten Chester any more.

# EPILOGUES

It was nurse Iris who found Magda Cribben's stone-cold corpse the morning after the big flood had hit the coastal village of Hollow Bay. Although such morning discoveries were not infrequent in a nursing home for the elderly, the nurse had to suppress a scream of fright when she walked into Magda's cell-like bedroom, for instead of lying peacefully in her bed, the old woman was sitting upright and fully dressed on her hard chair, facing the door, her body already stiff as if she had frozen there.

But it was the expression on Magda Cribben's face that upset Iris so: Magda's jaw was dropped, her toothless mouth open wide as if in a rictal cry of horror, and her lifeless eyes remained staring at the doorway – staring past Nurse Iris – as if her last sight was of something horrific entering the room.

They never recovered the body of Gordon Pyke, the man who had visited Crickley Hall on the night of what the locals called the Second Great Flood. They assumed that his drowned body had been carried by the underground river out to the sea and then to the ocean beyond. Either that, or it was still

632

trapped somewhere in the underground river, snagged by rocks or washed into some subterranean cavern. After all, two bodies that had been lost since the last world war had only recently been found.

No one knew much about Pyke, so no one cared very much that his body was lost. To the older villagers, he was just another victim of Crickley Hall's curse.


Crickley Hall has remained empty for a year now. Potential buyers or those looking to rent are not attracted to the place. Its architecture is too severe, its ambience too depressing, they say. Some even compare it to a mausoleum despite (or maybe even because of) its grand hall.

Even the estate manager hates his monthly check on the property's condition. It's creepy, he likes to tell anyone who is not a possible client. Sometimes he hears noises, he claims. Oh, he knows that most are the usual sounds of trespassing rodents, birds in the chimneys or merely the house settling, but sometimes they are different from all those. Always faint. Always from rooms that are empty when he looks into them. But they are distinct.

They sound like:

*Swish-thwack!*
*Swish-thwack!*
*Swish-thwack!*

extracts reading groups
competitions books new
discounts extracts
competitions extracts reading groups discounts
books new extracts events reading groups
events books extracts discounts
new extracts title reading groups
interviews events new
new events extracts extracts books
discounts events interviews new books extracts
new books events events
events new
discounts extracts discounts

www.panmacmillan.com

extracts events reading groups books
competitions books extracts new